THE GAME

"May well be the best King has yet devised for her strong-willed heroine . . . . The sights, smells and ideas of India make interesting, evocative reading . . . . All readers will appreciate the grace and intelligence of King's writing in this exotic masala of a book."
—*Publishers Weekly* (starred review)

"A wondrously taut mystery, ticking away like a malevolent clock . . . Fabulous reading, breathless excitement, and the myriad pleasures of watching great minds at work." —*Booklist* (starred review)

"Vibrant local color, described by Russell in the droll tongue of a woman with the wit to realize that, while she may be dirty and tired and in constant danger, she is having the time of her life!"
—*New York Times Book Review*

"A rousing adventure story made credible by the sheer force of its characters' personalities and the sharply realized details of their surroundings. Good historical fiction is as close as we'll ever get to time travel, and historical fiction doesn't get any better than this. Nor do literary pastiches, which, at their best, like this one, take on a life of their own." —*Denver Post*

"Imaginative . . . Dazzling. Lush, colorful and utterly compelling, this is a superbly wrought novel of suspense that evokes its period with enviable panache. Four stars out of four stars." —*Detroit Free Press*

"Of the many fine writers currently adding to the canon of stories about [Holmes], the nimblest is Laurie R. King . . . . Splendid fun, perhaps the rippingest of all of Russell's ripping tales." —*Seattle Times*

JUSTICE HALL

"A one-woman case for the defense of unauthorized literary sequels...intelligent, witty, complex and atmospheric...By making a woman possible who matches Holmes in brainpower, as well as in depressive tendencies of mind and spare elegance of manner, King has made marriage possible for the most famous and, surely, one of the most aloof detectives of all time....A spellbinding mystery...superb."
—*Washington Post*

"In King's delightfully inventive hands, Holmes' retirement is energized by a feisty, half-American wife and partner named Mary Russell—every bit the equal of the detective's fabled cranium and spirit....[King] uses her background as a theological scholar to spin richly textured subtexts and asides. The result is far superior to the average post–Conan Doyle canon of Holmesiana." —*Seattle Times*

"Audacious...Mary Russell [is] never less than fascinating company." —*Los Angeles Times*

"Sir Arthur Conan Doyle...would probably approve....Consistently smart and poignant."
—*Chicago Tribune*

"*Justic Hall* is *Gosford Park* with an Arthur Conan Doyle twist....Fascinating...Expertly combining history with mystery." —*Orlando Sentinel*

PRAISE FOR
LAURIE R. KING
and the
MARY RUSSELL MYSTERIES

LOCKED ROOMS

A Deadly Pleasures Best Crime Novel of the Year
A Seattle Times Best Mystery of the Year

"King not only marvelously evokes the bygone days of 1920s San Francisco but she adds layer after complex layer to this believably rendered relationship. A light touch, well-handed flashbacks, and excellent pacing make *Locked Rooms* a thoroughly entertaining read."
—*Baltimore Sun*

"Laurie King is not only one of the finest mystery writers in the country, but one of the most honored.... King trumps herself in Mary's homecoming—this outing will be hard to top."
—*Monterey Herald*

"Engrossing." —*Washington Post*

"Brimming with 1920s verve, this continues King's vividly imagined series about Mary Russell, Sherlock's younger [but equally smart and brave] wife."
—*Seattle Times*

"*Locked Rooms* is spectacular." —*Mystery News*

"King is [one of] the best American authors of traditional mystery fiction." —*New York Sun*

O JERUSALEM

" *O Jerusalem* returns to the fascinating, shadowy, psychological terrain of [Holmes and Russell's] courtship . . . . [King has] stepped onto the sacred literary preserve of Sir Arthur Conan Doyle, poached Holmes, and brilliantly brought him to life again . . . . *O Jerusalem* is a standout." —*Washington Post Book World*

"Inspired . . . King puts us into each scene so quickly and completely that her narrative flow never falters." —*Chicago Tribune*

"King's considerable talent makes history virtually leap off the page . . . . Readers can't lose." —*Booklist*

"King's impeccable research combines with her colorful, fully drawn characters to make this another memorable addition to a strong series." —*Ellery Queen Mystery Magazine*

THE MOOR

"There's no resisting the appeal of King's thrillingly moody scenes of Dartmoor and her lovely evocations of its legends." —*New York Times Book Review*

"Erudite, fascinating . . . by all odds the most successful re-creation of the famous inhabitant of 221B Baker Street ever attempted." —*Houston Chronicle*

"King has the tone, mood, and voice precisely right . . . . Very good—as satisfying at this time of year as a truly rich fruitcake." —*Boston Globe*

"Dazzling...mesmerizing...a superbly rich read that would please Doyle himself." —*Booklist*

A LETTER OF MARY

"A lively adventure in the very best of intellectual company." —*New York Times Book Review*

"The great marvel of King's series is that she's managed to preserve the integrity of Holmes' character and yet somehow conjure up a woman astute, edgy and compelling enough to be the partner of his mind as well as his heart....Superb." —*Washington Post Book World*

"An intellectual puzzler, full of bright red herrings and dazzling asides." —*Chicago Tribune*

"Top-notch stuff in a wonderful, feminist historical series." —*Mystery Lovers Bookshop News*

A MONSTROUS REGIMENT OF WOMEN

"As audacious as it is entertaining and moving." —*Chicago Tribune*

"Beguiling...tantalizing." —*Boston Globe*

"One of the year's best...Enormously appealing...Rich in atmosphere and a plot that will keep the reader breathing hard." —*Mostly Murder*

"Remarkable...delightful." —*San Francisco Chronicle*

LOCKED
ROOMS

LOCKED ROOMS

*A Mary Russell
Novel*

Laurie R. King

BANTAM BOOKS

LOCKED ROOMS
A Bantam Book

PUBLISHING HISTORY
Bantam hardcover edition published July 2005
Bantam mass market edition / April 2006

Published by Bantam Dell
A Division of Random House, Inc.
New York, New York

This is a work of fiction. Names, characters, places, and
incidents either are the product of the author's
imagination or are used fictitiously. Any resemblance
to actual persons, living or dead, events, or locales
is entirely coincidental.

Library of Congress Catalog Card Number: 2005048082

ISBN-10: 0-553-58341-7
ISBN-13: 978-0-553-58341-0

Printed in the United States of America
Published simultaneously in Canada

www.bantamdell.com

OPM   10   9   8   7   6   5   4   3

To the '06 survivors, especially
Robert John Dickson and Florence Frances Adderley,
"Dick" and "Flossie–"
my grandparents

LOCKED
ROOMS

Editor's Preface

This is the eighth chapter in the continuing memoirs of Mary Russell, based on a set of manuscripts I received in the early 1990s.* Some of the manuscripts were neatly collated and tied by ribbons; others, comprising as they did varied sizes and qualities of paper, required considerable work to decipher. Still others were mere fragments apparently unrelated to larger bodies of the work, and thus, for lack of a better approach, are best published as short stories.

The following episode in the memoirs looked, at first glance, like a collection of those fragments, but on closer examination I realized that they combined two separate narratives which had been either clumsily filed together, twenty pages here and fifty there, or else roughly inter-leaved, matching up the chronological progress of both story lines. One document was handwritten in Miss Russell's distinctive script; the other was a typewritten,

*The first of these, *The Beekeeper's Apprentice,* gives details of how I came to possess them.

third-person narrative following the actions of her partner/husband. Certain instances of grammar and punctuation would seem to indicate that the writer (or, typist) was Russell herself, but whether she is transcribing a story given her, or creating a more or less speculative document based on learned material, is anyone's guess. Personally, having had some time to consider the matter, I venture to say that she put together those chapters of her story based on at least two separate accounts, and found that typing them instead of using her customary handwriting provided her a necessary psychological distance from the tale, as did the shift from the personal voice to one of an objective narrator.

But as I say, it's anyone's guess.

I have preserved Miss Russell's third-person material as it appears in the original, although attempting to duplicate her crude day-by-day interleaving of the two viewpoints made me a bit dizzy. Instead, I have allowed the material to accumulate, following several days' story before resuming the alternative account.

Laurie R. King
Freedom, California

 # Prologue

The dreams began when we left Bombay.

Three dreams, over and over, rode the ship with me as we churned south around Cape Comorin and up India's eastern coast, lending their peculiar chill to the steamy nights. Three companions, at my back all the way around the coastline of Asia and across the misnamed Pacific to California.

In the first dream, objects flew.

The first time I dreamt about flying objects was just a day or two after we had steamed away from the port, and it seemed at the time an entertaining variation played on one of the day's events. That morning, sitting on a deck-chair beneath the canvas awning that sheltered us from the tropical heat, I had eavesdropped on a discussion of the *Alice* books between a child enthusiast and her disapproving nanny. So when I dreamt that very night of a deck of cards hurling themselves at me through the air, I woke startled, but amused as well.

The amusement did not last for many days, not when

the playing cards became winged bats, then fluttering books, then finally bricks, lamps, and pieces of furniture, all of them aimed at me with ever-increasing force and animosity. Within a few days I caught myself examining my skin in the morning, looking for bruises.

The second dream began after the first was well established in my nocturnal routine. In it, a completely faceless man stood before me, peculiarly terrifying in his utter anonymity, and appearing always in a similarly white and featureless room. He would sometimes speak—how, without a mouth? *Don't be afraid, little girl,* he would say. *Don't be afraid.*

Might as well say *Don't look down at the bear trap,* or *Take no notice of the shotgun on the breakfast table.* The sort of command intended to suggest its opposite: *Be afraid, little girl.*

Be afraid.

Then, as if two hauntings were not sufficient, a third dream began shortly after we had rounded the tip of India. The nights were stifling and would have made sleep difficult at the best of times, but with this third regular visitor, I nearly gave up sleep entirely.

Not that this one was as openly nightmarish as the flying objects or the faceless man, merely troubling. In the third dream, I would be strolling through a house, a large and beautifully designed building whose architectural style changed every time—Mediaeval stone one night and modern steel-and-glass the next, Elizabethan half-timbered or nineteenth-century brick terrace. My footsteps seemed to echo through the hall-ways, although I often had a number of friends with me, showing them around what seemed to be my own house. We visited a spacious bedroom here, they admired an ornate dining room there, stood and talked about a baronial fireplace in a great hall.

But neither the architecture nor the friends seemed to be the central thrust of the dream, for sooner or later, in dim stone passage-way or brightly windowed corridor, we would come to a door, silent and undemanding, and I would finger a key in my pocket. The door was to an apartment, I knew that, but it was so thoroughly concealed that no-one knew of it but me. My companions would pass by, unaware, while I thoughtfully played with the cool metal key and felt the unsettling pull of the rooms on the other side of the door.

It wasn't that I was hiding the apartment from them—indeed, some nights my illusory self would pull out the key and open the unnoticed door, showing my surprised friends around a set of richly comfortable rooms—Mediaeval or modern—that were only slightly dusty with long disuse. The importance seemed to lie neither in the existence nor in the secrecy of the locked rooms. What mattered—and what troubled me inexplicably when I woke—was my awareness of them, and of the hidden apartment's dim, empty stillness, comfortable and undemanding, tucked away in the back of my mind as the key was tucked into my pocket.

Almost as if the locked rooms lay deliberately waiting, knowing that someday I should have need of them.

BOOK ONE

BOOK ONE

Russell

Chapter One

Japan had been freezing, the wind that sliced through its famous cherry trees scattering flakes of ice in place of spring blossoms. We had set down there for nearly three weeks, after a peremptory telegram from its emperor had reached us in Hong Kong; people kept insisting that the countryside would be lovely in May.

The greatest benefit of those three weeks had been the cessation of the dreams that had plagued me on the voyage from Bombay. I slept well—warily at first, then with the slow relaxation of defences. Whatever their cause, the dreams had gone.

But twelve hours after raising anchor in Tokyo, I was jerked from a deep sleep by flying objects in my mind.

Three days out from the island nation, the rain stopped and a weak sun broke intermittently through the grey. The cold meant that most of the passengers, after venturing out for a brief turn on the decks, settled in along the windows on the ship's exposed side like so many somnolent cats. I, however, begged a travelling-rug from the purser and found a deck-chair out of the wind. There, wrapped to my chin with a hat tugged down over my close-cropped hair, I dozed.

Halfway through the afternoon, Holmes appeared with a cup of hot coffee. Actually, it was little more than tepid and half the liquid resided in the saucer; nonetheless, I sat up and disentangled one arm to receive it, then freed the other arm so that I could pour the saucer's contents back into the cup. Holmes perched on a nearby chair, taking out his pipe and tobacco pouch.

"The Captain tells me that we are making good time," he commented.

"I'm glad the storm blew itself out," I replied. "I might actually be able to face the dinner table tonight." Something about the angle of the wind the past days had made the perpetual pitch and toss of the boat even more quease-inducing than usual.

"You haven't eaten anything in three days." Holmes disapproved of my weak stomach.

"Rice," I objected. "And tea."

"Or slept," he added, snapping his wind-proof lighter into life and holding it over the bowl of his pipe.

That accusation I did not answer. After a moment, as if to acknowledge that his comment had not required a response, he went on.

"Had you thought any more about pausing in Hawaii?"

I stifled a yawn and put my empty cup onto the chair's wide arm, nestling back into the warmth of the rug. "It's up to you, Holmes. I'm happy to stop there if you like. How many days would it be before the next ship?"

"Normally three, but it seems that the following ship

has turned back to Tokyo for repairs, which means we could be marooned there for a week."

I opened one eye, unable to tell from his voice, still less his smoke-girt expression, which way his desires leant. "A week is quite a long diversion," I ventured.

"Particularly if Hawaii has embraced the austerities of Prohibition."

"A half-day would mean a long walk and sit at a table where I don't have to aim a moving soup spoon at my mouth. Both would be quite nice."

"Then another four days to San Francisco." The pointless, unnecessary observation was unlike Holmes. Indeed, this entire conversation was unlike him, I reflected, squinting at him against the glare. He had his pipe between his teeth, and was concentrating on rolling up the pouch, so I shut my eyes again.

"*Terra firma,*" I said. "A week in California, tying up business, and then we can turn for home. By train." I don't get seasick on trains.

"A week will be sufficient, you believe?"

"To draw up the papers for selling the house and business? More than enough."

"And that is what you have decided to do."

This noncommittal, pseudo-Socratic dialogue was beginning to annoy. "What are you getting at, Holmes?"

"Your dreams."

"What about them?" I snapped. I should never have told him about them, although it would have been difficult not to, considering the closeness of the quarters.

"I should say they indicate a certain degree of anxiety."

"Oh for heaven's sake, Holmes, you sound like Freud. The man had sex on the brain. 'Rooms in dreams are generally women,' he declares. 'A dream of going through a series of rooms indicates a brothel, or a marriage'—I can't imagine what his own marriage could have been like to equate the two so readily. And the key— God, you can imagine the fraught symbolism of playing with a key that lies warm in my pocket! 'Innocent dreams can embody crudely erotic desires.' The faceless man he'd no doubt equate with the male organ, and as for the objects that spurt wildly into the air—well, I'm clearly a sick woman. What does it say about my 'erotic desires' that reading the man's book made me need a hot bath? Or perhaps a cold shower-bath."

"You sound as if you've researched this rather thoroughly."

"Yes, well, I found a copy of his *Interpretation of Dreams* in the ship's library," I admitted, then realised that I was also admitting to a greater degree of preoccupation than I thought sensible. To lead him away from the admission, I said, "I wouldn't have thought that you of all people would fall for the Freud craze, Holmes."

His face darkened as he came close to responding to my diversion, then he caught himself, and counterattacked with a deceptively mild, "A knowledge of psychological jargon is hardly necessary when confronted with such an unambiguous statement as that contained in those dreams of yours."

"What do you mean, unambiguous?" I protested furiously, and too late realised that I had stepped into his own diversion with both feet.

"San Francisco's earthquake, which sent things flying about, is clearly the paradigm for the first dream. And the locked rooms may represent your family's house, which has stood empty for ten years while you pretended it wasn't there."

"A house is more often symbolic of the self," I told him, although I did not know why I wanted to argue.

"True, although a house may also be simply a house."

I threw off the rug so as to face him unencumbered. "Holmes, you're mad. I've only owned the place for three years, since I turned twenty-one, and I've been rather too busy to travel halfway across the world to take care of things. As for your earthquake fantasy, I wasn't even here in 1906. And what about the faceless man dream, anyway?"

"There is as yet insufficient data to identify him," he said, not in the least troubled by my words.

I drew breath to argue with him, but in the event, I couldn't be bothered. I rose with dignity, and said merely, "If you imagine we shall have time to uncover the relevant data in San Francisco, you are mistaken. We will be there only long enough for me to sign papers, then catch the train for New York."

Tucking the rug under my arm, I left him to his pipe. Earthquakes. Ridiculous.

He did not bring it up again, and neither did I, although over the following days I often felt his eyes upon me, and knew that at night he too lay awake, waiting for me to speak. But I did not, and he did not, and thus we traversed the Pacific. Between the dreams themselves and lying awake in dread, I scarcely slept, and began to feel as if I was walking in a wrap of cotton gauze.

Hawaii was a pleasant interlude, although the wind blew and the wide beaches were nearly deserted. We walked for hours, and I even managed to eat something, but that night I slept no better.

The following evening I wandered about the ship, up and down the various decks (trying to ignore the Freudian overtones of entering enclosed stairways) until I found myself at the furthest point of the ship, after which there was only water. The wind had stopped that morning, leaving the smoke from the stacks to trail straight back along the various layers of deck, which created a series of solitary if insalubrious places for meditation. I was on the last of those decks, with only a railing between me and the Pacific.

And there I meditated, about the dreams and what Holmes had said.

Clearly, I thought, the damage we had seen in Japan, with Tokyo still recovering from the previous year's devastating earthquake, had set the literalist idea of shaken objects into his mind. I was not worried about the possibility he had suggested; no, despite my words, it was the niggling fear that Freud might be right.

Since leaving England in January, we had marked the nine-year anniversary of our meeting and the second year of marriage. I was content in ways I had not thought possible, well matched mentally and—despite the difference in our ages, despite the regular clash of our personalities, and despite the leering innuendo of Sigmund Freud—well suited physically, to a man who interested my intellect, challenged my spirit, and roused my passions.

So, no: Psychology be damned—the dreams weren't about my marriage.

Yet there they were, keeping me exhausted and irritable and searching out a piece of quiet if smoke-covered deck where I could stand by myself and stare down at the endless sea.

The water stretched out as far as the eye could see in an expanse of gentle grey-blue swells broken only by the occasional white-capped wavelet and the line of the ship's passage, unrolling die-straight behind us until it faded into the glare of sun on the western horizon. Directly below where I stood, dominating my vision if I leant my upper body over the rail, the churn of the great screws dug an indentation in the surface, followed by a rise just behind. Like the earth from a farmer's plough, I thought dreamily, cutting a straight furrow across three thousand miles of sea. And when the ship reached the end of its watery field, it would turn and begin the next furrow, heading east; and after reaching that far shore it would shift again, ploughing west. Back and forth, to and fro, and all the while, beneath the surface the marine equivalents of earthworms and moles would be going busily about their work, oblivious of the other world above their heads. The farmer, the ship, above; the insect, the fish, below. So peaceful. Peacefully sleeping, while occasionally a seed would fall and take root in the freshly split furrow . . .

"Russell!" Holmes exclaimed, and the sharp voice and his sudden hand on my arm snatched me awake and sent my hat flying. I grabbed at it, but too late; the scrap of felt sailed out behind the ship, floating on the air for a long time until eventually it planted itself into the brine furrow. I turned to my husband.

"Why did you have to startle me like that?" I complained. "That was my last warm hat."

"Easier to purchase another hat than to fish you out of the sea," he said. "You were on the edge of going over."

"Don't be ridiculous, Holmes, I was just watching the patterns made by the propellers. What did you want, anyway?"

"The first bell for dinner went a bit ago. When you didn't come to dress I thought perhaps you hadn't heard it. And when I came down the stairs, it appeared as though you were trying to throw yourself over."

His laconic words bore just the slightest edge of true concern, as if a question lay behind them. I reached up to adjust my hair-pins, only to find them gone—weeks after chopping off my thick, waist-length hair (a necessary element of disguising myself as a British officer) my hand was still startled to find the weight of it missing from my head. Spreading my fingers instead to run them through the brief crop, I glanced back at the straight path laid out behind us, and felt a shudder play up my spine. Perhaps I shouldn't lean over any more rails while I was as tired as this, I told myself, and allowed Holmes to thread my hand through his arm and lead me back towards our cabins.

I picked at my meal, making no more response to the conversations around me than would a stone statue. Afterwards we listened to the ship's string quartet render a competent selection of Beethoven, and took a turn around the decks, Holmes chatting, me unresponsive. Eventually we took ourselves to bed, for another night's broken sleep.

The next morning the mirror showed a woman with stains beneath her eyes. Holmes had already risen, and I dressed slowly, drank several cups of strong coffee, and took a book up onto the sun-drenched deck. The pages, however, made no more sense than the conversations of the night before, and eventually I merely sat, staring at the almost imperceptible horizon of sky and sea.

After some time I became aware that Holmes had settled into the adjoining chair. My gaze came reluctantly back from the distance and settled onto the bit of brightness he held in his hand. It was, I decided, the silken scarf he had purchased in a bazaar on the first leg of our voyage out from England, a garish item perhaps useful for one of his gipsy disguises. He held it in his hands as if its bright dye bore a hidden message; it was his focussed concentration that finally caught my attention.

"What is that, Holmes?"

"The length of silk we bought in Aden. I thought to use it as an *aide-mémoire*, to bring back the details of that curious afternoon. The whole affair puzzles me still."

Recalling the events of Aden was something of a wrench, since so much had taken place in the intervening months—weeks in India tracking down a missing spy and jousting with a mad maharaja, followed by the better part of a month in Japan with all the complexity of events there, interspersed by the dream-plagued weeks at sea. Granted, we had nearly been killed in the Aden bazaar by a balcony falling on our heads, but near-death experiences were no rarity in my life with Holmes. I had in the end dismissed it as a curious series of events that might have had tragic consequences, and fortunately had not. Clearly, Holmes was not of the same mind.

"It had to have been an accident, Holmes," I objected. "The balcony fell because the bolts were old, not because someone tried to pull it down on our heads."

"So I tell myself."

"But yourself will not listen."

"A lifetime's habit of self-preservation leaves one disinclined to accept the idea of coincidence."

"Holmes, one event does not a coincidence make."

"But two oddities catch at the mind."

"Two?"

"The fallen balcony, and the ship's passenger who enquired about us, then disembarked. In Aden." He raised an eyebrow at me to underscore the importance of that last.

"The ship's...Oh, yes, Thomas Goodheart's little story. A Southerner, didn't he say?" Tommy Goodheart, American aristocrat and occasional Bolshevik, had led us a merry chase across India over the course of January and February. Deep in a tunnel beneath a hill palace, with the maharaja's guards close on our heels, Tommy happened to mention that a female passenger on board our ship, a passenger who mysteriously disembarked in Aden, had been talking to him about Sherlock Holmes. Later, in a spymaster's office one sultry afternoon in Delhi, Holmes had pressed the young man for further details, but there were few to be had.

"From Savannah, or so she'd claimed. It might be noted that the accents of the American South are among the easiest to feign."

"Holmes," I chided, "don't you find it difficult to mistrust that the sun will rise in the east come morning?"

"Not in the least. I am more than willing to operate under the hypothesis that past experience will continue to provide the paradigm for Nature's functions. Although I do not believe that witnessing the sun rising in the west would cause my heart to stop."

"Glad to hear it."

"Watching my wife go over the rail of a ship, however, might have done the job."

"I was only—"

"You were three degrees from overbalancing." His

hard voice brooked no argument, and although that in itself would not normally have prevented me from arguing, at the moment all I could think of was my inadvertent shudder at the alluring smoothness of the ship's wake.

When I did not answer, he sighed. "Russell, clearly something is tormenting your mind. And while I firmly believe that all persons should be allowed to wrestle with their own demons, it is nonetheless possible that two minds working in tandem on the problem might have more effect than one tired mind on its own."

"Yes, very well," I snapped. I set my feet onto the deck, then spent some time studying my hands while the words arranged themselves in my mind. "When I suggested that after Bombay we should go to San Francisco, it seemed a logical idea. My business in California is best served by my presence, and . . . Well, I thought it a means of saying my farewells, which I was in no condition to do when I left ten years ago. But I am finding that the nearer we get, the more I wish we'd just turned for home. I . . . I find I am dreading the entire thing."

"Of course you are," he said. "It is quite natural that you do not wish to go to San Francisco."

"What do you mean?" I protested, stung. "It's taken me days to admit to myself that I was wrong, yet you claim to have known all along?"

"I do not say you are wrong, merely that you are torn. Russell, the moment we turned for California you became irritable, insomniac, restless, and without appetite. When we paused in Japan, your troubles were suspended—you slept, ate, and concentrated as you normally do—but when we resumed our easterly progress, they began again. What else could it be? Some curious aversion to the ship itself? I think that unlikely."

I could only stare at him, openmouthed, until his face twisted in a moue of impatience. "Russell, we are sailing on a straight path for the place that holds the most troubling memories of your childhood. It is only natural that you feel concern about seeing the place that burned to the ground when you were six—yes, yes, you weren't there, but even if you were not present you would have been told about it, over and over. Furthermore, it is the place where, at the age of fourteen, you experienced the horrendous crash that killed your mother, your father, your brother, and nearly you. It would be decidedly odd if you were not fearful. What concerns me is that your degree of apprehension seems excessive. Those dreams, whatever their message, clearly spring from powerful roots."

"But these dreams have nothing to do with the accident. They're nothing like the dream I used to have when I was a child—the one I told you about. There's no motorcar, no family. No fire or explosion, no road or cliffs. Not the same at all."

He thrust the scrap of orange into one pocket, then drew his pipe from another and started packing tobacco into its bowl. As he rolled the top of the pouch shut, he remarked, "This faceless man of the second dream. He seems to alarm but not threaten."

"That's a fair description, yes."

"He does not reach for you, or harm you in any way?"

"He just appears, says 'Don't be frightened, young lady,' and leaves."

He paused with the brass lighter halfway to the bowl, and two sharp grey eyes locked on to me. "*Young lady*, or *little girl?*"

"*Young*—No, you're right, it's *little girl*. How did you know that?"

"That was the phrase you used the first time you told me."

"Well, it scarcely matters."

"I shouldn't assume that," replied my husband, in his customary irritatingly enigmatic style, and concentrated on getting the tobacco burning. When he had done so, he let out a fragrant cloud and sat back, his legs stretched out before him. "What do you suppose it means by his being faceless? Is it literal, or is something obscuring his features—a mask of some kind, perhaps, or heavy makeup?"

I gazed out over the sea for a minute. "I just think of him as faceless, but it could be a white mask, or bandages, or as you say, heavy makeup. Like those dancers we saw in Japan, only without the features accentuated. He's just...faceless." It was frustrating, trying to grasp a thing so firmly lodged in the dim recesses of the mind.

"And he appears in a white room."

"Yes, always."

"Tell me about the room."

"It's brightly lit, windowless, and crowded with an odd assortment of furnishings." I had already decided that this room was a place of importance to my subconscious mind, which had furnished it with elements from all the sides of my life. An almost mythic place, as it were, a sort of Platonic cave.

"But not the same as the locked rooms of the third dream."

"Oh, no, nothing like. Those are dim and solid, this is bright and, I don't know, soft somehow." Womblike, I thought—other than the brightness.

"Ah," he said, and bit down on his pipe-stem with an air I knew well: The case was coming together in his mind.

For some reason, that gesture made me uneasy; I got to my feet to walk over to the railing, looking down at the lower decks, refusing to rise to his bait.

"It's a tent," he said after a minute.

"From my childhood? Not very likely, Holmes—my mother wouldn't have been caught dead tenting. We did have a summer house, south of San Francisco, and although we left the servants behind when we went there, it was a far cry from roughing it."

"Not a holiday. Following the earthquake and fire, the parks of San Francisco were covered with the canvas tents of refugees."

"I told you, I wasn't there during the earthquake."

"So where were you?"

"I don't remember—I was six years old, for heaven's sake, and we moved around. England, most likely. Or Boston. Not in San Francisco."

"You were born in London, and lived in California fourteen years later; were you not resident in between?"

"On and off. Not the whole time," I said, far more decisively than I felt. Did anyone pay much attention to memories of childhood? Personally, I rarely thought about them.

"Where did you live when you were six years old, Russell?" he asked patiently.

"Oh, Holmes, leave it, do."

"Where, Russell?"

God, was the man out to drive me mad? "Boston, I think."

"Do you recall the house?"

"Yes," I said triumphantly, and turned to face him, my chin high. "A large brick mansion with a portico, a pianoforte in the parlour, and a stained-glass window over the stairway landing that used to cast its colours on the walls."

"Your house, or that of your grandparents?"

"Ours, of course." But the moment I said this, the stairway in memory became populated with a number of small white dogs, their fluffy bodies spattered magically with blue and red from the window. My grandmother's dogs.

No: I must have seen that when Grandmother came to visit.

Bringing her dogs with her? Reluctantly, I prodded at the memory, trying to locate a bedroom or nursery I could call my own; all I came up with was an uncomfortable trundle bed in a room that smelt of lavender.

Damnation. Why couldn't I remember such a simple thing?

My fingernails located a rough place on the wooden railing, and began to worry at it. "Honestly, Holmes? I don't know."

"Russell, I propose that in all likelihood you were, in fact, in San Francisco during the earthquake. That would explain the flying objects in the first dream, don't you think? And the soft white walls of the crowded room, a tent full of odds and ends rescued from a damaged or burning house."

"Damn it, Holmes, I was not there! Why are you so insistent that I was?"

"Why are you so insistent that you were not? Russell, you never speak of your childhood, do you realise that?"

"Neither do you."

"Precisely. Happy childhoods nurture memories; uncomfortable events cause the mind to wince away."

A splinter came abruptly up from the railing and drove itself into my finger. With a stifled oath, I sucked at the offending digit and shouted furiously around it, "I had a happy childhood!"

"Certainly you did," he retorted drily. "That is why you speak of it so freely."

"Later events made the memories painful."

"Russell, where did you live in 1906?"

"I'm going to go find a plaster for this finger," I told him, and went down the stairway at something close to a run.

I *had* a happy childhood.

I did *not* live in California during the quake.

And I did *not* intend to linger in San Francisco long enough to dig over what sparse portions of my past lay there.

Chapter Two

It is a characteristic difficulty of shipboard life that one cannot escape an interrogator or a boor for long. It is particularly true when one is sharing rooms with one's interrogator.

So it was that the next morning, Holmes knew as well as I did that the dreams had not plagued me during the night. I did dream of the locked rooms, but for the first time since we had left Japan, the flying-objects nightmare did not arrive to jerk me gasping from my bed.

The other two dreams persisted. The faceless man had returned, although he had stood clearly outlined in the door-way of a tent, and had not spoken. Still, his presence had not been as troublesome as before. Instead, that night and the following, the enigmatic concealed rooms became the focus for my sleeping mind, dimmer yet ever more sumptuously laid beneath the dust of disuse.

Had I been in the city as a child of six? Had I felt the earth leap and split, watched half the city go up in flames in the worst fire America had ever seen? The disappearance of the first dream forced me to consider the possibility that Holmes was right, for it seemed almost as if, by naming the demon, he had stolen its authority.

Later in the afternoon of our last full day at sea, another image came to me that confirmed Holmes' interpretation beyond a doubt. The day was warm and bright and, passing under the ship's white canvas sun awnings, I was suddenly visited by a vision of my mother, wearing men's trousers, a ridiculous wide-brimmed straw hat with an enormous orange silk flower, and a delicious, self-mocking grin. She was turning from an open fire with a cast-iron skillet in one hand, a large spoon in the other, the bright canvas of an Army tent behind her; for a moment it was as if a door had been thrown open, permitting me, along with that tantalising glimpse, all the sensations the room-dream held: a thud of heavy sound beneath the crisp noise of breaking glass, a sharp thrill of terror, the feel of arms wrapping around me, and over it all an angry red haze. Then the door slammed shut, and I stood motionless for a long time, until a child ran past and broke my reverie.

It was, I knew without question, real. For that brief glimpse of recovered memory, I could forgive Holmes any degree of meddling. I could even admit to him that he was right: I had been in San Francisco during the earthquake, a child of six.

Why, however, had I pushed away all memory of the event?

We came at last to my childhood home, the West's biggest, youngest city, which spread over the end of a peninsula between ocean and bay. Eighty years ago, a ship coming through the Golden Gate would have seen nothing but a handful of Indian shacks clustered around a crumbling mission. Then, in 1848, John Marshall picked up a gleaming lump of yellow metal from a creek near Sutter's Mill, and the world came pouring in.

I had relatives in that first wave, victims of gold fever who worked claims, made fortunes, and lost them again. I had other relatives who joined the second wave of those who supplied and serviced the miners; their fortunes were more slowly made, and not as quickly lost. But unlike the others who now reigned supreme in the state of California, my grandfather had clung to his East Coast roots: Although he had built a house in San Francisco, it had been on Pacific Heights, keeping its distance from the showy Nob Hill mansions of Hopkins and Stanford; and although he had kept his holdings and remained a financial power on the West Coast, he had also bowed to his wife's demands that they return to the civilised world of Boston to raise their children, and thus loosed his hold on Californian political authority.

Still, my restless iconoclast of a father had claimed San Francisco as his home, declaring his independence by settling his Jewish-English wife in the family house there, and taking control of the family's California business interests. My father loved California, that much I knew, and I remembered him speaking of San Francisco as The City, a phrase that from my mother's lips meant London. I remembered almost nothing about the place itself, but I looked forward to making The City's acquaintance before I turned my back on her for good.

Thus it was that on a morning in late April, seventy-five years after the gold rush began, I stood on the deck and saw the Gate that had welcomed my father's people, smooth hills bracketing the entrance to the bay—green now following the winter rains, but golden in summer's long drought. Stern gun placements protruded from the hills on either side, but as we entered the Golden Gate and followed the curve of the land to our right, the white-walled city that carpeted a dozen or more hills came into view, its myriad piers and docks stretching long fingers out into the bay.

Our pilot took us in to one gleaming set of buildings not far from the terminal where ferries bustled in and out. We eased slowly in, coming to rest with a barely perceptible judder; ropes were cast and tied; the crowds on board and on land pressed towards each other impatiently, while behind them rough stevedores lounged among the lorries and heavy wagons, smoking and making conversation. The first officials started up the board walkway; as if their uniforms made for a signal, the passengers turned and scurried for their cabins.

Holmes and I waited until the crowd had thinned, then went below to gather our hand-luggage and present ourselves for collection.

The only hitch was, no one appeared to be interested in our presence. We sat in the emptying dining room where the purser had told us we might wait, Holmes smoking cigarettes, both of us watching out the windows as the disembarking passengers went from a torrent to a stream to stragglers. I glanced at my wristwatch for the twentieth time, and shook my head.

"It's been nearly an hour, Holmes. Shall we just make our own way?"

Wordlessly, he crushed his cigarette out in the over-flowing tray, picked up his Gladstone bag, and paused, looking out of the window.

"This may be your gentleman," he noted. I followed his gaze and saw a portly, tweed-clad, sandy-haired gentleman in his thirties working his way against the flow of porters down the gangway. Sure enough, he paused at the top to make frantic enquiries of the purser, who directed him towards our door. A moment later he burst into the room, red-faced and breathless, his hat clutched in his left hand as his right was extended in our direction.

"Miss Russell? Oh, I am so terribly sorry at the delay the boy I sent to watch for the ship's docking appears to have a girl-friend in the vicinity, and he became distracted. Why didn't you have someone 'phone me? Have your bags been taken off? Hello," he inserted, his hand pumping mine, then moving to Holmes. "Good afternoon, Mr Holmes. So good to meet you. Henry Norbert, at your service. Welcome to San Francisco. And to you, Miss Russell, welcome back. Come, let's get you off the ship and to your hotel." He clapped his soft hat back onto his head, scooped up my bag, and urged us with his free hand in the direction of the doors.

"Why a hotel?" I asked. "Surely we can stay at the house?"

Norbert stopped and removed the hat from his head again. "Oh. Oh, no, no, I wouldn't think that's a good idea. No, you'd be much more comfortable at a hotel. I've made reservations for you at the St Francis. Right downtown, just around the corner from the offices."

"Is there something wrong with the house?"

The hat, which had been rising in the direction of the sandy head, descended again. "No, no, it's still standing strong, no trouble there. But of course, it's not terribly habitable after all these years."

I opened my mouth to protest that he'd been told to get it ready for us, then decided there was little point: Clearly, I should have to see for myself, and decide if the house was in fact uninhabitable, or simply uncomfortable after ten years of standing empty. Probably hadn't had the dust-cloths cleared away. I closed my mouth again, Mr Norbert's hat resumed its head, and we allowed ourselves to be herded gently from the ship and into a gleaming saloon car that idled at the kerb.

Eighteen years ago, I reflected as we drove—almost exactly eighteen years ago—this city had been reduced literally to its very foundations. There was no sign of that catastrophe now. The busy docks gave way to a land of high buildings and black suits, then to the commercial centre. We passed between shop windows bright with spring frocks and alongside a square that had patches of spring flowers around a high pillar with some sort of winged statue at the top. Then the motor turned again, dodged the rumbling box of a cable-car, and drifted to a halt before a dignified entranceway. Liveried men and boys relieved us of our burdens, and we followed Mr Norbert through the polished doors to the desk.

The equally polished gentleman behind the desk greeted us by name, with professional camaraderie, as if we were longtime guests instead of newcomers known only through our local escort. Another, even more dignified, man lingered in the background, casting a gimlet eye on the desk man's efficiency. While Holmes signed the register, I asked Mr Norbert if his office had received any messages for me.

"Hah!" he exclaimed, and dug into the breast pocket of his suit for a thick packet of letters. "Good thing you asked, I'd have had to come back across town with them when I got home."

I flipped through them—three from Mrs Hudson, Holmes' longtime housekeeper although more of an aunt to me, several from various friends that she had sent on for us, a post-card from Dr Watson showing Paris. Norbert noticed the disappointment on my face.

"Were you expecting something else?" he asked.

"I was, rather. It must have been delayed."

Back in Japan I had decided that the one person I wished to see in San Francisco was Dr Leah Ginzberg, the psychiatrist who had cared for me after the accident, in whose offices I had laboriously begun to piece together my life. I had written to tell her that I was going to be passing through the city, and asked her to write care of Mr Norbert.

Perhaps the mail from Japan was unreliable.

"Well, I'll certainly have my secretary check again," he said. "Perhaps it'll come in the afternoon delivery. Now, I'll have most of your paperwork together in the morning; if you'd like to come to the offices first thing, we could have a look."

"I could come now, if that's convenient."

"Oh," Norbert said, "it's not, I'm afraid. There were some problems with the records of the water company shares, I had to send them back for clarification. But they promised to have them brought to me no later than nine in the morning. Shall we say nine-thirty?"

There did not seem to be much of a choice. I told him I'd see him at half past nine the following morning, and he shook our hands and hurried off.

Holmes had finished and was waiting for me, but before we could follow the boy with the keys, the dignified man who had been lingering in the background eased himself forward and held out his hand. "Miss Russell? My name is Auberon. I'm the manager of the St Francis. I just wanted to add my own personal welcome. I knew your father, not well, but enough to respect him deeply. I was sad to hear of the tragedy, and I am glad to see you here at last. If there's anything I can do, you need only ask."

"Why, thank you," I said in astonishment. Holmes had to touch my arm to get me moving in the direction of the lifts.

In our rooms, while Holmes threw himself onto the sofa and began ripping open letters, I stood and studied the neatly arranged bags and realised that, between the hasty packing of our January departure from England and a most haphazard assortment of additions in the months since then, there was little in those bags that would impress a set of lawyers and business managers as to the solidity and competence of the heiress whose business they had maintained all these years. To say nothing of the long miles that lay between here and the final ship out of New York. I did have a couple of gorgeous kimonos and an assortment of dazzling Indian costumes, but my Western garments were suitable for English winters and two years out of date, which even here might be noticed. I wasn't even certain the trunk contained a pair of stockings that hadn't been mended twice.

"Oh, what I could do with that Simla tailor of

Nesbit's," I muttered, interrupting my partner's sporadic recital of the news from home.

"Sorry?" said Holmes, looking up from his page.

"I was just thinking how nice it would be if women could get by with three suits and an evening wear. I'm going to have to go out to the shops."

"Sorry," he said again, this time intoned with sympathy rather than query.

I gathered my gloves and straw hat, then checked my wrist-watch. "I'll be back in a couple of hours, and we can have a cup of tea. Anything I can get you?"

"Those handkerchiefs I got in Japan were quite nice, but the socks are not really adequate. If you see any, I could use half a dozen pair."

"Right you are."

Down at the concierge's desk, I asked about likely shops, receiving in response more details than I needed. I thanked the gentleman, then paused.

"May I have a piece of paper and an envelope?" I asked. "I ought to send a note."

I was led across the lobby to a shrine of the epistolary arts, where pen, stationery, and desk lay waiting for my attentions. I scribbled a brief message to Dr Ginzberg, explaining that an earlier letter appeared to have gone astray, but that I hoped very much to see her in the brief time I would be in San Francisco. I gave her both the hotel address and that of the law offices for her response, signed it "affectionately yours," then wrote on the envelope the address I still knew by heart and handed it to the desk for posting.

The doorman welcomed me out into a perfectly lovely spring afternoon. Far too nice to be spent wrangling with shopkeepers, but there was no help for it—no bespoke tailor could produce something by nine-thirty tomorrow morning. Grimly, I turned to the indicated set of display windows on the other side of the flowered square and entered the emporium.

An hour later, I was the richer by three dignified outfits with hats to match, two pairs of shoes, ten of silk stockings, and six of men's woollen socks. I arranged to have everything delivered to the St Francis and left the shop, intending to continue down the street to another, more exclusive place mentioned by the concierge for dresses that did not come off a rack. But the sun was so delicious on my face, the gritty pavement so blessedly motionless underfoot, that I decided a brief walk through the flowered square would be in order.

Union Square was full of other citizens enjoying the sunshine. The benches were well used, the paths busy with strolling shoppers and businessmen taking detours. Few children, I noted—and then a sound reached me, and my mind ceased to turn smoothly for a while.

A rhythmic clang, a rumble of heavy iron wheels, the slap and whir of the underground cable: That most distinctive of San Francisco entities, a cable-car, rumbled up Powell Street, its warning bell ringing merrily as it neared Post.

The combined noises acted like the trigger phrase of a hypnotist: I dropped into a sort of trance, staring at the bright, boxy vehicle as it passed. It paused to take on a passenger, then grabbed its ever-moving underground cable again to resume its implacable way down the centre of the street towards the heights. Before it had disappeared entirely, a passer-by brushed past me, waking me from the dream-world. I turned away from the tracks and began walking fast, head down, crossing the flower-bedecked square and fleeing up streets with whichever crowd carried me along.

I was dimly aware of changes: the standard odours of a downtown shopping district—petrol, perfume, perspiration—gave way to more exotic fragrances, chillies and sesame oil, roasting duck and incense. Then a splash of colour caught my eye, and I raised my head to look around me. A row of bright paper lamps danced in the spring breeze, strung between two equally colourful buildings. The streets were oddly discordant, strongly remembered yet utterly foreign, as if I'd known the idea of the place, but not the reality. I walked on, but after a while the streets changed again. The air became redolent of garlic, tomato sauce, and coffee. In a short time, those smells faded beneath the air of a waterfront, and suddenly I had run out of land.

I stood on the edge of a wide, curving roadway fronting a row of piers that bustled with machines and men, loading and unloading ships from a dozen countries. Wagons and lorries came and went, few business suits appeared, and the air smelt only of sea and tar.

Reassuringly like London, in fact.

After a while I began to walk along the waterfront road, turning towards the western sun. It felt good on my face, as the unmoving ground felt good beneath my feet, and the muscles of my legs took pleasure in the fact that they could stride out without having to turn and retrace their steps every couple of minutes. The claustrophobic air of shipboard life slowly emptied from my lungs, and I thought, maybe it actually was some *"curious aversion to the ship itself"* that had inflicted the insomnia on me. That and lack of exercise.

I stopped to watch some fishermen at work, all high boots and loud voices, repairing holes in their nets while wearing sweaters more hole than wool. The fresh, powerful smell of fish and crab rose up all around me, to fade as I continued on. An Army post intruded between me and the water for a time, then allowed me back, and with the water before me, a dark round mountain rising from the northern shore and the island of Alcatraz before me, I stretched out my arms in the late sun, half inclined to shout my pleasure aloud, feeling a smile on my face. I turned to survey the rising city—and it was only then I noticed the length of the shadows the buildings were casting.

"Damn," I said aloud instead: I'd told Holmes I'd be back for tea.

I crossed the waterfront road to re-enter the city, and in a couple of streets I spotted a sign announcing public telephones. At least three languages mingled in the small room, an appropriate accompaniment to the Indian, English, and Japanese coins I sorted through in my purse. At last I found some money the girl would accept and placed a call to the St Francis. Holmes did not answer, nor had he left a message for me, so I left one for him instead and walked out of the telephone office nursing a small glow of righteousness: Had I been at the hotel at the declared time, I told myself, I'd only have been cooling my heels waiting for him to return from heaven knows where.

I continued south, which I knew was the general direction of downtown—it is difficult to become seriously lost in a city with water on three sides. And I was beginning to take note of my surroundings again, raising my eyes from the pavement to look around me. This was a more heavily residential area, the houses both older and larger than they had been in the area I had fled through, the residents less strikingly regional. As the ground rose, steeply now in a delicious challenge to my leg muscles, the houses began to retreat from the public gaze behind solid walls and gated drives. Street noises diminished with the loss of restaurants and shops, the trees grew taller and more thickly green, and the paving stones underfoot were more even although the number of pedestrians was markedly reduced.

The hilltop enclave might have had a moat around it and signs saying *Important Persons Only*. From here, the bank manager's driver could take his employer to the financial district and easily return in time to run the man's wife to her luncheon date downtown. There was no risk of roving gangs of boisterous children here, or late-night revellers walking noisily past by way of a short-cut home.

Even the air smelt of money, I thought, crisp and clean.

I looked up smiling at the house opposite, an unassuming brick edifice of two tall stories, and nearly fell on my face over my suddenly unresponsive feet.

I saw: snippets of red-brick wall and once-white trim set well back from the street, now nearly obscured by a wildly overgrown vine and an equally undisciplined jungle of a garden; a grey stone garden wall separating jungle from pavement, in want of repointing and somehow shorter than it should be; one set of ornate iron gates sagging across the drive and a smaller pedestrian entrance further along the wall, both gates looped through with heavy chains and solid padlocks; the chain on the walkway gate, which for lack of other fastening had been welded directly onto the strike-plate—the very strike-plate that had reached out to gash open my little brother's scalp when he had tripped while running through it.

There was no mistaking the shape of the house: My feet had led me home.

Chapter Three

I don't know how long I stood there in the fading light, gawping at the house. I do know that it was nearly dark when a hand on my shoulder sent me leaping out of my skin in shock.

I whirled and found myself face-to-face with a tall, thin, grey-haired gentleman with sharp features and sharper grey eyes. I expelled the breath from my lungs and let my defensive hand fall back to my side.

"Holmes, for goodness' sake, do give a person some warning."

"Russell, I've been standing behind you clearing my throat noisily for several minutes now. You appeared distracted."

"You might say that," I said grimly.

"Am I to assume this is your family's house?"

I turned back to look at what was gradually becoming little more than a blocky outline against the sky. "I couldn't have told you for the life of me where it was, but my feet knew. I looked up and there it was."

"Do you wish to go in?"

"I don't have a key," I said absently, then caught my-self. "Not that the lack of a key would stop you. But frankly, I don't think your lock-picks would do much good against the rust on those padlocks."

"The wall, however, is easily scaled. Shall we?" So say-ing, he bent and hooked his hands together to receive my foot. I eyed the top of the stones, which indeed were scarcely five feet tall, although my memory of them was high—my childhood memory, I reminded myself. The wall was not set with glass or wire, and certainly there would be no watch-dog in that jungly front garden.

I set the toe of my shoe into Holmes' hands, braced my hands on his shoulder and the wall, and scrambled over the top with stockings more or less intact. He fol-lowed a moment later, brushing invisible dust from his trousers.

The walkway was buried under a knee-high thicket of weeds; five feet from the gate, the path disappeared en-tirely behind the press of branches from the shrubs on either side. Still, the drive was open, and we sidled along the wall until we reached it, then picked our way up the weed-buckled cobbles to the house.

The street-lamps had come on, but so thick was the vegetation, their light made it to the house's façade in fits and starts, allowing us a glimpse of downspout here, a patch of peeling trim there, the lining on a set of drapes through a grimy downstairs window.

We followed, initially at any rate, the path of least re-sistance, and continued along the drive that ran down the side of the house. The windows here were similarly closed and uninformative, the once-trim roses that fol-lowed the wall between our house and the neighbours (the ... Ramseys?) a thicket that reached thorny claws out to our clothing.

At the back of the house, the drive continued to a carriage house where my father had kept his motorcars. Holmes went on, standing on his toes to peer through the high windows, then came away. "Nothing there," he said, but of course there was nothing inside; my father's last motor had gone off a cliff and exploded in a freshly filled tank of petrol.

We stood looking at the impenetrable garden in back of the house. "Do you want to push through that?" I asked him.

"As there's no particular urgency, perhaps we ought to play the Livingstone-in-blackest-Africa rôle when we've had a chance to don thorn-proof outer garments."

"And snake-proof boots," I added. As we turned back towards the front, I shook my head in disgust. "The garden must have received some rudimentary attention, but it doesn't appear as if anyone has been inside the house for years. I thought there was an arrangement to keep the place up."

"I'd have thought it desirable, from a property manager's point of view. Undoubtedly your Mr Norbert will know why."

"He's got some explaining to do; no house should be allowed to get into this condition. It's a wonder the neighbours haven't complained."

"Perhaps they have," Holmes commented—but not, as I first thought, about the shocking condition of the paint. A motorcar had pulled up in front of the gate, and now I heard two doors slam shut as a pair of powerful torches probed the drive.

"You there," shouted a voice whose tones would carry

the same authority the world around. "Come out here at once."

"The constabulary have arrived," Holmes said unnecessarily, and together we moved to obey the command.

Our dress, our demeanour, and our accents soon had the torch-light diverted from our faces into a kinder illumination, and our claim to be the house's concerned but keyless owners was not instantly discounted. One of the policemen even came up with an orange crate from somewhere, so I could climb with dignity back over the fence. The last shred of suspicion fluttered away after we had been taken to the hotel and been recognised by the doorman. We thanked the two policemen for their concern over the property, and then I put to them the question that Holmes had raised mere moments before they had arrived.

"Before you go, may I ask? Which of the neighbours reported our presence? I'd like to thank them for their concern, don't you know."

The two burly men looked at each other; the older one shrugged. "It's the old dame across the street. She's kinda taken the house under her wing—'phones the station every so often to have us chase kids out before they can get into mischief."

"I do understand. Sleepless old lady with nothing better to do. She'll be disappointed we weren't stealing the doorknobs."

The two laughed and took their bulky blue selves away. Holmes and I made for the dining room, for our long-delayed meal. As we passed through the ornate foyer, it occurred to me that it was no longer necessary to search out a looking-glass to straighten hair mussed by the hours out-of-doors. A benefit of my new, if inadvertent, hair-style—Holmes loathed it, but I was not altogether certain that I did.

To our surprise, we were offered—quietly—wine with our dinner. It was local, but unexpectedly good, and although my appetite had yet to return, Holmes consumed his meal with approval. After our coffee, we went back outside for a turn under the lamps of Union Square.

"Holmes, I take it you followed me all this afternoon."

He was expecting the question, or rather, the question behind it, because he answered without hesitation. "I am concerned about the effect that coming to this place is having on you, yes."

My hand slipped away from his arm. "You were worried about me?"

"Not worried, simply curious to see where you would go. I thought it possible that, as one of your beloved psychological types might say, your sub-conscious would direct your steps."

"Indeed." A few more paces, and my hand went back through his arm. "Holmes, I honestly don't know what to make of it. I remember this city, and yet I do not. Before I found the house, I'd have sworn I didn't even know what part of the city it was in. How can that be?"

"I believe," he said after a moment, "that the process of discovering your ties to the place is one of the reasons we are here."

We finished our walk in silence, and went up to our rooms. The bed was soft and had the novelty of standing on an unmoving floor, and to my surprise and relief, the night passed in blessed dreamlessness.

I was at Mr Norbert's offices at the appointed hour dressed in one of my new frocks, my silk-wrapped legs taking note of the current length of hem-line. Between the Cuban heels and the curl of hair that barely touched my ears, I resembled a person who cared about fashion.

Norbert welcomed me into an office that would have satisfied the stuffiest of London solicitors, all dark wood and leather. It was his office, for this man, despite being scarcely ten years older than I, was now the senior partner in the august firm that had served my father in life and after. The elder Norbert and his contemporary partner had both succumbed in the influenza epidemic of 1919, leaving the son of one and a twenty-year-old grandson of the other in charge. Norbert had done his best to fill the impressive surroundings, but I thought that even now he was slightly intimidated, and would have been more comfortable among lighter, more modern furnishings.

Still, my London solicitors had never voiced a complaint about his handling of my California affairs, and I knew them to be scrupulous: The senior partner of that firm had been in love (secretly, he thought) with my mother, and had transferred his loyalty wholeheartedly to her daughter.

I settled into my chair, accepted the compulsory cup of weak American coffee, and made meaningless small talk for precisely three and a half minutes before Norbert eased us into business matters.

My California representatives had long been pleading that I apply my attentions to the holdings I had inherited in the state; having seen the house, I could only pray my other possessions were not as derelict. However, it soon appeared that the need for my presence was more for the sake of long-term decisions, re-investments and liquidations that I alone could make. What most of them boiled down to was, if I wasn't going to take an active rôle in the running of this factory, that company, and the other investment, I should sell my interests and move on.

Which was just what I had in mind.

We set up a number of appointments for the coming days so I could meet with my managers and directors. Looking at the brief synopses of figures Norbert laid before me, one after another, I had to agree: Electrical companies and copper mines did not run themselves for too long before they began to suffer from inattention, and thousands of acres of land adjacent to the recently discovered oil fields in southern California weren't going to join the boom without some help.

At the end of a long morning, Norbert pushed back in his chair with a sigh and stood. "Time for another cup of coffee," he pronounced, and went out of the door. I heard him speaking with his secretary for a moment, heard too the flush of distant waters a minute later. He returned with the secretary on his heels.

He poured the watery brown liquid, offered cream, sugar, and biscuits, then settled for a carefully measured five minutes of closing conversation. I broke it after one.

"Mr Norbert, I have to say you've done wonders with the entire estate. It couldn't have been easy, at this distance." I laid my spoon into the bone-china saucer. "However, that makes it all the more puzzling that the house has been allowed to go to ruin." I told him the outline of our adventures the previous evening, and he produced little noises of distress at our meeting with the police. I ended by repeating my comment about the state of the house, which observation he met with a sympathetic shake of the head.

"Terrible, isn't it?" he agreed, looking not in the least shame-faced. "Such a pity. But I hadn't much of a choice, really; the will was very clear on that."

"The will," I repeated.

"Yes, your father's will. Parents', I should say. Don't tell me you haven't seen it?"

"When I was fourteen, I must have done. Not since then."

"Oh, my, no wonder you're a little confused. And here I was hoping *you* might enlighten *me* on the matter. Hold on just a sec." He reached forward to toggle a switch on his desk-telephone, and said into the instrument, "Miss Rand, would you please bring me a copy of the Russell will?"

Miss Rand duly appeared with the bound document, handing it to Norbert, who passed it over to me. He sat back while I undid the ties and settled in to read it.

It proved to be one of the odder such that I had ever read. I went through the document closely, wondering why I had not seen it before—I was certain that it had not been among the stack of papers I had gone through when I had taken over my father's estate at the age of twenty-one. My eyes lingered on the two signatures at the bottom, my father's strong and unruly, my mother's neat as copperplate, and then went back to an earlier page.

"What does this mean, 'to ensure that no one unaccompanied by a member of the immediate family be granted access to the house for a period of twenty years after the date of this signing'?"

"Just that. It's actually quite straightforward, as these things go: If your father died, your mother inherited. If they both died, as sadly happened, you and your brother would inherit the house, however, no one else other than you, your spouses, and your children would be allowed to set foot in it except in your presence for twenty years after the—what was the date of signing?—yes, the fifth of June, 1906. It goes on to say that the house is exempt from the remainder of the disbursements until, as I said, the fifth of June, 1926—a little over two years from now. Now you're here, you and your husband are welcome to do what you like to the house. Except permit others inside without your being physically present, or to sell it before the given date."

"But why?"

"My father, who of course drew up this will, did not see fit to tell me the reasoning behind its details before he died," he replied, with the bemused attitude of one who had himself written so many odd wills that he no longer questioned them. "However, the requirement of the codicil is crystal clear, although it leaves to the discretion of this legal firm the means of ensuring that the house remain undisturbed. Within days of your father's unfortunate demise, my father, as head of the firm, arranged for a single lady relative of his to take the house across the street, Agatha Grimly is her name— she's my great step-cousin or something of the sort. Miss Grimly was later joined by her unmarried nephew. She was a schoolteacher most of her life, so she's got eyes in the back of her head. The nephew is a little dimwitted, but quite clear as to his job. They receive a bonus each time they run strangers off the property, which happens two or three times a year—the first time was within a few days of her taking over, the most recent—apart from last night's, of course—was a couple of months ago. And they live under the threat of losing their comfortable position were they to let an intruder slip past them. Frankly, it's a little game we play—I occasionally hire someone to try to break in, to see if he can get by them. They probably assumed you and your husband were such."

I supposed it was sometimes necessary that a solicitor not be too curious about his client's purposes. Clearly, my father had intended that no one get into that house but family. The why of that intent did not enter into Norbert's realm, merely the how. I gave a mental shrug and closed up the will.

"You may keep that, if you like," he said. "I have two other copies, one of those in a vault down the Peninsula. The lessons of 1906," he explained with a grimace. "We're still struggling with the consequences of City Hall burning."

He then reached into his desk's central drawer and drew out a lumpy, palm-sized brown-paper envelope, its flap glued down and signed across by my father's distinctive hand. Its contents gave off a slight metallic tick as he laid it onto the glossy wood of the desk.

"If you need assistance with cleaning ladies," he went on, "gardening services, anything, I hope you'll call on me. We do have a gardener come in once a year, to keep the front from becoming an offence to the neighbours—although as that is questionable under the will, I go down and stand watch while they work, always, to ensure that none of them approach the house itself. In the same way, my father supervised the cleaners who came in the week after the accident, when it became apparent that you...that the house would have to be closed up. He was never absolutely certain, because strictly speaking the codicil indicated that he should have allowed the milk in the ice-box to go bad and the moths to get into the carpets, but he decided that protecting the client's assets allowed for a degree of flexibility. He may even have consulted with a judge on the matter, I don't remember. However, that is neither here nor there. I'll 'phone Miss Grimly, and let her know that you're coming—wouldn't want you to be arrested again."

I stood up, tucking the folder under my left arm and putting out my right hand.

"Thank you, Mr Norbert. Although as I indicated, I have no intention of doing anything other than preparing the house for sale as soon as possible."

"Whatever you choose, I am at your service," he answered, shaking my hand. He retrieved the lumpy brown envelope and handed it to me with a small laugh. "Don't forget this—you'll be climbing over the walls again."

"Certainly not," I agreed, and slipped the envelope into my pocket. As we made our way to the door, I asked him, "Do you by any chance know how far the fire reached, in 1906?"

"I remember it vividly—I was seventeen then, and spent the whole time digging through rubble and helping people rescue their possessions from its path. The entire downtown burned. The only things left standing were the U.S. Mint down on Mission Street, a few houses on the peak of Russian Hill, and a handful more on Telegraph— everything else was gone, churches, saloons, Chinatown, and as I said, City Hall with all its records. But if you mean your house, the flames were stopped at Van Ness when the Army dynamited the entire length of it. Three blocks down from yours."

"I see. Thank you." I paused at the door, and reluctantly asked the question that had been hovering over me the entire time in his office.

"Mr Norbert, this may sound odd, but do you know if I was here during the earthquake? Actually during it, I mean?"

"Sure you were. My father took me to check on your

family the day the fire died down. That would have been the Saturday. Took most of the day to track you all down to the park where you were staying, but I remember your mother, making us coffee on an open fire as if she'd done it that way her whole life." His face took on a faraway look, and he smiled slightly. "She was in trousers and a pair of men's boots, but she wore the most extraordinary hat, with an enormous orange flower pinned to one side. It was as if she was thumbing her nose at the discomfort and fear all around her. She was an impressive lady, completely undaunted."

The pale hat with the orange flower dominated my vision as I took my leave of the lawyer and wandered towards the busy thoroughfare of Market Street. Trolleys and traffic were thick there, and the other streets met it at odd angles. Idly, my mind still taken up with the vision of the hat, I watched an ex-soldier with one leg negotiate his crutches through a flurry of female office workers in bright frocks.

Why would my father have written that codicil into his will?

When I put the question to Holmes some time later, he tossed the will onto the room's desk and shook his head. "There is no knowing at this point. But I agree that it is an oddity worth looking into."

Holmes had spent the morning getting the lay of the city, returning to the hotel with a sheaf of maps and scraps of paper scribbled with telephone numbers and addresses. He dug through the sheets now until he had found the detailed map; a green pencil had traced the streets to form an uneven outline around a large chunk of the Peninsula's eastern half, including all of the downtown. When I saw the straight line running more than a mile along Van Ness, I knew instantly what the pencil mark meant.

"This is the part that burned?"

"Wooden buildings, spilt cook-fires, broken water lines," he listed succinctly. "The city burned for three days, and almost nothing was left standing inside the line."

"Must have been absolute hell."

"You truly don't remember?"

"Oh, Lord, Holmes. I don't remember anything but my mother cooking over a camp-fire. Surely a child of six years would recall an event like the city burning?" I was beginning to feel as if someone had just pointed out to me that I was missing a leg. "Even a person with amnesia must be aware of some ... gap."

"I don't know that I should term it amnesia, precisely—that condition is extremely rare outside of ladies' fiction, and generally stems from a severe head injury. In your case I venture that it is the mind choosing to draw a curtain across the memories of your early childhood, for any number of reasons."

That I liked even less, the idea that my traitorous mind chose the cowardly option of hiding from unpleasant memories. "Holmes," I said abruptly, "last night you said that the process of discovery may be the reason we came here. What did you mean by that?"

"My dear Russell, think about it. Had you merely wished to rid yourself of your business entanglements in California, you could have done so in London with a command to your solicitors and a flourish of signatures. There would have been no need to traverse half the globe for the purpose. Instead, for the last three years you have delayed making decisions and refused to give direction until things here had reached a state of near crisis. And when my brother asked us to go to India, it seemed natural to you that we continue around the world to come here, although in fact it is both out of the way and considerably disruptive to our lives. What other reason could there be but that some well-concealed urge was driving you here, with purpose?"

A part of my mind acknowledged that he was right. The larger portion held back, unwilling to believe in such transparent machinations.

There was something else as well: Holmes was eyeing me with that awful air of expectancy he did so well, as if he had placed an examination question and was waiting for me to follow my preliminary response with the complete answer. He believed there was more in the situation than I perceived; were I to ask what it was, he would make me work for the answer.

That was more than I could face at the moment. Instead, I stood up briskly.

"I want to go look at the house. Norbert gave me the keys. Would you like to join me?"

"Shall we take lunch first?"

"I'm not really hungry. You go ahead, if you like, and join me later."

"No, I shall go with you," Holmes said. We assembled our possessions, and at the door he paused to ask, "Do you have the keys?"

"Of course," I said. "They're in my...No, they're not. What have I done with them? Oh, yes, here they are."

I had left the brown envelope on the foot of my bed, I saw, and went back to pick it up. As I turned back to the door, I thought about the walk before me and the condition of the house—and, no doubt, its facilities—at the end of it. "I'll be with you in a moment, Holmes," I said, and stepped into the marble-and-gilt room. When I had finished, I dried my hands, patted my hair (unnecessarily—the bob minded neither wind nor neglect) and strode to the door.

"The keys?" Holmes reminded me.

"They're—Damn it, where have I put them now?" I spotted the manila rectangle, half hidden between the mirror and a vase of flowers, and picked it up curiously: The wretched thing eluded me so persistently, it might have been possessed. With a spasm of irritation, I ripped it open and tipped its contents into Holmes' outstretched palm. His long fingers closed around the simple silver ring with half a dozen keys that ranged from a delicate, inch-long silver one to an iron object nearly the length of my hand. I tossed the scraps of paper in the direction of the trash basket, and marched out into the corridor.

Twice on the way I took a wrong turn; both times I looked around to find Holmes standing and watching me from up the street. The first time he had a frown on his face, the second a look of concern; when we finally reached the house itself he stopped before the wide gate, studying the keys in his hand.

"Russell, perhaps it would be best for me to enter first."

"Open the gate, Holmes."

He raised his eyes to my face for a moment, then slid the big iron key inside the padlock's hole and twisted. The metal works had clearly been maintained—oiled, perhaps, on the gardener's yearly visits—and the key turned smoothly.

I stepped onto the sunken cobblestones of the drive, my nerves insisting that I was approaching the lair of some creature with teeth and claws. I could feel eyes upon me, and not simply those of the guardian neighbour across the street. Yet there was no movement at any of the windows, no evidence of traffic apart from the footprints and crushed vegetation Holmes and I had left the day before. With Holmes at my back I walked towards the front door—and nearly leapt into his arms with a shriek when the branches above us exploded with sudden motion: three panicked doves, fleeing this invasion of their safe sanctuary.

I forced a laugh past my constricted throat, and gestured for Holmes to precede me to the door.

The solid dark wood was dull with neglect, the varnish lifted in narrow yellow sheets where the years of rain had blown past the protective overhang of the portico. Thick moss grew between the paving tiles; an entire fern grotto had established itself in the cracks where stonework met door frame. I heard the sound of the tumblers moving in the lock, a sound that seemed to shift my innards within me. Holmes turned the knob without result, then leant his shoulder against the time-swollen wood, taking a sudden step across the threshold as the door gave way.

The dark house lay open to us. I looked over Holmes' shoulder down the hallway, seeing little but a cavern; steeling myself, I took a step inside. As I did so, the corner of my eye registered an oddly familiar rough place in the frame of the door, about shoulder height. I stopped, one foot on either side of the threshold, and drew back to examine it.

A narrow indentation had been pressed into the surface, some four inches in height and perhaps half an inch wide. Screw-holes near the top and the bottom, and a gouge a third of the way down from the top where someone had prised the object out of the varnish that held it fast. A mezuzah, I thought, and suddenly she was there.

My mother—long rustling skirt and the graceful brim of a hat high above me—pushing open the glossy front door with one hand while her other came up to brush the intricate carved surface of the bronze object. A blessing on the house, laid at the entrance, mounted there by command and as recognition that a home is a place apart. My Jewish mother, touching it lovingly every time she entered. And not only my mother: My fingertips remembered the feel of the carving, cool arabesques protecting the tightly curled text of the blessing within.

My hand reached out of its own volition and smoothed the wood, indented, drilled, splintered, puzzling.

"What have you found?" Holmes asked.

"There used to be a mezuzah on this door. My mother's father gave it to her, the year I was born. It was his first overture after the offence of her marriage, her first indication that she might be forgiven for marrying a Gentile. And as it turned out, his last, since he died a few months later. It meant a great deal to her. And it's gone."

"Perhaps Norbert senior took it down, for safekeeping?"

"I shouldn't think it would occur to a Gentile to remove it."

"And your mother herself wouldn't have taken it down?"

"Not unless she didn't plan to return. And they died on a week-end trip to the Lodge—our summer house down the Peninsula. We intended to be back in a few days."

"A friend, then, who removed it, knowing what it meant to her?"

"Perhaps." I fingered the wounded frame again, wondering. I knew none of her friends. I had a vague idea that one or two women might have visited me in hospital after the accident, but I had been injured and orphaned, and in no condition to receive their comfort. Their letters that reached me in England went into the fire unanswered, and had eventually stopped.

Oddly, although the missing object should by rights have increased my apprehension, in fact the brief vision of my mother moving through the doorway served to reassure me, as if her hand had smoothed the back of my head in passing. When I turned again to the house, it was no longer the lair of a dangerous beast, merely empty rooms where once a family had lived.

The interior looked like something out of *Great Expectations*, an interrupted life overlaid with a decade of dust. The gilt-framed looking-glass in the entrance hall bore a coat of grey-brown fuzz, the glass itself gone speckled and dim. I stood in the door-way to the first room, my mother's morning room, and saw that the furniture had been draped with cloths before the house was locked up, all the windows and curtains tightly shut. The air was heavy with the odours of dust and baked horse-hair, unaired cloth goods, and mildew, along with a faint trace of something burnt.

Holmes crossed to the nearest windows and stretched his hand to the curtains.

"Careful," I warned, and his tug softened into a slow

pull, so that the dust merely held in the air instead of exploding back into the room.

A drift of trembling black ashes in the fireplace was the sole indication of the house's abrupt closure. Everything else lay tidy: flower vases emptied, ash-trays cleaned, no stray coffee-cups, no abandoned books. This had been my mother's favourite room, I remembered, and unlike the formal back parlour had actually been used for something other than the entertainment of guests. She had arranged the delicate French desk (one of the Louis—XIV? XV?) so that it looked out of the window onto what had been a wisteria-framed view of the bird-bath, and was now a solid green curtain. She'd loved the view, loved the garden, even keeping yearly journals of its progress—yes, there they were, pretty albums bound in silk that she'd pored over, writing the names of shrubs planted and sketching their flowers, recording its successes and failures in her precise script so unlike my own scrawl. I turned away sharply out of the room; as Holmes followed me, he gently shut the door, cutting off the watery sunlight and plunging the hall-way back into gloom.

The entire house was a stage set with dust-coloured shrouds. The long dining-room table was little more than a floor-length cloth punctuated by the regular bumps of its chairs, its long tarpaulined surface set with three blackened candle-sticks. The music room was home to a piano-shaped mound and a small forest of chairs; the pantry, its door giving way reluctantly to a third key on the ring, lay waiting, the house's silver, crystal, and china neatly arrayed in their drawers and on their shelves.

In the dim library, Holmes gave a grunt of disapproval at the smell of must. This had been my father's study, where he had kept accounts and written letters, typing with remarkable facility on the enormous Underwood type-writer, its mechanism so heavy my child's fingers could barely propel the keys to the ribbon. The Underwood, like the desk and the two chairs in front of the pristine fireplace, was draped; the carpets here had been rolled up against the wall, and emanated a faint trace of moth-balls.

The stillness in the house was proving oppressive. I cleared my throat to remark, "How many acres of dust-covers do you suppose they used?"

Holmes merely shook his head at the disused and mouldering volumes, and went on.

As we worked through the rooms, various objects and shapes seemed to reach out and touch my memory, each time restoring a small portion of it to life: The looking-glass near the door, for example, had been a wedding present that my mother hated and my father loved, source of much affectionate discord. And the fitted carpet in the back parlour—something had happened to it, some catastrophe I was responsible for: something spilt? An upturned coffee tray, perhaps, and the horri-fied shrieks of visiting women—no, I had it now: Their horror was not, as my guilty young mind had immedi-ately thought, because of any damage to the carpet, but at the hot coffee splashing across my young skin, mirac-ulously not scalding me.

My eye was caught by a peculiar object on the top of a high credenza: an exotic painted caricature of a cat, carved so that its mouth gaped wide in a toothy O. But shouldn't there be a flash of yellow, right where that stick in the middle ... ? Ah, yes: Father's joke. He'd found the cat in Chinatown and fixed a perch across its open mouth, then arranged it on the precise spot where my mother's canary, which was given the occasional freedom of the room, liked to sit and sing. How Levi and I had giggled, every time the bird opened its mouth in the cat's maw.

As I worked my way through the rooms, there was no entirety of recall, merely discrete items that sparked specific memories. I felt as if some prince was working his way through the sleeping events of my childhood, kissing each one back to life. Or tapping them like a clown with a trick flower that flashed miraculously into full bloom.

Not that I'd ever much cared for clowns, nor had I been one for fairy tales: The passivity of that sleeping princess had annoyed me even when I was small.

Only when we reached the very back of the ground floor and Holmes pushed open a swinging door did I discover a place that felt completely familiar, wall to wall: the kitchen. No cloth shrouds here, just white tile, black stove, shelved pots, a row of spoons and implements. The wooden table where I'd sat down with plate, glass, and home-work. The ice-box (unchanged from my infancy) from which I'd taken my milk, tugging at its heavy door. The pantry, startlingly equipped with foodstuffs: biscuits and coffee in their tins, flour in its bin, preserves in jars that had gone green beneath their wax seals.

Ghosts are most often glimpsed at the corners of one's vision, heard at the far reaches of the audible, tasted in lingering scents at the back of one's palate. So now the house began to people itself at the furthest edges of my senses: A wide-bottomed cook, her back to me, laid down the wooden spoon she was using to stir a pot and bustled away through a door. It happened in one short instant at the very corner of the mind's eye, and she was gone when I turned my head, but she lived in my mind. Then at the base of the door I noticed a trace of long-dried soil, and with that, through the window in the upper half of the door, a much-abused, sweat-dark hat the colour of earth seemed to pass: the gardener.

His name had been...Michael? No, Micah. I'd loved him, I knew that without question, although I remembered next to nothing about him. He had rescued a bird for me one time; the neighbour's cat had pounced and feathers flew and I—small then, perhaps four, sitting on the back steps (Were there back steps on the other side of that windowed door? I crossed to the window: yes, two of them, leading down to what had once been a neat gravel path-way)—I had screamed in full-throated protest at the sight, bringing Micah around the corner with one hand clamping down his hat and the other holding a rake, his stumpy legs so close to running that the very sight of him silenced me. The cat shot away into the shrubbery; Micah gathered the bird, gentled it, placed it in my sheltering hands where it lay for a time, stunned but not injured. Its heart thrummed nonstop, astounding the palms of my hands, until suddenly it jerked into life and launched itself into the air, flitting into the branches of the apple tree, then away.

I looked down at those hands, two decades older. Curious, the means by which memories were stored. The door-frame mezuzah, the bird, both lay in the skin of my hands. Why was the mind said to have an eye and not a hand, or a tongue? Perhaps touch, taste, odour, sound were linked to the heart rather than the intellect. Certainly both of these tactile memories I had retrieved carried with them profound and specific emotional charges, the one of homecoming, the other of competent authority, both of them immensely reassuring.

I raised my eyes to the grubby window, and in that instant it was as if the kitchen door flew open and the sun spilt into the room. I knew, beyond a doubt, what I wished to do: I would clean the house, restore it, remove the decay to which my neglect had condemned it; and I would find the people who had been here, friends and workers, and talk to them all, weaving myself back into the tapestry of community. For too long, I had turned my back on my past. Holmes was right: I had brought us here for a reason.

Feeling as if I had cast off a heavy and constricting garment, I spun on my heel to go in search of Holmes, to tell him what I had decided, and nearly fell over him. He was stooped to look into a small mirror placed awkwardly on the wall.

"Holmes, I—" I began, and then I took in his attitude, that sharpening of attention that put one in mind of a dog on scent. "What is it?"

"Does this not seem to you an odd location for a looking-glass?"

"For a man your height, certainly. But even in America, few cooks are over six feet tall."

"Yes, yes," he said, waving away my explanation. "I mean the placement itself."

Once my attention was drawn to it, I could see what he meant. It was a round glass set in an octagonal frame, somehow Chinese looking, but a looking-glass used by servants to check their appearance before entering the house would surely be located near the swinging door, not above the long bench used for pots and dishes on their way to the scullery. I took his place before it, bending my knees to bring my eyes to a more normal level.

"It's also too small to see one's entire face in it," I noted in surprise.

"Queer," he agreed, opening and shutting the cabinets to survey their contents.

"Could it be intended as a means of keeping one eye on the back door while working at the bench?" I speculated, but unless it had shifted over the years, its only view was the cook-stove, and there was no sign of a prop fallen from one side. While I was craning this way and that, taken up by the minor puzzle, Holmes continued on his circuit of the room.

"Did your family have a resident pet?" he asked, back again near the swinging door.

He was squatting before a roughly glazed porcelain vase or bowl that sat on the floor at the base of the wall. Six inches at its widest and five inches high, it was primitive in craftsmanship but oddly graceful—and precariously placed, considering the traffic there would have been in and out of the door.

"I don't believe we did. We had a canary, but cats made my brother sneeze, and my mother disliked dogs."

I could see why he asked, for when I picked it up to examine it, beneath the dust the mineral deposit left by a pint or so of evaporating water was unmistakable. Still, it was an odd utensil for the purpose, its sides narrowing at the top to an opening that would prove awkward for feline muzzles. Too, surely it would have been better placed in the corner between the sink and the back door, or even inside the scullery. I put it back where I had found it and cast my eyes around the kitchen for anything else out of place. All I could see was a long-dead pot of some unidentifiable herb withered on a window-sill—no doubt an oversight on the part of Norbert's cleaners, not a deliberate peculiarity.

"Was your cook Chinese?" Holmes asked.

"I shouldn't have thought so," I told him. As with most Western cities, the Chinese community in San Francisco was closely hemmed by judicial ordinance and societal expectations. They were allowed to run laundries, make deliveries, and perform menial labour, but a Chinese cook in a private home would have been unusual.

"You don't remember," he said, not a question.

"I am sorry, Holmes," I snapped. "I'm not being deliberately uncooperative, you know."

But even as I said it, his question had woken a node of memory; the ghost stirred again, that ample-bodied figure moving from stove to scullery. A cook: But now that I thought about it, the woman had been wearing loose trousers, and soft shoes. And a tunic, but colourful, not a thing a menial worker would have worn for hard labour.

"Mah," I breathed in wonder. "Her name was Mah. And Micah was her brother."

"Who is Micah?"

"Our gardener. He rescued a bird from the neighbour's cat one time. He wore a sweaty soft hat, and he used to bow when he gave my mother a bouquet from the flower bed. And…and he used to make me laugh with the way he talked. He called me 'missy.'"

"Did he wear a queue?" Holmes' voice was soft, as if not to disturb my attention.

"He…" I began to say no, he wore a hat, but again my hand knew the truth of the matter: my small fingers wrapping curiously around a smooth, glossy rope of plaited hair, hot from the sun. But the sensation seemed very distant, as if overlaid by something else. "Bless me, he did. His hair was once in a long plait all the length of his back, but that was a very long time ago. Later I just remember the Western hat, and that he dressed like anyone else."

"No doubt after the emperor was overthrown in 1911, your gardener would have joined the rest of the world in cutting the queue and taking on the laws and customs of his adoptive land. Before that, his assuming Western dress would have been dangerous for his family in China."

"That's why Chinatown seemed different," I exclaimed.

"How is that?"

"The streets. I remember them as filled with people in strange dress—funny hats, the queues, foreign clothes. But yesterday most of them were dressed like the rest of the city."

"And their children will now be going to public schools, and their laws will be those of America."

"But how on earth did you know? That he was Chinese, I mean?"

"The mirror, the water, the pot-plant. There is a Chinese belief that the psychic energies within a room can be shaped by the judicious use of objects that embody the elements. Something to do with the dragons under the earth. Symbolic, of course, but a belief in patterns of electromagnetic energies across the face of the earth is common—one need only note the prehistoric hillside carvings in Peru, the song-lines among the aboriginals of Australia, and the ley-lines across England."

I braced myself for a set piece on one of Holmes'

many and invariably arcane interests, but that seemed to be the extent of his lecture for the time being. With a last glance around, he went out the swinging door, leaving it standing open. A moment later I heard his feet climbing the stairs.

Chapter Four

I did not follow him. Truth to tell, I was feeling just a little shaky.

I am a person to whom self-control is basic. Over the course of the past few years I had been shot, knifed, and forcibly drugged with a hypodermic needle; I'd had Holmes abducted from my side, been abducted myself, come within moments of being blown to a red mist, and recently faced down a tusked boar mad with rage, all the while eating peculiar foods, wearing impossible costumes, and sleeping in scores of highly uncomfortable situations. Yet I had never really deep-down doubted my ability to meet the peculiar demands of life with Holmes, because I had always trusted my body and mind to function smoothly together. Will and intellect, in easy harmony.

And suddenly, what I had imagined was control now seemed mere passivity, what appeared to be harmony was merely a façade. I felt as if I were standing with my back braced against the door of an overstuffed cupboard, struggling to keep the avalanche of clutter inside from sweeping out and overwhelming me. Coming to this house had opened that door, and memories had begun to trickle out: Mah the cook, Micah the gardener. My mother's fingers brushing the door frame, her hand cupping the back of my head.

How many childhood memories does the average person retain? I suspect not many, and those either a generalised composite of experiences or striking events that lodge in the mind like boulders in a stream. And if the average person were to be told that those memories were unreliable, that the utterly familiar home never existed, that the vividly remembered fall from the tree never took place outside of dreams, what then?

That person would begin to mistrust his or her mind.

And that person would be right to do so.

Instead of going to the stairs, I turned the other way and found the library, tugging back one of the sheets to uncover a leather chair. I sat down, dimly aware of creaking floorboards overhead, more immediately interested in the ghosts this room might have.

It was a man's room. So I sat, waiting for my father.

I had been lucky in my parents, blessed for fourteen years to live in the vicinity of two lively, intelligent individuals who loved me, and each other, unreservedly. My self-imposed amnesia, if that is what it was, no doubt had its roots, as Holmes had said, with the double trauma of the accident that took my family's life.

My father had been driving a difficult piece of road in the autumn of 1914, a last family week-end at the lake-house before he enlisted and the war engulfed our lives. He had been distracted, and the motorcar had swerved, hesitated, and then plunged down the cliff into the sea. With the swerve, I had been thrown free; father, mother, and brother had sailed off the world and into the resulting flames.

I spent the rest of the autumn in hospital, and still bore the scars and twinges from my injuries. Worse than the scars, however, was the guilt that started up as soon as consciousness returned—not just the grinding offence of having survived when they had not, but the burning agony of knowing that I, myself, had been the cause of the accident. That I had distracted my father, by starting a loud and petty argument with my younger brother. That I had killed them, and lived to bear the guilt.

Impossible to live with the memory, impossible to leave it alone; within weeks, my young mind had learnt to suppress it during the daylight hours, although my nights had been haunted for years by the Dream, nocturnal memories of the sights and sounds of the car going off of the cliff.

Easier by far just to shove all the past into the same crowded cupboard than to pick and choose what to keep out on display and what to hide away. And because my mind, and my will, are both very strong, the door stayed so firmly shut that I managed to forget it was even there, until the ship had sailed out of the Bombay harbour and turned towards California, its prow a wedge, prising at the edges of the cupboard door.

My father had used this library daily. He had sat at that shrouded desk, taken a cigar from that enamelled box and clipped it with the tool that lay waiting, sat to read the newspaper in that other canvas-wrapped chair before that cold and empty fireplace. And being the kind of person he was, he would have allowed me free access, and I would have been in and out of this room at all times, with questions, with specimens of natural history, with discoveries and complaints and proposals. But was it a composite of experiences that told me this? Or was it hypothetical reasoning, a theory given flesh?

I did not know. Still, I felt that he had been here, once long ago, and that I had been with him, and for the moment, it would have to be enough. Leaving the leather chair uncovered, I absently adjusted a crooked painting and pushed a couple of misplaced spines back into place as I went out of the library on my way upstairs.

Holmes was nowhere to be seen, but I heard a movement from further overhead: the attic. I stood in the door of my parents' room, looking in warily, not certain if I was ready for the intimacy of a married couple's bedroom. However, the room did not feel particularly private, not with the afternoon sun streaming in through the south window where Holmes had drawn back the curtains. The dust of his passing still hung in the sunlight, muffling the rainbows cast by the prismed glass of the window onto the white cloths covering the dressing-table. He had also left a trail of footprints on the boards, coming and going and, by the looks of it, circling into various corners as he searched for anything out of the ordinary. Two white-painted wicker chairs sat in the bay window to my left, arranged on either side of a small, high table just large enough for a cup-laden tray. I had a vivid picture of the two occupants sitting in the morning sunlight, sharing their coffee at the start of the day; again, was it memory, or imagination?

I moved across to the lumpy dressing-table, cautiously raising its protective cloth to reveal hair-brush, powder, manicure implements, crystal scent bottle. My hand hovered above the delicate glass stopper of this last, pulled by the powerful memory stimulus the aroma might hold, held back by the fear that it might be more than I could endure. Either that, or nothing at all, which would be even more unbearable. Instead, my hand came down on the long red lacquer-ware box beside it, tipping open the top to reveal a collection of hair- and hat-pins and the single carved ivory chop-stick that she had used to tease loose portions of hair. It was a lovely thing, and I ran my thumb across the worn carvings before I closed the top of the box and withdrew my hand.

Tomorrow, perhaps, I would envelop myself in my mother's scent. Or the next day.

Instead of the bottle, my hand reached out for a picture, one of half a dozen tarnished silver frames lying face-down on the table's linen cloth. The one I lifted first was the largest, and showed my brother and me when Levi was on the cusp of walking—perhaps a year old, which would have made me six. But instead of the usual studio setting of curly-headed children before a painted rose bower or atop a bored Shetland pony, we were dressed in elaborately formal Chinese costumes, high-necked, glossy as only silk could be, the frogs of the front fastenings intricately worked. My brother and I stood before some kind of shelved cabinet, ornately carved although out of focus, and although he looked merely bewildered, my expression indicated that I appreciated the joke; I could see why my mother had chosen the photograph for her dressing-table.

I ran my thumb over the blackened frame, thinking it looked familiar. Slowly, it came to me: I had this one's twin at home, in Sussex, lying (also face-down) in a drawer under some meaningless papers; rarely glimpsed, never forgotten. My own photograph showed the entire family, not just its younger generation, but as I studied the arrangement of pictures on my mother's dressing-table, I began to suspect that mine had once balanced the other frame on this surface. I could even see where it had once stood, in the large empty space on the right-hand side of the table. Whoever had packed the trunk of clothing and effects that accompanied me on the boat to England in 1915 had come in here and removed the portrait from my mother's collection, that I might take something of them with me.

I placed the picture back upright on the cloth, and one by one, set the others upright as well. My father appeared, stretched out on a travelling-rug laid across a very English-looking stretch of pebbly beach, eyes closed behind his spectacles, the blonde infant tucked under his arm similarly asleep; my dark-haired brother as a small baby was next, his face surrounded by a cloud of lace in our mother's arms, a peculiarly enigmatic expression on her features; me by a lake, shovel in one hand, mud to my waist, a look of great stubbornness on my face. Then a surprise: a pair of strangers who could not possibly be related to me.

I knew who they were, though: Their shades had just visited me downstairs, in the kitchen and just outside its door. Mah and Micah, siblings or, I thought, studying their broad, foreign faces more carefully, a married couple. And if their employment here had struck me as unlikely, how much more so their presence in my mother's collection of intimate family portraits?

I sat down on the padded bench before the dressing-table with the small photograph of two middle-aged Chinese people in one hand, looking between it and the larger one of my brother and myself in Oriental costume. The edge of the carved cabinet could be seen in both photographs; they had been taken in the same room.

After a minute I reached out to prop up the remaining pictures. The first showed a curly-headed blonde girl of about five, bony knees drawn up into a large wooden chair, a book spread out in her lap, squinting in concentration at the pages. Portrait of a young scholar: Miss Mary Russell at her books. And finally, like a familiar face in a crowd, the picture of my house in Sussex. It had been a vacation cottage during the periods we lived in England, and I had insisted on going back there when I was orphaned, to the place where happiness had once lived.

Not that I had found happiness still in residence when I returned: Instead, I got my aunt. But I had held to myself the sensation of refuge, and restored the house to it when I came of age and turned that so-called guardian out. Clearly, my mother, too, had treasured the summer weeks there on the Downs.

My reverie was broken by motion. I looked up, and nearly dropped the pictures before my mind interpreted the ghost it was seeing as Holmes' reflection in the filthy looking-glass.

"Holmes! You startled me. Did you find anything?"

"Dried scraps of soap in the bath-room dishes, beds still made up, two half-packed trunks here and one in the child's room, and in the attic entire townships of mice. What have you there?"

I handed him the picture of Mah and Micah for his examination, watching his reflected face, seeing his eyes flick from the Chinese faces to the ornately wrought frame, then to the identical frames that graced the family pictures.

"Provocative," he said after a minute, and gave it back to me.

"Why were you so interested in my father's dressing-table?" I asked.

"That was not I."

Startled, I looked into his dim reflection, then swiv-

elled around on the bench to stare at the swirl of footprints I had taken to be his. This time, I saw: At least two
other people had walked through this room, one with
feet slightly smaller than Holmes', the other's considerably smaller. I slid the photo into my pocket and went to
see what had interested the intruders.

The other dressing-table, which had neither seat nor
mirror, stood just outside the door to the bath-room.
That it belonged to a man was clear even under cover,
since the shapes were those of a man's hair-brushes and
a clothes brush, and little else. Kneeling in front of it, I
could see that the dust on the top had been recently disturbed; I duplicated the disturbance now, folding the
cloth back to reveal a small drawer. It did not take a
magnifying glass to see the marks on its brass lock.

"Looks pretty amateurish," I remarked.

"They might as well have set a chisel to it," he agreed.

By habit, I hooked my finger-nails under the edge
of the drawer in case of finger-prints, and tugged. It
slid open freely, releasing a faint odour of cedar and
revealing a handful of small coins, a set of black shoe-
laces, some pen nibs, and an assortment of collar-
studs, the normal débris of the male animal. If there
had been anything of import in the drawer, it was not
there now.

I swivelled on my heels to study the prints. The people who made them had spent some time gathered
around my father's steamer trunk, then one of them—
the smaller feet—had investigated his bed-side table.
Not, however, my mother's, which was decidedly odd.
Unless, of course, they were not simply sneak-thieves,
and had already found what they were after.

"When do you suppose those footprints were made?"
I asked.

"Within the past month, or two months at the most."

"Did you find where they got in?"

"Judging by the traces of soil there and here, I should say they came in through the kitchen door."

I twisted to look up at him. "I saw no fresh soil there."

"You were . . . distracted."

"I did see the soil, but I'd have said it was old. And I'm certain the kitchen door showed no signs of tampering." That I definitely would have noticed.

"No," he agreed.

I slid the drawer shut, let the cloth fall over it, and got to my feet. "Which means that either their locksmith's talents deteriorated, or they had the one key and not the other. I shall have to ask Mr Norbert just how many sets of keys there were."

The rest of the house held neither ghosts nor clues. Even my bedroom might have belonged to a stranger, its fittings and knick-knacks curiously apt rather than familiar. I picked from a shelf a tiny porcelain baby-doll, all unruly brown hair and a lacy robe, which fit most satisfyingly into the palm of my hand. I had not been a child who played with dolls, but I vaguely thought that a friend had given me this one; perhaps I had kept it through affection for her rather than for the object itself. I put it back on the shelf, dusted off my hands, and continued through the upstairs rooms.

Each room showed signs of a recent passage through it, with disturbed objects and footprints in the dust. And not just footprints.

I went back downstairs and found Holmes in the library with a book, sitting in the leather chair I had uncovered. He had carried one of the candelabras in here from the dining table and filled it with candles; drips of wax on the floor-boards traced his progress along the shelves. The candles, half-burnt, now stood on top of the desk, but still gave sufficient illumination to the shelves that I could see that the dust-lines where the books had stood no longer coincided with the edges of the books.

I picked up the candle-stick and held it close to the shelf: dust along the tops, faint disturbance along the top ridge of some of the spines—the intruders had pulled the books back to look behind them, but not removed each one to rifle through the pages. It was something of a relief, for to have laboriously searched each book, then scrupulously replaced it on the shelf, would have indicated a particularly organised and potentially dangerous sort of mind. These people were just looking in the more obvious places.

But for what?

I put the candelabrum back on the desk, pinched out the flames, and gently pulled back the wrap of the other chair, allowing the cloth to slump gently to the floor. I sneezed and sat down.

"Any idea what they were searching for?"

"Something of his rather than hers. There is no safe in the house?"

"Not so far as I know. I know they kept Mother's jewellery in the bank, and had to remember to retrieve it in time when she wanted to wear it."

"I should say your intruders did not know that, going by the universal disturbance of the picture-frames."

And I'd thought time had misplaced them. As if to redeem myself, I asked, "You noticed that the two guestroom beds had been disturbed?" In response, he patted his suit coat, telling me that his inner pocket held envelopes of evidence. "Hairs?"

"Short grey on the one, long brown on the other."

"How long?"

"As long as yours—as yours used to be," he said, resigned to the necessity of my scant haircut, but not the fact.

"A woman? Good Lord."

He closed the book on his knee. "Russell, what precisely do you intend to do?"

"I don't know, Holmes," I said, taking off my spectacles to rub at my irritated eyes. "I really don't know."

After a while, he opened his book again and I went into the kitchen, unlocking the back door to step out into the wilderness. As I stood there on the damp, subsiding bricks, my naïve determination to restore my family's home to its former glories faltered beneath the enormity of the task. What was I thinking? It would take weeks, months to bring the house and gardens to a state of liveability, and what then? I had no intention of moving back to California.

Restoring the house would not restore my family.

Better to sell it now, before the building wormed its way into my affections. Let someone else worry about the brambles and the mice. Let someone else love it.

And as if to lay an omen of blessing on the decision, a small piece of Nature's magic whirred past me, a flash of red more brilliant than a maharaja's rubies, moving so fast I could not easily focus until it paused, hovering to drink from the pendulous blossoms of a fuchsia: a humming-bird. I hadn't seen one since I was a child, and I gaped at it with a child's wonder. When it darted away, I was aware of a smile on my face.

I returned to the library, and spoke to Holmes' back. "As I see it, there are two separate problems here. One is the house itself and what to do with it. The other concerns the puzzles we've found here—not necessarily the break-in, as nothing seems to be missing other than the mezuzah, but I've decided that I wouldn't mind, after all, knowing something more about my family. About the years I spent here. It is, after all, my past. I'll give it a week, in between my appointments with Mr Norbert. And then we'll leave and I'll tell Norbert to sell it once the restrictions are lifted, two years from now."

Holmes turned to look at me, and there it was again, that raised eyebrow of omniscience, asking me to reconsider some hasty judgement. I thought I knew what he was after this time, however, and sighed to myself. He'd been too long without intellectual challenge and itched to uncover more about the house's invasion.

"Holmes, they didn't take anything, they didn't damage anything but the lock on the desk." The eyebrow remained arched, and I raised a hand in surrender. "But please, go right ahead and investigate, if that's what you want to do."

"Very well," he said, depositing the book on the small table and getting to his feet. "I shall begin by applying myself to the finger-prints on your father's dressing-table."

"You brought your print kit?" I asked, surprised. His magnifying glass and evidence envelopes went everywhere with him, but the tin box containing powders, brush, and insufflator created unnecessary bulk in the pockets, unless he anticipated needing it. But his only response was yet another unreadable yet disapproving look as he went out of the door.

I was at something of a loss to know where to begin myself, so in default, I walked in the direction of the first room we had entered, my mother's morning room. I had my hand on the door-knob when Holmes' voice brought me up short.

"I shouldn't go in there while the kitchen door is standing open," he commanded. "The draughts might prove destructive, and I haven't any glass plates."

With that Delphic utterance, he continued climbing the stairs, leaving me with my hand on the knob and many questions on my lips. Draughts? Glass plates? What on earth was he on about?

Slowly, I put it together. Glass plates, used for the preservation of fragile documents. Documents, such as burnt papers. Burnt papers, such as a drift of trembling black ashes in an otherwise pristine fireplace.

Ah.

Was I being very stupid, or was he being unnecessarily scrupulous? I could not answer that, so I went back to the library to begin a methodical archaeology on my father's desk.

An hour or so later, during which Holmes had bumped about all over the upstairs, he came back in, brushing ineffectually at his sleeves with hands even grimier than mine. I looked up from my reading, blinked, and realised it was nearly dark. I reached for the lamp and switched its control, but without result. I closed the book and sat back.

"Any joy?" I asked him.

"They wore gloves."

"All the best-dressed villains wear gloves," I commented by way of commiseration.

"However, they remained in the house long enough to require sleep on the guest-room beds. Separate rooms, if you were wondering."

That they had slept in the beds seemed to please him. "They took off their gloves to sleep?"

"Possibly. But for other activities as well." With a smile, he took an oversized envelope from his pocket and held it for me to see. Inside lay the flowered porcelain pull-handle from a flush water-closet, detached from its chain.

"But surely there are layers of prints on it?" I asked.

"Oh, I'd say the maid your parents employed was a fine woman who took pride in her work. No short-cuts in her cleaning. Mrs Hudson would approve." Purring with satisfaction, he looked down at his unlikely treasure. "One lovely hand-print, from palm to fingertips, each one clear and precise."

"Well done, Holmes." Now all we had to do was ask the population of San Francisco to give us a comparison, I reflected—but no need to be churlish and say it aloud. "The man's or the woman's?"

"By the slim size of the fingers, hers. Her shoe size and length of stride suggest a height of slightly over five and a half feet, whereas her grey-haired companion is a short man, two or three inches under five and a half feet, whose broad feet suggest a broad hand. We shall have to make enquiries as to the weather over the past weeks," he added, folding away the pull-handle. "Their shoes left soil on the floor beneath their beds, but not enough to indicate they walked through actual mud."

"And if they came in through the kitchen, you're right, that ground would be a morass after a rain. Did you find any signs of lamps, candles, torches, anything of the sort?"

"The woman had a carpet-bag she set down several places, which could have held anything. But I saw no signs of dripped wax or any impression of a lamp's base. I think it probable they did their work during the daylight, so as not to alert the aged but sleepless watch-dog across the way."

"Coming in before dawn and leaving after dusk? I'd have thought that risky. Unless—"

"Yes," he said. "It would be satisfying to discover that the full moon coincided with a dry spell, would it not?"

And so it proved, in a pleasingly neat confirmation of how the intruders came and went unnoticed. When we repaired to the hotel an hour or two later, for supplies, soap, and sustenance, enquiries at the desk were followed within minutes by a simultaneous knock on our door and the ringing of the telephone. Holmes went to the door, holding it open for the man with the laden tea tray, while I received the information that February had been wet more or less throughout, but two weeks of dry weather in the middle of March had been broken by rain the morning of the twenty-fourth. The March full moon had been the twentieth.

I thanked the manager, then: "Oh, and Mr Auberon? Could you please have someone look into train reservations to New York, the middle of next week? That's right, two of us. Sorry?" I listened for a minute, then asked him to hold on, and covered the mouthpiece with my hand.

"Holmes, he says the hotel has another guest who is planning a cross-country aeroplane flight to leave the middle of next week, and wants two partners in the enterprise. Might we be interested?"

The vivid memory of our recent, nerve-fraying night-time flight over the Himalayan foothills winced across his face, but Holmes' upper lip was nothing if not stiff. "Up to you," he replied mildly, and returned to pouring the tea. I addressed myself to the telephone.

"Perhaps you could get the details of both, and we could decide which fits better with our plans. Thank you."

Holmes brought me a cup of tea and a selection of sandwiches, settling down at the window with his own refreshment. He ate two sandwiches in rapid succession, then sat back with his cup. "Have you a schedule for the morrow?" he asked.

"Norbert's arranged various appointments in the morning, but I have the rest of the day free. Would you like to see something of the city? We could go out to the ocean and sun-bathe, if the sun comes out. And there's a famous salt-water bath out there as well, if you'd like those."

He fixed me with a disbelieving gaze. "You wish to play the tourist?"

I kept the innocent expression on my face for as long as I could, but a slight movement of my mouth gave me away, and the answering relief on his face released the laughter. "Holmes, I wouldn't think of getting in the way of your glass plates."

He shook his head with disapproval, but said only, "You shall ask Mr Norbert about the keys?"

"Certainly, and if he knows where I can find Mah and Micah."

"You might also enquire if his watch-dogs saw anything out of the ordinary before the twentieth of March."

"I shall."

In the end, we did play the part of tourists, for that evening at least. We took a motorcar out to where San Francisco ended, and ate dinner at the Cliff House restaurant with the Pacific Ocean pounding at our feet, watching the sun go down. Wine again proved to be available, albeit decanted into an anonymous pitcher, and if the cooking was not as exceptional as the view out of the windows, the food was palatable. When we had finished our coffee, we walked down the steep hill and onto the sand, strolling along the beach. The wind had died down and the fog was lying well off-shore; it was quite pleasant.

At the far end, with the western sky darkening towards deepest indigo, Holmes settled onto a section of the sea wall that kept the sand at bay and took out his tobacco.

"Is this beach familiar to you?" he asked.

"It is, although the Cliff House I remember was a magnificently absurd Victorian monstrosity, so enormous and top-heavy it was a wonder that it didn't topple into the sea in the earthquake. We used to come here a lot with my father. Levi would build elaborate Gothic fortified castles using dribbled wet sand while I read a book, and my father would alternate between swimming and reading one of his dime novels. Which reminds me—do you know what I found on the shelves in the library?"

"Oh, Lord," he said.

"Yes, three of the stories Conan Doyle published. Oh, Holmes, my father would have been so delighted by the situation. He had a very droll and complicated sense of humour—you saw the cat carving on the high shelf?" I explained to him my father's canary perch, and he chuckled around the stem of his pipe.

"Were the library books his?"

"A lot of them were in the house when he took it over. You see, his parents badly wanted him to remain in Boston, but he refused to leave California, and lived on his own here for years before they decided that, for the sake of the family name, if their son wasn't coming home, he might as well comport himself in as civilised a fashion as one could in the wilderness of San Francisco. They gave him the family house and its fittings to permit him to do so. I think they'd bought the books by the linear foot when they built the library—you know how it is, books look good on the shelves, even if they're never read. Actually, my father wasn't a huge reader himself—you may have noticed that many of those books still have uncut pages. He used to come home with a book he'd bought, spend half an hour skimming through it to extract the essence, and never look at it again."

"Your mother was the reader, then?"

"A rabbi's daughter? Of course. Father used to say she was the brains in the family, but I think it was just that her intelligence was intellectual, his was practical. His mind grasped patterns—he could have been a superb chess player, if he didn't find the game so tedious. He loved gadgets, bought a new motorcar every year and tinkered with it himself. He was..." I thought a moment for a word that distilled his essence. "He was strong."

"And your mother?"

"Mother was...alive. She was dark and bright and very funny—she had a much quicker sense of humour than Father did, and the infectious giggle of a child. She was orderly—she didn't mind if things were turned upside-down in the course of the day, but she liked to see them restored to their places eventually. She was a natural teacher, knew how to present things so they caught the imagination of a child. She taught us both Hebrew, through the Bible, and with me she used an analytical approach—how slight changes in grammar affect meaning, for example—whereas with my brother she concentrated on the mathematics. She and his maths tutor worked out a system for integrating math problems and Torah studies, using the Bible to build problems in calculus and such; I never did understand it. Looking back, she might have been worried that Levi would turn his back on his faith, and wanted to ensure that Torah was in his bones from early on."

"Your brother was a brilliant boy, you told me."

"Levi was a genius, an extraordinary mind." I stared out over the water, white streaks appearing in the darkness as each wave peaked, then vanished with the crash of the surf. "He had three tutors. One for maths, one for Torah and Talmud, and one for everything else—he didn't care for history and English, but he could memorise anything, which served the same purpose as actual learning as far as he was concerned. I hated him, sometimes. I loved him, too, but he tended to dominate life, rather. It was always lovely to get one of the parents to myself. So relaxed. Actually, I think my parents were almost frightened by him. Certainly daunted—I would catch my father looking at Levi sometimes, as if wondering what sort of creature this was in his house."

I stood, brushing the sand from my skirt. "That's about all I have of them, vague outlines coupled with specific incidents. But I believe you'd have liked them, Holmes. I'm very sorry you never had a chance to meet them.

"And now I think our driver may be getting nervous, that we've fallen into the sea."

On Wednesday morning, I left Holmes at the front desk, puzzling the affable Mr Auberon with enquiries about glass-shops, and went to Norbert's office. Before we got started on the day's mountain of paperwork, I asked him about the Chinese couple employed on the property. He knew nothing about them, but said he would look into it. Then I asked how many sets of house keys he had.

"Just the one I gave you," he answered. "I do have another complete set, but it's down the Peninsula with my other papers. Do you wish me to have it sent up for you?"

"No, I just wondered. It appeared as if we'd had a visitor in the house recently."

At that, the lawyer's somewhat distracted air vanished and he sat upright, frowning. "A visitor? Oh, that is not good. The will clearly stipulates—"

"Yes, I remember. Tell me, you mentioned something about your elderly relative spotting someone about the place fairly recently. Would you perhaps recall when it was?"

"It must have been, oh, five or six weeks ago. Certainly well before the end of March—we send Miss Grimly a cheque the first of each month, and I do remember that April's included a bonus. But she did see them, and called the police immediately, although they didn't find anyone there. Most worrying. Is anything missing, or damaged?"

"No, nothing of the sort. They merely looked around, tracked some soil on the floor, may have burnt something in the fireplace—I take it the fireplaces were cleaned back in 1914?"

"Oh, certainly they would have been. We shall have to do something about the locks, I'm afraid—it just wouldn't do to have some vagrant moving in and lighting fires. And perhaps the old lady is getting beyond the responsibility. But nothing was missing, you're sure?"

"Not that I could see."

And he nodded and stretched out his arm for the first of many files.

When I left, three and a half hours later, my mind was so taken up with balance sheets and legal language that I was at the street before I remembered, and turned back to the office. Norbert's secretary looked up at my entrance.

"Sorry," I told her, "I forgot to ask, has a letter come for me?"

"Nothing today, Miss Russell."

I reminded myself that the United States postal system was not the English one, and that a letter posted one afternoon might not generate an overnight response, even within the city limits.

Perhaps Dr Ginzberg was too busy to speak with an old patient? No, that I could not imagine. She might be out of town.

If I hadn't heard from her by tomorrow, I decided, I would travel across town to her house and see if she was there. I wanted badly to see her, to let her know that I had done well, that I *was* well.

And perhaps to ask her how it was that a person could forget half her life.

At something of an impasse, I watched a trolley rattle past, considering my options. I could go to the house and join Holmes in his examination of the fireplace's burnt papers. Or I could interview the old woman and her halfwit nephew across the street, to pin down the date of the March intruders. Or I could see what I could discover about Mah and Micah on my own, without waiting for Norbert.

I retraced my steps to the hotel for the photograph and for directions, then followed the route I had wandered in a daze three days before. Soon I was standing at the gates of Chinatown.

Chapter Five

San Francisco's Chinatown had burnt to the ground in 1906; the blaze had scoured the infamous district of its noxious cellars and by-ways—a part of my sense of dissonance two days before had been merely the change in stage sets, that the neighbourhood which had always borne a trace of lingering wickedness and the sensation of things scuttling out of sight was now a place of gaudy chop-suey restaurants and tourist gee-gaws. Why, the streets smelt more of spices and incense than they did of rotting fruit.

Not that the place looked artificial: The hotchpotch of buildings was so hung about with extraneous pavement stalls and the grime of use that a person had to look closely to note the uniformity of building materials and the relative lack of wear, to see that they were none of them old enough to have seen the century's turn.

But the changes had not erased the essential nature of Chinatown. This was a place apart, a small, intricately crafted miniature city with rules and mores all its own.

The air here was not the same as that outside of its borders; the people moved differently. The Chinatown of my childhood survived in glimpses—the joyous exoticism of curlicued buildings; the unlikely fragrances, sweet and sharp; the dancing script on buildings and signs; an old woman in silks mincing along on bound feet; a man wearing a pole across his shoulders to carry his baskets of fruit—but even the girls in dresses that matched my own and the men in lounge suits and felt hats walked and spoke as if they knew their place in this delicate, perfect machine that was Chinatown.

Now that I stood on the busy pavement, caught between a lantern store whose rafters were solid with its wares and a noisy poultry shop stacked high with cages of ducks, geese, and roosters, my idea simply to ask among the residents began to seem simplistic. The bustle and press of people, the sheer number of shops and buildings whose signs bore only Chinese characters, made it clear that, Western dress and English-speaking schools notwithstanding, this dozen or so blocks formed a city unto itself—small, yes, but it was easily conceivable that not everyone here knew everyone else.

I did not even know their names, since "Micah" was a highly unlikely appellation for a Chinese man and Mah could have been short for anything. All I had was a photograph, at least fifteen years old, and the likelihood that they were interested in the art, or science, or perhaps even religion, of balancing the energies of the earth's dragons by the use of small bowls of water, mirrors, and plants.

It took conversations with three impatient shopkeepers to give me a name for this Oriental discipline: *fungshwei*, the fish-seller called it, shaking an octopus in my face, but no no, he didn't know no-one, go down to bookstore, please go now he busy. So I left him to his eels and squiggly things and went past the barber shop and around the pavement-seller of small decorated cakes, stepping into the street to avoid hitting my head on a platoon of flattened ducks, in the direction that he had indicated, only what appeared to be a bookstore turned out to be some kind of apothecary, odorous and shadowy with an entire wall of drawers marked only by characters. Further down the street, a building with curlicued roofs that I took to be a temple was revealed as a telephone exchange, so I turned back, narrowly avoiding collision with a heavily laden silver tray of fragrant covered bowls, and made a more methodical search. The bookstore, which I had passed twice, was tucked behind a pavement greengrocer's; I found it only by spotting a man coming out with a fresh newspaper in his hand.

I pushed between the crates of strange knobbly dark objects on the one side and baskets of strange smooth light objects on the other, to enter a world that was comforting in its familiarity. Books of all sizes, colours, shapes, and languages stretched from floor to ceiling, riding in neat piles on central tables, filling the hands of the half dozen patrons, all of whom glanced up as I entered and watched me unabashedly for a while before their books pulled them back in. The front of the shop displayed newspapers, mostly Chinese although I saw two San Francisco English-language dailies as well as a week-old *New York Times*. Nothing from England, though.

"May I help you?" asked a voice in lightly accented English, with no trace of the pidgin dialect. I hadn't noticed him before, as he had been standing behind a high desk, but now he rose up and seated himself on a stool. A Chinese man of about thirty, wearing a brown suit, flecked red tie, and wire-rimmed glasses much like those on my own nose.

"Yes, thank you," I said. With the recent experience of harried and impatient shopkeepers in mind, I thought I had better pin the man down in a commercial transaction before asking questions about Chinese cooks and gardeners. "I understand there's something called *fungshwei*. I'm probably not saying it right—it has to do with balancing energies in a room, or something?" I allowed my voice to rise into a question mark, to say that I was just a harmless white woman with money to spend on oddities that took her fancy.

"*Fungshwei,*" he repeated, and I took note of his pronunciation. "You wish a book on it?"

"If you have one. In English," I added with a self-deprecating grin. He responded to my silly-me attitude with a polite smile of his own, although something about it made me wonder if he wasn't aware that my act was just that. But he turned on the stool, and I was deciding to place the smile under general Oriental inscrutability when he all but vanished behind the counter. I watched the top of his head go past, realising belatedly that the man was only an inch or two more than five feet high.

As he walked towards the back of the store, I saw that his gait was slightly uneven, a twist more than a limp, as if his spine had a kink in it. He tugged a wheeled library ladder from its recesses, allowing it to run along its tracks for about fifteen feet before stopping it to clamber up into the reaches of the shelves. He pulled out two volumes, came down, returned the ladder to its place, and came back to the desk with the books, laying them in front of me on the counter.

"I do not have any English books entirely about

fungshwei," he told me. "Both of these have chapters on the science. The one in this book is longer, with more examples, but it suffers from slight inaccuracies. The other is shorter, the English barely adequate, but the author knows what he is talking about."

I looked over the offerings, finding among other things that the discipline was rendered as *feng shui,* and that the first book had clearly been written for an audience of Western ignoramuses and romantics. The second I found intelligible, if idiosyncratic; I placed it on the counter and told him I'd take it. His face did not change, but I felt as though I'd passed some sort of test.

When he had wrapped my purchase and given me my change, I pulled my mother's small framed photograph out of my coat pocket and laid it where the book had been.

"I wonder if you know these people? They may also be interested in feng shui."

Again, I could read no reaction on the man's face. But I felt a brief beat of stillness before he leant forward, adjusting his spectacles to look at the photograph obediently. After a few seconds, he raised his eyes to mine. "You think I should know these people?"

"They lived in San Francisco, at least they did ten years ago. I knew them as Mah and Micah, although I don't suppose those were their names. They used to work for my parents. I'm trying to locate them."

He did not ask why, although I expected him to. I even had a story prepared, about a bequest in the will. Instead, he reached out and ran a curious finger down the frame.

"I found the picture on my mother's dressing-table," I said without thinking.

That time, he reacted. Only a quick glance at my face,

and completely understandable—what kind of white woman would have a framed photograph of two Orientals on her dressing-table? But what could I say to that? I didn't even know myself, although I did know that it was very like my mother to look past society's restrictions.

When he sat upright, his face was once again polite and closed. "I am sorry, I do not think they live around here. But I will ask. How do I get in touch with you, should I find anything about them?"

I took out a visiting card and wrote on the back of it the address of the lawyer and, at a whim, the house itself. "I will only be in San Francisco a few days, but anything to the first address will be sent on to me, at any time."

He accepted the card, and inclined his head slightly. "I wish you luck, miss."

As I went out of the shop, I noticed a small mirror, located so low on a wall that only the proprietor would see it. And I wondered if, somewhere in the back of the store, lay a bowl of water and a small pot- plant.

Another waiter scurried past on his delivery, and as his heavy-laden tray trailed across before me, it emitted odours that tugged at me in a way I had all but forgotten. The hot breath of chilli pepper, the comforting aroma of fresh rice—for the first time in weeks, food had appeal. As I lingered on the pavement, waiting for the waiter to return, my mouth actually watered.

I had to wait for some time, jostled by black-clad women smelling of incense and spices, blue-clad men bearing the odours of laundry and labour, and bright, bobbed young things graced with the perfumes of the downtown shops, all of them intent on the greengrocer's peculiarly shaped wares, the impossibly long green beans and aubergines the size of eggs. Eventually, however, the young man reappeared, the tray tucked easily under one arm, a cigarette dangling from his lip, exchanging greetings with the people near the stall. I fell into step behind him; when he turned down a narrow alleyway and stepped down into a door-way, I did not hesitate to follow.

Once inside, however, I was not so sure of myself, for this was clearly not a restaurant that catered to outsider trade. A dozen Chinese people holding chop-sticks in their hands turned to see this exotic invader, and I offered them an uncomfortable smile, looking around for my unwitting guide. One of the customers called something in a loud voice, and the man popped out from a door-way, his eyebrows going up when he saw me.

"You like something?" he asked.

"Luncheon, if you're serving," I said.

"Sure, sure," he said, to my relief. "No problem, here, sit here."

He dashed a clean white cloth over the surface of a corner table, and pulled out the chair. "You need menu?"

Even if it was in English, I probably would not have been able to make much sense of it. Instead, I told him, "Why don't you just bring me something you think I'd— No, make that something you like yourself." Heaven only knows what pallid version of his native cuisine he might deem suitable for a white woman. Then I added, "Just nothing with pork or shrimp, please."

It was only when he had taken himself through the door and was carrying on a full-voiced and unintelligible conversation with the cook that the belated thought occurred: Chinese people were rumoured to enjoy eating dog, and rat.

I told myself not to be squeamish, and fingered the pair of chopsticks lying beside my plate, feeling the eyes of the other diners on me.

My food arrived quickly, although the earlier patrons were still waiting for theirs. One of them, a boy of perhaps fourteen, said something to his two older companions. All three watched me reach for the thin bamboo sticks.

They seemed more amused than disappointed when this white person's clumsiness with the chop-sticks did not come to pass—I had just spent three weeks in Japan, eating with sticks slicker and more delicate than these, and the skill had not deserted me in crossing the ocean. I grinned at the boy, cautiously seized and lifted a scrap of what appeared to be chicken, and held it out to him for a moment before slipping it into my mouth. He grinned back, and then frowned and said something to his companions.

Having been through this before, I knew what was puzzling them: I was using the chop-sticks in my left hand. I held up the empty sticks, clicked them together, and then bent over the rest of my meal.

The dishes contained neither dog nor rat, so far as I could tell. The soup held a tangle of chicken's feet, by no means the strangest foodstuff I had been faced with in recent months. The waiter watched surreptitiously until he had seen me suck the flesh from the bones in one quick between-the-teeth motion, then smiled widely. The other bowls appeared to be largely vegetable, although his English got us no further than the aubergine, which he called by the American name, "egg-plant." One dish was hot enough to bring sweat to my face, the second was heavy with garlic and tiny black beans, the third both tangy and sweet.

I paid, slid a generous tip beneath the side of my plate, and was halfway out of the door before I recalled my reasons for coming to Chinatown. With the experience of the impatient shopkeepers in mind, I hesitated briefly before I ducked back into the warm, fragrant room. The waiter again greeted me with raised eyebrows. When I took out the framed photograph and explained what I wanted, the eyebrows went down and the face closed. He handed it back to me with scarcely a glance.

"No, sorry, don't know them."

"Look, I'm not out to cause them any trouble, I'm not with the government or anything—" (although surely he could hear that in my English accent?) "but they worked for my parents until ten years ago and I'd like to see that they get a small pension. You understand pension? Income? Money?"

"I understand pension," he said. "We don't know them."

Stubbornly, I bypassed his authoritative stand and set the photograph on the table containing the largest number of diners, face up so they could all see the faces. "If anyone knows who these people are, could they leave a message for me at the St Francis? My name is Russell."

The picture was gathered back into my hands before more than six or eight people could have looked on it, and I was ushered, politely but inexorably, out of the restaurant. I thanked the waiter who was shutting the door in my face, and stood in the damp alley, buttoning my coat against the sudden chill and feeling somewhat queasy with the unwonted amount of food in my belly.

I showed the picture at twenty-five or thirty other places, sometimes leaving my card, other times only able to say my name and that of the hotel before I was deposited on the pavement again. By that time I had exhausted the Chinese quarter, so I continued into the Italian quarter then worked my way back on either side of the main streets of Chinatown, but with no luck.

Sadly, I slipped the pretty frame back into my pocket and turned back down Grant, Chinatown's high street. It was later than I had thought. Some of the shops were closing—the greengrocer's wares had been depleted, the bookseller's behind it was dark: Time to go.

According to Holmes' map, going due west on the grid of streets from this, the northern section of the Chinese district, would lead directly to the house. Two streets over, I came to a cable-car, parked in the middle of the street as if waiting for me. Hesitantly, I climbed onto it, inserting myself amongst the homeward-bound office workers and shop-girls. The brakeman's play on the bell, the shudder and rumble of the boxy vehicle and the constant sing of the underground cable that pulled it along the tracks, all teased out memories of childhood expeditions. Father's outings were best, I remembered, for he permitted us to ride standing within arm's reach of the posts, delirious with our daring. Mother, while she allowed us to ride outside, made us sit on the benches, while when Nanny was in charge we were forced to go inside, behind the steamed-up windows with the staid old ladies. Five streets up, the tracks turned north, and I jumped down from the quaint transport to watch it churn away, the cable singing through its slots.

How long had I lived here?

My body's memory was saying: *Longer than you thought.*

Connecting cable-cars rose up into Pacific Heights, but I continued on foot, caught in reverie. Names that shouldn't have been familiar, but were: Larkin and Polk, the wide Van Ness—I paused, to flow across the busy street with the other pedestrians—and the quieter reaches of Franklin and Gough. There was a park over to my left, I knew without looking, and down the hill to my right was a place where cattle were brought, although I could not remember if I had actually seen them, or if it was merely a story told by my father. But I did know that had I remained on the cable-car, I would have come to a busy waterfront smelling peculiarly of fish and chocolate.

I had been here. I had walked these pavements with my hand in my nanny's iron fist, and later with my adolescent head held high. I once had a friend in this house here, a friend named...Iris? No—Lily. Lily with the black hair that her mother insisted on curling, torturously and regularly, Lily with the red lips that always made her look as if she had been eating cherries. Lily with the dollhouse I had both scorned and secretly envied. She had moved away, to...where? Los Angeles, I thought, and as her farewell gift had given me—yes, the doll-family's porcelain baby, the figure I had found in my bedroom that fit so nicely into the hand. We had sworn undying loyalty, Lily and I, and I had never written to her after the accident.

As I walked through the gathering dusk, with each beat of my heels on the pavement the neighbourhood came more alive around me. Here was where I had been terrified by a dog that had bared its teeth until driven away by a delivery boy. And the strange old woman here had owned a pet monkey, letting it out in a big cage on the porch where it flung itself about and screamed curses at passers-by. And next to her, the man with the parrots, two of them that competed with the monkey in screams, so that my mother thanked heaven that we did not live any nearer. And behind those lighted curtains, a child had died of the polio; there, a woman had been rushed to hospital when she had fallen down the stairs (and the whispers that followed, saying she was pushed—my first experience with criminality); at the now-boisterous house next door had lived a boy with pale green eyes who talked to himself and...

And then without warning the slow unfurling flower of my past was hacked away, with a sudden fast scuttle of feet behind me and an urgent shout that I should *Get down, get down!*

I whirled, prepared for battle, but he was too close, and ploughed straight into my diaphragm with a sharp banging noise, driving all breath from my lungs and sending me flying backward. I struggled to do battle, in spite of a desperate lack of oxygen and the dizziness throbbing out from the back of my skull, but before I could so much as get my hands raised, my attacker was up and away. Completely confused, I fought to sit upright against the dizziness of the impact and the panic of no breath. After far too long, my compressed lungs finally remembered their function and, with a great whooping noise, sucked in several gallons of glorious cold night air.

Seated, my hands holding a head that threatened to fly off, I heard footsteps approach again. They seemed too slow to be threatening, so I simply sat and took pleasure in the act of breathing. A hand came into my vision, holding a pair of glasses; my glasses. I took them, straightened them on my nose, and squinted up.

Not very far up. The man was short. And Chinese.

"You're the bookseller." My head hurt, raised like that, so I allowed it to fall back into my supporting hands.

"I am. Are you all right?"

"I will be. What the hell did you do that for?"

"A man across the street was aiming a pistol at you. I feared that if I merely yelled, you would turn to see and he would hit you."

I reflected that I was probably the only woman in San Francisco who, if she heard someone yell *Get down!* might actually obey first and look around to ask questions later—unless, of course, the swift approach of footsteps took precedence. Still, he had no way of knowing that.

"That was a shot I heard?" The impact of shoulder to diaphragm had come simultaneously with the bang, creating a more direct link in my mind than in fact there was. I craned my neck again, trying to see him. He was holding his left shoulder, casually but firmly.

"God, you're hit," I exclaimed.

"An insignificant wound, I believe. If you can walk, perhaps we should do so."

With the impetus of someone else's blood to drive me, I staggered to my feet, stifling curses as my head swam and pounded.

By this time, three other men had come onto the street from their houses, all of them with the look of soldiers about them—men who would perceive instantly the difference between a motorcar's back-fire and the sound of a handgun. The nearest came to where the bookseller and I stood, and asked, "Ma'am, is this fellow bothering you?"

"Oh, no, this fellow has just saved my skin, thank you. And at the cost of his own. Mister . . . I'm sorry," I said to my rescuer, "I don't know your name."

He flung at me a series of Oriental syllables that found no foothold in my rattled brain, but I decided that here was not the place for proper introductions. "Yes," I said vaguely, and looked around me, trying to remember which way my house lay. "Down here, I think. We'll see if we can find some bandages that the mice haven't nested in."

Leaving three men to stare at our retreating backs, Mr Whosit and I made our wavering way up the street and around the corner to the familiar jungle-backed wall. Luckily, Holmes had left the drive gate open; in fact, he was standing in the front door-way, watching us approach.

"A bit of first aid, Holmes," I greeted him with. "Mr Something here took a bullet for me, and needs patching up. I could use a couple of aspirin for my head-ache. And I seem to have lost another hat."

"Why does it not surprise me that the sound of a pistol would herald the arrival of my wife," Holmes drawled, and stood away from the door so we could enter.

Chapter Six

Holmes had better luck with the bookseller's name, and was soon addressing the small man as Mr Long, which when I heard it caused a somewhat light-headed giggle to try to surface. I suppressed it firmly—he wasn't that tiny, really, just far from Long—and focussed on the tasks at hand.

We were sitting in the kitchen, bright lights pulsating off the white walls, as Holmes methodically assisted our guest in removing enough of his upper garments to allow treatment. He seemed uncomfortable with my presence, so I closed my eyes against the glare.

"Clever of you to get the power on, Holmes."

"It was simply a matter of locating the mains," he said. "The power company had not shut it off, just the caretaker."

"What about the water and gas?"

"I rang both companies from the watch-dog's telephone."

"Was Miss Grimly reassured to find you were a respectable English gentleman?" I asked.

"She telephoned to Mr Norbert's offices before she would allow me past the threshold; her nephew stood at the ready with a baseball bat."

"And did she have anything to offer on our intruders?"

A moment of silence served to remind me of our visitor, whose presence I had forgotten. To cover my mistake, I went on. "I took the photograph around Chinatown and must have asked a hundred or more citizens, none of whom recognised the two people. Or said they didn't. Although I had a very fine if somewhat *recherché* meal in a tiny cellar café haunted entirely by Orientals, and asked them to ring the hotel if they had any information for me." My brain, slowly subsiding into its proper setting, finally emitted an original idea, and I opened my eyes to squint at Mr Long. "One of the people whom I questioned was this gentleman, who runs a bookshop that sells, among other things, volumes on the Chinese art of feng shui. I trust I am pronouncing it correctly?" I asked. Mr Long nodded fractionally, then stifled a wince at Holmes' ministrations; I continued. "However, he has yet to tell me what he is doing rescuing me from assassins on my doorstep."

The bookseller stirred. "I have to say, Miss Russell, that your display of English—do they call it 'phlegm'?— is most impressive. I would have thought most young ladies would display more of a reaction to such an attack. Unless you think, sir, that she is suffering from a concussion?"

Holmes snorted. "Her brain wouldn't dare. No, the only time Russell becomes upset is when those near and dear to her are threatened."

"Is this—eh!" Long grunted.

"Sorry," Holmes muttered, and pulled more gently at the shirt.

"Is this common among the English?"

"Russell is not common among anyone. Good, it's merely winged you in passing—no permanent damage, I shouldn't think. Do you suppose there are any bandages in the house, Russell?"

"They would be either in the cabinet in my parents' bath-room, or in the nursery. Do you want me to go?"

"You sit."

So I sat, as his stride went up the stairs, and a few minutes later came down again. His search was successful, even to the presence of a bottle of Merthiolate. He sniffed it, then painted away at the bookseller's seeping upper arm, wrapping a length of gauze around the whole and tying it off in a neat bow. He handed Mr Long back his shirt, but carried the coat over to the sink, turning on the taps with an air of experiment. Nothing.

"I can't even offer to salvage your coat from the bloodstains," he apologised.

"That is of no importance," the bookseller said, gingerly inserting his arm into the ruined sleeve. Holmes moved to assist him, and between the two of them they got the man clothed without too much discomfort. The small man moved his shoulder experimentally, testing the limits of comfort, then turned to me.

"I am pleased that I could, as you say, rescue you from your assassins, but I cannot claim I came here with any such intention. No, I came to speak with you about your photograph, and as I paced the sidewalks in indecision, you came around the corner and the man with the gun showed himself. Pure felicitous accident. May I ask, are assassins a commonplace in your life?"

I might have returned his earlier question aimed at me, for his own demonstration of phlegmatic behaviour made me wonder if it was his own nature, Orientals in general, or a result of living in San Francisco, which after all was not so very far removed from its Wild West roots. But it was difficult to know how to answer his question, so I decided to consider it rhetorical rather than requiring an answer. Instead, I asked, "Why were you coming to speak with me?"

"The photograph you showed me. It is of my parents."

"Ah," Holmes said, and reached for his pipe.

"Mah and Micah were your mother and father?" I asked, with a dubious glance at the length of the man's legs.

"'Mah and Micah,'" Mr Long repeated with a faraway look on his face. "I had forgotten that. They adopted me when I was seven years old, and my mother died. As it happened, I was their only child. Their actual names were Mai Long Kwo and Mah Long Wan. They worked for your parents as gardener and cook, beginning in 1902. I did not know your mother had a photograph of them on her bureau. I suppose I should not have been surprised, for this was one of the few things my mother saved from the Fire, and it resided near the place she had her house gods." He drew from his inner coat pocket a portrait in a simple black wooden mounting, handing it to me. Smaller and set in a different frame, it was otherwise the same family portrait that lay buried in a drawer in Sussex: tall, blond American father, a secret smile under his trim moustaches; smaller, darker English mother, her eyes dancing as if she was about to burst into laughter; lanky blonde twelve-year-old with smudged spectacles, every inch of her shouting her impatience with the entire exercise; intense, dark-haired boy of perhaps seven, looking at the camera as if he intended to pull it apart to see how it worked.

I handed it back to him. "Where are your parents now?"

"They are dead." He put the photograph into his pocket, seeming to spend considerable attention getting it settled, then raised his face to mine. "Murdered."

A tingle of shock ran down my legs, and I was aware of Holmes coming to point, the pipe frozen in his hand.

"Tell us," I said.

"It was during the New Year celebrations of 1915—our New Year, not that of the West, which is some weeks earlier. I was not here. I was at medical school in Chicago, and Western universities do not recognise the celebrations of other calendars. They were both in the store—but I should explain first.

"The previous spring, your parents had made them a loan of money to start a business. My father had begun to find the physical demands of gardening increasingly difficult, and when he admitted as much to your mother, instead of merely dismissing him as most people in her situation would have done, she asked him what he intended to do. He trusted her enough to tell her his dream of running a bookstore, although their savings would mean they would begin with little more than a cart on the street. Medical school is expensive. But your mother would not hear of it, and insisted that they find a space large enough for a proper store, and that they could repay her over time."

He smiled in reminiscence. "Your mother was a most strong-willed woman. She would, as the saying goes, not take no for an answer, and even refused to sign formal loan papers, saying that if she were to drop dead suddenly, my father should consider it her thanks for the years of pleasure she had received from his work in the garden. And as it happened, my parents had recently seen a sign go up for a new shop-space, and eyed it wistfully.

"In the end, they accepted your mother's offer, and put up the money for the space that week. My father retired his aching knees from your garden to his shop, and began to order books and build shelves. He worked slowly, because he wanted the place to be perfectly balanced in itself. He wanted it beautiful.

"And then in early October came your family's tragic accident." He did not say he was sorry, did not mouth any platitudes, he merely made the statement. I thought, however, that he was in fact sorry, that he grieved for my parents alongside his own. I found myself liking him for his reticence.

"There was, as you may imagine, considerable discussion between my parents as to the status of the money. Your mother had been definite, but neither of my parents felt comfortable with the situation. And you, the sole survivor and heir, were not only a child but in the hospital as well, and clearly in no condition to make any decisions. In the end, my father went to the old lawyer who was handling your parents' affairs, and explained as best he could. The lawyer seemed more confused than anything else. There are men who require pieces of paper to give their world order, and cannot deal with the lack. In fairness, I believe the man had spent so much of the previous eight years wrestling with the lack of documentation in legal affairs following the Fire, that he simply could not face one more such problem, particularly when it involved such a—to him—paltry sum. In the end, he actually shouted at my father, saying that if Mrs

Russell wanted to throw her money away on a pair of…
Chinese people and not even make mention of the fact
in the will, there wasn't anything he could do about it.
And he invited my father to leave, rather rudely."

His smile was a wintry thing now. "You may not be
aware that even today my people, when they venture
outside Chinatown, risk being set upon and beaten by
drunks and young men. They throw rocks at us as if we
were stray dogs. Ten years ago it was far worse. I suppose
my father was fortunate not to be dragged away by the
police as a common thief.

"In any case, during my visit home over the
Christmas holidays we debated the problem, and in the
end, decided to let the situation stand. My parents
would continue with their plans for the bookstore, with
my mother working there now as well. They thought
that opening immediately after New Year's, which came
in the middle of February, would prove auspicious.
During the celebrations, they worked late at night to finish the preparations, shelve the books, arrange the furniture.

"No one heard the gun-shots. If they did, no doubt
they would have taken them for fire-crackers. Only the
following afternoon did it occur to the grocer next door
that the bookshop was strangely quiet. He went to see,
found the door unlocked, and discovered my parents in
the back, dead.

"When the news reached me in Chicago, I left my
studies and came home. And I have been here ever
since."

"And the police?" Holmes asked.

The dark, folded eyes behind the lenses regarded him
with gentle pity. "The murder of two elderly Chinese ser-

vants, in Chinatown? The incident made less of an impression than the police chief's missing budgerigar."

Holmes nodded, then asked, "After you took over the bookshop, were there any threats or . . . attempts against you?"

"None. Whatever my parents were killed for, it was not the store itself."

"Had they any valuables?"

"My father, unlike many men his age, was progressive when it came to money. He put his into a nearby bank that was beginning to take Chinese customers—the Bank of Italy, it was called. My father was very impressed with the actions of its owner, Mr Giannini, who went through the fires of hell, very nearly literally, in preserving the savings of his depositors during the days after the earthquake. So no, there was no store of gold under the mattress, no rare painting or Ming vase a collector would desire. No book worth more than a few dollars. And his bill-fold was in his pocket, untouched."

I spoke up hesitantly. "What about the Tongs? I've heard they are ruthless against those who stand against them."

"That is true, unfortunately, but unless it was a thing that came up in the few short weeks after I returned to Chicago, no point of conflict had been raised. My father paid what could be called his 'association fees.' And when I opened the doors of the bookshop, I was never approached for more than I owed."

"So the murder was because of something they were, or had, or knew," Holmes mused. "But you never caught a trace of what that might have been?"

"The life of the city closed over them as if they had never been," the bookseller told us.

After a minute, Holmes rose and stepped out of the

back door to slap his pipe out on the stones. He came back inside, locking the door as he spoke over his shoulder.

"Russell here has very clearly indulged in a pleasantly exotic meal, but I for one have not taken sustenance since a cup of tepid American tea provided by our watch-dogs some hours ago, and a supply of soap and water would not go amiss. Mr Long, would you care to join us in dinner and further conversation?"

"At your hotel?" the bookseller asked, sounding dubious.

"Certainly, unless you have to be back to your shop."

"My assistant will have closed up, but I don't know that I..." His voice drifted off.

"We can find you another coat," Holmes said.

"Holmes, I don't think that's the problem," I said. "The St Francis may have certain...exclusionary policies."

"Ah. Well, if they do, we'll take him to our rooms and have our supper brought up. Come, we can do nothing more here at the moment."

Three sets of eyes and ears scanned the streets for gun-wielding lurkers, but we walked two streets down and caught a cab on Van Ness without mishap. At the hotel, we avoided the question of the dining room's policies by simply whisking our guest past the desk and onto the lift; the operator did glance sideways at Mr Long, but his interest seemed to be more upon the small man's bloody sleeve than on the shade of his skin.

"Russell, would you like to order up a dinner while I remove a quantity of grime from my finger-nails? I won't be a moment," Holmes said, and stepped into the suite's bath-room. I consulted with Mr Long and then picked up the telephone and placed an order. When

Holmes emerged, scrubbed and damp, he made for the collection of bottles which, in a shallow bow to the Volstead Act, the hotel had placed behind the doors of a side-board.

"What flavour of analgesic may I offer you, Mr Long? Despite the strictures of your Eighteenth Amendment, we appear to have brandy, gin, whiskey, the inimitable American bourbon—"

"The brandy would be fine," our guest said, settling back a fraction into his chair. He took a healthy swallow, then took off his spectacles and cleaned them with a pristine white handkerchief. When they were back on his face, he seemed to relax, as if the cleaning exercise had clarified a decision as well.

"I hope you understand," he said to me, "why I hesitated to respond to your questions this afternoon in the shop."

"You wanted to think about it first."

"Indeed. And also to see you, as it were, *in situ* rather than in my place of business. However, when I saw a man with a gun aimed at you, it decided me that you were on the side of the angels. May I ask, though: When I ran at you—for which I apologise; I hope it is understood that I did not intend to injure you?"

"You need not apologise for saving my life, Mr Long."

"You are kind. However, when you turned to face me, it appeared as if you were assuming a position of the martial arts."

"Yes, I have some training."

"Interesting. And you, sir?"

"A discipline called *baritsu*. It's Japanese, a style of—"

"I am familiar with it, although I would have thought that few Westerners were. Thank you, it was merely a point of curiosity."

"Sir," Holmes said, with an air of drawing the meeting to order. "You have no doubt spent considerable time on the question of your foster parents' murder."

"Oh yes, I have. And cast out a hundred lines of enquiry, with no result."

"Yet you have never formulated a theory as to their deaths?" Holmes put it more as an accusation than a statement, and eyed him over the top of his glass.

The bookseller smiled. "I did not say that."

"Aha!"

"Yes. However, until this good lady appeared in my store this afternoon, there seemed little I could do about it."

"Wait, are you saying that I know anything about their deaths?" God, not another gap in my mind! Or was he saying—no, surely he couldn't think that I, a fifteen-year-old girl, would have come to Chinatown with a gun to do away with the family servants. To say nothing of the fact that in February of 1915, I'd been in England, on the verge of meeting Sherlock Holmes.

"No, of course not. But I have come to wonder if the actions of your parents might not have, unwittingly and posthumously, contributed to the deaths of my own."

Before I could summon speech from my dropped jaw, a rap at the door indicated the arrival of our meal. The distribution of linen and plates suspended conversation for a time, and the momentum of the actions and the odours from beneath the silver lids took us halfway through the meal. But eventually, I laid down my fork and said to the little man opposite me, "I think you need to explain how the Russell family brought killers to your door."

"It is a complex puzzle," he began, "and I do not have

all of its parts. But I will fasten together the pieces that I have, and you can tell me what design you see.

"The earthquake was the centre, April the eighteenth, 1906. But the story of our two families had its beginnings a number of years before that. And, I believe, its endings."

Chapter Seven

The man who would later be known as Micah by a family of mixed American-English, Christian-Jewish heritage was nineteen years old when he sailed from China with a shipload of his countrymen in 1877. Mai Long Kwo was an educated boy with an unfortunate interest in politics and the more unfortunate habit of allowing his hot blood to speak up when he should not. His family scraped together the fare and prayed that, by the time he had earned enough to return, his nature would have cooled and the memories of the authorities would have faded.

Long Kwo, known to his employers as Mike Long, worked as a paid slave for twelve years on the railroad and the docks, sharing rooms with other men in houses that had neither plumbing nor gas lighting. But because he did not gamble or drink, because he worked hard and had learnt to keep his mouth shut, his money belt grew thick, and by 1890 he had migrated to San Francisco and sent home for a wife.

It was a difficult time for a man to send for a wife. Five years after Long had arrived, the American government had established what it called the Exclusion Act, which reduced the numbers of Oriental immigrants effectively to none; after eight years, there was no sign of the Act being loosened. In the 1890s, this meant that the only practical means of bringing in a Chinese woman was on a smuggler's boat.

It took Long a while to find a smuggler who could be trusted with both money and wife, and a while longer for Long's family to locate a bride they could afford for their distant son. What they came up with was Mah Wan, a young woman who looked frankly like a peasant: tall and strong, with unbound feet, a plain face, and a questionable horoscope. However, she was known to be a hard worker, and her father was willing to risk her on the high seas. She sailed for Gold Mountain, as the land was known, in the spring of 1891, arriving on the tail of a storm that left her and the other would-be immigrants more dead than alive. They came ashore on a moonlit night in pounding surf, heaved bodily into the small boats and rowed ashore.

One of Mah's companions took one look at the dark figures standing on the beach and cried aloud, and would have dissolved into hysterics but for the hard slap one of the sailors delivered. Mah herself, filthy, terrified, and weak from seasickness, nonetheless managed to keep her spine straight and her feet underneath her.

The figures moved forward and began to divide up the immigrants—six women, four men. In seconds, it seemed, they were scattering, and Mah looked at the man who was left.

"Long Kwo?" she said hesitantly.

"Yes," said a voice, "come now, we must get off the beach before we are seen."

Obediently, she followed, stumbling over something on the invisible sand and nearly dropping the precious bundle she had guarded all this way. He stopped, and to her immense surprise took the bundle and seized her hand, guiding her to the road.

A half-hour's walk brought them to a dark house. Long Kwo led her to the back door and knocked quietly. It opened, and a small person let them in. When the door was shut again, the person lit an oil lamp, and Mah saw that it was a woman—a white woman.

This peculiar figure led them to a room, handed Long Kwo the lamp, and walked away.

He put the lamp on the room's shaky wooden table, then turned hesitantly to face his bride.

He saw a thin, pale woman as tall as he was, her hair marked by threads of premature grey, with more intelligence than most men would care for looking out of her dark eyes. She in turn saw a man a little rougher, and older, than she had been told to expect. He was wearing a Western-style suit, but it fit him ill; looking closely, she wondered if he could indeed read and write as she had been informed.

"There is hot water and a bath," he told her. "And cold rice and tea, unless you wish American food. I don't recommend it."

"Thank you."

"Tomorrow we will go to San Francisco, and you can have some proper food."

"Hot water is better," she said, and to her surprise, his face lit up.

"I thought you might want it. I remember all too clearly my own trip, and that wasn't with smugglers."

The next day, clean and dressed in the unfamiliar Western clothing he had brought for her, Mah and her bridegroom continued their illicit journey to the city. Before the day was out, Mah had seen his worth and been reassured. This man she was bound to was unfailingly polite to her. When he spoke to the white man who drove them in the man's own tongue, the driver, like the woman the night before, understood without a problem. And when they climbed out of the closed truck, she was in a place where the people had familiar faces and the air smelt almost normal.

The rooms he took her to were clean, if sparsely furnished, and held a surprisingly large number of books in both Chinese and foreign writing. And he might appear rough, but he was in fact so gentle as to be almost shy, and she found herself telling him that she was able to read, a little, forgetting momentarily that her mother and father had been adamant that she was not to let slip the admission until the marriage had been legally formalised.

Both were relieved, and satisfied, and the two strangers set about forming a partnership.

There was much work to be had in San Francisco, if one did not mind sweat and dirt. The city was growing so fast it seemed to be tumbling over itself, and Long Kwo's mastery of the white man's language meant that he was often chosen to supervise the crews of workmen.

Mah was slower to learn English, but learn she did, and work she did. The money was steady. They bought a house, a building with a shop on the ground floor to give an income, and they made themselves a part of the tight community of Chinatown.

The only thing they did not have was a child.

After nine years of marriage, not one of Mah's

pregnancies had spent more than three months in her womb. She had been sad and angry at first, and frightened that her husband would put her away. But Long seemed honestly not to mind, and gradually she became resigned to their state.

And then in the closing weeks of the Western year 1899, a woman in their apartment building died, leaving her seven-year-old son an orphan in fact where before he had been one in practice. The woman had no relatives, and her dead husband, too, had been alone in this country, but still, had the boy been a more attractive proposition, he would have been welcomed in any of several homes. However, the child was small and bent, scrawny from neglect, and he looked at a person strangely—in part this was his habit of squinting, but also a sort of aloof manner, as if despite his unprepossessing exterior, he looked upon the adults around him and found them wanting.

But Mah rather liked the child. He was well mannered, other than the look of superiority, and intelligent. Which, she reflected, might account for the look as well.

They talked it over, went before the community association responsible for orphans, and offered the boy a home. Their friends argued with them, saying that there was something very wrong with the child, that the boy must have attracted the evil eye somehow, to be so consistently cursed, and that he would bring his disastrous heritage with him. Mah's soft heart could be understood, but surely Long could see that the best place for the child was a nice anonymous orphanage? His friends' arguments, however, fell on ears that had been deafened by the faint ring of hope in his wife's voice. Long determined to go ahead; his friends and neighbours shook

their heads, saying that his weakness for injured creatures would get him into trouble.

With spectacles, the boy's squint went away; with affection and stability, the superior gaze faded. Nothing
much could be done about the boy's stature and
crooked back, although good food, corrective shoes,
and a regimen of traditional exercises helped, but in the
end, it did not matter. He was very bright, and with a little luck and a lot of planning, he might not have to depend on manual labour for a living.

School was easy enough, for the teachers in the
Chinese school appreciated a student who did his work
and more. And with care, the family savings would
stretch to teacher-training college, and the boy would
teach others, not carry loads like his adoptive father or
scrub floors and iron shirts like his mother.

Four years later, the gods decided to intervene in the
family fortunes.

Divine whim being by its nature both capricious and
deceptive, the intervention began with catastrophe. One
foggy morning in June 1902, when Long was working
with a gang of brick-layers on the third story of a new
building, the prophecy concerning his disastrous sus-
ceptibility to small, weak creatures was fulfilled. For
some reason, a mother cat had decided to shift her litter
during the night. And since cats, like ants, have a habit
of tracing an impossibly labyrinthine path to their goal,
this one had wound her way up some planks, dropped
into a half-finished chimney, and come to a rest inside a
wall that was due to be bricked in that day. The man
with the brick in one hand and a laden trowel in the
other had heard the rustle and faint mewing sound, and
paused to peer in.

No one particularly wanted to leave the cats inside

the wall, but stopping work to dig them out risked getting them all fired. The brick-layer went on with his job, but slowly, sending his hod-carrier to fetch Long who, while not exactly a boss, had a margin more authority than the man with the brick in his hand.

Long came, and saw that, short of tearing down the previous day's work, the only way to reach the litter was from the scaffolding on the outside of the building. And being the tallest man on the crew, his long arms were the clear candidates for the rescue operation.

Mother and two kits were soon in a burlap sack. He was stretching for the third, fingers out and brushing the tantalising softness that was hissing furiously from a niche just beyond his reach, when the board of the precarious scaffolding jerked, trembled for a moment, then slid with a sickening airiness into space. Arms flung out to catch at the framework of lashed-together boards scrabbled briefly at the fog-slick surfaces, then gave way, clawing a path through the intervening structure until Long finally smashed down on a surface that did not give. He lay on his back, staring up at the faraway faces of his horrified coworkers, at the slowing sway of the traitorous scaffolding, at the grey of the sky above, wondering if this was what the transition into death was like.

He waited for the shock of injury to drift away into the afterlife, but it did not. And then he heard the yowl of the mother cat, fighting her terrified way out of the bag, and somehow the noise told him that no, he was not yet dead.

The fall hadn't killed him, miraculously enough, or even crippled him. It hadn't snapped his spine or crushed his skull or ruptured some vital inner organ. It had dislocated three fingers and broken six bones—both those of his left forearm, one in his right ankle, two ribs, and his left collarbone—but the healer who pressed the expensive herbs on Mah assured them that he would heal.

And he did, slowly, although it was a month before he could hook a pair of crutches under his arms and hobble from one side of the apartment to the other. And two months before his leg enabled him to negotiate the stairs and stand on the street again.

Mah worked all the hours she could, and twelve-year-old Tom, strong despite his stature and the twist in his spine, was hired by the downstairs grocer to make deliveries all that summer. Still they went into debt to the money-lender. When the school year started up again, Tom demanded to keep working for the greengrocer, but Long was even more adamant that the boy needed to be in school, and his edict carried. Tom did work after school and on the weekends, but only on condition that his homework got done as well.

In October, Long began to look for employment, but building crews wanted the able-bodied and offices the formally educated. He picked up a few hours a week keeping the grocer's accounts, and tutored some men in English, but it was not enough. The money-lenders bit deep, and deeper.

The rains came, and if California in November was not as cold as China had been, nonetheless the air in an underheated apartment chilled the bones, especially bones that had been broken eighteen weeks before. On the days he did not have work, Long often walked, with an idea that he was building his strength. He also kept his eye out for potential jobs, along the docks or in the industrial edges of the town, although he was wary about the shopping centre, and avoided the residential areas assiduously: A forty-four-year-old man with a gimpy leg would be easy prey for a gang of toughs.

One Saturday in late November, Tom came upstairs from the greengrocer's and told his father that he had been asked to deliver a crate of exotic vegetables clear the other end of the city, all the way out at the western shore. The boy was both excited and apprehensive about the lengthy expedition, and Long offered to accompany him. In fact, he even convinced the grocer to throw in a second cross-town street-car fare, to ensure that the produce would arrive without mishap. The month before, another, older delivery boy had been set upon by a gang of white boys, leaving the fruit he had been carrying crushed and worthless. Even limping, Long's presence might serve to deter the vandals.

The trip went smoothly, other than a few disapproving glances. And the restaurant at the end of the world was so pleased at the freshness of the crate's contents that the cook gave Tom a dime tip and two thick sandwiches. Father and son took the food down to the beach at the foot of the cliffs, settling in against the sea wall for shelter.

It was a cold afternoon, the wind fitful from the previous day's storm, the waves erratic against the cliff. Although the Playland carnival rides were going full-strength, there were few other beachgoers that day to object to a Chinese boy. Tom happily stuffed the remnants of his sandwich into his mouth and ran off to see what the waves had thrown up. He stopped regularly to swipe his glasses clean on his shirt-tail, and squatted occasionally to examine some treasure or other.

Another family was making its slow way up the beach in their direction. They were white people: a tall man with that yellow hair some of them possessed and, behind a pair of gold spectacles, the peculiar blue eyes that often went with the hair; a woman with dark eyes and tendrils of normal-coloured hair blowing out from under her warm hat; between them, half hidden between the woman's dark red skirt and the father's tall legs, toddled a young child. The father had taken off his hat and tucked it under his arm against the wind. The man and the woman, both of them warmly bundled, were talking and watching the ground. The woman, too, bent from time to time, holding up whatever small thing she had found to show to the man or the child.

They did not see Tom; Tom did not see them; the two paths were set to coincide. And although Long did not worry that this man would perform any act of actual violence against the boy, he did not want his son's day ruined by a white man's crushing remark. So he got to his feet, as if his limping gait might actually interrupt the meeting.

To his relief, however, the progress of the trio was broken when the child's small foot caught on a length of kelp and she was sent sprawling face-first into the sand. Both parents lifted her, brushed her off, comforted her. The father held her to his chest and seemed to be engaging her in conversation, which made Long warm to him: White men so seldom talked with their children. And then the father turned away from the sea, carrying the child to the shelter of the sea wall. Long could not hear her, but he could tell when she laughed, and he was smiling himself when the father sat down with his great arms wrapped around her slim, well-padded body.

The woman, meanwhile, had been distracted by the approach of Tom. Long's face twisted in concern and he strode as quickly as he could out onto the damp sand, but half a dozen steps and he slowed again. The woman said something to Tom, but whatever her greeting, it had been friendly, and Tom answered her by holding out something in his hand. She leant over to examine it, and the two discussed it for a while. She must have asked where he had come upon the object, because Long saw his son's arm go out to point up the beach towards the rocks. The woman straightened to look, and then she nodded at the boy. They both continued in their original directions, Tom down the beach, the white woman in the direction of the cliffs; in a minute she was passing between Long and the water, greeting him with a polite nod before her eyes returned to the rocks.

It happened so fast that, if Long had paused even an instant to consider his actions, he would have been too late. The long-skirted figure strolled around the spit of boulders, comfortably above (or so she thought) the waves that broke and sank into the sand eight or ten feet away from her boots. But on this sea, the waves were unpredictable, and turning one's back on the water invited that seventh wave, or seventieth—the big one. The woman had bent to study something in the lee of the boulder or she might have noticed the uncharacteristic retreat of the waters, sucked back to feed a growing swell like the lungs of a man preparing to shout. The husband saw the danger—Long heard the man behind him, his call faint and snatched away by the wind. But the woman remained oblivious, the wave built and swelled, and Long stumbled into a run, ignoring the pain in his leg.

"Miss!" he screamed. "Miss, come away, oh—"

But the great wave was already surging on, its summoned waters rising, cresting to hurl itself at the shore. Its ridge began to show white, the cap dwarfing the woman even as she stood upright, stared in alarm at

Long with his lurching run and flailing arms, then whirled to see what threat lay behind her. The monster wave leapt at her like a falling wall, like the slabs of pavement at the base of the scaffolding. It pounced and scooped her up and hurled her over the small spit like a twig—a booted foot and a swirl of red skirt above the white foam the only signs of her as she skidded over the rocks and onto the sand, then turned, tumbling and gaining speed as the weight of the water sucked her down to the bowl of the ocean.

Long saw only a flash of red in the turmoil of foam and launched himself at it. The fingers of his right hand met only liquid grit and the bite of rock; his left felt the tease of wet fabric darting rapidly past them and he grabbed hard.

Even with two of them struggling, even with four legs and two sets of arms digging into the sand and clawing at the rocks, the ocean nearly had them. Long's heels dug in first, came to rest with a jolt against a half-buried outcrop of rock, and the sudden jar of the woman's weight shot a bolt of hot pain up his arm. The half-healed collarbone snapped; he cried out, but he did not let go, his fingers clenched into the wet fabric as he prayed that the seams did not give way, that his muscles not fail, that his bones . . . And then the predatory water turned its back on its prey, retreating into the sand; out of its foam appeared a tangle of red skirts and undergarments, a moving tangle as the woman choked and pushed herself upright against the immense weight of her sodden clothing. Long staggered upright, curled his right arm around her waist, and hauled her up into the air and away from the greedy fingers of the waves.

They collapsed onto sand that was damp but not wet, the woman retching and crying, blood and hair casting red-and-black fingers across her face as she fought to free her arms from the ripped and constricting garments. Only when he saw that she was safe did Long sink to his knees, gagging up quantities of sea water.

The husband was there then, the little girl in his arms screaming with alarm at their startling flight across the sand and the state of her mother and this strange man, both of whom were bleeding and making frightening noises. After a minute, Tom arrived, stark-faced, bending over his father, dabbing at Long's bloody hand with his schoolboy handkerchief.

Slowly, the woman's vomiting passed, to be replaced by deep shudders of cold and shock. The husband, satisfied at last that her bleeding was superficial and her skull and bones unbroken, dashed tears of relief from his eyes and lowered the child down to her mother's lap, where the two clung to each other. He glanced over his shoulder to measure the distance to the road, then looked at his wife's rescuer; taking in Long's pinched expression and the care with which his right hand was cradling the other elbow, the pale eyes shifted from relief back into alarm.

"You're hurt."

English was an effort, but Long managed to retrieve the words. "Old injury, sir. It will heal."

"You must see a doctor. Do you live around here?"

Tom answered. "We live in Chinatown."

"Then you'll have to come with us in the car." Long tried to protest, but the man was already speaking to the child, his voice measured and reassuring. "Mary, my brave girl, I need you to help me. Your mama's all wet and cold and she needs me to carry her to the car. This nice man here hurt himself helping Mama; can you take care of him and his boy? Do you think you can bring them to the car for me?"

The child's pale eyes considered the situation, and then she clambered out of her mother's sodden embrace and extended her hand to Tom. The man swung his wife up easily, waited until Tom had got his father upright, and led the way across the sand.

It was Tom's first ride in a motorcar, and he was torn between the softness of the upholstery and the hisses his father let out, like a prodded kettle, every time the car bumped and swayed. At the end of the ride, the white man pulled into the drive of a house so grand Tom wondered if he was the mayor. He turned off the motor and trotted around to lift his protesting wife out of her seat and carry her to the door, which opened an instant before they reached it. They vanished inside; a stern-looking white woman peered out of the doorway, and appeared to be coming out until a command from within made her hesitate. She said something, at which a voice so sharp it could be heard from the car made her turn and retreat inside, leaving Tom, his father, and the little girl seated in the car.

Child and boy looked at each other in the silence, self-contained blue eyes meeting apprehensive black ones.

"What's your name?" she asked. Behind the piping lisp of youth, her voice sounded like her mother's, some kind of accent, Tom thought.

"My name is Tom."

"Mine's Mary. Is your papa okay?"

"He hurt his shoulder in a fall a while ago. I think he's hurt it again helping your mother."

The pale gaze travelled from the cradled arm to the Chinese face. "I'm sorry," she said.

Long had to smile at her seriousness—he did not know young children well, Tom having come to him half-grown, and the size of Western infants always confused him, but despite her fluent speech he didn't think this one could be older than three. "It will be fine, missy," he reassured her.

"Does it hurt?"

"A little, yes."

"My papa will make it better for you," she said, without a doubt in the world. "Would you like to come in?"

"I think your father will have someone take us home," Long said. He couldn't afford any more doctors, and in any case there was little to do but strap the shoulder and keep it still. He just wished the man would hurry; the sun had gone and his clothes were soaked. He stifled a shiver, then grunted at the effects the motion had on his grating bones; the child saw, and frowned.

"Are you cold?" she asked, and without waiting for an answer, stood and pulled herself over the front seat, balancing over the seat with her feet dangling free while she stretched down, then slid back clutching the corner of the plaid travelling-rug the man had wrapped around his wife. Ignoring Long's protests, she arranged it over him, tucking the thick, soft wool around his knees in a child's imitation of adult nurturing. "There," she said, admiring her handiwork, and then looked up at an approaching figure.

It was the stern woman from before, come to snatch her employer's child from the wicked Orientals. She yanked the car door open and, without sparing the Longs a glance, pointed one finger at the ground by her feet.

"Come out here." Her command brooked no argument, but to Tom's astonishment, the infant's chin came up and her eyes narrowed.

"Papa said to take care of them."

The woman's eyes flashed and she reached over Long's knees for the child. "Your father didn't intend for you to sit in a dark motor with a pair of heathen—"

"Miss MacPherson!" The male voice from behind her gave the woman pause; with a glance at the wide-eyed faces of Tom and his father, she stood back from the car door.

"The child—" was as far as she got.

"We'll be fine, Miss MacPherson. Perhaps you could go and heat some water for the doctor, and see if Philips needs any more warm bricks for my wife's feet. Thank you."

The woman hesitated on the brink of insubordination, then thought the better of it and stalked away. The blond man laid one arm across the roof of the car and leant inside, his unruly hair falling forward onto his high brow.

"Sorry about her," he said. "She becomes a bit mother-hennish. Let's get you in and comfortable. The doctor will be here in a minute."

Long tried to protest, but the man already had his hands on Long's legs to swing them to the ground. He seemed to sense which motions would be difficult for a man with a bad shoulder, and his supporting hand was there to help. In moments, the man was propping his damp, sand-clotted Chinese guest on an immense leather sofa before a fire and giving succinct orders to the servants who appeared.

The fire was built up and a hot drink fetched. When the doctor arrived, although he was allowed upstairs to check on the woman first, he was soon retrieved and told firmly to patch Long together. When the re-snapped collarbone had been securely if excruciatingly strapped and Long's wet clothing replaced by ridiculously long but dry substitutes, a thick soup was brought, oddly flavoured but restorative. And at the end of it, a car arrived to take Long and Tom home, not a taxi, but commercial nonetheless.

"You're not to take any money from these people," the blond man told the driver. Then he moved to the back window and took out a slim bill-fold.

"Sir, please," Long protested. "I hope you are not offering me payment."

The man hesitated, glanced briefly with his peculiar blue eyes at Tom's heavily worn, too-small shoes, and stood uncertainly, slapping the bill-fold against his hand. "You saved my wife's life."

"As you would have done for mine," Long replied firmly.

The look the two men exchanged seemed to go on a long time, and said a great deal. Would this tall, beautifully dressed white man have thrown himself into the waves after the wife of the short Chinese man with the much-mended trousers? Most would not. But this one?

In the end, the man slid the bill-fold away into his breast pocket, and held out a hand to Long.

"Thank you," he said. And then he closed the door of the car, which negotiated the streets from the heights to Chinatown. The driver stopped before the greengrocer's, even getting out to hold the door for them as if they were white, or rich. A very worried Mah bustled onto the pavement, coming to a dead halt at the sight of the uniformed driver. The man tipped his hat to her, got into his vehicle, and drove away before Long could search his pockets for a tip.

The next afternoon, while Tom was off with a delivery for the grocer's and Mah was scrubbing shirts at the laundry down the street, there came a knock at the door of the apartment. Long, who had ached all day as if all his broken bones had come to pieces instead of just the one, laboriously got to his feet and answered it. The blond man filled the door-way.

"The driver gave me your address," he said to Long. "How's the shoulder?"

"It is nothing."

"The doctor said you'd broken it last summer, along with a couple other bones."

"That is true. They healed, this will too. I trust your wife is well?"

"She's fine, thanks to you." He simply stood there, leaving Long no option but to invite him in. The house, as always, was spotless, but having sat on the man's leather sofa and drunk soup from the man's gold-rimmed bowls, Long knew that the man would see nothing but the poverty.

But to his surprise, the man's surveying glance betrayed no distaste. If anything, he seemed appreciative of the simple ink drawing on the wall, and of the soft quilt lying across the chair which Mah had laid over her husband's legs before she left that morning.

"Would you care for tea?" Long offered.

"Thank you, I'd like a cup." The man seemed curious at the pale beverage, which reminded Long that Westerners polluted their tea with sugar and the milk from cows' udders.

"Would you like me to get some milk?" Long offered, wondering where on earth he would find the stuff in Chinatown.

But the man shook his head. "Don't worry, I

sometimes take it black." And when he had taken a sip, he added, "Actually, this is nice without milk. Refreshing." He drank the cup, accepted a second, and when it was cradled in his big hands, he got around to the reason for his presence.

"Mr Long," he started, then paused. "Am I saying your name right?"

"Yes, that is fine," Long reassured him, surprised. It was a question he'd never been asked before—and indeed, it was close enough, considering that the man's tongue was unaccustomed to a tonal language.

The man nodded and went on. "My wife and I are responsible for your injury. She, not being native to these shores, has never fully realised how potentially treacherous the Pacific surf can be, and yesterday I neglected to renew my warnings. Had you not been there, had you not been willing to risk your life for hers, she would have drowned. I do accept that one cannot pay a man for acting a good Samaritan, but one can at least reimburse him for the losses he incurs."

Long had no idea what a Samaritan was, good or otherwise, and a number of the other words were not in his vocabulary either, but his English was sufficient to follow his visitor's general meaning. What was crystal clear, and of far greater importance, was that this stranger referred to Long, a person whose eyes and skin made him less than human to most of the city rulers, as a man, and moreover one whose dignity was a thing to be taken into consideration.

Unwittingly, Long's chin came up and he met the pale eyes as one man to another.

"Sir," the tall Westerner said, "I would like to offer you a job."

It was the *Sir* more than anything else that clinched the deal.

Long came to work for the Russell family the following day, walking up the hills to the grand house each morning, descending home again to Chinatown in the afternoon. At first, his work was one-armed and somewhat pointless, but with the second healing of his collarbone, he took over responsibility for the grounds, and discovered in himself an unexpected quiet pleasure in working the earth and growing flowers and lettuces. Within the next year, Mah came as well, to work inside the house, helping in the kitchen and slowly absorbing this odd Western style of cooking. When the cook fled the city after the events of April 1906, Mah took over, and the Long family ran the Russell household, inside and out.

Unlike the Scots nanny, who had left the establishment soon after their arrival, the Longs never lived in the Pacific Heights house. The Russells offered, but did not press after the refusal, because both sides knew the problems the neighbours might raise. Instead, Long would clean his spade and tidy the walks, leaving the house in the afternoon so he might be home when young Tom was let out of school. Often as he walked, Long took with him some book or another that one of the Russells thought their gardener might enjoy. And during the periods when the Russells were away, in England or on the East Coast, one or the other of the Longs would go to the house every day, to be sure all was well.

When Tom went east to university in 1909, a Russell gift allowed him to take up somewhat more comfortable rooms than his parents alone could have provided. And when the deep aches that had settled into Long's bones made his work in the garden more difficult, it was Russell money that kept the family from having to approach the usurious money-lenders of Chinatown to create the bookstore.

Theirs was a symbiotic relationship of two species, different yet alike, that might well have lingered into old age, but for a car going off a cliff, some miles south of San Francisco.

Chapter Eight

Holmes reached out to refill Mr Long's glass. The story had taken nearly an hour in the telling, and now our guest sat forward with his drink clasped in his hands.

"That much I know, for a certainty. And it was necessary to tell you in detail so that you might understand the links between our families. It began with the rescue of a woman, but it was not simply a matter of rewarding a service."

"I do see that," I told him.

"And as you were young when you knew my parents, I did not think that you would have understood the ways in which they were something other than mere servants. I think your mother would not have spent hours discussing Chinese philosophy with her gardener, were she not aware that he was more than a man who could make plants grow. And your father would not have felt so free to lend him books, and later talk about them, were the things between them not more solid than a job and a payment."

"I am grateful to you. I...I don't remember a lot about my parents."

"That would be true of any child who is not given the opportunity to know his or her parents as an adult." The way he said this reminded me that he, too, had lost his mother and father—twice over, in fact.

"As I said," he continued, "it is necessary to perceive the strength of the links between them in order to make sense of what happened in 1906. Although that, I fear, is precisely where my tale falls into thin ground.

"You may have been too young to remember, but the catastrophe of those first days after the earthquake was unimaginable. Block after block of buildings collapsed, often on top of those trying to rescue their belongings. Men and women wandered the streets, driven mad by shock or simply with no place to go, no possessions to guard. People would be trapped under rubble, and the fire would reach them before the rescuers could—more than one was shot, through mercy, to save them from burning alive. The police feared riot and disorder so much, it was ordered that any person caught looting would be shot on sight—with no suggestion as to how the soldier or policeman might tell if the person in his sights was a looter or a rightful homeowner. It was an absolute hell of irrational behaviour against a backdrop of flames and shattered brickwork.

"In that macabre and unearthly setting, something happened that involved your father and mine. And there my story falters, for I do not know its details, I could merely see the shape of the thing in the aftermath. I was fourteen at the time, no longer a child, not yet seen as a man. I was left with my mother as the fire grew near, to

pack our goods and prepare to abandon the house. My
father needed to go and see to the Russells, to make certain they—you—were alive and uninjured. A portion of
the fire lay between us, so he did not know how long it
would take him to work his way around it, but my
mother urged him to go, insisted that we would be fine.
He left at four o'clock on the Wednesday afternoon, and
we did not see him until eight o'clock on Friday morning. In the forty hours he was gone, the fire reached and
consumed Chinatown, driving us all to the edge of the
sea. When he could finally return, he found all of
Chinatown pressed between the docks and a wall of fire,
the air thick with explosions and panic, everyone half
suffocated from the smoke. I tell you these details to illustrate the urgency of the demands, to have kept him
away from his responsibilities to us.

"He was near despair when he could not find us
among the crowd, but a neighbour saw him and told
him that we had already made our way to the Presidio,
where the Army had permitted us an area to shelter, and
provided food. He finally caught up with us there, and
wept when he found us safe, saying over and over that he
should never have left. He told us that your house was
damaged but standing, that you were all living under
canvas in a nearby park, that he had helped your father
move some valuables. And that was essentially all he
told us, that day or ever.

"But whatever it was he had done with, or for, your father, made him uneasy. One might almost say it
haunted him."

"What do you mean? Was he frightened?"

"Frightened," Long repeated, considering the word.
"It is difficult to imagine one's father frightened. No,
I don't believe so. It was, rather, as if he had done

something without considering the results, and reflection made him wonder if he had made the right choice. Or as if he had begun to suspect that what he had been asked to do actually concealed another purpose."

"As if he no longer trusted my father?"

"Not your father, but as if some underlying question threatened to betray them both." He shrugged, wincing at the motion. "It is difficult to put into words, a vague impression such as that."

"But you can't think what it was based upon? Was it something that happened to him, or that he saw, that he did?"

"Any of them. None." His spectacles caught the light as he shook his head. "He would never talk about it."

It was by now late, and I could see little sense in playing Twenty Questions with a man who could describe the object only by its outline. Holmes clearly felt the same, for he reached out to knock his pipe decisively into an ash-tray.

"Mr Long—" he began to say.

"There is one other thing," Long interrupted, and Holmes obediently settled back. "Again I do not know what it means, but your father came to see mine in the middle of September 1914. Two weeks before he died. They talked for a long time, and when he left, my father was quiet, but somehow as if a burden had been lifted from him. And when they shook hands, they seemed friends again, as they had not for some time."

"But you don't know what they talked about."

"They walked across to the park and sat on a bench, going silent whenever another person came near."

"Well, thank you, Mr Long," I said, wishing I did not feel so dissatisfied.

"If we think of any questions, Mr Long," Holmes said, "may we call on you in your shop?"

"Either I will be there, or my assistant will know where I have gone."

"Let me go downstairs with you and arrange a motor to take you back. It is late, and your arm clearly troubles you."

Long protested that it was but a short walk, but Holmes would not be swayed. He retrieved our guest's hat, standing at the ready should the man have any difficulty rising from his chair. He did not, although as Holmes had said, the wounded arm gave all indications of paining him. By way of support, Long gingerly worked his hand into the pocket of his jacket, but when he had done so, he paused, and drew the hand laboriously out again. In his fingers was a paper-wrapped object the shape of a very short cigar, secured in neatly tied twine, which he held out to me.

"In the turmoil of the past few hours, I forgot to give this to you. My father said that it was an object precious to your mother, and removed it for safe-keeping, lest vandals take it."

I turned the object over in my hands and saw, in a precise, spidery hand:

Removed from the Russell house, November 13, 1914.

Inside the paper lay the front door's mezuzah.

Whatever Long saw in my face caused him to take a half-step forward as if to grasp my arm, but he wavered, and instead merely asked, "I hope my father's actions did not create problems for you. He seemed to think it was a kind of household god, perhaps not literally but—"

"No," I said, my hand closing tightly around the cool metal. "It's fine. I'm very glad to find it safe. Thank you."

I felt Holmes' sharp gaze on me, but I did not look at him. He caught up his own hat and stick to accompany our guest out, so I was not surprised when he did not return for the better part of an hour, approximately the time it would take to make a slow and thoughtful foot trip back from Chinatown.

When he came in, he found me where he had left me, curled on the sofa with the mezuzah in my hand. When he had shed his outer garments at the door, he came and sat down beside me, taking my hand—not, as I thought at first, in a gesture of affection, but in order to prise my fingers away from the object. The palm of my hand was dented red with the shape of it, my fingers stiff. He examined it curiously before laying it on the low table before the sofa, then reached into his pocket to pull out a handkerchief.

I blew my nose noisily and drew an uneven breath. "I never had a chance to say good-bye to them. Not before they died, not even at their funerals, since they had to be buried before I got out of hospital. Dr Ginzberg took me to their grave site, but I was so full of drugs at the time, it made no impression on me.

"It's the . . . unfinished quality of their deaths that is hard to set aside."

"Yes." There was an odd intonation to the monosyllable, almost as if he had asked a question: Yes, and . . . ?

"What do you mean, 'yes'?"

His grey eyes, inches away, drilled into mine, his expression—his entire body—radiating an intensity I could not understand. He did not answer, just waited.

I shook my head wearily. "Holmes, you apparently believe you see something I am missing entirely. If you want me to react to it, you're just going to have to tell me."

"Your parents died in October 1914."

"And my brother, yes."

"And you were either in hospital or under your doctor's supervision until you came to England in the early weeks of 1915."

"Yes."

"Your parents' cook and gardener—ex-gardener—were murdered in February 1915."

"According to Mr Long."

"Your house sits vacant for ten years, then is broken into in late March, approximately the time you would have been here had we not stopped in Japan. And within forty-eight hours of your return to San Francisco, someone is shooting at you."

"Or at Mr Long. Or simply at a Chinese man who dared to venture from his assigned territory."

I might not have been speaking, for all the impression my voice made on his inexorable push towards his ultimate point. "And during the earthquake and fire of 1906, some experience troubled a brave and loyal servant into a change of heart towards his employer."

"Holmes, please, I really am too tired for this."

"Within two months of that event, your father's will was given an addendum to ensure that the house be left untouched by anyone other than family members for a minimum of twenty years."

"So?" I demanded, driven to rudeness.

"And finally, your emotional turmoil over the unfinished nature of your family's death has led to a series of disturbing dreams."

"Damn it, Holmes, I'm going to bed."

"The evidence is clear, yet you refuse to see it," he mused. "Fascinating."

"See what?" I finally couldn't bear it another moment, and blew up at him. "Holmes, for Christ sake, I'm absolutely exhausted, I have bruises coming up all along my shoulders and skull, and my head is pounding so hard I'm going to have trouble seeing my face in the bath-room looking-glass, and you persist in playing guessing games with me. Well, you'll just have to do it in my absence." I stood up and stalked into the bath-room, where I ran a high, hot bath and immersed myself in it for a very long time. Holmes was asleep when I came out; at any rate, he did not stir.

For the brief, dull, businesslike venture that I had expected of our trip to San Francisco, it had already proved remarkably eventful. Even before we arrived, dreams had been pounding at the door of my mind; in the three days since the ship had docked on Monday morning, I had been arrested, confronted with a bucket-load of oddities, seen the evidence of a house-breaking, met a large slice of my past, been attacked on the street, and had a serious argument with my husband.

But the deadly ambush laid for us Thursday as we walked in all innocence across the hotel lobby reduced the rest to little more than specks of dust on our way.

We'd had a pleasant breakfast—or Holmes had, while I drank coffee and ate a piece of toast while reading the newspapers. Holmes had the *Call*, I had the *Chronicle*, working my way from NEW WOMAN IN POISON CASE and past an advert for MJB coffee with two finger-prints accompanied by the statement "No two are alike—People differ in their coffee tastes as well as their thumb prints." I consulted Holmes, and we agreed that the prints in the advert were those of fingers, not thumbs, so I went on to GAY GATHERING ON YERBA BUENA FOR SWIM PARTY and RESCUED GIRL TELLS COURT BONDAGE STORY.

All in all, a satisfying day's headlines.

We drained our cups, dropped our table napkins beside our plates, and made our way towards the lift.

The first volley of the ambush rang out across the dignified lobby, startling every inhabitant and sending Holmes and me into immediate defensive posture. The next shot fired hit home and froze me where I stood.

"Mary! It's Mary Russell, I'd never be wrong about that, you're the spitting image of your father. When I read you were in town I—"

I straightened: The previous night's argument notwithstanding, I had no wish to inflict on Holmes a bullet aimed at me. I fixed him with one of those glances married people develop in lieu of verbal communication—in this case, the urgent glare and slight tip of the head that said (to give its current American colloquial), "Scram!"

Holmes faded away as no man over six feet tall ought to be able to do, leaving me alone to face my attacker.

The top of her hat might have tucked under my chin, had I been foolish enough to allow her that close. Its waving feathers and bristling bits of starched ribbon were ferociously up-to-date, her well-corseted figure was wrapped in an incongruously youthful dress whose designer would have been outraged at the sight (although it testified well to the tensile strength of the thread), and her hair might at one time have been nearly the intense black it now was. Her fingers sparkled with a miscellany of stones, and the mauve colour of her sealskin coat came from no animal known to Nature. She was making for me with both arms outstretched, and although she looked more likely to devour me than to embrace me, I did the English thing and resisted mightily the impulse to place the outstretched heel of one hand against her approaching forehead to keep her at arm's length. Instead, I allowed her to seize my forearms and smack her painted lips in the general direction of my jaw.

It appeared that I had a dear friend in San Francisco.

"Mary, Mary, why on earth did you never write? My, you've become so grown-up, and so tall! Taller than your mother, even, and I thought she was a giraffe! Oh, dear, you poor thing, whisked away from your friends and your home like that—I said to Florence—you remember little Flo, your good friend?—that someone should just get on a train and go fetch you back. Imagine! Nothing but a child, and all alone in the world."

"Er," I managed.

"And you've kept your blonde hair, like your dear father—it never did darken like your mother said it would, now did it? Do you rinse it in lemon, like I told you to when you were twelve years old? It looks a nice thick head of hair, too, although this fashion for men's haircuts is so unfortunate."

"I'm terribly sorry," I pushed out into the storm of words. "I'm not sure I know who you are."

The sound she emitted—laughter, I suppose—was a string of seven notes descending from a soprano's high shriek to a low sort of chortle. The gaiety of it was somewhat undermined by the hurt expression in her eyes, but it was hard to know how I might have posed the question any less bluntly.

"I'm Auntie Dee, dear child. Your mother's very best friend in all the world. She used to bring you over to my house so you could play dollies with my Flo. Although you usually ended up in a tree or down the street with her brother Frankie's friends," she added reluctantly, as if the memory was a somewhat shameful one.

I had to admit, in a tree with the boys sounded more like me than dollies with Flo. Although what my quiet, intelligent mother would have seen in this woman was beyond me.

Still, I did what was required of me. "Auntie Dee, of course, how ever are you, and dear Flo?"

During the course of the monologue that followed, I glimpsed Holmes coming out of the lift, dressed for the day. Give him credit, he did raise a questioning eyebrow in my direction. But there was little point in inflicting this female person on him, so I gave him an impercepti-ble shake of the head and lowered my eyes until I was gazing soulfully into my companion's face. The motion, or perhaps the fact of her audience actually turning at-tention onto her, silenced her for a moment, a gap I took advantage of.

"Er, Auntie Dee, I haven't had breakfast yet. Would you care to join me?" A lie, but casual interrogation of this woman might prove informative.

Again came the wince-making seven descending notes of laughter, and she reached out to slap my hand playfully. "How silly of me, of course you're standing here starving to death, when all the while I came to your hotel to whisk you away to breakfast at your old Auntie Dee's own table. If you're free, that is, of course." She looked vaguely around, showing that she had registered something of Holmes' presence before he had faded into the palm trees. But before she could spot him, I took her hand in an imitation of childish glee.

"Of course I'd love to come. Shall we get a cab, or do you have a car?"

She looked at me askance, speech for once difficult to retrieve. But only for a moment. "Don't you want to go and get your hat or something?" she asked.

I might have been proposing to walk into Union Square wrapped only in a bath-towel. However, I thought perhaps I wouldn't take her to our rooms, even if Holmes had left.

"Oh, I'm only going to my old second home, aren't I?" I asked. "No need for formality here, is there?"

Thus bereft of hat, coat, and gloves, I walked out of the hotel in my half-nude state towards the waiting car, only to pause at the sound of not-so-distant drums.

"What is that noise?"

"Oh, the Loyalty Parade down on Market Street," she answered.

Now that I looked more carefully at the flow of traffic and pedestrians, it was obvious that some major disruption was going on a couple of streets down to my right.

"I hope we don't have to get across it," I said, climbing into the car, but fortunately she too lived in Pacific Heights, five streets up from the house I was slowly beginning to think of as mine. Aunt Dee's, however—I could not call her otherwise for the moment, as she had yet to provide me with her full name—was higher up, far more ornate, and possessed a front garden no one would mistake for a jungle. The car rolled to a halt under the imposing Greek pillars of the portico and a man with a face like an ebony carving came out, surreptitiously tugging his white gloves into place. He held the door for my companion, allowing the driver to do the same for me.

"This is Miss Mary Russell," she told her servant. "Tell Mrs La Tour that we require breakfast."

"Yes, Mrs Greenfield," the man murmured. I was grateful for the name, which rang not the faintest chime of familiarity. His, however, was another matter.

As Dee Greenfield turned to the door, she told me, "You won't remember Jeeves, Mary; he's only been with us for two years."

Startled, I looked straight into the black eyes of the butler, seeing in their depths a well-concealed spark of humour. "*Jeeves?*"

It was she who answered, over her shoulder. "Yes, his name was Robert, but we could hardly have that, could we, it was my husband's name. So I let him choose another and that's what he came up with. Silly, but what can one do?"

My involuntary grin fanned the spark of humour for an instant, then he turned to open the ornate wooden door for us. As I went past, I said, "Carry on, Mr Jeeves."

The smooth dark skin around the man's mouth twitched briefly, but nothing more.

The inside of the house was as needlessly ornate as the outside, although it reflected a very different era. The exterior decoration dated to the house's period of construction some forty years earlier, but the original Victorian interior had been transformed, and recently by the looks of it, into a showcase of modern design. The Deco movement contributed its whirling patterns of rich colours on the walls, a tangle of wire and glass around every lighting fixture, long and languid chest-high marble figures of standing women and seated greyhounds in every corner—it was like taking up residence in a box of chocolate crèmes, chokingly rich.

As Mrs Greenfield unloaded her gloves, handbag, and the extraordinary mauve coat into the white-gloved hands of Mr Jeeves, she babbled without pause. "Isn't this room just the most beautiful place you've ever seen? I shouldn't say so myself, I know, but we just finished it last Christmas and it still gives me a little thrill whenever I walk into it. We had a dress ball to celebrate, and oh, you should have seen it with all the candles glowing and an eighteen-foot Christmas tree in the corner there! Every guest here oohed and aahed like they were children, it was so lovely. Oh, do run along, Jeeves, Miss Russell is utterly famished. Tell Mrs La Tour we'll start with coffee in the conservatory."

Although I was prepared for nearly anything in the realm of the spectacular, the conservatory had apparently resisted the efforts of Mrs Greenfield's modern-minded decorator, and sat, Victorian and defiant, attached to the back of the house. It was a pleasant room, white-painted wood and basket chairs, although the plant life showed an unfortunate preference for orchids so ornate they appeared artificial.

The coffee arrived, blessedly strong and served in eggshell-thin bone china, a combination that soothed the spirit. Mrs Greenfield rambled on, regaling me with elaborate tales of people whose names she seemed to think I should know. I began to suspect that her mind might be none too firmly rooted in the here and now, that perhaps she imagined that I was my mother, but then I decided that no, it was more a matter of her self-absorption being so profound, she simply assumed that the rest of the world saw through her eyes.

A person like this is the easiest of all to interrogate, as they never look beyond the opportunity to talk about themselves to question why their audience might be asking along certain lines. It is mildly exhausting, to be sure, as it requires close attention to tumbling streams of nonsense in order to pluck out the occasional nugget being washed one's way. And since it would hardly do for me to take notes, I had to hold in my mind all the glimmering bits, gold and pyrite alike.

If this woman knew my mother, then she would know when my family had lived in this city, and when they had not. It took many circuitous loops and back-tracks, and a number of the reference points she used would take some research on my part to pin down as to their date—for example, that we had arrived back in San Francisco, baby brother in tow, the very week that that exclusive French couturier on Post Street had opened.

The cook also very evidently dated from before the modernisation of the house. Mrs La Tour presented us with a breakfast that was solidly Edwardian in its sensi-bilities, and although I was not in the least hungry, I had begun by telling my "auntie" that I was on my way to breakfast, so I could scarcely claim to have eaten already. I pushed my eggs, grilled tomatoes, and various fried ob-jects around on the plate until she noticed, and then forced down a quantity of the congealed food before she could pick up my fork and feed me. The meal left me feeling as if I ought to set off for a brisk march around the circumference of the city, and it was with gratitude that I pushed away from the table.

This time she led me into a morning room from which the sun had already retreated. But a fire had been laid and more coffee stood ready on the low table between two comfortable chairs. I was handed a cup without being asked if I wished it, and before I had done more than blow across the top of the cup, we were interrupted by a person whose presence went far to explain the vast and recent changes in the household.

A bustle in the hall-way and an exchange of words at the door warned of an impending invasion, and indeed, seconds later the door was flung open and in whirled a petite, black-haired, absolutely perfect specimen of the species *Flapper Americanus*. She was quite obviously just coming in from the night's entertainments, although it was well past nine o'clock in the morning, and her clothing and makeup were very much the worse for wear. Both of her silk stockings were out at the knees—stockings that I knew from my earlier bout of shopping cost nearly five dollars—an English pound for a pair of stockings! The hem of her abbreviated skirt cried out for the attention of an expert seamstress, her collar was smudged with face-powder, and unless wearing a single earring was the fashion here, she'd lost one of her diamond pendants.

What I found most shocking, however, was the lack of reaction on the part of her mother, who merely shook an affectionate head at the bedraggled state of the newcomer.

"Mummy, darling," the jazz-baby was exclaiming before she had cleared the door-way, "Jeeves says you have a guest—what on earth are you doing bringing a guest home at this hour, I thought that kind of goings-on was reserved for the younger generation? And even I only drag friends in for breakfast after we've been out all night, I don't begin the day with abductions. Oh! I've been with Trudy for the past three hours, stuck on the other side of Market Street with that pig of a parade the children are putting on—twenty thousand boys, they say, God, what a nightmare thought, all of them banging away on instruments and marching and pulling floats, so that even if you weren't drunk beforehand you'd need to be by the time you'd got past it—*and* she's just given up smoking and I'm dying, just *dying* for a smoke, tell me you don't mind, Mummy dearest, and if your friend objects I'll just have to skulk away into the conservatory and puff away among the orchids."

In the course of this speech, the girl had made her way across the room in that languid, loose-limbed shuffle characteristic of her species, moving as if her shoes were too large and threatened to fall off, or to trip her up. Neither mishap occurred, however, before she reached a swooping sort of octopus-armoire whose many arms were each topped by a small Benares-ware tray, seven in all. Drawing a brightly enamelled cigarette holder a good eight inches long from somewhere about her person, she flipped open the lacquered box that sat on one of the trays and pulled out a cigarette, sliding it into the holder with a frown of concentration. She lit it with a grenade-sized cigarette lighter that matched the enamel of her holder, drawing in a dramatic lungful of smoke and emitting a small cloud along with a sound of satisfaction. She then hurled herself onto the chaise beside the fireplace, crossed her knees in a manner that would have had her grandmother swooning, and looked at me brightly.

I was hard put to keep my hands from applauding.

"But this is Mary, my dear," Mrs Greenfield explained. "You remember Mary, your best friend when you were a little thing? She used to play dollies with you."

This was, as I had suspected, my former playmate, Flo.

"I remember she used to play a vicious game of kick-the-can with Frank's friends, and one time climbed up to the top of that tree that Billy Murrow broke both legs falling out of." The flapper's tired face creased in amusement, and she gave me a languid wave of her cigarette holder by way of greeting. "Hi."

"Hullo."

She tipped her head a fraction, and asked, "Do you have an English accent now?"

"Didn't I before?"

"I suppose you did, and I'd forgotten. You live in England, then? So what are you doing here?"

"She's touring the world," Mrs Greenfield broke in. "I opened the paper this morning to the society page and what should jump out at me from under the 'gossip from hotel lobbies' section but the name Miss Mary Russell, and I just knew it had to be her, had to be. So I had Jeeves send for a car and went right down to welcome her home. We've just had breakfast, although we'd have waited if I'd known you were on your way."

Flo grimaced, making me suspect that there might be a link between the red of her eyes and her lack of enthusiasm over Mrs La Tour's cooking. "Thanks but no thanks," she said. "So, Mary—shall I call you Mary?"

"Of course."

"What are you doing in the City?"

"There's some business to take care of here; my father's holdings need attention. As I was sailing the Pacific, it was easy enough to stop here for a few days."

"But is that all?" Mrs Greenfield cried. "You must stay longer and see your old friends. Flo, tell her she must stay on."

"I'd be happy to show you something of the night life, such as it is," Flo drawled, and stifled a yawn.

"Oh, what a good idea!" exclaimed her mother. "I was going to invite some of her mother's friends over for a morning tea and perhaps treat her to a night at the theatre, but you young things might have a better time dancing and having fun."

Neither jazz-dancing nor provincial theatre was high

on my list of passions, particularly while inhabiting a skull that still gave twinges of protest at the previous day's crack on the pavement, but it was difficult to say so in the face of the mother's enthusiasm. Or of the daughter's flagging attention. Flo yawned again hugely, not bothering to pardon herself, then stood up to grind her cigarette out in an ash-tray.

"There's a party on for tomorrow night that doesn't sound too frightful. Shall we pick you up at nine, then?" she asked me. "That's early, I know, but we could have a bite to eat first."

Nine o'clock as the opening hour of a night's adventures sounded ominous, but I was trapped for the moment. Well, I thought, I could always telephone to the house and say I had developed a sudden rash from oysters or something. "That would be grand," I told her.

She merely nodded, and directed her steps towards the door-way, already half asleep on her feet.

Mrs Greenfield shot me an apologetic smile. "She's a good girl, just going through a silly phase. She worked so hard with the decorator, when it was finished she was at something of a loss what to do. Blowing off steam, you know?"

I nodded to say I knew, although it seemed to me the girl might find a manner of release less destructive to both body and possessions. But Flo's involvement in the renovations wrought on the house did explain the style better than if Mrs Greenfield had been supervising them. And I thought that, once a person got used to the vigorous style, there was an appeal in Deco. In small doses, preferably.

Flo's departure gave an excuse for my own, although it took many promises and an acceptance of the Greenfield telephone number to free me from the establishment.

Mrs Greenfield told Jeeves to have the motor brought up, but I countermanded the order.

"No, really, I'd rather walk a bit. It's a lovely morning, and I could use the exercise."

"Oh, you young girls," she gushed, "it's all faddishness with you, isn't it? Exercise and education—why, next thing you'll be running for public office and joining the Army!"

The descending seven notes of her laugh followed me down the steps to the drive.

Running for office; what a mad idea.

I suppose Mrs Greenfield thought I was strolling the five streets over to my house, but in fact, I had an appointment with Mr Norbert and two managers at ten o'clock. I stood at the gates to the house, searching up and down the street for waiting figures. I had more or less decided that whoever took a shot at me had been a random madman, but I wasn't about to be foolish enough to ignore another explanation. And I admit, the possibility made my spine crawl. To put off making a decision, I settled onto a section of low wall in the shelter of the gate, and spent a minute scribbling notes in my little book. I might have done it in any event, since I did not wish to forget any of what Mrs Greenfield had told me. And when I was finished, I closed the notebook, hopped down from the wall, and without hesitation turned towards the solicitor's office.

The brisk hike from Pacific Heights settled my nerves somewhat and cleared all manner of cobwebs from my mind, and the equally brisk and pleasantly efficient meeting with Norbert gave me the feeling that things were moving with admirable purpose. I signed papers; agreed to commissions for selling various stock; agreed, too, although with a degree more reluctance, to remain in nominal control of my father's division of the company for a year, or at the most two, until the most opportune time to sell my interests came about. I was on my way shortly after noon, having declined to join the three men for a luncheon at their club (the ladies' room, of course). I stood in the door-way, my hand on the heavy bulge in my hand-bag as I studied the adjoining street-corners and building entrances, but the most dangerous character I could see was a boy on roller-skates, zipping in the direction of the parade. I told myself that no-one was about to shoot at me on a crowded street. And during the time I was walking to the hotel, no-one did.

Holmes was not there, so I changed my formal business attire for clothing better suited to a dusty house, and left again. The cable-car passed by the front of the hotel, but instead of joining it I walked up to Post Street, studying the shops until I found the one Mrs Greenfield had mentioned. When I went in, the sales-girl looked at me with one plucked eyebrow raised past her hair-line, but she answered my question politely enough, and I thanked her. Only then did I hop onto a cable-car, and rattled up the hills with the working girls and the tourists.

Getting off at the same place I had disembarked the other night, this time I waited for the connecting line to carry me into Pacific Heights, and I reached the house without being shot at, tackled by Chinese men, or otherwise assaulted.

The padlock was off the gate, and when I rang the bell, the house responded with motion. In a minute, I could hear Holmes' footsteps approaching, and the door popped open.

"Ah, Russell," he said, stepping out rather than back. "Just in time. Glad to see you survived the affections of your adoptive aunt."

"Wait 'til you see her daughter. Just in time for what?"

"Luncheon, of course," said the man to whom meals and clocks were only faintly linked.

"Holmes, I've just eaten."

"I, however, have not, and am in need of sustenance. Come, I passed a small Italian bistro whose morning odours were most promising."

With the door securely locked in my face, there was little to do but follow him down the drive (he, too, peered sharply all around before he stepped out of the gates) in search of his fragrant Italian bistro. My lunch consisted of a glass of wine (which the waiter solemnly called "grape juice") and a crisp bread-stick; Holmes, on the other hand, did the menu justice.

When he had mopped up the last of his tomato sauce and drained the inky coffee from his cup, we returned to the house, and spent the afternoon trying, with small success, to rescue any portion at all of the blackened papers in the fireplace. Holmes had taken a closer look at them the previous morning and, after having the first flake dissolve into dust, decided that four hands were better than two for the job. But even with both of us, Holmes to raise each remnant a fraction and me to slide the glass beneath it, they were still heart-breakingly fragile. No matter how gently we worked and despite all the art in Holmes' hands, time after time they crumbled into flakes and dust.

At the end of it, we were left with sore knees, black hands, and seven fragments large enough to preserve words.

Five of them, rather to my surprise, were type-written, as far as we could tell on the Underwood in my father's library, which had a marginally skewed lower-case *"a"* from when a curious child—me—had tried to commit surgery on it. Holmes judged it the letter's original, rather than a copy, which is why it was so disappointingly preserved: Carbon would have survived the fire better than the ink had.

From the top sheet, three fragments survived:

```
United States Army
having cleared my cons
```

```
                     Since nei-
            me forward under
          I may not reveal the
```

```
          d his stalwart
          both friend and
```

From later pages, the two fragments we deciphered were:

```
          e mayor's order
          was announced
          earthquake—an
          the man had
          ffers. Offici
          ally executed
```

```
     healthy to be a scorche
  ull of money.
```

The newspaper cuttings appeared to be from the period immediately following the quake, for one had the bold headline "URNS!!" which was more likely, considering the size of the font, to be an article concerning the destruction of the city than the archaeological discovery of some Greek jars.

The other appeared to be about a man and his new wife who had lost each other for days after the Fire, then discovered that they were half a mile apart in Golden Gate Park. With either of the newspaper bits, however, it could have been the opposite side that was of importance, and in both cases that obverse was illegible.

We left the plates arranged on my mother's writing desk and went through the kitchen to sit on the stoop, where Holmes lit a pipe and I worked to find a comfortable niche for my kinked spine.

The jungle of the garden was oddly appealing, particularly in the quiet of late afternoon. I could hear the sound of children's voices somewhere far away, and closer in, a woman singing softly.

"Do you make anything of those fragments, Holmes?" I asked.

"Very little. The words might be provocative, suggesting some act of violence during the earthquake, and money, but any conclusions built upon them would have foundations of air. If the fragments have any value, it may come to light later in the case. Clearly, the house was fairly thoroughly cleaned before your Mr Norbert turned the key and walked away—unless the fireplaces were scrubbed and the carpets rolled up before your parents actually left. I don't suppose you remember?"

"Norbert senior arranged for the cleaners to come in and roll up the carpets, to 'protect his clients' assets' as his son put it, put on the dust-covers, and clear out the ice-box. They may have scrubbed the fireplaces then, although September tends to be warm in San Francisco, warmer here than the actual summer. They could have been cleaned at any time."

"We need to know if Norbert senior left them all clean."

"Yes, I know," I said. I sighed—but quietly, to myself—at his insistence that we were investigating a case. There was no point in saying that it was quite likely that the papers were the remnants of some last-minute business letters of my father's, draughts later rewritten and dropped into a post-box, so I got out my note-book and wrote down the instruction to myself: *Norbert——fire-places cleaned?*

I glanced over the previous pages, added one or two facts that I had neglected to make note of earlier, then said to Holmes, "Mrs Greenfield was actually very helpful in sorting out our times in San Francisco."

"And she assured you that your family was all here during the earthquake and fire."

"She did, yes. You were right, Holmes. But we did come and go a number of times, so my memory of England isn't entirely wrong, either."

I had been born in England, in January 1900: That much I knew. What I had not known was that we came here when I was just over a year old, in the spring of 1901, at which point Mrs Greenfield met my mother. Eighteen months later, according to Mr Long, my parents and I had gone walking on a wave-swept beach and met him and his father.

We lived in San Francisco for three years that time, leaving again for England in the summer of 1904. My brother was born in February of 1905, so it was probable that Mother, finding herself pregnant, preferred to give birth among her own people. However, once he was six months old, they returned here, arriving just after the couturier on Post Street had opened in September 1905—although my "aunt" vaguely thought that we had stopped in Boston for a time on the way, with my father's family.

Which may have been when the coloured window and the small furry dogs had lodged themselves into my young mind.

We lived in San Francisco from September 1905 until the summer of 1906. Many of my parents' friends had fled the shattered city in April, but Mrs Greenfield was quite clear that Mother had insisted on staying on until at least June, assisting with the early weeks of the emergency, before the demands of her young family took her back to England.

This time, without my father. For the next few years, he had lived half the year here and half in England, taking a train to New York and sailing back and forth across the Atlantic in order to be with his family, until finally in the summer of 1912, Mother relented and joined him in California. Two years and three months later, they died, and I had gone away for good.

I laid my scribbled notes in front of Holmes, who glanced at them thoughtfully. "When I first met you," he said, "I heard a solid basis of London in your voice, with a later overlay of California. Clearly, the influence of very early childhood had been put aside. I shall have to look into this—it would make an interesting monograph."

"Why don't I remember it?" I protested, then flinched at the tight strain of agony in my voice. "I can understand the early years, but don't people remember things from when they were five or six?"

He studied me appraisingly. "You do honestly wish to know?"

"Don't be ridiculous, Holmes. Why wouldn't I want to know about a large chunk of my missing life?"

"I can think of a number of reasons," he said, his grey eyes unwavering in their intensity.

"Well, I can't. It's vexing. And more than a little humiliating. Why wouldn't I want to feel whole?"

"If, for example, you discovered that your parents were not the paragons you think them?"

"I loved my parents and respected them, but they were hardly paragons," I scoffed. "My father was easily distracted and my mother could be cold. And after all, disillusionment is a part of growing up."

"And if the disillusionment was more serious? If, say, you discovered your father was involved in some act of criminality during the earthquake?"

"What sort of criminality?" I asked sharply.

"Perhaps whatever it was that happened during the Fire, the thing that so upset Mr Long's loyal father."

I tried to picture my father in the rôle of a criminal, and failed. I shook my head. "Holmes, he was an ethical man. And my mother enormously so—she never would have put up with a real wrongdoing. No, I can only say that, if he did something criminal, there would have been a reason for it."

"She would not have put up with it, you say. And she left for England a few weeks after the Fire."

"Wouldn't any woman with two small children?"

His gaze neither changed nor left me, and I shifted

uncomfortably. What was he getting at? Why did I feel suddenly uneasy, as if a masseur were closing in on some bruised and tender spot?

But Holmes said nothing further; in its way, that was even worse.

Chapter Nine

Friday morning, faced with a plethora of urgent tasks and troubling questions, I decided that the two things preying most heavily on my mind were my need for a dress for the evening and the continued lack of communication from Dr Ginzberg. As soon as we had finished our breakfast, and after a glance at the changeable spring sky, I put on a light rain-coat and crossed Union Square to the dress shops.

It took a couple of hours to find a frock and shoes sufficiently formal for an evening out, but since my other options were a kimono or *salwaar kameez*, I persisted, arranging for the necessary alterations (my height exaggerated the hem-lines past current fashion and into a concern for propriety) and to have my purchases sent to the hotel. Back on the main street, I threw out my hand for a taxi, ducking quickly inside it and watching the street behind us for a while: no tail.

I gave the driver Dr Ginzberg's address, which was both her home and the office where we had met those last times, after I had been released from hospital and before I had left for England. The taxi pulled up in front of a building that looked almost right although the walls were a different colour, and when I got out to ring the bell, the plate said "Garbon."

A small woman answered, but that was her only similarity to my psychiatrist. I explained about my search in increasing detail, but so little was her response that I began to suspect that she was either dim or deaf.

"I'm sorry," I said. "Do you speak English?"

"But of course I speak English," she said with a light accent of Southern France. "However, I do not know the person for whom you search."

"Perhaps she has moved. Do you mind telling me who sold you the house?"

"It is merely let, through an agency on Geary Street, but I do not believe the owner is named Ginzberg. Something with a B, I think it was. Baker? Bolton?" She shook her head. "No, I can't remember. It has been five years we live here, and always we pay to the agency."

"Perhaps they can tell me. They're on Geary, you said?"

"Not too far from the start of the Panhandle—you know the narrow strip of green that leads into Golden Gate Park? One or perhaps two streets to the east."

"Thank you," I said, and had stepped off the small landing when her voice stopped me.

"Are you the person who sent a letter?"

"I wrote to this address, yes. Twice in fact."

"There was one last month, from some place with the most interesting stamp. I did not remember the name on the address."

"That was from Japan, yes."

"Most such letters are caught by the mailman, who sends them to the agency. The Japan letter came here, and I gave it to him the following day, to take there. Perhaps as you say, they will know."

I thanked her and went back to the waiting taxi and asked the driver if we might explore the area to the south of the Panhandle for an estate agency, but it turned out that he knew the place, and drove directly to the door. Again, I had him wait in case this, too, proved a brief visit.

The office was staffed by a solitary woman, who should have been three or four. Two 'phone lines rang the moment she put down the receivers, three people waited to speak with her, and clearly she was not going to give me much of her attention.

I waited with limited patience, and when I reached the head of the queue, I took from my purse a five-dollar bill and laid it, and a piece of paper bearing the Ginzberg address, on the desk in front of her. She looked at it, looked at me, and rang off the telephone she was speaking on, laying it and its brother onto the desk so they would not interrupt.

"Thank you," I said, giving her a smile. "I can see you're busy, but I need to find a woman who used to own one of the houses your agency manages. Her mail gets forwarded here, so I assume you know where she is."

"What's her name?"

"Dr Ginzberg. I think her first name—"

"Sure, the mental doctor. She doesn't own the house, and I don't know where she is. We just stick anything that comes for her in an envelope and send it along with the monthly cheques to the hospital. Not that she gets much anymore."

"Do you have a name there?" I asked, ignoring the impatient shifting of the man behind me.

"Not particularly. Just the business office."

"Thank you," I said again, and left her to her popularity.

At the hospital, I suggested to my driver that he might want to leave me, as I could easily find another taxi at the busy door, but he shrugged and said he'd go and get some lunch, and wait for me down the street. I paid him off, in case he decided to leave, put my head down, and forced myself to enter the dwelling-place of fear and pain.

One step inside the door, and the smell seized me by the throat, making my legs go weak and my head begin to whirl. If coming to San Francisco had filled me with dread, this building was the very centre of that horror, and the smell of cleaning fluid and illness made the memory of those weeks rise up in the back of my mouth. Physical pain and raw abandonment and an excoriating sense of guilt slammed into me, fresh as the week I first woke here. I would have turned on my shaky legs and bolted for the door had a nurse not noticed my distress, and come to take my elbow.

"Miss," she repeated, "come sit down, you're about to faint."

Obediently, I took the chair she dragged me towards, and felt her cool hand pushing gently but firmly against the bare nape of my neck, forcing my head down. I took a breath, then a few more; the dizziness passed somewhat, and I sat upright.

"Goodness," I said with an embarrassed laugh. "I hadn't expected that."

"Not to worry, it's always the strong ones that get the feet knocked out from under them by hospitals," she replied cheerfully. "Had an Irish longshoreman in here this morning, one look at the needle and—*phht*—out cold. Were you looking for someone?"

"Actually, it's the business office. I'm trying to track down a doctor who worked here ten years ago."

"I couldn't help you there, I've only been here three, but I can get you to the office."

Several turns and a stairway later, the more distressing odours and sounds faded, and the office itself could almost have been anywhere. Almost. I thanked my guide, and went through the door.

Two more recitations of the details of my quest were required before I was set before an authority in a suit and tie instead of dress and stockings. I gratefully sank into the indicated chair, pulled off my gloves as an indication of my intention to see this enquiry through, and gave a third, somewhat more detailed version of the story.

At the end of it the man in the suit sat back and laced his hands together over his waistcoat.

"You were a patient here?"

"After the accident, yes, in October and November 1914. After November, I moved to a convalescent home, and saw her in her private office until I went home to England."

"And you saw Dr Ginzberg during that whole time?" I detected a note of apprehension in his voice, at his awareness that he was seated across from a former mental patient, and I tried to look reassuringly sane. However, this did at least indicate that he was familiar with Dr Ginzberg's practice; I gritted my teeth behind my friendly smile, and prepared to grovel.

"I did, yes. I was fourteen years old and had just lost my entire family. Dr Ginzberg was extremely helpful to me. I thought I should return her kindness by showing her how things turned out." Was this the place to drop casual mention of a donation to the hospital, I considered? Perhaps not just yet.

"I see," he said, reassured that I was not about to launch myself in a lunatic rage across the desk. He seemed to be wrestling with a decision; I was just opening my mouth to play the money card when his eyes came up to meet mine. "Well, Miss Russell, I'm very sorry to have to tell you this, but Dr Ginzberg died several years ago. It must have been shortly after you knew her, and she was ..."

But the growing noise in my head obscured his words, although I could see that he was talking, could see too when he stopped talking and his eyebrows came together in an expression some part of me recognised as concern. Then his mouth moved again and his hand came out but I couldn't hear him, couldn't hear anything but the roaring of a great waterfall, and for a while it was hard to see anything as well.

With no helpful nurse around to press her cool hand against the back of my neck to force my head down, it was a wonder I didn't end up on the floor. I came back to myself to find that my body had assumed the head-down position under its own power, my forehead resting on the heels of my hands, lungs pulling in, slow and deep. It could only have been seconds that my awareness faltered, because two suited legs had scarcely had time to clear the desk on their way to the door.

"I'm all right," I croaked.

He paused, out of sight, and I cleared my throat and

repeated the assertion, with sufficient strength this time that he could understand me.

"Can I get you something?" he asked, sounding nervous. "A glass of water?"

"That would be good, thank you."

By the time he returned, I was sitting upright, feeling the colour seeping back into my face. I drank the water, thinking somewhat nonsensically that Holmes would have given me brandy, and placed the glass on his desk. My hands were steady enough to reassure him.

"I'm terribly sorry," he said. "I should have realised that the news would be a shock."

"How did she die?"

His long pause made me think that perhaps he had already told me, while my ears were filled with the rush of receding blood, but by that time I was more concerned with the information than reassuring him as to my sanity. I looked at him sharply and said, "Please, how did Dr Ginzberg die?"

"She was hit on the head. The police thought..." and for the second time, his mouth moved while no sound reached me. I waited calmly until his face muscles were still before I asked him to repeat himself. His gaze flicked to the door and back, and I thought that if he got up to summon help, I would physically stop him and force the information from him. Fortunately, assault proved unnecessary.

"Someone broke into her office at home, where she met patients. Apparently he thought she was out, but she was not, and she disturbed him in the process of ransacking her desk for money. He hit her with a statue she had on the desk, and left her for dead. She wasn't found until morning. She never regained consciousness."

There. I had it now, and hadn't fainted or gone deaf again. I could handle this. I heard myself speak, and sat wondering at my ability to appear rational.

"When was this, precisely?"

"Precisely, I don't remember. But it was in the early weeks of 1915."

"That's not possible."

"Er, well, I suppose I could be mistaken, although I think—"

"I'd appreciate the date, if that's available." It could not have been so soon after I left for England, simply could not.

"I could have my secretary research it," he said, clearly uncertain why it would matter.

"Thank you. Another question: Why is the hospital still receiving the mail addressed to her home?"

That question made his body relax into surer ground. "We administer Dr Ginzberg's estate. She left everything to the hospital, for the benefit of mental patients. Some of her holdings we sold, others we retained as income. The house is one of those."

"Where do letters go?"

"She didn't have much family. We generally open letters, and if they are business we answer them, if personal—there are few of those anymore—we send them to a cousin of hers who lives near Philadelphia. I believe the cousin is getting on in years; her communication has become quite . . . eccentric."

"Was an arrest made?"

"Not that I've heard."

"Do you know the officer in charge of the investigation?"

"I met him, but years ago. His name slips my mind."

"Perhaps your secretary could look that up as well?"

"If you like. Although as you are not family, I don't suppose he'd have much to tell you."

"We'll see," I told him, a trifle grimly. Although Holmes tended to travel under an assumed name—currently he was using a favourite, Sherrinford Holmes—if necessity called I would not hesitate to send him in under his own name. There wasn't a policeman in the world who would turn down a conversation with Sherlock Holmes. "Well, thank you, Mister, er..."

"Braithwaite," he provided.

"Of course." I pushed myself out of the chair, obscurely pleased that I did not fall on my face. My feet seemed remarkably far away.

"Miss Russell, let me arrange a car for you."

"That won't be necessary; I have a taxicab waiting for me. I think."

Still, his sense of responsibility demanded that he arrange for an escort, who proved to be the secretary occupying the desk outside of his office door. The woman was at least sixty and so thin she might have snapped in two had I leant on her firmly, but fortunately that did not prove necessary: The tonic of leaving the confines of the hospital restored me to a degree of normalcy. Once outside of the doors, I thanked her, and even remembered to give her my various addresses for the information she would be unearthing for me.

The taxi pulled up, and as I climbed in, I told my faithful driver that I wished to return to the hotel.

I believe he chatted at me the whole way back; I heard not a word.

And it never occurred to me to look around for a gunman.

In front of the St Francis, I got out, and was a good way up the entranceway when I realised that he was calling me—I had forgotten to pay him. I returned, thrust some money at him, and turned away, but his voice persisted, to be joined just inside the entrance by his person as he tried to press some dollar bills into my hand. My fingers closed over them automatically—anything to be rid of the man—but I did not pause in my path to the lift.

Inside the humming enclosure, I gave the attendant my floor number and stood staring down at the change for my fare. The bills were quivering slightly. I could feel the boy, looking out of the side of his eyes at me. The upward thrust slowed, the door slid open, and I walked to the room. The key even turned the lock, an event I found mildly amazing, considering the uncertain state of the rest of the universe.

Granite pillars, in the general course of events, did not simply crumble and fall. Trollies did not leave their tracks and set off down the side streets. Lightning did not strike out of a cloudless sky.

Psychiatrists who made for the only secure hold in a time of catastrophe did not bleed to death on their office floors.

I stepped out of my shoes, ripped off hat, gloves, and coat, and burrowed deep among the bed-clothes.

Which was where Holmes found me, five hours later.

BOOK TWO

Holmes

Chapter Ten

It is a singularly disconcerting experience to discover a supremely competent individual brought to her knees; even more so when that person is one's wife.

In the course of his long career, however, Sherlock Holmes had with some regularity been faced with a client or witness in a state of shock, and long ago recognised the benefits of the traditional remedies: either a stiff brandy or large quantities of hot, sweet tea to soothe the nerves; some readily digestible food-stuff to set the blood to flowing; and at the properly judged moment, a sharp counteractive shock to restore the patient to useful coherence.

So when he came into his hotel room and found his young wife huddled inertly beneath the bed-clothes, he picked up the telephone to summon tea and biscuits, administered a quick dose of contraband brandy, and then proceeded to an alternative not generally permitted a consulting detective when faced with a distressed client: He bundled Russell into the bath, undergarments and all, and turned the taps on hot and full.

The tea came, the water rose, and he spent the next quarter of an hour bent over the steaming porcelain tub forcing liquid and sweet morsels of cream-filled cakes into the silent woman. Slowly, her eyes returned to a focus. He went into the next room to look for her spectacles, stripping off his coat and rolling up his wet shirt-sleeves as he studied the room for any indication of what had put her into that state. No out-spread newspapers on the table, no crumpled telegrams in the wastebasket, nothing but the trail of discarded possessions and garments from door to bed.

He found her hand-bag just inside the door and turned it upside-down on the bed: money purse, handkerchief, note-book, pen-knife, pistol, and investigative tool-kit—all the usual paraphernalia and nothing out of the ordinary.

He abandoned the hand-bag, eventually found the spectacles under the bed, and took them into the steam-filled room, setting them in a corner of the soap-dish for her. He then poured himself a cup of tea, refilled hers (just one sugar this time instead of two, although usually she took none) and settled onto the vanity stool to wait for her to speak.

Which she did before his cup had reached its dregs.

"She's dead, Holmes."

He went still, surveying the possible meanings of the pronoun: The death of one of the Greenfield women would explain the shock, but not the despair beneath it. That left one likely candidate. "Your doctor friend?"

"Murdered in her office by someone looking for money, the police say."

"I am sorry," he offered, and he was, although it was

habit more than anything that caused him to mouth the phrase—generally meaningless, yet its recitation often prompted valuable reminiscence.

"She's the end. There's no-one left now. All these years—I never wrote to her, you know? I always thought I would see her one day, stand in front of her and tell her that it had all worked out. And all these years she's been gone."

Holmes stifled his impatience at this unhelpful production of data, and said merely, "She died some time ago, then?"

"Even before I met you. Just weeks after I left here. Gone, all this time."

"How did you find out?"

At last, Russell's eyes came to his. She blinked, spotted her glasses, and put them on; under their influence she pulled together some degree of rational thought. It was a considerable relief.

The story of her afternoon's search for information had more gaps in it than substance, but it did provide a place to begin. As she arrived at the portion of the tale that took her to the hospital, she seemed to become aware of her surroundings and, without pausing in her narrative, stood up from the bath and wrapped herself in a towelling bath-robe. He followed her into the sitting room and turned up the radiators to keep her warm.

"She'd left everything to the hospital for their mental patients, you see," Russell said, absently running one bath-robe sleeve across her wet, lamentably butchered hair. She looked like a child when her hand came away, hair tousled, pink-faced, and wrapped in an oversized robe—again Holmes was struck by how thin she was looking, and pushed away the urge to retrieve the tea tray with its sticky sweets.

"You believe the hospital administrator knew nothing other than what he told you?"

"I don't think he did. His secretary was going to find the name of the investigator for me. And something else as well, what was it? Oh, yes, the precise date of her death. I wonder why she hasn't 'phoned yet? Maybe I ought to—"

"Sit, Russell. Have another cup of tea and one of those cream cakes."

"Holmes, I'm fine. What time is it, anyway? Good heavens, I've slept the day away, what a ridiculous thing to do."

"Russell, the only reason for you to be on your feet is to accompany me to the restaurant for a meal."

"Holmes, I've just consumed half a pound of buttercream. I'll wait until dinner-time, if you don't mind."

"I do mind. Russell, you have lost nearly a stone in recent weeks, and haven't eaten a proper meal since we left Japan. If you don't feed yourself, I swear on Mrs Hudson's rolling-pin that I shall call for a doctor."

It was something of a turn-around, to have Holmes encouraging someone else to take nourishment—for most of the past forty-some years it had been Dr Watson or Mrs Hudson cajoling, bribing, or berating Holmes not to starve himself. In fact, so extraordinary was this approach that Russell subsided without protest, and if she did not take a large meal, it was nonetheless meat and bread—or in any case, an omelette and toast. Her colour was better at the end of it, and Holmes' features had relaxed a fraction.

After the meal, they took a turn through Union Square, settling onto a bench in the far corner that caught a stray late ray of sunlight. Holmes pulled out his tobacco pouch; Russell closed her eyes and raised her face. A nanny hurried past with her charge in a pram; two boot-boys sauntered through, glancing with professional disdain at the toes of passers-by; a pair of police constables strode the other way, their gazes probing faces, watching for signs of shiftiness.

Finally, Russell stirred. "So, what have you been doing today, Holmes?"

"I have been conducting my own research."

"Into what?"

"Into your family."

One bright blue eye opened to look at him sideways. "Really? What aspect of my family interests you?"

"All manner of aspects."

"Pray tell," she said, although her voice told him not to.

He ignored her tone, let out a thoughtful cloud of smoke, and said, "Your parents met in the spring of 1895, when your father did the Grand Tour and met your mother at the British Museum."

"Over the display of Roman antiquities, yes."

"They married, despite the objections of both sides, little more than a year later, in the summer of 1896."

"His parents objecting to Mother being a Jew, hers outraged by his being a Christian. Holmes, I've told you all this."

"And came here, to San Francisco, although his parents had long ago returned to Boston, the Russell family centre. California being, like the Colonies, a place one sent younger sons to try themselves, and with luck to add something to the family fortunes before they came back home to the castle."

"I thought they'd first come here in 1900, after I was born."

"Not at all. According to the account books in your father's study, they lived here from 1897 to 1899, before returning to England for your birth. They returned in May 1901. As we heard, they met the Longs eighteen months later, and as your honorary aunt told you, lived here, apart from the period of your brother's birth, until the summer after the earthquake."

"At which time my mother got nervous about the house falling down around her and took my brother and me back to England. I know."

"Whatever your mother was nervous about, it did not include houses falling down."

"What do you mean?"

"According to two of your neighbours, your family moved back into the house ten days after the fire, at which time your mother seemed remarkably light-hearted about the damage, and sanguine about any future catastrophes."

"Then why would she leave?"

"Precisely what they wondered. And why leave so pre-cipitately, taking only a few bags, and following a loud argument?"

"An argument? My *parents*?"

"The postman heard it. He said it was unusual. Said, too, that to find your father's motorcar in the drive in the morning was most unusual. You do not remember any degree of discord between your parents?"

"I don't remember them fighting, no."

"Yet they separated for large parts of the years between 1906 and 1912. What would have caused that if not marital discord? A child's health? Some threat here in California?"

"Threat from what?"

"In June 1906 your father also wrote the codicil to the will specifying that the house be closed to outsiders. Two months following the fire."

"I imagine a catastrophe of those proportions would have caused many people to add codicils to their wills."

"And two months following some incident that caused a shift in the relationship between your father and Micah Long."

"Again, the experience of the fire itself could have done that. Or even Long's guilt and resentment that he had been seeing to the safety of my family when his own family was driven from their home and nearly killed."

"That is true enough," he conceded. He thought for a minute then asked, "And over the following years, whenever your father came to England, how did your parents seem?"

Russell looked uncomfortable at this autopsy of a marriage. "They seemed . . . normal. Well, when he first arrived we would all be somewhat stiff and formal. But within a few days everything would be fine. And Mother was always very sad when he left again."

"So why leave, and so suddenly?" Holmes asked, but he was only musing aloud, not asking her.

"I was at school," Russell said suddenly, as if a memory had been startled from her. "I came home from school one afternoon and found her throwing things into bags and telling me we had to go. I'd finished my exams, but I didn't even have a chance to say good-bye to my friends. I had to write home to Father from New York and ask him to send certain books I'd forgotten in the rush. I always assumed it was because they'd discovered the house wasn't safe to live in."

"There was damage, but less than some of the

neighbouring houses withstood. I think it more likely that the cause lay in some threat. Possibly linked to the happenings in the fire."

" 'Possibly' this, 'theoretically' that—you keep harping on some mysterious event of a criminal nature, Holmes. What sort of a crime are you imagining?"

"That I have yet to discover," Holmes said calmly.

"Or even if there was one." She rose and said coldly, "Holmes, I have things to do. I shall be out with Flo until late, so don't wait up for me. And please, I beg you, find something to keep yourself busy. This stirring about in my past is becoming a vexation."

She walked away; he sat with his pipe, watching her retreat with hooded eyes.

Chapter Eleven

It was both a challenge and an irritation to follow an individual such as Russell without being seen. Had she been another person, Holmes would simply have trailed along in her wake, confident that a young woman in the hold of social impulse and illicit alcohol would be oblivious of a tail. Russell, however, even without her glasses, normally had eyes in the back of her head.

Not that she'd noticed him following practically on her heels all those hours on Monday afternoon. Still, Holmes kept his distance. He had his taxi park down the street from the St Francis until Russell's friend arrived, then followed behind, stopping a street down from where the gaudy, bright blue Rolls-Royce disgorged its passengers. He studied the motor's driver closely, taking note of the noise he made and the speed with which he drove—outside of a city's streets, the taxi would never have kept up with him—but noting also the way the apparently careless young man gave wide berth to a woman walking with her two children, and how he always kept both his hands on the wheel and spoke over his shoulder instead of turning his head to speak to the passengers in back.

When the blue car had been driven away by the club's valet, Holmes paid off his curious driver and took up surveillance in a more or less illicit dive across the way from the cabaret, a small and dingy space with air that looked as if the fog had moved in. He used his thumbnail to scrape a patch of paint from the window-glass, which looked to have been applied half-heartedly at the descent of Prohibition five years before, absently cleaned the grime from underneath his nail with a pen-knife, then settled in to his surveillance with a glass of stale beer before him on the table.

An hour passed. Motorcars came and went from the sparkling gin palace, music spilt out onto the street, the uniformed doorman chatted unconcernedly with two passing policemen (confirming Holmes' suspicions that the police department in this town was not as free of graft as one might wish—a two-year-old would have known that the alcohol inside flowed like water). And slowly, he became aware that he was himself being watched.

The man was good. Holmes had taken no particular note of him when he wandered in, other than noticing how tall, thin, and tidily dressed he was. He was simply one thirsty man among a dozen others—but when the man settled into the dimmest corner, when he nursed two whiskeys over the course of the hour and seemed uninterested in the company, and particularly when he seemed to relax into his corner and displace less air than a normal man, Holmes' antennae twitched. He pondered his options: keep guard over the street and Russell, or pursue this new avenue?

After an hour and a quarter, with a full glass on the table, Holmes rose and headed towards the back of the establishment, weaving slightly. He felt the other man come to attention in the dim corner, and smiled to himself as he heard the soft clink of coins being laid on the damp table: The man was preparing to follow if Holmes did not return in a reasonable time, but not immediately—he wouldn't want to risk a face-to-face meeting in the hall-way.

The noxious facilities were out-of-doors, in the delivery yard that was closed up for the night. Holmes slipped past them to the yard's wooden gates. The lock was a joke, and he let himself out into the ill-lit alleyway beyond, leaving the gates ajar.

Four minutes after he'd come through it, the back door to the speakeasy opened and closed. There came a stifled oath and the quick sound of a man hurrying across sloppy paving stones. The stranger shouldered his way out of the gate, took two steps—and came to an immediate halt at the clear sound of a trigger being pulled back, a dozen feet away.

"Are you armed?" the stranger heard, in the drawl of an Englishman.

After a minute, the American answered. "I'm not much of one for guns."

"Does that mean no?"

"No, I don't have a gun."

"Take off your coats and toss them over here," came the command. The tall American unbuttoned his overcoat and tossed it in the direction of the other's voice, then did the same with his jacket, standing motionless in the cold in his shirt-sleeves. "I trust you'll pardon me if I don't take your word on the matter. Would you be so good as to turn and place your hands against the wall?"

The man hesitated, loath to turn his back to a gun, but he had little choice. He faced the wall and leant against it with his hands. The bricks were briefly illuminated by the flare of a pocket-torch, and in a moment a hand patted all the obvious places for a weapon, and one or two not so obvious. Then the light winked out and he stood in the dark, listening to the sound of his garments being gone through. The overcoat was a good one, and relatively new; he'd be sore to lose it.

But after a minute the English voice said, "You may turn around again," and in a moment, the two coats were flying out of the darkness at him. He put them on, grateful for the warmth, and coughed gently.

"Now your notecase—wallet, if you will."

The American slid the leather object from his inner pocket and threw it across the alleyway, rather less concerned than at the loss of his coat. There wasn't all that much in the wallet to lose.

The torch flared again, dazzling him at the same time it showed the Englishman the contents of the wallet and its various business cards and identifications. All but two of the cards were inventions that placed him in the employ of agencies ranging from insurance to newspapers. The two valid cards were those the Englishman unerringly pulled out.

"Pinkerton's, eh?" he said. "And Samuel's Jewelers." The alleyway fell silent for a minute, then there was a faint click followed by the rustle of clothing, and the

Englishman stepped out into the alley. Accident or intent placed him in a patch of light, and the American could see the man's hands, the left one holding the wallet, the other outstretched and free of weaponry. "Holmes is my name, in the event you don't know it already. Might I buy you a drink while we talk about why you're following me?"

The American retrieved his wallet, looked at the open hand, and slowly extended his own. "The name's Hammett, Dashiell Hammett. And I guess we might as well have a drink."

They shook hands, with a certain amount of probing on both sides, and then Holmes released his grip and clapped Hammett on the shoulder. "I sincerely hope you do not wish to return to that...would it be called a 'joint' in American parlance? My palate may never recover."

"You like our Volstead Act, huh? Sure, there's a place up the street with liquor that's never seen the inside of a bath-tub."

"Actually, I have to say I've been pleasantly surprised at how civilised this city is when it comes to the availability of drink. I'd expected the whole country to be as dry as the Sahara."

"This side of the country, it's a bit of a joke, the cops don't even charge much to turn a blind eye, but like you say, in some places, things are getting tough. Chicago—wow."

Down the alley and out onto the street, and Hammett asked the question that had clearly been tormenting him since the moment he'd heard the trigger go back. "How'd you know I was on your tail, anyway? I've got something of a reputation as an invisible man."

"Invisible, yes. But the Pinkertons might wish to reconsider their policy of sending out a man with a tubercular cough on surveillance, particularly on a cold night. When one hears the same cough coming from a lounger outside the St Francis, and later on the other side of a speakeasy, one begins to wonder."

"Yeah," Hammett admitted with chagrin. "It's sometimes hard to sit quiet. But most people don't notice."

"I, however, am not most people."

"I'm beginning to think that. C'mon, it's down here."

The place Hammett led him to was more neighbourhood pub than urban speakeasy; one table hosted a poker game and at another a friendly argument about boxing. There was even a darts board on the back wall. When they walked in, the man drying glasses behind the bar greeted Hammett as a longtime acquaintance.

"Hey there, Dash. Guy was looking for you earlier."

"Evening, Jimmy. What sort of guy would that be?"

The man's eyes slid sideways to take in Holmes, and his answer was oblique. "The sort of guy you sometimes work with, seen him with you once or twice a while back."

"Well, he'll find me if he wants me. I'll have my usual, Jimmy. This is my friend Mr Smith. He's got a doctor's prescription you can fill."

"What's your medicament, Mr Smith?" the man asked as he reached for a bottle of whiskey, poured a glass, and set it in front of Hammett.

"No chance of a decent claret, I take it?" Holmes said wistfully.

"I could give you something red called wine, but I'm not sure a Frenchman would recognise it."

"Very well. What about a single malt?"

The barman shook his head sadly. "The state of my cellar's tragic, that's all you can call it."

"Never mind, I'll take a—"

"Now, don't be hasty. Said it was tragic, didn't say it was completely empty. Just explaining to you why the good stuff's limited and the price'll make you wince."

The quality was fine, although the price did truly make Holmes wince. But he counted out his money and followed Hammett over to a quiet table, taking out his cigarette case and offering one to his companion. When the tobacco was going, the two men sat back with their drinks, eyeing each other curiously.

They were of a size, Hammett an inch or so taller, but he possessed the folded-up quality of the man whose height fit him ill, and was so emaciated that his suit, nicely cut though it was, nonetheless draped his shoulders like one of the shrouded chairs in Russell's house; when he spoke, one was aware of the skull's movement. By comparison, Holmes looked positively robust. Hammett's thick, light red hair, combed back from his high forehead, showed a great deal of white at the temples, although he couldn't have been more than thirty. His clothes were good, his collar white, his ever-so-slightly flashy tie was precisely knotted beneath a face composed of watchful brown eyes, thick brows, knife-straight nose, and a mouth that skirted the edge of pretty. Strangers seeing the two men at the table might have taken them for father and son; certainly their long, thin, nervous fingers were of a type.

"So," the American finally broke the silence. "You

want to tell me why you didn't shoot me in the face back there?"

"Personally, I've always found leaving a trail of corpses inconvenient, although I admit it has been some time since I lived in America—perhaps strictures have relaxed in the past ten years. However, as it was I who got the drop on you, perhaps I should be permitted the first questions."

"Fair enough. Shoot."

"Clearly, the most fundamental question in our relationship has to be, Why were you following me?"

"I was paid to."

"By the Pinkertons?" Holmes had had dealings with the American detective agency before; not all of them had gone smoothly. His manner gave away none of this, merely his familiarity with the company.

"By whoever hired the Pinkertons."

"You don't know the identity of your employer?"

"Nope. Which also gives you the answer to your second fundamental question."

Holmes took a swallow of the passable single-malt Scotch, slumping back into his chair in a way that made the other man think the Englishman was enjoying himself, and said, "That question being?"

"Why didn't I have my pal Jimmy there pull out his shotgun and take your pistol away from you?"

"Two men having a drink together, Mr Hammett— surely that indicates a truce agreement, even in these farthest reaches of civilisation?" Holmes rested his cigarette in the flimsy tin ash-tray and picked up his glass again, left-handed; it occurred to Hammett that, other than their hand-shake and when he'd been paying for the drinks, the Englishman's right hand was always kept free and never more than a few inches from the pocket holding the gun.

Hammett gave a sudden laugh, his haggard face lighting up unexpectedly. "Mr Holmes, something tells me that you only trust a truce when it's fifty pages long and freshly written in the other guy's blood."

Holmes gave a small smile. "Superior strength is indeed a desirable component of negotiation."

"Fine then, let's negotiate away—you with your gun, me on my home ground."

"Am I to understand that your version of my 'second fundamental question' indicates a certain lack of trust in the very people who hired you?"

"Now why would you say that?"

"Had you been wholeheartedly committed to the cause of your employer, I suspect that you would have made a play for the weapon, either on the way here or with the bar-keep to back you up. Not that you would have succeeded, mind you, and in the process of demonstrating that fact someone might have been hurt, so I do commend your decision. However, I assert that your willingness to go along with abduction is somewhat unusual, considering the Pinkertons' reputation for professional behaviour."

Hammett scowled. "The Pinkertons are in it for the money, that's true. And they don't always look too closely at where their clients' cash comes from. It's one of the disagreements I've had with them over the years. Why I only work for them from time to time, nowadays."

Holmes squinted through the smoke at the younger man, thinking over the man's words. "If I hear you aright, you are telling me that you prefer to act in cases that suit your moral stance, and that this particular case you are on is making you suspect that your employers are not on the side of the angels."

"Yeah, well, a man's got to live with the person in the mirror."

Especially, thought Holmes, when the man's own mortality stood so clearly outlined at his shoulder.

"Your doubts therefore explain why you came with me so willingly. To see if my side, as it were, suited your ethics more comfortably."

"I thought I'd listen to what you had to say."

Which suggested the possibility, Holmes reflected, that the man had not only willingly permitted himself to be taken in the alley, but might even have set it up with precisely that end in view. He raised a mental eyebrow, reappraising the thin man before him: It had been a long time since he'd come across that combination of intelligence and fearlessness.

Russell had it, and half a dozen others he'd known through the years.

One of whom had been Professor Moriarty.

"So, do I get to ask a question now?" Hammett said.

"You may ask."

"Yeah, I know, and you might not answer. But that would be the end of a beautiful friendship, wouldn't it?"

Again the faint glint of amusement from the grey eyes. "Your question being, Why didn't I shoot you in the face when we met in the alley?"

"That's as good a place to start as any."

"I suppose one might say, better a known enemy than an unseen potential."

Hammett blinked. "You have a lot of 'unseen potentials' around?"

"One, at least. Unless that was you who took a shot at my wife the other evening?"

The thin man's jaw dropped as his features went slack for a moment, an expression of shock that only the most subtle of actors could produce at will; Holmes did not think this man an actor. "Your wife? I didn't know— Wait a minute. Is that the girl you were following tonight?"

"In the dark green frock, yes. Although I don't know that she has been a 'girl' in all the years I've known her."

"And someone took a shot at her?"

"Wednesday night, about six o'clock, in Pacific Heights."

"At the house?"

"So you know where her house is?"

Instead of answering, Hammett sat for a minute drumming the finger-tips of his right hand on the table while he studied the man across from him, weighing the fancy accent and clothes against the man's undeniable competence and the vein of toughness Hammett could feel in him. Toughness was a quality that Hammett respected.

"Why'd you take those two business cards from my wallet?" he asked suddenly.

Holmes reached into his pocket and laid the scraps of pasteboard on the table, pushing them slightly apart with a long finger. "Because they're yours. The others are fakes." He looked into Hammett's eyes, and smiled. "You're an investigator, of some kind. The Pinkerton's card was real because no sane investigator would disguise himself as an investigator. Of the others, all of them provided you with a front for asking questions— insurance, municipal water company, local newspaper, voting registry—except for the jeweller's. Therefore, that is real, too."

"Yeah," Hammett told him. "I write ad copy for them, sometimes. Pays the rent."

He looked at the cards for a moment, then his right hand clenched into a fist and beat gently once on the table-top, the gesture of a judge's gavel, before the fingers spread out to brace his weight as he rose.

"Come on, I need to show you what I got."

Holmes did not hesitate: Russell would simply have to look after herself. Outside the bar, Hammett threw up a hand to hail a passing taxi, giving an address on Eddy Street. Hammett knew the driver by name, and during the brief ride the two residents tossed around speculations concerning "the Babe's" homers this season (Babe, Holmes eventually decided, being the name of a sports figure and neither an affectionate term for a female nor a mythic blue ox; from his earlier time living in Chicago he knew that "homer" referred not to a Greek philosopher but a baseball play—the home run); Harry Wills' chances against Dempsey in the September fight that had just been announced (Wills and Dempsey apparently being professional boxers, not street thugs); the ludicrous conversation the driver had overheard recently between two passengers concerning the bridging of the Golden Gate, which both he and Hammett agreed would provide a huge opportunity for graft and never so much as a jungle foot-bridge to show for it; and the ever more lamentable state of the city's traffic. Holmes contributed nothing but sat absorbing local vocabulary with his ears while his eyes studied the passing streets. He also noted Hammett's careful survey of his surroundings before he climbed out of the cab, as well as the fact that the house number he had given the driver was down the street from the one they eventually entered.

He'd have been one of the better Pinkerton operatives Holmes had seen—if he'd been a Pinkerton.

The Eddy address was an apartment house. Just inside the door, the air was thick with the smell of alcohol.

"Boot-leggers," Hammett explained. "It's not usually this bad, but they dropped a box last night."

Upstairs, the Hammett residence proved to be a small, worn, scrupulously clean space with aggressively fresh air overcoming the reek of alcohol. Hammett left his coat on but dropped his grey hat onto the stand before he led his guest into the front room, closing its door quietly and crossing over to close the wide-open windows. "My wife's a nurse," he said. "Fresh air's a religion to her. It'll warm up in a minute."

He took a half-full bottle from a cluttered table set against the wall, poured two glasses, and brought them to the chairs in the front window, picking up a limp rag-doll from one. He brushed its skirt straight and set it on the sofa, where it made a miniature third party to their discussion, then took the other chair and pulled a tobacco pouch and papers from his pocket. With the windows closed, a faint trace of ammonia did battle with the boot-legger's accident: a child's nappies.

Holmes took one sip of his drink, to demonstrate that the declared truce still held, then set the glass down firmly on the little side-table.

"Mr Hammett, you may at one time have been a Pinkerton operative, but you are no longer. For whom are you working?"

The man's brown eyes flew open in surprise, and he held them open as a show of innocence. "Why do you say that?"

"Young man, you bring me here yet expect me to

believe you an active operative? Do not take me for a fool. You receive an Army disability pension because of your lungs, and you have no doubt supplemented that from time to time with work for the agency, but you are a man who at times is so debilitated you cannot make it from one end of the apartment to the next without stopping to rest. At the moment you are attempting to support your wife and small daughter by writing for popular journals."

The bone-thin fingers slowly resumed their movements, automatically taking a precise pinch of tobacco and arranging it along the centre of the paper without his looking. "You want to tell me how you know all that?"

"Eyes, man: have them, use them. The doll, a woman's magazine on the side-table, two envelopes from the United States Army in a pigeon-hole, the Underwood on the kitchen table, and a pile of manuscript pages and copies of such literary works as *Black Mask*. Mr Hammett, I of all people should recognise the signs of a struggling writer."

"The *Smart Set* on the side-table is mine, not my wife's," Hammett asserted, but weakly. "I write for them. But how could you know of my occasional...debility?"

"A series of chair-backs have worn marks into the wall-paper where they are occasionally arranged to allow you to walk the thirty feet from chair to bath without falling to the floor," Holmes told him dismissively. "Satisfied?"

Hammett's eyes fell at last to the cigarette his fingers had made. He ran a tongue along the edge, pressed it, and as he lit a match his eyes came back to

Holmes'. "You're that Holmes, aren't you? The detective."

"I am, yes."

"I always thought..."

"That I was a fictional character?"

"That maybe there'd been some...exaggerations."

Holmes laughed aloud. "One of the inadvertent side-effects of Watson's florid writing style coupled with Conan Doyle's name is that Sherlock Holmes tends to be either wildly overestimated, or the other extreme, dismissed entirely as something of a joke. It used to infuriate me—Doyle's a dangerously gullible lunatic—but apart from the blow to my ego, it's actually remarkably convenient."

"You don't say," Hammett responded, clearly taken aback at the idea of the flesh-and-blood man seated in his living-room being considered a piece of fiction. And no doubt wondering how he would feel, were someone to do the same to him.

It was all a bit dizzying.

Fortunately, Holmes had his eye on the ball. "Now, will you tell me who hired you to follow me?"

"Okay. You're right. But it was through the Pinkertons. I used to work for them, and like I said, I still do little jobs for them from time to time, when I feel up to it. I had a bad spell recently, but the rent's due, so when one of my old partners there called and said they needed a couple nights' work I said sure. But after I'd got the job, I began to wonder if he hadn't thought the job stunk and decided to palm it off on me. Here, let me show you."

He went to the table and opened the top drawer, pulling out a thick brown file folder, which he laid on the small table and flipped open, sliding the top piece of paper over to Holmes. On it was printed:

> *I wish to know all possible details concerning the whereabouts and interests of Mr S. Holmes and Miss M. Russell, staying at the St Francis Hotel. She owns a house in Pacific Heights. I shall phone you at 8:00 on the morning of Tuesday, 6 May for news.*

"That's what I got, that and a 'phone call. Now, it's not unusual to get a case over the 'phone, but I like to meet my clients face-to-face, and the lady didn't seem all that eager to meet with me. Refused, in fact. And paid cash in an envelope delivered by messenger—not a service either, just a kid, a shabby one. The whole set-up made me feel pretty uncomfortable."

"Thinking that perhaps you were being brought into something less than legal?"

"That there was something shady here, and I don't like being played for a chump."

"'Played for a chump'," Holmes repeated to himself as he bent over the note with his pocket magnifying-glass. "A flavourful sample of the vernacular. Hmm. What can you tell me about your telephone caller?"

"Woman, like I said."

"Woman, or lady?"

"I guess I'd call her a lady, if we set aside the question of whatever it is she's up to. Anyway, she talked like someone who'd been educated. In the South—deep South, that is."

Holmes' head snapped up from the handwritten note. "A Southern woman?" he said sharply. "From what part of the South?"

"That I couldn't say. Not Texas, deeper than that—Alabama, Georgia, maybe the Carolinas, that sort of thing. Slow like molasses, you know?"

But Holmes was not so easily satisfied. "Did she use any words that struck you as slightly unusual?" he pressed. "What about her vowels—what did her *a*'s sound like? Did she employ any hidden diphthongs?"

Hammett, however, could be no clearer than he had been; Holmes shook his head and returned to the note, leaving the younger man to feel that he had let down the Pinkerton side rather badly.

"You getting anything out of that?" he asked, sounding a trifle short.

"Very little," Holmes admitted, but before Hammett could make a pointed display of his own impatience, Holmes continued. "Criminals print because it conceals everything about them up to and including their sex. I see very little here, other than the obvious, of course: that she is right-handed, middle-aged, in good health, and educated; that she is probably American—hence the profligate scattering of full-stops—but has spent long enough in Europe that 'six May' rather than 'May six' comes to her pen; that said pen is expensive and probably gold-nibbed but the ink is not her own, as it shows an unfortunate tendency to clump and dry unevenly. The paper itself might reward enquiries from the city's stationers, although the watermark appears neither remarkable nor exclusive. And I should say that, behind its careful formation of the letters, the lady's hand betrays a tendency toward self-centredness such as one sees in the hand of most career criminals."

"The lady's a crook? Well, that sure narrows things down in a town this size."

"I shouldn't hold my breath," Holmes agreed, folding his magnifying-glass into its pocket and handing back the brief note. "Businessmen and even mere social climbers often display the same traits."

"You don't say?" Hammett mused, holding the note up into the light as if to follow the track of the older man's deductions.

"Graphology is far from an exact science, but it does reward study." Holmes sat back in the chair, took out his pipe and got it going, then fixed his host with a sharp grey eye. "So, Mr Hammett, am I to understand that you wish to terminate your employment with the lady from the South?"

"Not sure how I can do that; I took her money."

"Have you spent it?"

In answer, Hammett opened the file again and took out the envelope that gave it its thickness, handing it to Holmes. "I opened it to see how much there was, and since then it's sat there, untouched."

Holmes opened the flap and ran his thumb slowly up the side of the bills within, taking note of their number and their denomination. His eyebrow arched and he looked at Hammett, who nodded as if in agreement.

"Yeah, way too much money for a couple days' trailing."

"But as, what is the term? 'Hush money'?"

"You can see why I got nervous."

Holmes dropped the envelope back in the file; Hammett flipped the cover shut as if to put the money out of sight. "What I can see," said Holmes, "is that I'm dealing with a man who prefers to choose his employer."

"Mr Holmes, I've got a family. I'm not a whole lot of

good to them, the state I'm in, but I'd be a lot less good in prison."

Despite Hammett's explanation, Holmes thought that the threat of gaol was less of a deterrent than the young man's distaste for villainy. As unlike Watson as a person could be physically, nonetheless the two were brothers under the skin—and he had no doubt that, like the externally sensible Watson, Hammett's fictional maunderings would lay a thin coating of hard action over the most romantic of sensibilities.

"Very well, Mr Hammett. How would you like to work for me instead?"

"Turncoating has never had much appeal, Mr Holmes."

"Have you spent any of the lady's money?"

"I told you I hadn't."

"Has she given you a means of getting into contact with her?"

"That note was it. The boy brought it with the money, stuck it in my hand, and left. When I phoned my buddy to ask what the hell it all meant, he hadn't a clue, didn't know who it was, just some woman who needed a job done that he couldn't take on right away."

"Then you've done no more than keep the lady's money safe for a few days until you might return it with your regrets. Is that not so?"

Hammett sat in thought, not caring for the situation, torn between the implied but undeclared contract represented by the money in the folder and the undeniable pull of curiosity. And another thing: "You think this has something to do with the person who took a shot at your wife?"

"Pacific Heights is an unlikely venue for a random madman with a gun," Holmes pointed out grimly.

"Yeah, you're right. Okay, Mr Holmes, I'll take your job, so long as it doesn't involve outright betrayal. If it turns out that coming to me is what opens that lady up for a fall, I'm telling you now that I'm going to stand back and take my hands off both sides of it."

"Your rigid sense of ethics, Mr Hammett, will have done you no good in the world of the Pinkertons. But I agree."

The two men shook hands, and Hammett reached for the bottle again to seal the agreement.

"So, where do you want me to start?"

"First, you need to know what might be called 'the full picture,' " Holmes said, rapping his pipe out into the ash-tray and pulling out his pouch. "It would appear to have its beginnings a number of years ago, when my wife's family died on a road south of the city."

Hammett scrabbled through the débris on the table and came up with a note-book and a pen, which he uncapped and shook into life. His cigarette dangled unnoticed from between the fingers of his left hand as he hunched over the note-book on his knee, listening. After a few minutes, however, his occasional notes stopped, and his back slowly straightened against the chair-back, until finally he put up a hand.

"Whoa," he said. "Sounds to me like you're laying pretty much everything out in front of me."

"More or less," Holmes agreed mildly.

"Her father's job, the falling balcony in Egypt—"

"Aden," Holmes corrected.

"Aden. Do you honestly think all that's got anything to do with what's going on here?"

"Do I think so? There is not sufficient evidence one way or the other. But the balcony was a recent and unexplained event, and the possibility of its being linked should not be ignored."

"If you say so. But really, are you sure you want me to know all this?"

"If you do not know the past, how can you know what of the present is of importance?"

"I just mean—"

"You mean that, seeing as our initial meeting was adversarial, I ought not to trust you too wholeheartedly."

"Yeah, I guess I do."

"Mr Hammett, are you trustworthy?"

The thin man opened his mouth to answer, closed it again, and then began to chuckle. "There's no answer I can give to that—'yes' would probably mean 'no,' and 'no' would mean I'm a complete boob, and 'I don't know' means you'd be a damned fool to trust me with so much as a butter-knife."

Holmes was smiling in response. "Precisely."

"So what you're saying is, 'It's my look-out, shut up and listen'?"

"Mr Hammett, you have a way with the American vernacular that bodes well for your future as a writer of popular fiction."

"Okay, it is your look-out. So I'll shut up and listen."

And he did, attentively, his dark eyes alive in that gaunt face. His occasional grunt and question told Holmes all he needed to know about the man's brains, and he told Hammett even more than he had originally intended. Very nearly everything.

It was late when they finished, or early. Hammett took out his package of Bull Durham again, glancing over his notes as his fingers sprinkled the tobacco and rolled the paper, every motion precise.

Eventually he nodded. "Yeah, I can see that you need another set of hands here."

"And eyes. In the normal run of events, those would belong to Russell—to my wife. However, of late she has been...indisposed."

"Too close to things to see clearly," Hammett suggested.

"It is temporary, I have no doubt. But until she returns to herself, she is...." Again Holmes paused, searching for a word that might be accurate without being traitorous; he was unable to find one, and finished the sentence with a sigh and the word "unreliable."

"So what do you want me to do first?"

"Do you know anything about motorcars?"

"They have four wheels and tip over real easy—when I'm driving, anyway. I usually ask a friend to drive me."

"You don't like guns and you don't like motorcars. Are you certain you're American?"

"I've hurt people with both of them, didn't like the feeling."

"Very well, then; ask a friend to drive you."

Holmes reached into his inner pocket and pulled out his long leather note-case, taking from it a slip of paper with some notes in a small, difficult, but precise hand: his handwriting. "This is what I know about the motorcar crash. What we're looking for is evidence of foul play, any evidence at all. The police report is quite clear that it was an accident, so the best we can hope for is a faint discrepancy." He watched to see if Hammett looked puzzled, but the man was nodding.

"Something that smells off."

"Quite. It is, after all this time, highly doubtful that there was enough of the motor to salvage, and even less of a chance the wreckage has anything to tell us, but it is just possible that no-one could decide what to do with the thing, and either left it on the cliffside or pulled it up and hauled it into a corner until its ownership was decided. The convolutions of the American legal system," he added, "occasionally have inadvertent benefits."

"Can't you just ask your wife's lawyer what happened to the car?"

"I'd rather not bring him into it."

"I see. You'd rather pay me to go down on a fool's task and look at a ten-year-old burned-out hulk."

"It is an avenue of enquiry that must be pursued to its end, no matter how soon that end is reached."

Hammett studied the piece of paper for a moment with a faint smile on his expressive mouth, then he picked it up without comment and tucked it away in his note-book. Sure, investigating the car might be a red herring designed for nothing more than getting him out of town for a couple of days, but what of it? There was trust, and there was stupidity, and despite his snooty accent, this Holmes was no jerk.

And the Limey's money couldn't be any dirtier than the pile of bills in the file.

As if he had followed the line of thought, Holmes addressed himself to the leather wallet again, pulling out five twenty-dollar notes and laying them onto the table. "That should be sufficient as a retainer. You see, I do not make the mistake of paying too generously."

"No, Mr Holmes, I don't think you make too many mistakes. Anything other than the car you want me to be getting on?"

"That is the first order of business, I think. Oh, but Hammett? You saw my wife tonight. Well enough to recognise her again?"

"Girl with glasses, her height, hair, and posture—she doesn't exactly fade into the crowd. But if she was sitting, had a hat on? I don't know."

"Quite." Holmes bent his head for a moment in thought before he slid two fingers into the note-case, this time drawing out a photograph—or rather, a square neatly snipped from a larger photograph. Reluctantly (Reluctant to show it to me? wondered Hammett. Or to show he had it at all? The Englishman seemed a person who would not reveal his affections readily.), Holmes slid it across the table for Hammett to examine.

It was of a young woman on a street, clearly unaware of the camera. Her head was up, showing a determined chin and graceful neck. The day had been bright but not sunny enough to make her spectacles throw shadows or reflections, so that behind the wire frames were revealed a pair of light-coloured eyes. Her hair was fair and gathered on top of her head in a way Hammett hadn't seen in years—and hadn't seen on the woman getting out of the car the night before.

"She's cut her hair since this was taken?"

"Yes," Holmes said, with a trace of regret that made Hammett's mouth curve again, although he did not comment.

"And her eyes—blue or green?"

"Blue. And to American ears, she speaks with a pure English accent."

Hammett handed the photograph back across the table. "Okay," he said, making it a question.

Tucking the photograph back into its hold, Holmes said, "I showed you this because I think it possible that Russell will decide to travel in the same direction you are going, sometime in the next day or two. It would be as well if she didn't take too much notice of you."

"I hear you." Hammett put the money into his own wallet, dashed the last contents of his glass down his throat, and stood up to shake the hand of his new employer. "Mr Holmes, this has been an interesting evening."

Grey eyes looked into brown, understanding each other well.

Chapter Twelve

At that hour, with only the occasional vehicle to impede a walker's straight line, Holmes' long stride took him back to the hotel in twenty minutes—and that included doubling back twice to ensure that he had no one else on his heels. The doorman was dozing in his corner, the man on the desk jerked around, startled, at this late entrance, and the dim sea of posts and chairs that made up the lobby resembled a theatre after the curtains had fallen.

The boy on the elevator, by contrast, was bright-eyed and longing for company. He commented on the weather, mentioned a Harold Lloyd comedy showing at a nearby cinema house the following afternoon that Holmes might care to avail himself of, and admired the cut of Holmes' hat. The lad seemed disappointed that Holmes did not seize the opportunity for conversation, and threw open the door in a subdued manner that not even a coin could assuage.

Russell was still out. He stood uncertainly inside the

door, wondering if he should return to the bright cabaret where he had left her, then shook his head and closed the door firmly. It was unlikely that the young people had remained at one gin palace during the course of an evening, and he should end up haring all over town for her. She would return.

He exchanged his outer garments for a dressing-gown, then picked up the telephone to ask for a pot of coffee. When it had come, he assembled a nest of cushions and settled into it with coffee, tobacco, and his thoughts.

Two hours later, the faint rattle of the lift door was accompanied by voices raised in a manner guaranteed to wake the other guests: Russell and the elevator boy, exchanging jests. A moment later the key clattered about in the door, giving her problems before it finally slipped into place and Russell tumbled into the room.

"Good Lord, Holmes, are you still up? Had I known, I'd have rung you and had you come along. I know it's not exactly your kind of music, but you might have found the experience interesting. There was this extraordinary singer named Belinda Birdsong," she said, and regaled him with the details of music, dance, and conversation. As she talked she wandered in and out of the room, kicking her shoes in the direction of the wardrobe, washing her face, putting on night-clothes. She finally got into bed, but once there she sat bolt upright in the most exulted of spirits, prattling on—Russell, prattling!—about her evening with Miss Greenfield's cronies. Spirits of the liquid variety contributed to her mood, he diagnosed, but they simply enhanced the feverish look she had worn for longer than he cared to remember.

If she went on in this manner much longer, he would

have to locate some morphia and knock her out forcibly.

He scraped out the cold contents of his pipe into the ash-tray, extricated himself from the cushions, and went about the business of emptying pockets and undoing buttons, getting ready for bed. Russell looked as if she might be up for the rest of the night.

A name, or perhaps the way in which she'd said it, caught at his attention from the spate, and he paused on his way to the bath-room to listen. "—and a friend of Flo's friend Donny, who's a few years older than she is, was very kindly sitting out a dance with me and I mentioned what I had been doing today—or yesterday, I suppose—and he said that he remembered her."

"Remembered whom?" asked Holmes, just to be sure.

"Are you not listening to me?"

"I was pulling my vest over my head."

Sure sign of her state of mind was the ready way in which she accepted it, without even stopping to consider. "I was talking about Dr Ginzberg. Apparently she was rather well known in the city before ... Anyway, this friend of Donny's—his name was Terry, I think, or was it Jerry? I don't know, the music was rather loud—he said he remembered that people used to say she was good at getting her patients to remember things, 'mesmerism,' he called it although that's rather an old-fashioned name—even when I knew her she called it 'hypnosis.' You remember her techniques, Holmes."

"I remember you made use of them yourself on the Chessman woman, last summer, for just that purpose."

Russell's head dropped back against the padded head-board, and for a moment her face went quiet. "Good Lord, only last summer? What a long time ago it seems, since that afternoon poor Miss Ruskin came to tea and gave us her inlaid box. And then we had your friend Baring-Gould, then Ali and—" As if she had become aware of the unshed tears trembling in her eyes, her head snapped forward, her eyes dried instantly, and she was away again. "You're right, although I'm terribly clumsy at hypnosis compared to Dr Ginzberg. She was so gentle and convincing, she'd have you recalling what you had for dinner on your sixth birthday. But in any case, Jerry or Terry remembered that she was something of a celebrity in town, so that when she was…when she died, people talked about it for weeks, and it was in all the papers."

Holmes looked at his wife's hands, wringing each other with enough force that he could hear the sound from across the room; she was completely oblivious to both sound and gesture. "So I was thinking, Holmes, if it made such a stink at the time, surely the police would still have the file open. I mean unless they've decided she fell and hit herself on the head with the statue. Which going by what I heard tonight would only be likely if they were paid to decide that, did you know, Holmes—"

He walked into the bath-room and shook tooth-powder onto his brush, but even with the noise of the running tap and the brush, he could hear the words spilling out of the next room. Drugged, drunk, hysterical, or simply infected by the mood of a flock of partying flappers, he couldn't know, but it was tiresome and it was worrying and it was not Russell, not at all.

At last, near dawn, she slept. Holmes, who had spent most of his life in complete disregard of the hours of light and dark, wondered if age was beginning to slip up on him, for the long hours they'd kept the past few days had left him feeling light-headed with exhaustion. So he, too, slept, so deeply he did not hear her rise, dress, and go out.

It was past ten o'clock when the door opened again. This time, he came awake swiftly.

"Russell?"

"Good heavens," she said. "Are you still asleep? Sorry, I felt sure you'd gone out and I missed seeing you."

"How long have you been up?" A faint heaviness at the edges of his voice gave away his sleep-clogged state, and he cleared his throat to rid himself of it.

"Oh, two or three hours," she answered cheerfully: If that was true, she had slept for less than three hours, in spite of which she showed no signs of hang-over. She was probably still intoxicated. "It's a lovely morning, a bit of fog earlier but it looks to be warm today. I'll just fetch what I came for and leave you."

"That is not necessary, I was on the edge of waking. Have you had your breakfast?"

"Oh, yes."

"Six cups of black coffee."

"Two, and toast," she protested.

"Then you'll be ready for a proper breakfast. I shall meet you in the restaurant after I have shaved. Unless your current task cannot wait."

"Oh no, that's fine. I was just coming for the key, I thought I'd go up to the house this morning, but it can wait. I'll order coffee." And so saying she left. Holmes rubbed his face, grimacing at the stubble, and swung his long legs to the floor.

The restaurant was nearly deserted at that hour, and Russell was at a window table, the bright sunlight turning her into the silhouette of a young woman bent over her morning paper. She looked sleek and alien in her bobbed haircut and new clothes, and the arm that stretched across the paper had something of the modern fashion for bone without muscle: In another few days, her thinness would become alarming.

She looked up when he came to the table, and permitted the waiter to fill her cup along with Holmes'.

"Have you ordered?" he asked.

"I'll just have a piece of toast. I had an omelette at Flo's house."

"Seven hours ago. You will have a breakfast," he said flatly, and turned to the waiter to order two large meals. She raised an eyebrow at his tone and his action, and when the waiter had left, Holmes addressed himself to her again. "Occasional periods of self-starvation benefit the mental processes; over the long term, it can be destructive. The body is a machine, and needs fuel. Think of your porridge and eggs as petrol."

"They will have about as much savour."

"The body cares not what the palate thinks. What is in the news today?"

He listened with half an ear as she read to him a number of political and criminological stories that concerned him not in the least—"3 FLUNG TO ROAD FROM CABLE-CAR" was one admittedly evocative headline, less so the lengthy tale of a woman who came home from filing for divorce to find her three children and the husband shot to death by his hand. When their food came, he waited until she had begun before he picked up his fork, and felt he was nearly counting the number of times her own rose and fell. After a time, the habits of her own physicality took over, and he relaxed his vigil, and paid closer attention to her words.

By the end of the meal, he couldn't have said precisely where his wife had been the night before or recalled the peculiar names of the dances she had assayed, but two things were clear: She had eaten enough for the moment and, although she had not expected to do so when she'd left the hotel the night before, she had in truth enjoyed the company of Flo Greenfield. Holmes commented on the latter fact.

Russell looked mildly surprised. "Yes, I suppose so. She's not exactly my sort, and hasn't much of an interest in anything but fashion and decorating, but she does have a brain beneath the flutter. Sooner or later she's going to get tired of night-clubs and hang-overs, and when she does, I have a feeling she'll make something of herself. Are you asking for a reason?"

Holmes was not altogether pleased to see the evidence of Russell's quick common sense—it was good to see a flash of normality, but it meant that he'd have to proceed cautiously. He took out his cigarette case. "I don't suppose you've any meetings with Norbert until Monday?"

"I do have a brief appointment this morning, just to sign a few papers. The manager of the Sacramento property wanted to meet today, but unfortunately his mother's been taken ill and he's cancelled it until Tuesday or Wednesday."

"I see."

"What are you up to, Holmes?"

"Me? Why do you imagine—"

"You're asking far too many innocent questions."

"Ah. I was simply concerned...well, never mind. We shall plan an outing for the week-end."

"Concerned that what?"

"Russell, I don't know that it's good for you to be without something to employ your mind," he replied bluntly. "You're dwelling too much on the past. We shall hire a motor and take the Sausalito ferry to—"

"*Me?* I'm not the one who's 'dwelling on the past,'" she snapped. "And I certainly don't need a nurse-maid."

"Good, fine. You've no doubt made plans for parties with your friend. In town, I take it?"

"Why?"

"I don't…I would hate…" Holmes took a deep breath and began again. "I rather trust you won't do something foolish such as going to see your parents' summer house on your own."

"'Foolish'?" Russell's chin came up and her eyes flashed; with the raised colour in her face, she looked nearly herself. "Holmes, I should appreciate it if you would not try to tell me what I am and am not to do. If I choose to drive down the coast and look at the Lodge— *my* Lodge—then I shall do so. I need not ask your permission."

"Russell, I merely request—"

But the heat of her response was only fed by placation. "You think it 'foolish' when *I* investigate a matter, and not when you do it? Thank you, Holmes, I shall let you know what I decide to do with the week-end." And with that she rose, dropped her table napkin on the cloth, and strode from the restaurant.

It was as well she did not look back. She might have seen Holmes, leaning back to tap his cigarette into the ash-tray, smiling gently at the rising smoke.

An hour later, while Russell was grappling with legal terminology in Norbert's office, Holmes presented himself at the Greenfield mansion. He took off his hat and handed it to the man who opened the door, saying, "You must be Mr Jeeves? My wife was here the other day. I had hoped to find Miss Greenfield at home, Miss Flo Greenfield?"

"Yes, sir, I shall see if she is at home. If you'd like to wait in here?"

"In here" was a room whose purpose could only have been the temporary parking of callers, as the seats were too far apart to be of any use for conversation and the décor was intended to impress rather than to please or entertain. It was, in the end, more pleasing than a room more lived in, for the cool, sparse furnishings set off the modern sculpture and fireplace tile as a more cluttered room would not. It reminded Holmes somewhat of the Japanese rooms they had seen on the other side of the ocean, rich materials used in an austere fashion. Restful.

After a quarter of an hour, he was shown into a warmer, more lived-in room. The young woman seated before the fire with a coffee service put out her hand to greet him, her dark eyes alive with interest although she showed all the signs of hasty dressing.

"Mr Holmes? Mary's husband? It's fantastic to meet you. Mary said you wouldn't like our kind of fun or I'd have had her drag you along. But I'm glad you tracked me down at home. Is she coming, too? Oh, manners, Flo!" She pulled together a mock-formal face and manner. "Sir, would you care for a cup of coffee?"

"No, thank you, Miss Greenfield, I've just come from breakfast. Actually, my wife doesn't know I am here. Tell me, have you spoken with her this morning?"

"She woke me up about half an hour ago, 'phoning to see if I had plans for the week-end."

"And you've found yourself dragooned into a drive along the coast to her summer house in the mountains."

"Yes," she said, happily unaware that this plan ought

to have been a surprise to him. "Although I wouldn't exactly say 'dragooned.' There's a couple of boring parties
going on but it's the same old people, and I'm happy to
tag along. She's only here for a few days, after all."

"Miss Greenfield, are you aware of the circumstances,
and the place, of her family's death?"

"Well, sure, but why—oh, I see. Oh, I promise you,
we'll drive the other way, through Redwood City. I
wouldn't want to worry her."

"You may find that she insists on the coastal route.
She may feel it necessary to face the place where she survived, and they did not."

The cup dropped into its saucer with a clatter. "Oh.
Golly, yes, there is that. I hadn't thought..."

"May I be frank, Miss Greenfield?"

"Well, sure."

Holmes took a breath, and committed treason
against his wife. "For some weeks now, my wife has not
been herself. Something about this place has been preying on her mind. I should appreciate it very much if you
were to keep an eye on her, in my absence."

"What do you mean, 'keep an eye on her'?" She asked
it warily; Holmes could see the plots of a hundred lurid
novels springing up in the girl's eyes, and hastened to
turn them aside.

"I only mean to say, she does not care for herself sufficiently. She has not been eating well, and sleeps briefly
and restlessly. If you were to insist that she eat, and take
exercise, and perhaps go so far as to swallow a sleeping
draught..."

"Ah," she said, her eyebrows descending with mingled relief and disappointment. "I was afraid you meant,
oh jeepers, suicide or something." She gave a merry little
laugh, to illustrate that she was exaggerating, but for an

instant Holmes was seized by the memory of Russell tee-
tering over the shipboard rails, a thousand miles of
empty ocean waiting to swallow her. He pushed down
the image, and gave the young woman his most reassuring smile.

"Oh, she's far too sensible for that. No, just careless of
herself. She needs a friend at the moment."

"Sure, I can be that. It was nifty to meet Mary again—
I remember her from when we were kids." The thought
startled Holmes a little, as he had never thought of his
wife as any sort of a child, not even the day they'd met.
But this young woman, just Russell's age, was still
young in ways Russell had never been. She did not notice his momentary distraction, but continued on. "And
her family—Mary's father was just a card, and her
mother, gosh, she was amazing. Did you ever meet her?"

"I regret I did not have the pleasure."

"No, that's right, Mary met you after the...after-
wards. Well, don't you worry, Mr Holmes, we'll take
good care of her."

" 'We'?"

"Yes, I thought Donny—he's my boy-friend—might
drive us down, if you don't mind? He's a very responsible boy, when he hasn't been drinking, anyway, and he
never drinks when he's driving, honest."

"Quite. Yes, that should be fine." And if this relatively
sensible child and her strong young escort with the
bright blue motor weren't enough to keep Russell from
harm, little would be. "And if I might ask one more
favour: I believe Rus—Mary would be happiest if she did
not know I'd been here. Collusion between husband and
friend might prove...alienating."

"Right-o," she said cheerfully.

He stood up, taking her hand again, holding it for a

moment so that he was bent over her almost like a courtier. Then he left, and Flo watched him go; he was, she thought, really pretty swell.

That, thought Holmes, took care of Sunday and Monday at the very least. Which left only the afternoon and evening to get through.

Walking towards the lawyer's office, Holmes noticed a news-agent's with a small sign in the window advising OUT-OF-DATE JOURNALS LOCATED. He wrote down Hammett's name, told the proprietor that he'd take anything the man could locate by the fellow, and was strolling up the street (for the seventh time) as Russell came out of Norbert's office, pulling on her gloves with little jerks of irritation.

"Holmes," she said in surprise when she spotted him. "What are you doing here?"

"I was finished with my business, and thought I might accompany you on this fine afternoon."

She looked at him sideways. "Holmes, I hope you don't mind, but I'd rather like to spend some time in the house on my own."

"But of course, that was merely the direction in which I was headed. You remember the Italian café we ate at the other day? The owner happened to mention that his great-grandfather was a childhood friend of Paganini and had a sheaf of the composer's early attempts at music. I thought I might add a section on my monograph concerning childhood patterns of behaviour that extend into maturity."

"Yes? I didn't know you had such a monograph in process; it sounds interesting."

So they walked the mile in amicable discussion of the nonexistent monograph, and after Holmes had seen her safely into the house (using the excuse of seeing if the 'phone and electrical companies had done their duties) he went off, whistling a brisk tune the Italian had composed for violin.

At the end of the block, he paused to look back at the house that was holding his wife, in both senses of the word. The place reminded him of one of those primitive societies so beloved of archaeologists, where a people had stood up from their breakfast and walked into nothingness. The kitchen cupboard still held the packet of coffee used the morning the Russells had climbed into their new Maxwell motorcar and driven away, now so stale that, when he had tried it the other morning, it had given him little more than a brown colour and a sour taste in the cup. The half-packed trunks in all rooms but Russell's bore mute evidence of a future that would not exist for three people. He wondered if Russell had found her mother's night-gown inside the laundry hamper.

He shook his head and turned his back on the house of the dead.

Holmes had no intention of visiting the Italian's café (although its owner did in fact own two or three sheets of music in what he swore was Paganini's hand). Instead, he set about a systematic interview of those inhabitants of Pacific Heights he hadn't yet spoken with.

Eighteen years in London is nothing—there, even eighty years after an event one might expect to find a high number of houses inhabited by the families' descendants. In San Francisco, however, particularly given the circumstances of the past two decades, this was not the case. He had already discovered this when he had questioned the immediate neighbours on Friday and discovered that only two of the eleven houses contained the same residents as they had in 1906. Those two had, admittedly, proved useful, one of them describing how the Russells had been among the first to move back into their damaged house, the other providing the name of the postman who had worked the streets for many years. It had been the postman—or mailman—who had come up with the piquant information concerning the Russell argument, a detail of which Holmes had been very dubious and which had necessitated an interminable round of enticing similar feats of recall, until he finally was forced to admit that the postal gentleman had a perfectly extraordinary memory, prodigious in its powers of retention when it came to tit-bits of gossip.

He'd left profoundly grateful that the man had not delivered to Baker Street, and that he seemed to have not a sinew of the blackmailer's impulse in his makeup.

Still, the interviews with the neighbours had taken most of Friday morning, and hunting down the mailman the bulk of the afternoon. He could only hope that today's research proved more brisk.

It did not. Worse, the day's ratio of 1906 residents to newcomers was even lower than Friday's. Of the first ten dwellings to receive his enquiries, four had no idea who had lived in their house in the year of the fire; three knew the names but not their current location ("somewhere down the Peninsula" seemed a hugely popular dwelling-place for those who had fled the city); two were new householders in new houses, having bought cracked and leaning wrecks and built anew; and one alone had lived in that house at the time of the earthquake, and even recalled a period spent under canvas in the nearby park; unfortunately, that person had been twelve years old at the time, had been visiting from his home in that mythic land "down the Peninsula," and had been ushered back to that safe haven within days, as soon as motorcars could traverse the littered streets. The man remembered no-one named Russell.

The pattern held with a depressing reliability. At the end of four hours, Holmes had drunk enough tea to bring him to sympathy with the Boston rebels, found the coffee no better, taken to refusing the offers of a "quick one" through concern for his liver, and come up with a mere handful of residents who had been present at the time of the quake. Five of them had remained in the city during the weeks that followed; three of those had fled the approaching flames as far as Golden Gate Park; the other two had lodged with friends in relatively undamaged houses in other parts of the city. The maids who opened the doors to him suggested that a visit in the morning might be more productive, and he reluctantly agreed, although Sunday was often a difficult time to interview persons of this class, for reasons different from those on a week-day.

Then, when the afternoon sun was going soft with the incoming fog, he met Miss Adderley.

Chapter Thirteen

Miss Hermione Adderley was ninety if she was a day, and might have admitted to ten years more if he'd been her doctor, or priest. She was well guarded by a butler who looked nearly as old, and a house-maid in her late forties who bore a striking resemblance to the butler. All three had spines as straight and unbending as one of the gleaming brass pokers arrayed beside the ten-foot-wide marble fireplace, and Holmes would never have got inside had he been mere trade. But the old lady, whose shoes had the unbent look of those whose owner spent most of her waking hours in one chair or another, was fiercely curious about the world outside her window, and before the fragile old man at the door could turn the visitor away, the maid was behind him, whispering in his ear.

Disapproval and suspicion stiffened every thread of the butler's spotless black suit, but its wearer stood back, bowed Holmes in, and accepted hat, walking-stick, and overcoat, handing them over to the maid. He then picked up the gleaming silver tray from the polished teak table, held it out for Holmes' card, and showed the visitor into the room to the left of the doorway. His gait as he went to take his mistress the card told Holmes that the man was a martyr to rheumatism, but he crossed the freshly waxed marble floor without event and was back in moments, murmuring that Holmes should come with him.

The old lady in the brocade chair was so tiny her head did not clear the chair's oval back, and her creaseless shoes rested on a needlepoint hassock. Her hand in his felt like a bird's foot, so delicate he was afraid to close his fingers lest he leave bruises. But her cornflower blue eyes were undimmed by age, her pure white hair soft but full, and the myriad wrinkles that made up her face seemed to quiver with interest.

"Mr Holmes," she said in a high, thin voice, "from London. Pray have a seat so I don't get a neck-cramp looking up at you. How do you find London these days?"

He settled onto a chair across the bay window from her, trying to arrange his knees so his legs didn't rise up around his ears. "I left London in January, when a person would find it cold and dreary. I imagine that in April it is most pleasant."

"And are the fogs as bad as ever they were?"

"So long as the town continues to heat its homes, there will be yellow fogs."

"I have very fond memories of your 'pea-soupers,'" the old woman confided. "We spent some months there when I was a young sprig of a thing, and I escaped the eyes of my governess under the blessing of just such a fog. I had a beau," she explained, one eyelid lowering in a manner that would have been coquettish had it not also been self-mocking.

Holmes laughed aloud, and the old blue eyes danced. Tea was brought then, and as the maid poured and offered the sugar, she surreptitiously watched the visitor. Whatever she saw in him assuaged her suspicion; her spine relaxed and with it her tongue, so that before she left them, she raised an admonitory finger and said to Holmes, "Now you watch that she doesn't get over-tired. And if she tells you she wants you to take her out dancing, she's not allowed out on a Saturday night."

"I hear, and obey," Holmes said with a small bow of his head. When the door had closed again, Miss Adderley picked up her child-sized eggshell cup.

"Mimi has lived in this house her whole life. I think she forgets that I'm not actually her grandmother. Her mother worked in the kitchen, and Hymes—the butler— is the child's grandfather. So, Mr Holmes, what brings you to San Francisco and to my door?"

Holmes assembled his words with care, aware that too long a story would tire his hostess cruelly, and too little would not satisfy her.

"I am acting on behalf of a woman whose family was here at the time of the earthquake and fire."

"This would have been 1906?"

"Yes."

"I ask because the city shakes and burns with regularity. I remember the 1865 quake vividly."

"No, this was the recent one. Her parents have since died, but she wishes to know more details about the weeks following the fire. They had a house here in Pacific Heights, and I believe lived in a tent for some time."

"As did a number of us, in Lafayette Park."

"Ah. You were here, then?"

"I was. And Hymes, and Mimi, and the rest. We had a staff of, let me see, seven at the time. It was normally nine, but the footman and an upstairs maid had just eloped."

"Did you by any chance spend some time in the park yourself?"

"Certainly. Best time of my life, those three weeks, an absolute lark. Other than the bathing facilities, but then, an old lady doesn't need to be too fussy about her toilette. No, Hymes found a tent somewhere, the Army I think, and Mimi and three of the others moved in with me. Hymes stayed in the house, at first to fight any fire that might blow in, and later to discourage any looters. I told him not to be silly, that it didn't do any of us any good if he saved the house only to have it fall down on his head, but he wouldn't listen, nor would the other men. They buried the silver, in case of robbers—silly boys, they lost one of the spoons for the longest time, unearthing an entire flower bed before they came across it in the branches of a rose-bush—and took turns watching over the house and over me at the park. They enjoyed the adventure, too—we even had concerts while we were there, around a grand piano one of the families had pushed through the streets from the other side of Van Ness. Yes, everyone was quite restless for a while after we moved back inside."

"So, you lived in the park for about three weeks?"

"Twenty-three days, I believe it was."

"The people I'm interested in were named Russell. Charles was an American, would have been in his early thirties, tall, blond hair. His wife—"

"His wife's name was Judith. English girl, Jewish I think. And weren't there children?"

"Two."

"A little girl, and a baby. Can't remember if the baby was a boy or a girl."

"A boy, in fact. And it's the daughter who is now asking me to make the enquiries."

"What sort of enquiries?"

"Details about her parents. As I said, they died, in a motor accident some years later. In particular, she would like to know about the period in which the family was living in a tent."

He picked up his tea to cover the intensity of his interest, sipping the smoky brew from the paper-thin teacup, larger brother of the child-sized model on the saucer beside her. But he need not have worried; she was sitting, head bent, brows furrowed in concentration. After a moment she said, "Mr Holmes, would you be so good as to bring the sherry and two glasses from that cupboard over there?"

The sherry was dry and smelt of the Spanish sun, and under its influence, memory stirred. The tiny hand reached out for a silver bell and rang it. The door came open so quickly, it was evident that Mimi had been standing just outside it.

"Yes, Mum?"

"Dear, I need you to bring me the photograph album of the fire. You remember where it is?"

"Yes, Mum." The door shut, and silence fell, the old woman occupied with her inner images. In minutes the maid returned with a large morocco-bound album, laying a white cloth on the table before she set the book before her mistress. She adjusted the book slightly and stood back. "Would there be anything else, Mum?"

"No, thank you, Mimi."

"Beg pardon, Mum, but Cook asks if you'll be wanting dinner delayed?"

The question was nicely phrased, Holmes thought. It served to ask Miss Adderley if she was going to need another place laid without setting the question out in the open, while at the same time reminding Holmes that it was getting on to evening and he'd promised not to tire the elderly woman.

He was the one who answered. "You needn't delay on my behalf," he said. "I have an appointment before too long, and won't be staying. If we haven't finished our business by that time, perhaps I might impose on you for a second visit?"

The offer of a return pleased both women, the protective Mimi and the lonely Miss Adderley. Mimi sketched a curtsey and left them alone, the frail hand already lifting back the album cover.

She turned half a dozen pages until she came to a photograph of the city burning. It had been taken from a hill above the downtown, long shadows indicating that it was early morning. The buildings were crisp and clear, those closer to the camera revealing their missing cornices, shattered windows, and huge cracks running up the brick. The streets were adrift with brick and rubble, the mounds studded incongruously with chairs and wardrobes that had been carried so far, then abandoned. Men and women stood about, staring up at the cloud of angry smoke billowing grey against the lighter sky. To one side, a dead horse lay in the traces of its wagon, half buried by the collapsed wall of a building.

After a minute, she turned the page.

The next photograph was at once shocking and oddly reassuring. Again from a hilltop, again the fires raging in the background, but along the front of the picture, picnics were taking place. A group of young men, some of them hatless but all in ties and tidy suits, sat and lay back on their elbows on the grass around a cloth arranged with sandwich rolls and bottles of lemonade. In the centre of the photograph, with the smoke cloud huge and furious above them and the dapper young men glancing at them from the sides, stood a pair of young women—girls, really—dressed in their spring finery. Hats elaborate with feathers, new spring frocks, their postures shouting their awareness that the youths at their feet were of greater interest and importance than the city burning at their backs. It might have been an illustration of the careless self-obsession of the young, yet somehow it was not. For some reason, the posture of the young ladies and the ease of their admirers conveyed a sense of defiance in the face of catastrophe: One knew somehow that these young people were quite aware of the horrors creeping up on them, yet one suspected that they were merely biding their time until they might do something about it.

Reassuring, the assertion of young strength in the time of the city's need.

Holmes found himself smiling, and she turned the next page, her fingers swiping back the tissue protector to reveal a refugee camp.

The profile of the hill on which the camp was laid was the familiar park a few streets away—Lafayette Park, little more than a grassy knoll with the incongruous house parked among the trees at the top, the whole of it two streets wide and two deep. In the first photo, the grass was a jumble of possessions—bedrolls and steamer trunks, strapped orange-crates and disassembled bedsteads. All the women wore the elaborate hats of the period, and most of the men were missing.

In the next picture in the sequence, a tent city had sprung up in front of the elaborate Victorian houses that faced the park. Here, the rising smoke was closer, possessions had been gathered into rough heaps, and a few canvas tents had been raised, the whiteness of their sides and the unbeaten grass around their bases clear signs that the photograph had been taken soon after they had been installed. The women were mostly bare-headed, and the men had returned, to stand about in their shirt-sleeves.

"The Army brought the tents over," Miss Adderley said, "I believe from Fort Mason. At first there were sol-diers to set them up, but then they were called off to guard the downtown from looters and we were left to our own resources. Fortunately, a number of old sol-diers lived in the area, so we managed. This was our tent, here." A gnarled finger touched a taut white peak near the house at the top of the hill, then continued down to the bottom to turn to the next page.

Now, the Lafayette Park tent city was well established, peopled by an affluent group of refugees, long-skirted women with the occasional hat, their prized bits of fur-niture and statuary bulging the sides of the tents—a sofa here, two candelabra on a packing-case table there. All the children wore shoes, and the men, though still not as numerous as the women, invariably wore waistcoats and bowler hats.

As the days went on, the tents began to sag, more men appeared, the children started to look more un-kempt, and the women took on harried expressions. The grass turned to mud; sloppy tarpaulins draped posses-sions.

Then, five pages in, the small hand splayed across the page and Miss Adderley leant forward with a noise of satisfaction.

"Yes, I thought so. You see the figure in trousers there? If you look closely, you'll see it's a woman. That was Mrs Russell." Holmes already had his magnifying-glass from his pocket and was bending over the page. "That lamp on the other end of the settee is quite bright, if you like," she suggested.

He carried the album over to the lamp, resting the top edge of the book against the arm of the settee. He switched on the lamp, brought his glass into play, and Judith Russell looked back at him from over the years.

Her daughter's hair, eyes, and height all came from the father's side, but the tilt of the chin was instantly recognisable, and the tug of amusement at the corner of the mouth was exactly as Holmes had seen it a thousand times.

For the first time, Holmes felt a stab of regret, as a personal element entered the case: His wife's mother was a person he'd like to have met.

He shook off the distracting thought, and shifted the glass to one side.

Only to find, on a chair at the woman's side, feet dangling and a book in her lap, his wife as a small child. Her blonde hair was a bird's-nest of curls, and she was as utterly oblivious to her surroundings as ever she was when similarly bent over one of her Hebrew texts. His glass lingered here even longer before he tore it away and moved on.

The only indications of a younger sibling were the small tin cup and spoon piled with the other plates and a silver rattle discarded atop a sack of flour, although the closed tent door suggested a sleeping child within. Some days had clearly passed since the first photograph of the tent city—the wear on the grass alone told him that—and in that time, standards had relaxed somewhat, yet para-doxically others had asserted themselves. Thus, hats and even skirts had given way to head-ties and the occasional trousers, and drying laundry peeped from the tie-ropes as the distance between park (with its water supply and living quarters) and home (where laundry might be decently hung to dry) grew ever more onerous; however, at the same time the demarcations between one family's quarters and the next had become more formalised: chairs lined up along the agreed-to boundaries, facing inward to the informal court-yard before each tent; one such division had even been neatly drawn with a line of white pebbles. "Streets" had formed themselves between the ranks of outdoor "drawing rooms"; children played there, a woman with a bucket of water walked away from the camera, and a man approached.

Holmes' interest quickened again, and he moved the glass over the distant figure. What came into focus was a tall, light-haired man with a moustache, eerily familiar despite his gender. His spectacles caught the light, his bowler hat blurred slightly as he returned it to his head, having raised it to the woman with the bucket. The photographer must have called his subjects to attention in some manner because several faces were raised towards the lens, including that of the man trudging up the hill.

The blond man's twill trousers were spattered with dark stains and one knee looked in need of mending. On his upper body he wore only a shirt, the collar missing, sleeves rolled up his forearms to reveal a clean bandage on one wrist. He appeared to hold himself erect by will alone, and Holmes did not need to see his face to know that it wore the look of a soldier in the trenches, the gaze both interior and far away. This man ached with fatigue and with the things he had witnessed, longed to collapse into sleep for a day and a night, yet equally clearly he was only here temporarily, for his shoulders were braced against the labours to come.

Speaking over his shoulder, Holmes said, "I should like to borrow one of these photographs, if I may? I shall take care to return it undamaged."

"Certainly," the old woman replied.

Only then did Holmes stand upright, taking the album back to the table to allow her to turn the remaining pages, none of which proved of any interest to him. He turned back to the picture showing Judith Russell, eased it out of its mounts, and laid it before the old woman.

"That is Judith Russell. What can you tell me about her?"

"A very fine young woman, full of spirit. English, she was—you'd have expected her to be one of those who found the conditions trying, who burst into tears and wrung their hands uselessly at the merest nothing. I remember, one silly young thing found lice in her son's hair a few days after the fire, and collapsed into utter hysterics. And it was Mrs Russell with her fancy accent who put the girl back together again, getting her calm, sending for the barber, helping her boil the child's bedding. Most of the families left fairly quickly, as soon as they could find other arrangements and store their valuables. Others moved in as soon as the tents went vacant, of course—persons whose homes were in areas less prosperous than Pacific Heights." She laughed suddenly, her eyes sparkling. "I remember when a bevy of ladies of the evening from the Tenderloin arrived and began to set up ... Well, they were not made welcome by the local residents, and were sent on their way. A pity, really, they were much more cheerful than my neighbours by that point."

"Miss Adderley, do you recall any incident in particular, involving a strange man coming to the Russell tent?"

"There may have been any number—my tent was in a different area of the park, and after the first days I spent most of my time down in neighbourhoods that needed help, serving soup and distributing bread."

"I understand," he said, taking care not to show disappointment. However, she was not finished.

"There was a thing I heard about, walking one morning with some of the women down to where the bread was distributed. I am not absolutely certain that it concerned the Russells, you understand, but I believe it may have. It had happened the previous evening, three or four days after the earthquake itself, because the fire was out and the rain had just started. Might that have been the Sunday? Yes, I believe so. At first, the rains were welcome—we gathered it in buckets, the children ran about wildly, all we ladies washed our hair. But that evening, very early, everyone retreated inside their tents—what with the huge relief of knowing that the fires were at an end, and the blessedness of having shelter, and general exhaustion, this visitor came and found most everyone inside, so that he'd had to ask his way. He stopped at one tent, and the woman's children were asleep so she stepped outside to answer him quietly. She said he was dressed like a tramp, all dirt and mismatched garments. However, that would have described most of us by that time, and underneath everything he seemed polite and nicely spoken, so when he asked where Charles Russell might be found, she directed him to the Russells' tent and stood in her door-way to see that he found the right one.

"As soon as she heard the little girl scream, she knew what had happened, and she felt just terrible. Not to have warned the man first, you see. He'd very clearly been caught in a fire, possibly some sort of explosion—you know how a puff of burning gasoline can singe off eyelashes? Well, that's what had happened to this poor fellow. Swollen eyes, raw-looking skin, and no hair at all, lashes, brows, and even the front part of his head that his hat didn't cover. And he'd smeared some sort of white ointment on it as well—he startled this lady, so he must have scared the little Russell girl half to death. I can't think . . . Why are you smiling?"

"My . . . client remembered what she called a 'faceless man.' I think you've just found him for me."

"An apt description, I should think. We depend largely on hair for facial definition, do we not?"

"What about his beard?"

"I don't know that she mentioned a beard. But then, lack of a beard is not as startling as a lack of eyebrows, is it?"

No, thought Holmes, but it would take severe burns indeed to prevent a man's beard from growing in, and a man "all dirt and mismatched garments" would be un-likely to have visited a barber for a shave—to say nothing of submitting his burns to that degree of discomfort. Which would suggest that either the burns were recently acquired (and this was twenty-four hours after the fires were quenched), or that Russell's "faceless man" was a person without much of a beard in the first place.

Miss Adderley had begun to flag. Her back was as straight as ever, but the creases beside her mouth were growing pronounced and she had interlaced her fingers as if to keep them from trembling. Any moment the maid would burst in and send him packing.

Best to be found already preparing to leave.

He slid the photograph carefully into his breast pocket. "I shall bring this back as soon as I've had it copied."

"Take your time, Mr Holmes. And feel free to come back anytime. You will generally find me at home."

"May I also ask, Miss Adderley, do you know of any

other persons from the tent village who might still live in the city?"

"Off-hand, I can't think of any," she said, her voice quivering faintly with tiredness.

"Perhaps you'll think of someone. If you do, a note to the St Francis will reach me."

He rose and bent over her hand like a courtier, then walked across the quiet room to the door. It opened before he could lay his hand on the knob, but his departure was interrupted by the thin voice from behind him.

"She's not your client, is she? Is she your wife, or your ... 'friend'?"

"Both," Holmes told her.

The old eyes closed, and the withered lips curved up at the corners.

"Good," she said.

Chapter Fourteen

Holmes strode fast along the streets, the houses around him growing obscure with dusk and incoming mist. A fog-horn had begun its periodic moan from the north and the passing motorcars had lit their head-lamps. He turned the corner, his eyes seeking out the jungle-shrouded house, expecting to see the windows dark and to find the doors locked tight: He'd been longer with Miss Adderley than he had intended.

However, the narrow window set into the front door glowed dully, and when he stood before it he could see the light coming from the back of the house. He tried the knob, and gave an approving grunt: At least she'd had the sense to lock it.

He rapped one knuckle onto the door and waited, long enough to be visited by a brief pulse of alarm. His hand was going out for the raucous bell when the light dimmed as Russell stepped into the door-way of her father's library. She had, inevitably, a book in her hand, closed over one finger as she walked down the hall-way to work the bolts on the door.

"Hullo, Holmes. I thought you'd gone back to the hotel."

"I rather hoped you might be interested in a meal."

"Oh. Goodness," she said, peering over his shoulder at the gathering darkness. "It's later than I realised. Yes, I suppose I'm more or less finished here. Let me just get a couple of things."

Holmes ran an analytic eye over the signs of her passage through her parents' home: The drawer in the small inlaid table near the front door was ajar; the various decorative jars and boxes inhabiting the shelves in the morning room had all been disturbed, as well as the cubby-holes and drawers of her mother's writing desk in the front window. The blotting-paper there had even been turned over, although the stack of glass plates containing the ashes he had found and mounted looked to be untouched. She'd even shifted the furniture, with every wooden foot resting to one side of its decade long dust shadow.

He raised an eyebrow of disapproval at her haphazard methods, and followed her to the library. There his eyebrow climbed again: The room was scrubbed clean and clear of dust-cloths; the rolled-up carpets were now more or less flat on the floor. On the low table across from the fireplace, between the two leather chairs, a rough fistful of flowers from the garden had been dropped into a graceful crystal vase. The chairs had been rubbed into a gleam, and a fire laid, but not lit; probably just as well, he was thinking when she noticed the direction of his gaze.

"I was going to warm it up in here, but then it

occurred to me that I ought to have the chimneys looked to first. I wouldn't want to smoke up the place."

"Or burn it down."

She looked ill at the thought, although Holmes was beginning to wonder if it wouldn't be for the best: The polished chairs and laid fire, the child's gift of flowers, suggested that she was becoming more interested in re-creating her past than she was in recalling it. He held the door for her until, reluctantly, she pulled herself away from her father's laden desk and joined him in the hall-way. He helped her into her coat, handed her the hat and gloves from the stand, and waited while she locked the door behind them.

"You want to go to your Italian friend again, Holmes?"

"No, I've spent rather enough time there. I suggest we investigate the culinary exotica of Chinatown."

Wordlessly, she turned towards Grant Avenue. They walked the evening pavements, out of the heights and across the busy thoroughfare of Van Ness, climbing again and then dropping down into the bright lights and lurid colours of the Chinese district, where the gathering mist pulled like gauze across the street-lamps and coloured lanterns.

All the way, she said not a word and kept her hands in the pockets of her coat, making no effort to take his arm. This in itself did not concern Holmes, but that she also kept her eyes on the pavement did. She appeared oblivious to threat, as if the shooting seventy-two hours earlier had happened to another woman in another place. With another person, he might have thought that she was leaving the necessities of defence to him, but she was not that person.

He felt like seizing her by the shoulders and shaking her.

Or like giving her a hard shock in a less physical manner. But he could not decide if the shock he had in mind would clarify matters for her, or only make them worse. As with any blow, once delivered it could not be retracted; and so he kept his silence, although his eyes never ceased from probing the dim, fog-soft streets around them.

Halfway down the bright cacophony of Grant Avenue, Holmes touched her elbow. "Mr Long appears both fully recovered and at his till," he noted. "Shall we invite him to join us?"

They were, indeed, before the greengrocer's stand, with the door to Long's bookstore open to reveal the owner making change for a customer, moving his arm with no apparent distress. Without waiting for her approval, Holmes stepped around the displays of *bok choy* and flat Oriental peas to stick his head inside of the door. The conversation went on for two or three minutes, and then he emerged, touching her elbow again with one hand and indicating the street with the other.

"He'll join us in half an hour, we can have a drink while we wait."

He led her down the street to a building whose entrance was encrusted with carved dragons highlighted in gilt. Just inside the door was a tiny old woman all in black holding a clutch of large red leather menus to her breast, braced foursquare as if to guard the virtue of a granddaughter. Holmes delivered the message that they were friends of Mr Tom Long, who would be joining them in half an hour. The glittering black eyes scowled up at them, and then she turned and stumped away into what proved to be a large, warm, comfortable-looking restaurant peopled entirely by Chinese. She seated them at a table that was not visible from the front windows yet in close proximity to both front and kitchen doors, dropped two of the menus on the table, and hurried back to her post. Holmes held Russell's chair, then took the one beside her. She opened the menu, glanced at its pages, and closed it again. It was in Chinese.

"Are you up to a cocktail," he asked solicitously, "or would you prefer to stick to wine?"

"I'm fine," she automatically protested. "A gin and tonic would be good."

He ordered for them both. When their drinks were before them, she inflicted a dose of spirits onto her mistreated insides, then set down her glass sharply and announced, "I'm going down to the Lodge tomorrow."

He arranged a look of mild surprise on his face. "Do you think that's a good idea?"

"I don't know, but I think it's necessary."

"Do you wish me to come?"

"I telephoned to Flo this morning, and she'd like to go—her friend Donny will drive us. We'll be back on Wednesday; there's some museum opening Donny wants to attend."

"Hm," he grunted. "I'd have thought you'd want to drive yourself." Russell disliked being driven anywhere.

"I'm sure he'll let me have the wheel part of the time," she said, although Holmes, having seen the lad's pride in that gaudy motor, had his doubts.

"How many people know of your plans?"

She fixed him with a glare. "Holmes, I know you

think I'm being particularly stupid lately, but give me some credit. Neither of them know precisely where the place is, although I had to tell them roughly where we were heading. And I asked them to keep it quiet—I said I didn't want anyone else to know, because they'd want to join us and make it more of a bash than I wanted."

"'Bash.'"

"You know what I mean."

"Of course."

"I hope you don't mind. That I'm abandoning you here," she said, belatedly concerned for his welfare.

"Not in the least. I have plenty to keep me busy."

"Your Paganini research?"

"Actually, it's proving quite intriguing. Do you know, there is a theory that Paganini was commissioned by the Duke of..." but between the alcohol and her own concerns, she soon stopped listening. Which was precisely what he had intended.

When the drink was half gone and her eyes had begun to glaze with boredom, he dropped the diversion and told her, "I believe I've identified your faceless man." Then he corrected himself. "Not identified, perhaps, although I've got a lead on him."

She stared, picked up the glass and gulped down the second half, coughed a while, then, eyes watering, asked, *"What?"*

"The faceless man of your second dream. I found an elderly woman who spent some time in the park following the earthquake, and remembered your family. She also gave me the tale of a man coming to the tent city the day the rains began, which was the Sunday, who'd had his facial hair scorched off and wore some white ointment on his skin. Probably zinc oxide," Holmes noted.

"Ointment," she repeated, and reached for her empty glass. Holmes raised a finger to the waiter for another.

"The chap was looking for your father. He went to your tent, and his appearance frightened you. Miss Adderley's informant remembered your shrieks."

"My God."

The shock—or reverence—of the phrase was tempered by the effects of alcohol on an empty stomach. She seemed scarcely to be listening as Holmes described the old lady and her establishment, the aged butler and his protective granddaughter. He did not tell her about the photograph in his breast pocket, judging that its introduction would drain any rationality from the remainder of the evening. Other than that omission, he piled every conceivable detail into the narrative, until the sheer complexity and the second drink allowed her to attain a degree of distance from his revelation.

She interrupted his description of the old lady's shoes. "So two of the dreams depict actual events. First the earthquake, then an event shortly afterward."

"So it would appear."

"That would suggest that the third also refers to a concrete event. That there is an actual hidden room somewhere that I know about."

"Of that I would not be so certain."

"Why not?"

"The three do not run in precise parallel. The first two have powerful emotional overtones, yet the third is emotionally neutral, or even mildly reassuring. Of the first pair, the only element that changes is the description of the flying objects, but with the third, change itself is the constant factor—the details of the rooms are different each time; the only similarity in them is that only you know where the hidden apartment is to be found, only you have the key."

"Which I don't," she retorted angrily. "Holmes, I tore that place apart today, attic to cellar, and didn't find so much as an out-of-the-way broom closet. I'd have to take a wrecking hammer to it to find any more."

He nodded: Having measured the rooms scrupulously on Wednesday morning, he would have been astonished had she found any hidden spaces larger than a few inches wide. "When you discover the dream's message," he told her, "I believe it will be, as it were, out of the corner of your eye, not through use of a sledge hammer and crow-bar. Ah, here comes Mr Long."

The bookseller was being led through the room by the entrance crone, but his progress was uneven, as one table after another called its greeting and caused him to detour to shake a hand here and exchange a word there. Half the people in the restaurant seemed to know him; all greeted the small man with affection and respect. Even the elderly door-guard seemed to be smiling when they finally reached the table.

He shook hands with the only two Caucasians in the place, then turned to the old woman and began a vigorous conversation. They were joined after a minute by the waiter and, shortly afterwards, by one of the cooks from the kitchen. The discussion escalated into an apparent argument, voices climbing and gestures becoming ever wilder—Long ticking off points on his fingers, the cook's face twisting in incredulity. Then it ended as abruptly as it had begun. Waiter, woman, and cook all turned on their heels and set off in separate directions, leaving Long to sit down, looking pleased.

"What did that concern?" Holmes asked.

"That? Just dinner."

"Dinner? They weren't asking that you remove us?"

"My goodness, why would they want that? No, we just had to settle the menu. I needed to reassure them that you did not require a slab of beef and boiled potatoes, but to assert that you did not eat pork or shellfish. I recall hearing of this religious peculiarity of your mother's, Miss Russell, and thought perhaps it was yours as well."

"That was very thoughtful of you," she said.

"Not at all," he responded, but he looked pleased as he shook out his linen table napkin and draped it across his lap. "So, have you two been busy since we met? I don't suppose you've had a chance to look at the feng shui book?"

"I have, actually," she replied, dredging up intellect from the muddying effects of drink. "It presents an interesting theory of geomancy, but I have to say, it leaves out a great deal of the *practicum*. I had understood that feng shui includes the idea that a building's . . . energies can be influenced by the judicial placement of certain items. Water, plants, mirrors and the like."

"That is true," Long said, "although its precepts are used not only for architecture, but for investments, farming, planning battles, and a thousand other activities. Here, let me show you." He patted through his pockets until he found a mechanical pencil and a scrap of paper, smoothing it out on the table-cloth and sketching an octagon. He then connected each angle with the centre, and ascribed to each of the eight resulting triangles an area of influence: family, wealth, knowledge, and so on, with the all-important health at the confluence. After a few minutes, the minutiae of detail became more than even a sober Russell might have asked for, and she interrupted his explanation of the *"chien"* side of the octagon.

"What I would really like to know is, why would someone put a mirror, a bowl of water, and a pot-plant in a kitchen?"

He unfolded another piece of paper and pushed it across to her, laying his pencil on top. "To answer that, you will have to draw the room for me."

"It's the kitchen in the house here. I would assume that your parents were responsible for the items."

"My mother. Although she would have called in an expert. Yes, I see. However, it has been some years since I was inside that room."

She took up the pencil and sketched the kitchen's outlines, locating the sink, scullery, cook-stove, and entrances. At his direction she indicated the lights and windows, as well as the locations of the small mirror, the water bowl, and the dead plant. Then she pushed it back across the table at him.

Soup arrived, and he moved the sketch to one side, keeping his hand on the edge of the paper. "As I remember, the kitchen faces the back of the house, its windows to the west, is that correct?"

"Yes, it is."

He picked up both sheets and laid them in front of her, next to each other. "The objects you name would have been intended to correct the *chi,* the energy patterns, within the room. And thus, of course, within the lives of the residents."

"Of course," she murmured.

He heard the irony. "I apologise, I know it is complex, and with little logic for the literalist Western mind."

"Perhaps I should ask, is it possible to analyse how

these... additions were intended? Can you tell what was wrong with the *chi* in the room?"

Long looked down at the two pieces of paper, his lips pursed in consideration. "That is an interesting question," he said at last. "I am by no means an expert, but it looks to me as if there was a perceived external threat to the internal harmony. The items were placed to strengthen the internal harmony—the family."

But "harmony" was not the word that caught Russell's attention. "A threat? Of what kind?"

"That I cannot know. Some force that threatened to pull the family off-centre into disharmony. Which, I agree, is so general as to be considered witchcraft, or mumbo-jumbo." With an apologetic smile he turned to his soup; after a minute, the others did the same.

"Apart from the articles of feng shui," he said when the bowls had been removed and fragrant plates were beginning to appear, "I hope you have found the house in satisfying condition?"

"I found it run-down, dreary, and most uninformative," Russell replied.

"I am sorry." Long scooped shreds of vegetables in some dark, piquant-smelling sauce on top of his rice, then ventured, "You had hoped to learn something from the building?"

"Oh, not really. But it would have been nice." The bookseller's face wore a look of confusion, although he was too polite to persist with his questions. But to Holmes' surprise, Russell relented.

"I've had a series of peculiar dreams. Two of them served to remind me about the earthquake and the period afterwards, events I had forgotten entirely, but the third is still puzzling. It involves a secret compartment in a house—nothing particular happens, I just pass by and know that it's there. I don't know what the imagery means. Probably nothing, but it would have been satisfying to have discovered a hidden vault under the house or something."

Long nodded impassively and the conversation turned to the collection of furniture the cellar contained, some of which was going to have to come out through the coal-cellar doors. They ate the food and drank wine and pale tea, and when they were replete, Long patted his lips with his table napkin and spoke hesitantly.

"I wonder, about your hidden room. Do you know of the writings of Father Matteo Ricci?"

Russell shook her head, but Holmes got a faraway look on his face.

"Ricci was a Jesuit in the sixteenth century who went to China, as a missionary of course, although as was the habit of the Jesuits, he learnt as much as he taught. Many of his writings are in Chinese, which somewhat limits his fame in the West. But one of the things he tried to teach the Mandarins concerned the mnemonic arts. I believe Western philosophers have something of a tradition of memory training."

"Ignatius of Loyola," Holmes supplied, his own memory having performed its retrieval, "founder of the Jesuit order. And Pliny has a section on memory experts, I believe, as do several Mediaeval works on oration."

"What does this have to do with locked rooms?" Russell asked.

"Ricci's technique involves the construction of memory palaces," Long told them. "One visualises a large building—real or imagined, palace or basilica—and furnishes it with items that stimulate specific memories."

"The problem being," Holmes commented, "that the

formulation and retention of the myriad rooms and furnishings alone requires a prodigious memory."

"And," Long added, with an air of finally being permitted to reach his central thesis, "there is nothing to guarantee that a room once furnished will not be closed off and forgotten. To have its lock turned, as it were."

"I see," Russell said. Her chin had come up and one light brown eyebrow had arched delicately above the frame of her spectacles: scepticism, and a trace of indignation that this stranger would presume to know her mind. Before she could voice her objections aloud, Holmes firmly turned the conversation to books and Chinese philosophy, and in a while they were lighting their after-dinner cigarettes and arguing amiably over the bill.

She was still silent when they stood to leave, rousing herself only to say the necessary words of farewell to the bookseller. Outside, the fog had thickened into a clean, grey version of a London particular, and Holmes relaxed into its protection, hooking her hand through his left arm as they set off for downtown.

Holmes was intensely aware of the physical sensation of her arm on his. He generally was aware of her presence, that sturdy physicality wrapped around a magnificent brain and the stoutest of hearts. One flaw alone had he found in this incomparable hard diamond of a woman, an imperfection that had long puzzled him, and cost him no small amount of sleep.

Five years ago he had sat in a dark cabin on a boat heading to Palestine, listening to the details of her family's death, hearing of the guilt that had been bleeding her like an invisible wound. Ever since that night, he had waited for Russell to question those things that she believed to be true. She was, he had reminded himself time and again, one of the most competent natural investigators he had ever known, unerring and undistractible. If her ears would not hear and her eyes refused to focus, there might well be a reason.

Even so, over the years it had been on the very end of his tongue a score of times to push matters into the open. At first, he had not done so because she was so very young, and clearly needed to shield herself against further injury. Later, he had come to realise that forcing her into a confrontation with her beliefs, tempting though it might be, could well drive a steel wedge between the two of them: She would blame him for introducing the troubling question, then further blame him for having waited so long before doing so—if there was a thing Russell hated more than a stranger presuming to know how her mind worked, it was the sensation of being protected. The resulting disquiet and mistrust would have made an already difficult relationship unbearably, perhaps fatally, complicated.

And nearly literally fatal: On the boat out from Japan, he had ventured a slight step, suggesting that the flying dream was a reference to the earthquake; the very next day he'd found Russell at the rail, moments from overbalancing.

Yes, fear had kept him silent.

Later, a growing and perverse fascination with his wife's single, glaring blind spot had stayed his hand. It had felt at times like watching a child's block-tower continue to grow and wondering when it would topple and crash.

Abject cowardice, compounded by intellectual curiosity.

And then in January, his brother Mycroft's commands had prised them out of England and flung them halfway around the world, and Russell had decided—on her own, without the faintest suggestion from him—to come to this place. He had known it was coming, then, and held his breath. Even when he'd come up the stairway on the ship and seen her about to tumble over the rail, he'd held back.

She was coming to it: The mounting pressure of the things she had seen yet not perceived would break down her blindness. She knew, yet kept it from herself; she had the key, and had only to draw it from her pocket. He would force himself, as he had all this time, to continue trusting that she would face the question before she failed to notice a man with a gun, or absent-mindedly stepped out in front of a taxi. Sooner or later, something would drive her to a confrontation with all the things she knew and did not see.

He, Holmes, had known the question's answer the moment he saw that intent young man making his way up the hill in Miss Adderley's photograph: This was not a man to be fatally distracted by a pair of argumentative children.

Russell should not require a photograph: She knew her father.

And there were any number of ways to send a motorcar off a cliff: steering wheel, brakes, a score of parts vulnerable to sabotage.

Russell knew that as well.

Soon now, she would look down at her hand and see the key lying there; she would ask herself a simple question that would teeter an edifice of ten years' belief.

Was it indeed an accident? Or had my family in fact been murdered?

Chapter Fifteen

The fog had ceased its teasing around the street-lamps and taken possession of the streets. However, the fog here was a very different thing from that stinking, inert yellow blanket that settled over London every winter. This seemed a living thing, shifting and breathing across the city, and it sheltered their walk, wrapping these two wayfaring strangers in anonymity. No shots rang out, no gaunt figures with tubercular coughs dogged their heels, and they walked arm in arm in mutually distracted silence, physically linked but mentally miles apart, through the Chinese district and downtown to the welcoming lights of the St Francis.

Between the excess of drink and the shock of two complete meals that day, Russell succumbed quickly to the warmth of the bed and did not wake until Holmes placed a cup of coffee on her bed-side table. She opened one eye, winced back from the brightness as the curtains went back, then threaded out a hand to fumble with the alarm-clock, holding its face up before her own. When she had focussed, she slammed it back down and made to throw off the bed-clothes.

"Nearly nine o'clock! Holmes, why didn't you wake me earlier? I told you that Flo wanted to get an early start, and I haven't finished packing my things."

"Your friend telephoned five minutes ago to say that she was only now putting her things into a bag, that she would be here in an hour. The word 'early' appears to have a different meaning in Californian English."

"Only in the dialect spoken by a certain sub-genus of nocturnal Californians," Russell said, pawing the bed-clothes back into place and reaching for spectacles, then coffee. With lenses and the beverage, her vision improved, and she looked more closely at her husband's attire and his purposeful movement through the rooms.

"Are you going somewhere, Holmes?"

By this time he had his coat and hat in hand, and it was apparent that he was indeed on his way out of the door. "Yes, if you don't mind I shan't wait for your friend to arrive. There's a gentleman with a collection of manuscript papers across the Bay in Oakland, and a ferry that leaves at ten-thirty. If that's all right with you?"

"Of course it is," she answered with just the faintest edge of too much protest in her voice. "I'm glad you have something to keep you busy, so I won't worry that you're going to be bored silly in my absence."

"No danger of that," Holmes replied lightly. "Do you wish me to mention at the desk that we won't be leaving San Francisco on the Wednesday as you had intended?"

"Oh! I forgot to do that. Yes, would you? I have a few more days' business with Norbert, so perhaps another week?"

"The fourteenth," he said, pulling on his gloves, and carefully not bringing up the topic of cross-country aeronautical pioneering.

"Or maybe the next day; that ought to give Norbert sufficient time to finish things off."

"Thursday the fifteenth it is. Have a pleasant time, Russell."

"I'll ring you if I'm going to be delayed past Wednesday," she said, but the door had closed on the final words. She frowned; he'd seemed merely distracted, but perhaps he was in truth affronted by her abandoning of him for Flo and the cabin.

No, she decided in the end; it was merely a piece of academic investigation that had caught his imagination, nothing more.

More cheerful than she'd felt in some time, she went to dress and consider an appropriate wardrobe for a none-too-rustic cabin in the woods.

Holmes, in the meantime, made straight for the front desk. Auberon handed his guest the heavy Gladstone bag Holmes had left there earlier, and after informing the manager of the change in their departure date, Holmes lowered his voice to ask, "Is my car here?"

The gentleman responded in kind. "Around the back, Mr Holmes, as you requested."

One man's palm lifted slightly from the polished surface of the desk and, so smoothly it might have been rehearsed, the other's palm came down and slid the note away. Before it had reached Auberon's pocket, Holmes was halfway to the kitchen.

He passed through that steamy cacophony with

scarcely a glance from the white-clad workers, slipping out of the delivery door into the passage-way through which flowed the great hotel's supplies. A shiny Pierce-Arrow with velvet curtains across its back windows was idling off to his right, its driver immersed in a garish journal entitled *Weird Tales;* Holmes opened the door, gently laid the Gladstone bag on the seat, and got in beside it; the motor's tyres were moving before he had the door shut.

"Morning, sir," said the young man at the wheel. Holmes opened his mouth to ask if this connoisseur of pulp fiction had read anything by Hammett, then changed his mind at the number of complicated conversational path-ways this would open up. Instead he said merely, "What's your name, lad?"

"Greg Tyson, at your service."

"The name's Holmes. Auberon told me you were a relative."

"His wife's nephew. And he told me that you needed a fair bit of driving today and a lot of shut mouth afterwards."

"An accurate description. You know the coast road south?"

"Know it well, sir."

"I shall let you know when to stop."

"Very good," the boy said, and set out to provide what Holmes had required, both the driving and the closed mouth.

Holmes dropped his soft hat on the dark green leather of the seat beside him and went about making himself comfortable, tucking one foot beneath him, loosening his overcoat, and arranging the travelling-rugs behind him. When he had got things as close to a nest of cushions as he was about to achieve in a motorcar, he took out his tobacco pouch—cigarettes were for social occasions and for stimulation, but a pipe was for thinking. And a peaceful review of the past seven days had become increasingly necessary.

He'd rather have stayed to see Russell safely into the motorcar with Flo Greenfield and her friend Donny, but from what he'd seen of that young man and his blue motorcar, once pointed on the road out of town, there would be no catching him up. And Holmes very much wanted to be in front of the carload of merry-makers.

No, he would have to trust that nothing would happen to Russell before her new friends arrived, and that they would quickly out-distance any potential pursuers. Russell was safely out of the way for the next three days.

By the time she returned to the city, he intended that their as-yet-unidentified opponents would no longer be in the equation.

He grimaced with the irritation of it. Cases were far more congenial when there was no personal element in them, and this sensation of being his wife's fond fool was highly unsatisfactory. Urging her to eat, fretting about her safety—he must put Russell out of his mind before the distraction could interfere with rational thought.

The case had started slowly, but was now progressing somewhat, despite the distances it involved in both time and place. While Russell had been immersed with her solicitor and business affairs, he had been occupied with things far more demanding than Paganini sheet music.

Tuesday morning, their first in San Francisco, he had used the time while she was busy with Henry Norbert to get the lay of the land, assembling maps and creating the initial contacts among the local vendors of news-papers and flowers, the shoe-shine boys, the local police-men, and the all-important street-sweepers: his eyes on the world.

He had also succumbed to a growing urge and laid out the beginnings for a line of enquiry into some unfin-ished business. This had begun with a trip to the P. & O. Line's offices. With considerable difficulty, he had fi-nally determined that the ship on which he and Russell had sailed to Bombay in January, the *Marguerite*, was currently on its way back across the Mediterranean and due to dock in Marseilles late on Saturday. Immediately he left the steamship offices, he had sent a telegram home to Sussex, asking Mrs Hudson to find the where-abouts of his old comrade-in-arms, Dr Watson. After a bit of thought, he had also sent one to his brother, Mycroft, requesting that he find out if anyone had been enquiring in early January about the absence, and whereabouts, of one Sherlock Holmes.

That damnable incident in Aden bothered him mightily. He wanted to be quite certain that the falling balcony was just an accident.

He still was not sure what had driven him to appeal to those two for assistance—an ill Mycroft and an arthritic Watson. No doubt it was at least in part due to the unexpected and highly disconcerting absence of his partner-wife's usual competence; in her mental absence, he had turned to her predecessor.

In any case, turned to Watson and Mycroft he had; there was little point in agonising over the why of it.

With past events cared for as best he could, he turned to present concerns, and cast out for information regarding Russell's city, family, and history. With a visit to the offices of the *Chronicle,* he'd come up with an obituary for the Russell family—Charles (age 46, born in Boston), wife Judith (age 39, from London), son Levi (age 9), survived by daughter Mary (age 14)—and the article about the crash, from which he gleaned a description of the actual location.

Most of Wednesday had been spent at the house, first in a quick survey of the house records—the financial accounts he found shelved in the library, a set of garden journals from Mrs Russell's morning room. Then he had taken out the graph paper and measuring tape Auberon had provided for him, going over the house inch by inch until he was satisfied that no rooms hid between the walls. His knees had suffered and his lungs filled with dust, and he had scarcely finished before the sound of a gun-shot had drawn him inexorably to the front door where he'd stood, his blood running cold as he strained for the sound of another shot or of wailing, only breathing again when his wife and her new acquaintance had appeared at the gate. He'd enjoyed meeting Mr Long, although he rather wished the means of their introduction had been somewhat less dramatic.

Thursday morning he had continued to unearth the family's past, examining the social registers for the early years, interviewing neighbours and post office employees. In the afternoon he had finally got those burnt scraps between glass, although he'd had to put off scouring the newspapers for the pertinent articles until the following day. That night being free, they had passed up the cinema offering of Harold Lloyd and the advertised "SF Musical Club High Jinks" at the Palace Hotel in favour of a small, private recital of *lieder* by a visiting coloratura soprano to which Auberon had

arranged an invitation. It had brought him pleasure
and given Russell an hour's sleep, and served as a reminder of culture after long months in the wilds of the
Far East.

Friday morning had been spent digging through
mountains of old newspapers, at the *Chronicle* building,
City Hall, and the public library. Now in his possession
were Photostat copies of the pages that had been burnt
in the morning room fireplace: The bold, heavily leaded
"URNS!!" had indeed been a headline about the city
burning, from a newspaper outside the area of damage
whose presses were still functioning. Nothing in it
seemed to explain its presence among the papers burnt,
other than its possible value as a souvenir, for the page
was primarily concerned with names of the missing,
availability of shelter, news about looting, and the expected recovery of the fire chief (who, Holmes had later
read, in the end died of injuries caused by his house
falling in on him). The other piece of burnt newsprint,
smaller than the first to begin with, was from the following Monday, long enough after the original disaster
and the cessation of the fire that urgent news was being
supplemented by human-interest stories. Prominent
among those was the tale of a newlywed couple who had
been separated in the hours after the quake and driven
apart further by the track of the fire. Each had spent
days convinced that the other was dead, until a chance
encounter with a mutual friend had led the husband to
his wife. On the obverse were several small articles no
more than a paragraph or two long: the theft of a number of Army tents from Golden Gate Park; an infant rescued from wreckage; a dog gone mad with grief; the
burnt body of a policeman amid the charred ruin of a
house; and the departure from San Francisco of the

great tenor Caruso. Holmes set aside the Photostats, for
further consideration.

Later in the day he'd tracked down that other source
of inside knowledge into a neighbourhood, the Pacific
Heights milkman of 1912. He'd been forced to hare
across town twice in the process, wasting huge blocks of
time, and all for nothing. The man might as well have
been deaf and blind for all he knew about the Russells,
or anyone else for that matter. Now, if Holmes could tell
him of any unusual standing orders the family habitually placed, he might remember....

It happened in every investigation, hours wasted. Age
cannot wither nor custom stale her infinite tediousness,
he reminded himself, and scraped out his cold pipe into
the motor's ash-tray, filling the bowl anew.

Friday had also seen the utter collapse of Russell,
knocked flat by the news of Dr Ginzberg's death. All in
all, not a good day, Friday.

But not without its bright points. Mrs Hudson's
answer, typically long-winded, had finally come into
his hands during one of his cross-town trips on Friday:

MR HOLMES GLAD TO HEAR FROM YOU AND
SORRY FOR THE DELAY I WAS VISITING MY FRIEND
MRS TURNER IN SURREY. DR WATSONS
HOUSEKEEPER SAYS HE IS AT THE BADEN SPAS
BADEN GERMANY FOR HIS ARTHRITIS POOR MAN
WHAT A MARTYR HE IS. I TOOK YOUR BROTHER
SOME ELDERBERRY WINE HE LOOKS WELL.
SEVERAL PEOPLE RANG TO ASK WHEN YOU WERE
RETURNING PLEASE DO LET ME KNOW. LOVE TO
MARY. MRS CLARA HUDSON

Seeing that Watson was off taking the cure, Holmes had hesitated before sending his request.

But only briefly. After all, someone had to interview the ship's pursers about the mysterious Southern woman, and although he would naturally have preferred to do it himself, he was far from home, and the idea of letting it lie for weeks until he could do it himself made his skin crawl with impatience.

So he'd sent it:

WATSON URGENT NEED ENQUIRIES STAFF
ESPECIALLY PURSERS ON P AND O SHIP
MARGUERITE DOCKING MARSEILLES SATURDAY
EVENING. WOMAN POSSIBLY FROM SOUTHERN
UNITED STATES ASKING QUESTIONS ABOUT US
DURING JANUARY RUN AND WHO LEFT AT ADEN.
ANY AND ALL INFORMATION VALUABLE BUT
CHIEFLY DID SHE KNOW WE WERE CALIFORNIA
BOUND QUERY DID SHE ARRANGE OWN FURTHER
TRAVEL QUERY WAS SHE WITH ANYONE QUERY
AND FINALLY HER NAME AND DESCRIPTION
QUERY. SORRY OLD MAN. HOLMES.

Only later in the morning, cooling his heels waiting for the milkman, had it occurred to him that Watson could as easily have made a leisurely journey to London on Thursday and intercepted the ship when it arrived there. He nearly turned back and sent another missive to say that Thursday would do, but in the end he did not.

Knowing Watson, Holmes reassured himself, he'd have left Baden immediately, and the second telegram would miss him anyway.

And the information received from Mrs Hudson

provided its own form of solace. Mycroft had been ill since the winter, and it was good to know that Mrs Hudson had found him well.

Watson and Mycroft would come through, he reassured himself, and set a match to his pipe.

He wished he could be as certain about his other assistants, who were abundant if somewhat questionable. He was accustomed to working with Irregulars, to be used and discarded when their purpose was served. He was also well acquainted with the problems of finding reliable help, particularly as he was generally forced to draw from a pool of candidates consisting of society's dregs: One was less likely to find honour amongst thieves than simple thievery, and one developed the habit of not placing too much weight on any one helpmeet.

Take this Hammett fellow, for example. He appeared to be an ideal Irregular (apart from his chronic infirmity), a man whose ready knowledge of the ground, and especially the underground, could save an employer a great deal of superfluous footwork. However, the niggling question of whether he might be too good to be true had already cost Holmes a hurried trip cross-town Saturday morning, returning to the telegraphist's near the P. & O. offices to request that they retain any messages for him there, and not (as he had arranged earlier) have them delivered to the St Francis. A local ex-Pinkerton might well have as close an agreement with the Western Union boys as he had with the taxi drivers, and if Hammett was in fact currently under employment, that employer was likely to be the very subject of the telegrams from Mycroft and Watson. Better to keep them from leaving the telegraph office under any hands other than his own.

And then there was Tom Long, another convenient assistant dangling before his nose, tantalising in his intelligence, experience, and personal commitment to the cause. If, that is, Tom Long was what he appeared to be.

Or even the driver of this motor. Tyson, as with the motor, had been provided by the hotel manager, Auberon. Driver and vehicle made for an unlikely pair—the motor had been chosen to give an impression of an aged employer out for a sedate drive, but beneath the livery and cap he wore, its driver was a bright young man with carroty hair and a cheeky grin. Tyson's own motor, according to Auberon, was of a colour to match his hair, along with chrome-yellow seats and a throaty engine—ill suited for the sort of surveillance they were conducting today. Tyson appeared to be a simple young man with a passion for motorcars and a deplorable taste in literature; on the other hand, he could conceivably be an agent of the faceless enemy, planted on Holmes by yet another agent, Auberon.

Even Henry Norbert bore a question mark above his head, as the lawyer knew more than anyone else about Russell's business, whereabouts, and life in general. He had keys; he was in a position to manipulate the Russell fortunes; and he might indeed know more about the Russell past than he was saying.

The only person Holmes could be sure of was currently *hors de combat*, so distracted by her problems that she was effectively half-witted. She hadn't even noticed that morning that he did not actually say he was taking a ferry to Oakland, merely that there was a manuscript and there was a ferry-boat. In her right mind, she'd never have missed that.

So, here he was, Sherlock Holmes on his own again with the dubious assistance of an unlikely trio of

Irregulars: a cadaverous Pinkerton who ought to be abed, a diminutive Chinese bookseller with a wide knowledge of arcane topics, and a red-headed modern-day barrow-boy trying out for a part in one of Conan Doyle's bits of airy nonsense. His most reassuring partner at the moment was good old Watson, halfway across the globe and launched on another desperate dash across Europe on the business of his longtime friend.

Holmes smiled around the stem of his pipe at the image of his erstwhile partner, thinner of hair and stouter of girth, limping with bulldog tenacity across a crowded German railway station. If anyone could intercept the *Marguerite*, it would be the doctor.

Soon, however, he would need another pair of hands and feet—very soon, if Watson had succeeded in catching the ship in Marseilles. Whom to trust? The story-teller, the bookseller, or some sturdy young man picked at random from the street?

With luck (a commodity in which Holmes placed no trust whatsoever) today's outing would settle at least one of those questions.

And in the meantime, he would hold up for consideration four points.

First, those burnt scraps they had salvaged from the fireplace, from a document written on the machine in Charles Russell's study. The surviving words made it clear that the document had concerned matters of some import: "Army...looters...stolen...executed"—these were not from the draught of a chatty family letter.

Two: That they were burnt, and so close to the source of their writing, indicated a certain urgency, or at the very least an emphatic quality, in the act of destruction. A more sanguine individual would merely have carried them off rather than risk discovery through lighting a fire in the fireplace of a vacant house.

Two points did not an hypothesis make, but taken with the third—that persons unknown had broken into the Russell house with, to all appearances, the sole purpose of destroying that document—they formed a shape. And the shape was one that Holmes had studied closely the whole of his professional life: blackmail.

Point four: Although the victims of blackmail often turned on their tormentors, he could not recall a single incident when a blackmailer had deliberately killed his victim.

This was the most troubling of all, for in the midst of those four salient points lived the growing and awful possibility that the blackmailer had been none other than Charles Russell himself.

Holmes had always despised the sly and verminous quality of the blackmailer, and his every instinct shouted that the stalwart young man in the photograph was no extortionist. However, that was emotion talking. Certainly he would say nothing to Russell—not yet, perhaps not ever, if no further evidence came to light. And perhaps, under certain circumstances, if Charles Russell had been given no choice, if he had been driven to the detestable weapon by the needs of his family, if one could accept that blackmail was a weapon like any other...

He hoped very much it did not come to that.

On the other hand, there remained the question of the relationship between Charles and Judith Russell: Two months after the fire, husband and wife have a furious argument; that very day she packs up the children to leave for England; for the next six years he sees them only periodically, in England, for slightly less than half the year. According to Russell, her parents were easy and affectionate with each other when they were together, but the fact remained that the family was divided for much of the year from June of 1906 until the summer of 1912.

If Judith Russell had discovered that her husband was a blackmailer, that could have driven her away. But if her outrage against his morals had caused her to flee, why then welcome the man when he came to her in England? And why return to San Francisco after six years?

That was more the behaviour of a woman protecting her children from threat than a woman disillusioned with her husband.

He shook his head and, noticing that the pipe had burnt itself out, he slid it into a pocket. Too many questions, not enough data.

The remainder of the journey he spent divided between a study of the maps and watching the landscape go past.

Eventually, the motorcar's bonnet shifted west, and soon the grey Pacific stretched out into the distance. Holmes folded the map away and set both feet on the floor, intent now. He'd read the newspaper report that suggested where the crash had happened, and he had studied the maps closely until he had narrowed down the possibilities to one.

"Drop your speed somewhat," he said to the boy in the front. "Not as if you're watching for something or about to stop, but as if you're under direction from a nervous passenger."

"Got it." The car's progress became more stately, and Holmes resumed his hat and sat back. It would take very sharp eyes indeed to see the vehicle as anything but the means of an elderly gentleman's progress.

Half a mile from the spot where he had decided it happened, the road climbed, then abruptly turned and dropped away at the same time. Young Tyson's foot came down hard on the brake pedal, and Holmes nodded grimly to himself.

Near the top of the hill, a battered bread-delivery lorry—truck, as they called them here—had been pulled into an inadequate flat space on the eastern side of the road. On the other side, overlooking the sea, stood a short, bow-legged man with close-cropped hair, his garments tossed by the wind. His knees were against the guard-rail as he craned to look over the edge. As they went past, Holmes raked the figure with a glance, then resumed his straight-ahead gaze, frowning slightly.

At the bottom of the hill the waves had deposited a small beach, a golden crescent of sand. At the far end of it, two people were making their way up the sand to the road, a picnic basket and bright blankets in their arms, heads ducked against the wind. Even from a distance, Holmes could see their Model T rock with the wind.

Holmes spoke to Tyson in a taut voice. "Park where those two young people are just leaving, but turn around on the other side of them so as to be facing north. I want to have an open view of the cliff." The young man nodded, performed the turn and, once the Model T had left, eased cautiously off the road onto the edges of the sand. As he slowed, Holmes said, "Pull your wheel a few more degrees to the right and go forward ten feet." When he had done so, Holmes dropped the back window and looked out at the cliff, seeing what he had feared. With a shake of the head, he told the boy to shut off the motor.

"We shall be here for an hour or two, possibly longer.

You may stay or go, as you like; if you remain in the motor, you must keep quite still; if you go, you merely need to stay within the sound of my voice." While speaking, Holmes had retrieved the Gladstone from the floor and yanked open the top. He now drew out a stubby brass telescope, not new but with the polish of care, which Auberon had conjured up for his guest. Laying it on the seat, he went back into the bag and took from it a tripod with extendable legs, which he set up on the floor, arranging his long legs around it. He fastened the telescope onto the tripod, raised it so it reached the height of his eyes, and leant back to examine it. The sun was well away from any reflective portion of the instrument, but he tugged the velvet drapes a few inches closer together, rendering the interior invisible.

Only then did he lower his eyes to the eyepiece and put his hand to the adjustments.

A six-foot-two-inch man with tubercular lungs was hanging from the cliff face while waves were reaching up to catch at his feet.

Damn the man, thought Holmes, angry and apprehensive; what was he trying to prove? That he was better than the famous Sherlock Holmes? A sickly man with a family to support, risking his neck for the sake of what? The faint possibility of ten-year-old evidence? He'd been told to look at the wreckage, which very clearly was not on the rocks, and to interview the locals, which equally clearly the man standing up on the road was not.

As Holmes watched the thin figure pick his way from one precarious hand-hold to the next, he felt precisely as he had whenever he had placed Watson in danger—a thing he'd generally done as inadvertently as he had this man. Scarcely breathing, he watched the man on the cliff, expecting at any moment to see those long arms flail and the body crash down into the foam: one assistant shot, another smashed; this case was proving hard on the Irregulars.

Ten minutes later, the young man in the driver's seat shifted and the hillside scene leapt and danced through the lens.

Holmes said coldly, "Mr Tyson, you may feel free to get out and watch the sea-birds."

After a minute, the door opened and the abashed lad got out, shutting it with care. Holmes settled again to the eyepiece.

Taking into account his poor physical condition, Hammett was making a remarkably thorough job of his investigation of the cliffside. With an intervening decade of high waves and Pacific rain, there could be little evidence left among the rocks, but twice now Holmes had seen the man pick his way cautiously towards some invisible object. The first time, hanging like a three-legged spider, he had worked some object loose with his fingers, examined it (to all appearances completely unconscious of the precariousness of his stance) and tossed it away. The second time he had pulled something from his back trouser pocket and gouged at a crack in the rocks, retrieving some long, narrow object; that, too, he held close to examine, only this time he kept it, lifting his coat to secure it through the back of his belt.

His greying hair and coat-tails tossed wildly in the wind as he continued to scan the rocks, and Holmes found himself muttering under his breath: "Hammett, it must be damned cold out on that exposed rock; this won't be doing your lungs a bit of good. The tide's on its way in and in another ten minutes you'll get wet. Look, man, I'm not your father; you've nothing to prove to me."

It took another twenty-five agonising minutes,

during which time Hammett had found one other item of interest, nearly fallen down the cliff twice, and shifted upwards on the cliff three times to keep free of the wave splashes, before he finally threw back his head to study the return route.

From where he stood, the cliff must have appeared nearly vertical, because he then pulled back to survey the terrain to his right. He appeared to stare straight into Holmes' lens for a moment before it became clear that he was merely estimating the possibilities of the beach route. The horizontal must have appeared preferable, because in a minute he waved widely at the bow-legged man who had been pacing to and fro on the cliff-top road all this time, and pointed towards the sand.

Immediately, the other man waved his response and turned away to the bread van—only to leap back at the unexpected approach of another motor.

A sleek blue motorcar driven by a fair-headed boy, with two young women passengers. He'd been right: Russell had insisted on coming by this route. He'd also been right that she wouldn't succeed in getting that car-proud young man to relinquish the wheel.

Holmes raised his face from the instrument and lifted the curtains to one side so as to see unimpaired. The gaunt man was beginning to work his way along the cliff above the line of wetness, his entire being concentrating on the effort. Above him on the roadway, the bow-legged man gave him a glance before turning to face the three young people emerging from the motorcar. The slick-haired driver tumbled over the side with the practiced agility of a monkey, trotting around to open the passenger door for the black-haired girl; the other young woman, the one with the absurdly short blonde hair, was standing up so as to follow. Holmes put his head back to the eyepiece.

Russell moved stiffly, as if she were in pain, or fear, climbing out of the car and onto the surface. She wrapped her heavy coat around her against the wind. Flo Greenfield said something, then reached out as if to take her arm, but Russell had stepped away from her in the direction of the precipitous edge. Holmes risked a quick glance down at the man near the water, but Hammett was still intent on his spider-act along the rocks.

Russell stood at the very lip of the cliff, leaning over the inadequate railing as she'd leant over the ship's rail the week before. Flo Greenfield picked her way near, but the shoes she wore were inadequate for the terrain, and she wobbled dangerously until her beau's arm flashed out to steady her. The two young people stood on secure ground, apparently pleading with their English companion, but Russell did not respond. She seemed hypnotised by the breaking waves, but Holmes could see the moment when her attention was caught by the figure far below: Her mouth came open in surprise and her hand came out, but to Holmes' immense relief, the bow-legged man stepped forward and took her arm, urging her back from the cliff. Holmes began to breathe again.

The driver of the delivery van seemed to be explaining Hammett's presence, and Holmes would have paid a great deal to be able to hear what he had to say. Whatever the explanation was, it did not immediately strike Russell as impossible; she looked at the man doubtfully, but her head did not go back into that intensely familiar posture of disbelief that allowed her to look down her nose at the offender. She just listened to the man, craned forward to see how far the grey-haired climber had got, then said something over her shoulder.

The three young people got into their motorcar and the bow-legged man into his, driving in procession down the long curve to where the cliff gave way to the beach. Holmes lifted his face from the eyepiece for a moment to rub the tension out of his muscles. When he pulled his hands away, Greg Tyson was walking quickly towards the car, brushing the sand from his trouser-legs. He jumped in behind the wheel and slammed the door.

"Do you want to scoot?" he asked.

"No, I believe the two motors will stop at the other end of the beach. No need to flee unless they continue down here—you are welcome to resume your reading material. However, be ready to move quickly."

"Whatever you say."

Both men in the closed car sat tensely until the two other vehicles had come to a stop far up the road, Tyson's hand hovering near the starter button. Holmes unfolded his legs and rearranged the tripod holding the telescope, pulling the curtains together until they brushed the very edges of his field of vision. He also reached into the Gladstone bag and took out a pistol, surreptitiously laying it beside his leg: He had no reason to believe that Hammett and his bread-truck assistant were on any side but that of the angels, but he had not lived this long by depending on trust. If either man made the slightest move against Russell, he wouldn't hesitate to make a dramatic entrance with engine roaring and gun blazing. He fervently hoped, for many reasons, that it would not come to that.

It took Hammett a quarter of an hour to sidle his way off of the rocks. He stumbled when his feet sank into the sand, then set off, hunched against the cold, staggering with the soft surface and his own exhaustion. His hair was awry and his light grey suit had suffered from the treatment, and he looked a far cry from the dapper man Holmes had met.

At the bread truck, Hammett accepted his hat and a flask from the driver, propping his back against the vehicle and ignoring the approaching newcomers. Eyes shut, he took a deep draught from the flask, then another, shuddering slightly in reaction. He handed the flask back to the bow-legged man, then peeled himself off the wall of the truck, wrenching open its cargo door to drop onto the floor where he sat, head bowed and feet resting on the ground, clearly gathering his energies. After a minute, his right arm reached surreptitiously around his back, as if scratching an itch at the belt-line, then he straightened. His hands came up to run through his hair, returning it to a semblance of order, then adjusted his neck-tie, dashed ineffectually at the stained knee of one trouser-leg, and finally shifted to his inner chest pocket to pull out his pouch of Bull Durham.

Hammett's fingers shaped the cigarette with an exaggeration of their normal care, and eventually lifted the object to his tongue to seal it. He was fumbling for his matches when the young blond swell who'd been driving the other car stepped forward and stuck out a hand with a lighter in it.

The lighter was sleek and gold, of a piece with the coat and the car; the blond man was maybe a year or two younger than Hammett himself, but he looked like a kid—family money and no responsibilities will do that for you. But Hammett bent to accept the light and sat there, eyes half shut, for the length of three or four steadying puffs. Then he moved the cigarette to his left hand, pushed his hat-brim up with the forefinger of his right hand, and at last looked up into the face of the tall blonde girl whom his new employer had been watching from the speakeasy on Friday night.

Mary Russell, married to Sherlock Holmes, gave him a smile meant to be reassuring. "That looked a rather dangerous climb."

"Not something I'd do for fun, no."

"So why were you doing it? If you don't mind my asking," she added.

"What's it to you?" he said bluntly, putting the cigarette back to his lips.

After a moment, she said, "I know someone who was killed on that piece of hillside. It was odd, seeing you at the same exact place."

"Yeah, well, as I understand it, there's a number of people that corner's killed. But my company's only interested in two deaths that happened last December. That the same accident as yours?"

"No."

"Then I can't help you."

"What's your company?"

"Mutual of Fresno," he replied, reaching for his wallet and drawing out a business card with a salesman's automatic habit. "Somebody phoned in a tip to say we might've paid death benefits on an empty car. Always a problem, you see, when there's no body."

"I see," she said, looking at the card.

"Well," he said, sucking the last draw from his cigarette and tossing it out onto the sand, "I'm afraid I didn't. Risked my neck and a case of pneumonia for absolutely nothing. And now, if there's nothing more I can do for you, I need a drink and a fire and a pair of dry socks." He stood, tipped his hat, and threaded his long body into the back of the van.

Smooth, thought Holmes admiringly as he studied the scene through the lens. Not once had Hammett given away the presence of the object he had retrieved from the cliffside—even Russell had taken no notice of the man's surreptitious motions as he slid the thing from the back of his belt to the floor of the van.

Holmes would have liked to hear the conversation, but his lip-reading abilities were lamentably rusty, and in any case best suited to closer work. He had only been able to follow scraps of it—almost none of Hammett's words, since the man's face had been in profile much of the time, but what he had perceived of Russell's side of the brief exchange had reassured him oddly.

With his unlikely passenger stowed away, the bow-legged driver raised his own hat a fraction off his scalp, then slammed the cargo door and trotted around to the driver's side. The bread van started with a violent cloud of blue smoke, causing Flo and her young man to back hastily away, but Russell just stood and watched the ve-hicle back-and-fill into a turn before it accelerated up the steep hill north.

The three young people did not immediately climb back into their own vehicle. Instead, there was a discus-sion, during which Flo gestured towards the road ahead, Russell stared at the wake of the bread van, and Donny sat on his running board smoking a cigarette and watching the waves. Eventually, consensus appeared to be reached. Flo straightened and dug something from her pocket, offering it to Russell. At first Holmes thought it was a cigarette, but after Russell had shaken her head and turned away, the other young woman worked at the object for a moment, put something into her mouth, and followed Russell towards the gaudy car. Holmes risked one last glance at Russell's face as she sat down in the back, then swept the machinery away and tugged the curtains down to a crack.

"Mr Tyson, please remain where you are. Slump back into your seat and look bored with your lot in life, and watch the blue motor go past as if it was the most interesting thing that has happened in an hour."

The sound of a starter and an engine catching reached them, then the car was in gear and accelerating onto the road. It roared past, and away, until the beat of waves against the shore was the only sound. Holmes pulled the velvet curtains aside a fraction with one finger to peer out, not entirely certain that Russell wouldn't have chosen to solve the disagreement by staying behind, but the road and the hillside behind it were empty of humanity.

He settled himself onto the green leather, sliding the pistol back into the Gladstone. As he began to unfasten the telescope from its tripod base, he said to the boy, "Now we return to the city."

"That's it?"

"That's it."

Greg Tyson radiated a palpable sense of outrage all the way back to the hotel, clashing gears in a way the big car had never before experienced and taking corners at speeds that made its tyres squeal in protest. His potentially thrilling outing had fizzled into anticlimax like a damp firecracker.

And here he'd thought he had a real Philo Vance in his backseat.

Chapter Sixteen

Sundays were invariably a source of frustration for Holmes: Why was the world so enamoured of its day of rest, rendering itself largely unavailable to a decent, hard-working detective?

This Sunday was no exception. Once the car returned to the hotel and Holmes had paid the disgruntled young driver, it was still only the late afternoon, and long hours stretched out before him. He took the Gladstone to the room and changed his warm tweeds for a more formal City suit, then persuaded the restaurant to serve him a hot dinner despite the hour, but when he had finished it was still daylight outside.

He read the newspapers, pored over the city maps for a while, smoked a pipe and two cigarettes, and finally set out on a circuitous walk to the telegraphist's, on the chance that a reply had come from Watson. But the man was ill pleased at having his Sunday evening interrupted, and told him brusquely that the shop was closed and no, he hadn't had a telegram from Europe that day.

At least it was dark by the time Holmes returned to the hotel.

What was more, the desk man had a message for him from Hammett.

He went out of the hotel and down the street until he came to a public telephone, where he rang the number given. It was picked up by a man who grunted, "Yeah?" In the background he heard the sound of half a dozen male voices in conversation, and the *ting* of glass on glass: a bar.

"Is Mr Hammett there?"

"Yeah," the voice said again, without the rising inflection, and thumped down. In a minute, the thin man's cough could be heard approaching the earpiece.

"That you?" Hammett's voice asked.

"I had a message from you to ring this number."

"You're at the hotel?"

"Down the street from it."

"Good idea. Can you find the place we had a drink at the other day?"

"Yes."

"There's a chop house two blocks up, same side of the street. I'll be there in five minutes."

They both rang off.

In five minutes, Holmes arrived at the small restaurant on Ellis in time to see a plate of chops and grilled tomato set in front of Hammett. The thin man had gone home and changed his stained grey suit for one of a subtle brown check, and looked himself again. His eyes caught Holmes' entrance, but he continued bantering with the pretty waitress, although it seemed to Holmes that the man was so fatigued that the flirtation was little more than habitual motion. Hammett picked up knife and fork with determination, addressing himself to the plate as if eating was just another job to be got through. Holmes waited in growing impatience while the man sawed, chewed, and swallowed, but before long Hammett allowed his utensils to come to a rest on his plate, drained the glass of orange juice he had been drinking, and searched his breast pockets, coming out with a small note-book.

He flipped it open on the table and resumed his knife and fork, working now with a degree less intensity.

"Saw your lady this morning," he said when he had swallowed.

"Yes? Did you have conversation?"

"Just an exchange. She saw me climbing the rocks where the accident took place, asked me if I was having fun. I said no, not really, and gave her some guff about an insurance company investigating a 'fatal' accident that might have been a set-up."

"Did she believe you?"

"Seemed to." Holmes thought this was probably the case: If Russell had been suspicious, she would have asked more questions than she had.

"Why did you wait until today to go down there?"

"I thought I'd get some answers about the car, first, and then snoop around the local garage down there, second. Couldn't do either of those on a Sunday, but the cliff would be there anytime."

"But why did you find it necessary to climb down the cliffs?"

The words were mild enough, but some vestige of anger in Holmes' voice brought Hammett's head up. After a moment, his eyes narrowed. "Wait a minute. You knew I was there today. Did you have me watched?"

"I did not."

"You were there? Where—the old Pierce-Arrow with the velvet curtains, right?"

"Correct."

Holmes waited to see if the man became angry, saw him consider it, then lay it aside with a shrug. "Your business, I guess."

"You didn't answer my question."

"What, about why I climbed around on those cliffs? Because it needed to be done. From up at the top, it looked to me like the waves would push things in behind a couple of those rocks, and it seemed worth a look. I took a piece of wire from the truck and went to see. Or are you asking about whether I'm not too weak to be doing things like that?"

"Clearly you were not. But I mistrust derring-do even more than I mistrust cowardice. With a coward, one at least knows where one stands. With a fool, anything can happen. And most frequently does."

"It's not derring-do, just common sense." Seeing Holmes' sceptical eyebrow, the younger man sighed and picked up his fork, pushing the half-eaten chop around on the plate. "Look, this disease I have, it respects toughness. In the TB ward, it was the ones who babied themselves who died the fastest. The ones who got on with life had the best chance of shaking it. I sleep a lot, but I don't baby myself."

Holmes studied the young man's features, bone-thin but unbending, and his shoulders relaxed.

"I suppose I've been called reckless myself, from time to time. But don't risk your neck again for the sake of my case, you hear? In any event, what have you learnt?"

"I guess your wife's father was something of a nut about cars," Hammett said, his irritation fading as his attention returned to the plate. "The Maxwell dealer remembers him well, one of his first and best customers. Seems Russell bought a new car every year from 1908 until this one that killed them, which he picked up about two weeks before the war broke out in Europe—middle of July 1914. The owner seemed to think Russell might even have intended to ship this one out to Boston, where his family was going after he enlisted."

"Not to England?"

"Said Boston, because England might not be the safest place for a while. Looking back, I'd say your father-in-law was a clever man."

It was true: In the summer of 1914, most of the world had thought the war would be over by Christmas, and most men would not have hesitated to send an English wife home to her family.

The waitress decided that her customer had eaten as much of his dinner as he was going to, and without being asked she set two thick white mugs of coffee on the table, removing the half-eaten dinner with a shake of her head. Hammett wiped his fingers on his table napkin, took a swallow of the coffee, and picked up something from the seat of the chair beside him, laying it on the table between them.

"You know what this is?" he asked.

"This" was a pair of bent and rusted steel rods, although it did not take a very close examination to see that they had originally been two parts of a still-longer whole. The longer of these two sections, about eighteen inches from the still-attached ball joint to its broken end, was pitted from long exposure to the elements; grains of sand still nestled in the rough surface. Holmes fingered its uneven end: not merely broken, but half sawed through, then twisted hard to shattering.

The other piece was slightly shorter, just over a foot long, and although it, too, was rusted, its lack of pitting and sand indicated that it had spent its life in a slightly more protected environment. One end was a twin with that of the longer piece—half sawed, half wrenched apart. Its other end, however, was neatly, and freshly, sawed through.

Hammett gestured at the tidy end of the shorter piece. "I didn't think we really needed to haul the whole thing around, so I just cut off the hunk we needed. Seemed to me the two ends said it all."

Holmes laid the two pieces of rod on the table, the broken end of the rusted one resting against the broken end of the cleaner.

"I have long feared it might be something of this order. Yes, Mr Hammett, I know what this is. I spent some time as a garage mechanic in Chicago, just before the war broke out. A little case for His Majesty. That's a brake rod, or rather the better half of a brake rod, and I agree, you were right to cut it off—as far as evidence is concerned, there's no need to drag around a piece of steel half the length of a motorcar. Which side of the motor was it from?"

"The left."

"So whoever did it knew they would be travelling south on that road."

"I . . . Yes, I suppose they would have."

"No supposition involved. Failure of the left-side brake rod under pressure would cause the motor to swerve to the right, and with that hill-top turn it didn't even require an on-coming motor to break the rod." Russell's father would have braked hard at that spot in any event—without the other motor, without two squabbling children in the back. Mary Russell's disagreeable behaviour had nothing to do with it.

"Whoever did it was clever," Hammett agreed. "And according to my guy, if it'd been cut all the way through, your Mr Russell would never have made it as far as the top of that hill without crashing."

"Although I'd have thought he'd had to have been a remarkably cautious man to drive all the way from San Francisco with brakes in that condition."

Hammett's starved-looking face relaxed into a satisfied grin. "They stopped for lunch in Serra Beach. That little town about a mile before the hill."

"Parking the motor out of sight?"

"Actually, he left the car at the garage while they ate, to be filled up and to have a slow leak in one tyre repaired. The man took the wheel off and fixed it, and once I'd jogged his memory it all came back to him, because when he'd first heard about the accident, the day it happened, he'd been scared to death—thought maybe he'd failed to tighten the rim bolts enough. He even went out to see, and was hugely relieved to see the burnt-out shell, turned turtle, with all four wheels safely in place."

"And this cleaner half of the brake rod was in his possession?" Holmes nudged the stub with one finger.

"Yeah. A week or so after the accident, he and his older brother, who ran the garage, took a pair of draught horses up and hauled the wreck off the rocks. Because it had landed upside-down, the fire had just erupted into open air—*poof,* hot and fast and it's over— and his older brother thought they might be able to salvage some of the engine parts. Which, as it happened, was true. The chassis is still around the back of the garage, the bones of it, and pretty thoroughly picked over. The brother, by the way, died in a racing-car crash, the summer of 1920."

"The man doesn't remember anyone interfering with the machine, while it waited?"

"Nope. Wheel off, patch it up, wheel on, then fill 'er up and shift the car around to the side."

"Was it common practice, for the Russell family to pause there on their way south?"

"I don't know, but it would've made sense to stop there halfway along, let the kiddies stretch their legs."

"A thing anyone might have anticipated."

"Yeah." Hammett's eyes came down to the twisted lengths of rod, and he shook his head. "Killing a woman and a kid in that way. I'd sure like to help you solve this case."

Until the man had come up with these two lengths of rusted steel, Holmes thought, there hadn't been a case to solve. He owed him a great deal, already. Too, he could not see that a man working for the other side would have given him the only hard evidence the case had yet generated. This new lieutenant of his threatened to have as much independence as Russell, and he lacked the physical stamina of Russell or Watson, but Holmes found himself warming to the man. He'd trust him a little further.

"Do you have any reliable contacts among the police?"

Hammett laughed. "You haven't been here long enough to hear about our cops. They're the best money can buy."

"I see. Any you can trust to take your money and not sell you as well?"

"One or two. What do you want?"

Holmes took out his bill-fold and removed a piece of paper with some writing on it, putting it in front of Hammett. "I'd like to know a little more about these three men. Charles Russell was my wife's father, killed in that accident. That's his home address, and I think he had an office in the Flood Building. I picked up a rumour that he was involved in some what you might call 'shady' activity during the fire in 1906, thought it would be good to make sure he was clean."

"What sort of deal?"

"That's all I know."

"Okay, I'll see what I can come up with."

"The other two, it's just to be certain that the help they offer is not in fact a hindrance. The first, Auberon, is the manager at the St Francis; I don't know his Christian name or his home address. The last is a Chinese bookseller who goes by the name of Tom Long; his Chinese name could be almost anything. The address is for his store, just off Grant in Chinatown."

"Auberon and Long, got you."

"Shall we meet here tomorrow night, at say, eight o'clock?"

"That's fine."

"And Hammett? Don't try to do anything else tonight. Get some sleep."

"Right you are," he said. He put some money down next to his mug, waved two fingers at the waitress, put on his hat at a rakish angle, and walked off into the fog of the evening, shambling bones in a dapper brown suit.

With the satisfaction of two lengths of old steel rod nestled in the sock-drawer across the room, Holmes slept the sleep of the just.

He was up early on Monday morning, fed and brushed and out of the hotel before eight o'clock, taking the lengths of brake rod with him. He found a photographer's studio nearby, where he left Miss Adderley's picture with instructions. When he left the shop, he walked a route sure to reveal anyone on his tail, but he reached the telegraphist's office without detecting anyone. The man, rather curtly, told him that he'd barely opened his doors and that nothing had come in, try again later. So Holmes went looking for a bank.

When he found one that was open, he went in and hired a safe-deposit box, giving the name "Jack Watson." Into the box he put his evidence. It probably would have been perfectly safe lodged with Mr Auberon, but one did not place more weight on a reed than one knew it would bear, and Mr Auberon was as yet unproved.

Next, after consulting his mental street map, he located the street-car that ran to the end of the city, to the Cliff House and Sutro Baths. There he got off, walking south in the direction of the beach where he and Russell had strolled at sunset on Tuesday. This time, he was interested less in the beach than the place where the bookseller's father had saved the rabbi's daughter from drowning.

The cliff on which the restaurant perched rose sharply out of the sand, with a scattering of boulders to mark the transition and a sharp tangle of white-capped rocks scattered off-shore, sunning spots for sea-birds and bellowing sea-lions. Down the beach children played in the sand; two boys flew bright kites out over the water. Holmes climbed onto a rock and took out his pipe. It was indeed a vicious spot to be taken unawares by the sea. The waves rose fast into their long, white curls to break hard against the black cliffs; every so often one would show extra vigour and reach wet tendrils around the base of the rock where he sat. He could well imagine, come the winter, that these waves would be killers.

When the pipe had gone cold, Holmes knocked it out on the rocks and retraced his steps, presenting himself at the telegraphist's door just after noon. This time, the man glared at him, but slapped two envelopes down on the counter as well.

"You know," he remarked sourly, "it's much easier on everyone if you just let the boy bring it to you."

To appease him, Holmes counted out the tip the boy would have got, not in the least expecting that it would be passed on to its intended recipient. Mollified, the man pushed the envelopes over, and Holmes left the shop.

Three doors down, the smell of cooking pulled him in. He ordered more or less at random, wanting a quiet table more than he did a meal. When eventually it was granted him, he took a swallow of the coffee (which was typically American: scalding, pallid, and apparently compulsory) and pulled out the thicker of the two flimsy envelopes, running a thumb through the seal. It was from Watson, in Marseilles, probably the longest telegram the good doctor had ever had to pay for:

FOUND YOUR PURSER BUT LETTER OF REPRIMAND
FROM THE COMPANY FOR DELAYING DEPARTURE
FOLLOWS. POSSIBLE FINE. SAVANNAH WOMAN
LILLY MONTERA BOARDED IN PORT SAID AND
JOINED WITH A BAND OF ENTERTAINERS BOUND
FOR CALCUTTA FROM LONDON VIA BOMBAY.

PURSER NOT CERTAIN BUT THOUGHT HER
ARRIVAL WAS UNEXPECTED. MONTERA UNWELL
THOUGH GOOD APPETITE THROUGH SUEZ CANAL
AND DEAD SEA AND KEPT TO HER ROOM
DISEMBARKING SUDDENLY IN ADEN. PURSER
REMEMBERS HER QUESTIONS CONCERNING YOU
BOTH REPEAT BOTH AND YES SHE KNEW YOUR
TICKETS WERE FOR CONTINUED EAST INCLUDING
CALIFORNIA. NO TRAVEL ARRANGEMENTS MADE
BEFORE ADEN BUT SHE ASKED ABOUT OTHER
SHIPS EAST AND POSSIBLE AEROPLANES.
DESCRIPTION TALL FULL FIGURED LIGHT BROWN
HAIR BROWN EYES PROBABLY WEAK VISION
WEARING DARK GLASSES AND AVOIDING BRIGHT
LIGHT ALSO WEARING ENTERTAINERS POWDER
AND ROUGE. OCCASIONALLY SHARED CABIN WITH
NEW YORK BAND TRUMPETER FERDIE KNOLL HOPE
YOU DON'T KNOW THIS WOMAN HOLMES.
ANYTHING ELSE I CAN DO QUERY. WATSON.

On his third time reading the words, Holmes became
aware that he was halfway finished with a bowl of unexpectedly acceptable fish chowder. He ate it more slowly,
absorbing the information.

It was not as complete as he or Russell would have
come up with, but it was enough, and it was certainly
every bit as timely as he could have wished. And clearly,
Watson had been forced to lay down every bit of authority he could muster to keep from being thrown off so
the ship could get under way. Good old Watson.

He pulled open the other, briefer telegram.

COULD FIND NO PERSON MAKING ENQUIRIES RE
HOLMES RUSSELL IN SUSSEX OR LONDON SORRY.

COULD IT HAVE BEEN THE LETTER TO THE TIMES
REGARDING YOUR STUNT WITH THE KENT TRAIN
QUERY. IN CASE YOU MISSED THAT ISSUE OF
JANUARY FIVE A READER NOTED THAT JANUARY
FOUR ARTICLE OF THE STOPPED TRAIN
NEGLECTED TO SAY THAT THE STOPPER LOOKED
REMARKABLY LIKE ONE MR HOLMES. THE WAGES
OF FAME. MYCROFT.

Holmes sat with the spoon suspended, considering
the implications. He had seen the newspaper for the
fourth of January, which did, as Mycroft said, contain a
small piece about the train he and Russell had been
forced to catch at an unscheduled stop in the snow-
covered wilds of Kent. He had not seen that of the following day, as by that time they were out to sea and the
papers themselves became so sporadic and delayed as to
be superfluous. Plus, he'd been otherwise occupied.

And Mycroft had not, of course, thought to take the
question a step further, since Holmes had not let his
brother know what the problem was. Another telegram
would be required.

It did, however, solve one knotty part of the problem,
he thought as he broke a slice of chewy bread into pieces:
that of the very beginning. Their trip to India had been
sudden and unexpected: If the Savannah woman—"Lilly
Montera" had to be a pseudonym—had been on their
ship, it was due either to coincidence or deliberation. If
coincidence, Holmes could live with that: Heaven knew
he had made enough enemies over the years to stumble
across one with some regularity. But if her presence had
been deliberate, an entire Pandora's box of problems
opened up, for it could only indicate that she knew
everything about their movements in England, almost

before they themselves did. That degree of intelligence coupled with the almost instantaneous planting of an operative on board the very ship they were joining would have indicated an enormously, even frighteningly, sophisticated operation.

On the other hand, the woman had openly questioned the young American Bolshevik, Thomas Goodheart, about the older man he had befriended on board the ship. In addition, if indeed the collapse of a balcony on their heads in the Aden bazaar had been purposeful and not an accident, it was hardly sophisticated. Clever, perhaps, and very nearly effective, but a group who had been given time to plan could have arranged for a sniper on a hillside or a bomb in a cabin or any of a hundred other deadly ambushes.

Coincidence, or deliberate? Watson's information could easily lead to the first conclusion: an old foe who boarded the ship, happened to spot Holmes before he saw her, and spent the rest of the voyage hiding in her cabin, leaving the ship at the first possible opportunity—though not without first making an attempt at murder-by-balcony. If that was right, the spectre of an organisation of considerable size and expertise receded considerably.

Mycroft's news, however, rather complicated the issue, introducing the remote possibility that a person had seen the name Sherlock Holmes in the *Times* Saturday morning, then spent the next three days (and considerable resources) racing to Port Said before the boat put in there. It would have been very difficult, but possible.

However, no matter if she came to be there by coincidence or talent, once on board the "Montera" woman had enquired specifically about them, and knew that

California was in their plans. Putting aside for the moment the question of how she came to be there, he would work under the hypothesis that, once aboard, her enquiries had not been the sign of some casual and self-effacing acquaintance, but purposeful. And as a corollary thesis, that she had come before them to California, awaiting their arrival, where she intended to take action.

He had a great deal to do before Russell returned Wednesday.

Not the least of which was to decide which of his two potential allies, Hammett or Long, he could trust the furthest.

He retraced his steps to the telegraphist, and wrote out a second telegram to Mycroft:

HIGHLY URGENT NEED KNOW IF WOMAN
ARRANGED EMERGENCY TRANSPORT TO PORT
SAID JANUARY SIX SEVEN OR EIGHT. HOPE YOU'RE
WELL. SHERLOCK.

He hesitated over that last, unwonted burst of sentiment, but allowed it to stand. He did, actually, hope that his brother was well.

Outside the telegraphist's office, he pulled out his watch. Just gone two o'clock, which gave him six hours before meeting Hammett. He took a bus down to the hotel and found two messages waiting for him. One was from the hospital where Russell had gone Friday, with the information that Leah Ginzberg had died on January 26, 1915, and that the investigating officer had been one James Roley. He started to pocket it, thinking to give it to Hammett that evening, then stopped and copied the information instead, leaving the original on Russell's dressing-table. The other was a list of four names written in a hand so spidery and feminine he did not need the embossed address at the top of the paper to know it had come from Hermione Adderley.

This one he did pocket, then spent the rest of a frustrating afternoon trying to chase down the four individuals.

Shortly after eight o'clock, Holmes walked wearily into the Ellis Street grill to find Hammett looking even wearier, a half-full bottle on the table before him. Holmes accepted a glass of the raw whiskey without comment, and allowed the fire to warm his bones for a few minutes. When the waitress came to their table, Hammett ordered, and Holmes told her he'd have the same, although he couldn't have said what it was the man had ordered. Hammett sat back with his second drink, lit a cigarette, and exhaled.

"You look like your day's been as lucky as mine," he told Holmes.

"What universal law, I wonder, determines that all potential witnesses be either missing, amnesiac, or comprehensively stupid?" Holmes reflected. "The retired milkman is off visiting his sister in San Jose; one of the Russells' old neighbours took an hour to decide that the 'nice Jewish girl' he remembered was not actually Judith Russell but one of the good-time girls who moved into the park in early May; another of the neighbours insisted that I was a 'Fuller Brush Man' and chased me down the street with a broom he had bought which had fallen apart, only stopping when his daughter caught up with him and told me that he'd been fixed against broom salesmen ever since his wife ran off with one in 1903; and the rabbi of the synagogue Judith Russell attended is a young man who will have to consult with the elders before he submits any names for my attention.

The only thing I have accomplished of even marginal import all afternoon has been to arrange for a chimney sweep, so that one corner of the house might be inhabited without risk of a conflagration."

Hammett was grinning like a greyhound. "The fast life of a private dick—ain't it great?"

"I hope to heaven that the stories you write don't glamorise the job as much as Watson's did. He was generally so occupied with his practice or his wife, he had no idea how many hours I put in while he wasn't there to see."

"Nah, my stuff's a little harder edged than his. But you know, when you're putting together a story, sometimes you just have to skip over the boring bits."

"I suppose necessity must. In any case, Hammett, what have you to show for the day?"

"Not a heck of a lot more than you." Their food arrived as he was taking his note-book from his pocket, but he unfolded it on the table and reported in between bites. "The paper the Southern lady used is a bust, just too common to trace. Spent a couple hours on that, and decided it was a waste of my time and your greenbacks. I'll keep going if you want, but—"

"Let's abandon the lady's note-paper for now," Holmes said. The chops on his plate were more mutton than lamb, but nicely grilled and he was hungry. Hammett went on.

"The rest of the day I spent with the cops. They've got nothing at all on your Chinese friend. You knew his parents were found murdered at that same address you gave me? It's still on the books, more or less—not exactly near the top of the pile. They did question him, but he said he was at school—training as a doctor, back in Chicago— and as soon as they got confirmation of that, he was cleared. The only funny thing in the file was, someone wondered how two Chinese servants could afford to buy a three-storey building in Chinatown. There wasn't a follow-up to that, probably decided the old folks ran an opium den on the side or something. Might be something to look into."

"There's nothing there," Holmes reassured him. "What about the others?"

Hammett's fork and knife paused while he studied the older man, then he shrugged. "If you say so. Auberon's name is Howard, he's got one charge of running a card game back when he was a teenager, but nothing since then."

"Wait a minute, he must be in his late forties now. I thought all the records burnt in 1906?"

"Police records were saved, though they're in a hell of a mess. It was the City Hall stuff that went—births, property rights, you name it. If you own a house, you might have God's own time proving it, but an ancient arrest for drunkenness will follow along like a stink on your shoe. Anyway, talk is that your boy on the desk doesn't run anything too organised, but like any desk man, he can get you anything from a bottle to a companion, for the right bill."

Auberon, then, was about as clean as could be expected.

"And as for your wife's old man, he was a positive paragon of virtue. He came from money, but then you'd know that. Picked up once when some of the boys he was with had a little too much to drink, broke some windows, that kind of thing. He spent the night in the jug, paid for the repairs, stayed clean after, at least in San Francisco."

"When would this have been?"

"Oh, let's see. Yeah, here it is, 1891."

Charles Russell would have been twenty-three years old, and fresh out of university; four years later he'd gone to Europe, there to meet and marry Judith Klein. "Did you get the names of his companions in drunkenness?"

By way of answer, Hammett reached for his notebook, tore out a page, and slid it across to Holmes:

Thomas Octavio Hodges (San Francisco)
Martin Sullivan (San Francisco)
Robert Greenfield (New York)
Laurence Goldberg (New York)
Calvin Francis O'Malley (San Francisco)

Holmes studied the names: The only one he might identify was that of Robert Greenfield, who could be the father of Russell's childhood friend Flo. "You know any of these men?"

"No, I only got the list about an hour ago. You want me to find out about them?"

"Let's leave that on our list of Things To Do. Before that, however, we need to look into this one." He took from his pocket the piece of paper he'd copied at the hotel. "This woman was killed two weeks before the Longs were. That address is her home and her office as well. She was a psychiatrist. She was treating my wife."

Hammett's eyes came up from the scrap of paper, meeting those of Holmes. "Your wife's doctor, your wife's family servants, your wife's parents. The same wife who got herself shot at the other day."

"I want this settled before she gets back into town the

day after tomorrow." The grey eyes had gone cold and hard.

After a minute, Hammett looked away, and folded the page with the name into his note-book.

"Then I guess we'd better get to work."

BOOK THREE

Russell

Chapter Seventeen

I stood on the roadway that bright and blustery Sunday morning, inches away from the continent's edge, and looked at the rocks that had taken my family. In ten years, some things had changed; others were the same. The guard-rail had been repaired, for example, but the outline of the rocks against the sea—were I to walk over to a spot fifteen feet from Donny's front head-lamp, drop to the ground, and turn my head due west, the jagged shapes would match precisely those seared onto my brain. I had been thrown from the motor's backseat onto that place on the rough-graded roadway; the brother with whom I had been arguing, the father who had turned from the wheel in irritation, the mother who had sat sharply forward, her hand on the dash-board and her mouth open to cry a warning—all three of the motorcar's other passengers had remained where they were. I alone had shot out over the side and hit the road, hard and broken, and only chance had determined that I came to rest with my face pointing towards the sea. My stunned eyes had been open to receive the impression of the motorcar dropping out of existence, had stayed open to witness the rotund flare of exploding petrol, had remained open and passively staring as the other, on-coming motor swerved and slithered to a halt before disgorging one pair of legs, then another. One set of feet had hurried to where I lay, accompanied by unintelligible squawks of sound; the other went to the shattered guard-rail for a moment, only to retreat rapidly from the cloud of oily smoke roaring up the rocks.

As the second pair of shoes came towards me, my eyes had drifted shut.

I had been fighting noisily with my brother, as my father's brand-new Maxwell motorcar had climbed the hill; I had distracted my father at a crucial moment, a fatal moment. I had killed my family, and survived, and in ten years, I had told only two people of my rôle in the disaster: Dr Ginzberg and, five years later, Holmes. She had soothed me, a temporary solution; Holmes had given me an emotional safe-box in which I could lock the knowledge, knowing its shape but no longer consumed by it.

Had I been told that I must return to this place, my first act setting foot in San Francisco would have been to hire a lorry-load of dynamite to blow the entire cliffside into the sea. I still was not certain how I had ended up here, staring at the great grey Pacific. Something Holmes had said, or rather the way he had said it, had made it seem not only necessary, but essential.

"Mary?" Flo's voice made me think she'd said my

name more than a couple of times, for it sounded worried, and was accompanied by a hand on my arm. She'd been hovering near me, I realised, ever since we'd left the motor. "Mary, do you want to go now? I don't think we need—"

"No, I'm fine," I told her. I blinked, and the past retreated a fraction. I was on the piece of ground I hated most in all the universe, ground I should gladly have consigned to the waves below, but it was also merely a piece of precipitous roadway built far too close to the edge of the world.

There was another motor there, as well, I noticed. Some sort of baker's van, although the bow-legged man standing across the roadway from it looked nothing like a baker. As I walked up to him, my first impression was confirmed: Grease, not flour, lay in his finger-nails, boots, and pores. And although he wore a cap, he also held in his hands a grey soft hat, turning it round and round in his blunt, blackened fingers. I stopped at the edge of the cliff near the baker's mechanic (Sunday, my mind processed automatically: no bread deliveries, good day to borrow the van) and looked out across the sea, the expanse of green merging into grey-blue with specks of white here and there, and a trace of mist lingering over the horizon. Then I looked down.

A man was working his way along the rocks, a dozen feet above the waves. His head was bare, a shock of greying red hair blowing about in the wind, the brightest object in sight against the dark grey of his overcoat and darker grey of the wet boulders below. His sideways progress was purposeful, undelayed by any consideration but the safest place for his hands and feet. Whatever he'd climbed down after, he'd either already found it, or decided it was lost. I did not even entertain the possibility that he was there for sport, a dare, or drunken whim: A man his age did not launch himself into danger for no good reason. And his companion, the mechanic with the grey hat in his hand, showed even less sign of intoxication than the man picking his deliberate way along the hazardous surface.

I raised my voice against the stiff wind. "What has he lost?"

The man looked up, startled, although I could not tell if his surprise was at my words or at my unexpected presence breaking into his intent concentration. "What?" he asked, half shouting.

"Your friend, what has he lost down there?"

The mechanic shook his head and returned his gaze to the cliff-side. "I don't know. And he ain't a friend, just some guy paid me to drive him out here. Insurance, he said. Didn't think he'd be pulling a stunt like this." He shook his head again and began muttering; I moved closer to hear his words. "Hands me his hat and down he goes. Didn't even have a rope in case he falls, and seeing the kind of shape he's in, it wouldn't surprise me a bit if he did fall, damned fool, and what'll I tell the wife if I let the guy kill himself down there? Shoulda said no, call yourself a taxi, shoulda." His voice drifted off and his eyes remained locked on the man who'd hired him, as if the strength of his gaze might be all that held the climber to the cliff face.

In a few minutes, the man below had crept around the worst of the boulders, and appeared to have a straight, if laborious, scramble to the sandy beach. The mechanic stirred and slapped the felt hat against his leg, his back straightening with the beginnings of relief.

"Well, I'll go down and pick him up. Oughta charge him extra for the years he's taken off me."

I stood at the cliff's edge for a moment longer, then turned away and said to Flo, "Shall we go down there, too, and see what on earth that man was doing?"

I climbed inside the car expectantly, giving them little chance to argue. Donny held Flo's elbow across the uneven ground, as her ankle-strap sandals were more suited to urban pavements; her right hand remained firmly clamped to her hat.

At the bottom of the hill Donny pulled into the lay-by near the bread van, and we got out to wait beside its driver. The climber emerged from the rocks, stumbling in exhaustion as he came up the beach. I revised my estimate of his age, and his condition, downward. His hair was thick and its grey premature—he wasn't much older than Donny. But as the mechanic had said, this was not a well man, in no condition, I'd have said, to go clambering around dangerous rocks for a lost article. When he'd dropped heavily onto the floor of the van and put together a cigarette with shaking fingers, Donny reached around me to light it for him— less a gesture of good manners perhaps than for fear the man would set his coat alight if he tried to manipulate a match. The man accepted it, and after a moment's silent appreciation, raised his eyes to give me a look that was oddly appraising, as if we'd met sometime before. I was sure we hadn't, however—I'd have remembered that face.

"That looked a rather dangerous climb," I said mildly, by way of breaking the ice.

"Not something I'd do for fun," he said dismissively.

So the gentleman did not care for amusing repartee;

very well, I too would be blunt. "So why were you doing it? If you don't mind my asking."

He was not interested in giving out any information, but I had often found that by handing over a revelation of my own it served to, as it were, prime the pump.

So I told him that someone I knew had died there, and with that his words began to flow.

It seemed that he was an insurance investigator looking into a death claim that might have been faked. It also seemed that this corner was infamous as a killer of motorcars.

Indeed.

He finished his cigarette, and by the looks of it the driver's flask, then with a tip of the grey fedora he climbed into the back of the van. The other man slammed the door behind him and hurried around to the driver's side; in moments he had the van turned around and headed back north.

Flo held out a packet of something in my direction. "You want a piece of chewing gum, Mary?"

"Thanks, no," I said, and she helped herself, folding the stick into her pretty mouth. "Well, can we go now? It's too windy to smoke and I'm freezing to death standing here."

"I was thinking we might go back to Serra Beach and have a drink or something."

"Back? Mary, we're running late as it is. And it's a pig to drive a strange road in the dark. Wouldn't you say, Donny?"

"Oh, it's not so bad," he said, but we could both hear the doubt in his voice. "If it's a jolt you want, I've got my flask."

Body-temperature gin was not what I needed at the moment. "As I said, I'm happy to take over the driving,"

I told him, but was not much surprised when I received the same response I'd got when I'd made the offer out in front of the St Francis: a polite and disbelieving smile. Clearly to Donny's mind, "girls" didn't drive unless there wasn't a man around to do that job.

The van had reached the tight curve at the top of the hill, and disappeared around it. My thoughts followed it for a few moments, but I decided that yes, the episode had been slightly odd, but it could hardly be judged as ominous: As coincidences go, this one was scarcely worth noting.

"Okay," I told my companions, resigning myself to the backseat again. "Let's keep going."

Flo bundled herself back into her fur rug as Donny worked the starter and put the powerful car into gear. Another motor was parked at the far end of the little beach, I noticed as we drove past; a closed Pierce-Arrow, about as far from Donny's blue monster as could be imagined, with a bored-looking driver and half-shut curtains in the passenger compartment: old lady come to the beach for a Sunday drive, I diagnosed. No more ominous than finding a Fresno insurance agent hiring a local mechanic with a temporarily unemployed bread-delivery truck. I was, I realised, looking for something—anything—to distract me from the empty sensation that had been growing since we had left San Francisco.

And even before that—what else would explain my having asked two perfect strangers to accompany me to the Lodge? When I'd telephoned to Flo the previous morning, I had only meant to tell her that I wouldn't be joining the Monday party she'd talked about, but in the process of telling her where I was going, I'd somehow ended up inviting her. And then she suggested that

Donny could drive us, and—I'd had qualms the instant I hung up the earpiece.

I told myself that, if their presence became too much of a strain, I could as easily send them back and hire a car to take me when I was ready.

I did not know why the death of Dr Ginzberg was hitting me as hard as it was. Yes, the woman had been an important influence at a vulnerable time in my life, but that was ten years past, and during that time weeks, even months might go by without my so much as thinking of her. Still, hitting me it was.

Looking back over the previous two days, I had to be grateful to Holmes for having pulled me out of Friday's deep funk, first by dumping me into a hot bath and then force-feeding me tea and conversation.

However, there is a drawback to allowing Holmes to involve himself in a project, particularly when he is bored to begin with—for example, following a long and tedious ocean crossing: The machinery of his mind cannot bear to run without engaging, so that he tends to adopt hobbyhorses.

Even before my emotional collapse on Friday, the minor conundra surrounding the house and the death of my parents had shown every sign of becoming his latest project, into which he had thrown himself with all the intensity that he would have given to a crucial case of international relations. There was no point whatsoever in telling him that the mystery of the house-breaking was of less import to me than the eternal mystery of why a woman cannot buy a pair of shoes that fit: His teeth had seized the bit, and he would run with his chosen investigation until it was either solved or had reached an insoluble dead-end.

It was, at times, trying, to live with a man constitutionally incapable of relaxation. Despite the emptiness within, I was more than a little relieved to get away from him for a couple of days.

Then it occurred to me, a mile or so south of where we had met the insurance man, that my embarrassing display of weakness on Friday might possibly have unexpected benefits, in setting Holmes another problem at which to worry. Dr Ginzberg's nine-year-old murder might not be of a complexity worthy of Holmes' efforts, but it was a case I would like to see solved, if he could do so in the few days left to us here. And if it turned his attentions away from the pointless and uncomfortable mysteries of the house and my past, so much the better. He hadn't seemed terribly interested in it this morning, headed to the ferry on one of his odd scholarly pursuits, but in any event, it would be difficult to ferret out any official sources of information before Monday.

I smiled: Sundays were often a vexation of spirit to Holmes.

My companion in the front seat must have been keeping a surreptitious eye on me and seen a degree of relaxation on my features, because my distant thoughts were interrupted by a solicitous question directed at me.

"Feeling a bit warmer, Mary?"

"Sorry? Oh, yes, I'm fine. It's very beautiful, isn't it?"

Satisfied, either with my answer or that I could make one, Flo gave me a smile meant to be encouraging and left me to my thoughts.

Watching the back of her glossy black hair dancing in the breeze, I realised that I liked her, and her friends, more than I had expected.

Our beginnings on Friday had not been auspicious: Flo Greenfield and her entourage were late. I was in the lobby by nine, more than ready to put the day's shocks behind me; by nine-thirty, I was pacing and considering a return upstairs. Three minutes later, gathering myself up to go, I became aware of a riot approaching rapidly down the street, a cacophony of horns and shouts. The Rolls-Royce that squealed to a halt before the doors was the colour of a cloudless sky in June, and throbbed with power from within its elegant bonnet. As the man behind the wheel attempted to perform the contortionist manoeuvre of threading himself out from behind wheel, brake, and shift levers, the passenger by-passed the entire issue of male chivalry by flinging open her door before either driver or hotel staff could reach it. A slim figure in a dress that complemented the colour of the motor stepped unescorted onto the pavement, and I realised belatedly that Flo had arrived.

She was dressed in a costume every bit as extreme as that in which she'd come home the previous morning, although this one was still in good repair. Tonight's frock was silver with a spray of beads the precise blue of the motorcar, a brief lamé frock that clung and outlined a body patently unencumbered with a surfeit of undergarments. Her hair clung to her head with careful spit-curls in the height of fashion, her cheeks and lips were redder than Nature had granted, and her legs glistened with silk. Around her right wrist clustered a mass of silver and turquoise beads that I thought had been originally intended as a long necklace, now twisted over and over her hand to form a thick bracelet. Around her sleek hair she wore a silver bandeau, from which rose a bright blue ostrich plume, and her light fox-fur coat was spilling negligently from her near-bare shoulders.

She looked gloriously young and beautiful and light-hearted and *fun,* and my spirits lifted the instant I laid eyes on her.

The motor contained at least six other people, although it might have been ten or eleven. As I allowed myself to be inserted into the front, ending up on the lap of a young man who told me to call him "Dabs," Flo waved a genial hand towards me, shouted my name at the passengers in the backseat by way of introduction, and wedged herself in beside me. The throbbing engine roared into life and we spun into the oncoming traffic.

The driver, according to Flo's running commentary, was called Donny. He was a tall, elegant figure with slick blond hair parted down the centre as if he'd invented the style, a pencil-thin moustache a shade darker than the hair on his head, a warm and humorous voice, and an immaculate tuxedo. He appeared to be something of a beau, although Flo bestowed her affections equally on the young man beneath me, on the gentlemen in the back, and on the occupants of several passing motorcars as well, blowing kisses and giggling flirtatiously at their shouted remarks.

I was coming to regret the evening long before we pulled up in front of the club. It was not in a salubrious part of town, and did not at all appear the sort of place that justified the degree of fashion we were wearing: Across the street was a warehouse, and next to that the sort of speakeasy for which bath-tub gin had been invented. The building Donny parked before was something of a warehouse itself, ill-lit, in want of paint, and with boards nailed over its few windows. There were attendants, however, one of whom hopped into the motor and drove it away while another pulled open the door, greeting some of our party by name.

Inside lay a gilded cavern with some sort of Oriental theme to it, rich colours and a surfeit of patterns. When we had been shown to a table near the band and had our drinks placed before us, I looked around and realised that the theme was intended to be that of an opium den. A highly romanticised version of an opium den—I doubted any of the patrons of the establishments I had been inside would recognise any similarity. Instead of a filthy, claustrophobic room littered with equally filthy and near-comatose individuals, this glittering palace was bursting with more energy than a classroom full of eleven-year-old boys. The only thing I could see that was at all similar was the thick fug in the air, although this had the smell mostly of tobacco instead of the cloy of opium.

Mostly, I say. There was also cannabis in the air, and the smell of illegal spirits, served openly and without apology. I accepted the glass of champagne handed me, and could only hope that there was not a raid of the premises.

Now, in the normal course of events, I have no great appreciation for a raucous setting and great lashings of alcohol, but the course of events that week had been nothing like normal. The alcohol went down smoothly, the conversation seemed more witty than I'd have expected, the entertainment more stylish, the dancing feverish but physically satisfying—all in all, it buoyed my spirits beyond measure.

When we first got there, a band was playing some tune with a syncopated beat that my companions seemed to know, for two or three of them sang snatches of words in between swallows of their first drinks. With the next number, several of my companions got up to dance, and shortly after that, the band took a short break, to return with a fanfare and the announcement of the singer.

"Ladies and gentlemen," the band-leader purred to the crowd, "the Blue Tiger is just thrilled to present, fresh from her triumphal tour of Paris, Berlin, and New York, our own home-town girl…Miss Belinda Birdsong!"

The singer with the unlikely name appeared in a sudden burst of spotlight, dressed in a shimmer of white, head bowed; the hall erupted in applause, cat-calls, hoots, and intoxicated laughter. It was evident that Miss Birdsong was well known here. And as soon as she opened her mouth to sing and the sound died down a bit, it became clear why.

She was a Personality, in the tradition of Lily Langtry and the like who had come to the city through the dance-halls and cabarets of the West. Pretty if not beautiful, saucy yet preserving an air of innocence, Miss Birdsong had the crowded hall wrapped around her nicely manicured little finger. And I had to laugh myself, when I recognised her first song—I'd heard just that tune coming from a peculiar dive in Delhi some weeks before, a 'Nineties ditty about a bird in a golden cage.

It was apparently her trademark song, because the patrons made no attempt to dance to it, even those already out on the dance-floor. Instead, they hung on her every syllable and note. When it ended, a wave of cheers arose that put the earlier cacophony in the shade; when that finally died away, the singer started another song, and this time, the couples on the floor started to move.

I knew none of the modern dances and would have sat most of them out, but Flo would not permit it, and demanded that Donny pull me out onto the floor. That night I learnt the ridiculously satisfying moves of the Charleston, as well as several variations, and between the various males in our party, and later from adjoining tables, I spent a respectable time gyrating beneath the lights. It is a dance of unbridled energy, making it impossible to feel anything but strong and filled with the invulnerability of youth. It was breathless and pointless and fun, and the thirsty work of it made the champagne flow. In time, another singer took Miss Birdsong's place, a rather raw-boned female with an uncertain voice and a practiced line in raunchy jokes, but then the local heroine returned, wearing scarlet sequins this time, and saw out the rest of the night.

I was, truth to tell, disappointed to call the evening to an end. Donny drove us all (or mostly all—I thought we numbered fewer than we had, and a couple of those newcomers) to Flo's house, where he opened cupboards and drawers with the readiness of long practice and whipped up cheese omelettes, after which Flo hacked uneven wedges off a slightly stale cake and served them with a bowl of strawberries dipped in sugar, and mugs of cocoa.

In the end, Donny piled the rest of us back into his blue Rolls and drove through a city where only the milkmen and paper boys were stirring. When I walked into the dim hotel, I looked around for the clock, and found to my astonishment that it was nearly four in the morning.

Holmes was still awake, so we'd talked for a while before turning out the lights. I was too elevated to sleep much, and rose a few hours later to take a walk through the waking city. It was very beautiful, San Francisco, its uneven terrain and highly varied inhabitants making it both distinctive and worldly. It resembled London, in that it seemed to be made up of hamlets that had been joined but which had not lost their individuality. Here, however, the air was clean, the buildings fresh, and working men met one's eye straight on (an egalitarian reaction one tended to find only in the docks area of the English capital).

I came back to find Holmes, astonishingly, still abed. And also, unfortunately, watching me as if I were about to relapse into the previous afternoon's quivering mass. The only answer to that sort of concern is to assume a brisk manner and an assertion of strength, and although it did not entirely convince him—his ongoing fixation with the amount of food I required, for example, was vexing—it did allow him to draw away sufficiently that I could breathe. It may even have reassured him, when I responded to his mother-hen overprotectiveness by declaring that I would do as I please, whether that involved finishing my plate of food or going to see the Lodge on my own. He was not pleased at the latter decision, but as I said, I think my spirited defence of the choice he found reassuringly normal.

As a result, he made no attempt to linger during Saturday afternoon, leaving me alone in the big house while he went about his own business. When he came back before I had finished in the house, I found that he'd persisted in his fixation and spent the afternoon interviewing the neighbours—although I couldn't be completely annoyed, because in the course of his interviews, he had come up with the solution to the second of the dreams. It was, I had to grant him, a nice piece of work, and he seemed pleased with himself when we went to dinner with Mr Long. Then this morning, he'd appeared to be so convinced of my rehabilitation, he had not even insisted on hovering over me when Flo and Donny were delayed. He had merely told me to have a good time, said he'd see me on Wednesday, and left.

And if I'd regretted his absence the moment I climbed into Donny's motor, the regret had faded under the bright day and the coastal beauty and Flo's friendly and not unintelligent conversation. Perhaps this trip would not be a complete disaster, after all.

The road continued to flirt with the sea, coming near and ducking away again, before we turned definitively towards the hills and the engine noise deepened with the climb. My body knew the twists and turns, the scattered farms and cattle lots rang a familiar note in my heart, but the hollow space at the core of me grew: I should not have come; Holmes was right, it was a mistake; it would be bad if I were to find something of my family still inhabiting the Lodge; it would be worse if I did not. I wanted to seize my savaged hair in both hands and scream aloud, just to relieve the building pressure, but I knew that if I screamed, it would be impossible to stop.

So I sat and quivered, staring in hope and apprehension, responding to Donny's questions with silence or a brief gesture—a flick of the finger to say, "Go right, here" or a nod to say we were on the correct road. I was conscious that Flo was watching me out of the corner of her eye, wary as a horse about to startle, but at some time in the previous couple of miles I had also become aware that Flo was riding in the place my mother had sat, and my mother had usually done something—very soon now, she used to...what?

We cleared a corner and the hillside of trees dropped away, and I threw off my rug and shouted, "Wait! Stop!"

Donny slammed on the brakes, causing Flo to choke on her chewing gum and the heavy motor to skid to the edge of the loose gravel roadway, but he managed to stop the machine before its front tyres entered the drop-off. I swallowed hard to push my heart back out of my throat—I emphatically didn't like being a passenger—and then scrambled over the side of the car to the ground. Donny turned off the engine. Silence took over, broken only by the crunch of their shoes on the gravel as they joined me, the *ping* of cooling metal, and the call of some rude-voiced bird.

Mother used to call out for Father to stop, so she could see the view.

The trees were lush, dark redwoods interspersed with brash young maples, the native oak, and some leathery-leafed tree with peeling red bark. At precisely this point on the road, as if stage curtains had been parted by a pair of huge hands, the forest drew back, revealing a sparkle of blue water.

But something was missing. I stepped to the side, then further, until the very tip of a dock came into view behind the trees. I wondered if the dock had been truncated, by decay or purpose, or if it was simply that the trees had grown up and obscured its length. Studying the vista, I decided the latter was the more likely explanation: The end of the dock appeared to be as square as ever, and the slice of lake revealed by the parted boughs seemed narrower than it should be. I nodded, satisfied, and climbed back into the motor.

Flo and Donny glanced at each other, and I realised belatedly that some kind of explanation might be in order, considering that I'd nearly sent us off the road with my sudden shout. Their hearts were probably still racing.

"I'm sorry," I said. "I'd forgotten until we reached this point that we always stopped to take a look at the lake. If I'd noticed what a state the road was in, I'd have suggested it more gently."

"No problem," Donny said. "My baby's got good brakes."

He was, I believed, speaking of the motorcar.

We drove on, slowing as we went through the village that was not as tiny as it had been. The general store had sprouted a petrol pump in front, which would mean that the residents no longer had to remember to stop in Serra Beach or Redwood City to fill up their tanks, and the café next door to the store had nearly doubled in size—it now might seat as many as twelve people at one time. The post office looked just the same, and the minuscule library, but I could never have imagined a day when I would see that brief stretch of village lane with more motorcars than horses.

"Half a mile or so, and the road will divide," I said to Donny. "Keep right and circle the lake. I'll tell you when to stop."

The lake was small, and in five minutes, I was saying, "We can pick up the keys from that house with the white picket fence. Flo, would you mind awfully going in and asking for them? If I go I'll get involved in offers of coffee and she'll stir up some biscuits and it'll be dark before we get away. Just tell her I'm feeling rather tired, and I'll call by tomorrow. Oh, and make sure she knows we brought a picnic for tonight, and that we don't need her assistance to make up beds." Mrs Gordimer's garrulous streak was a steady-flowing stream whose levee required constant shoring, lest the flood of words wash over the cabin's lovely quietude. She more than made up for her husband, whose speaking voice I had heard perhaps a dozen times over the years.

"Sure," Flo said, and hopped out to trot up the spotless stones of the front path between brutally pruned standard roses, all an identical peach-pink, that hadn't changed in as long as I remembered. Nor had the face that appeared at the door before Flo could touch the bell, the face that frowned mistrustfully at her explanations before peering past her at the motor. I leant forward, trying to look even more wan than I felt, and waved a feeble hand. Before the caretaker could come and deluge me with sympathy and questions, Flo laid a gentle hand on her, no doubt reiterating her lie about the state of my nerves.

In a moment, she had retreated; a minute later, and Flo was coming back down the walk with the keys swinging from her finger-tips. Mrs Gordimer came out onto her porch—whiter of hair and more stooped, but I'd have sworn wearing the same exact gingham dress she'd worn when I was a child. I waved at her again, and silently urged Donny to get the motor under way. He heard me, and did.

The track down to the Lodge had been maintained to the extent of having the ruts smoothed and the branches trimmed away, but Donny had to creep the last few hundred yards, chary of ripping out some vital piece of the underpinnings. Finally, the trees opened up, and we were there, at the living centre of my childhood.

Chapter Eighteen

Not much to look at, actually. Certainly nothing grand enough to impress our Pacific Heights neighbours: an original one-storey house made of stripped logs with a newer two-storey addition to one side, cedar shingles going slightly mossy on the roof. However, standing and looking at the way it sat on the earth, one became convinced that here was a house whose doors would shut true, whose windows would not rattle in a breeze, whose porch floor would not attack a child's running feet with splinters.

Father had called it the Lodge, and although Mother had complained that the name made it sound like the gate-house to a manor, the name had prevailed. In this basic summer house on the lake, we had been Family. When we were in San Francisco, my father had worked long days, appearing in our lives briefly in the evenings, generally granting us one whiskey-and-soda's worth of time in the parlour or library before he wished us a good-night and sat down to dine with Mother.

Week-ends were better, but often he and Mother were taken away by social obligations—either that, or Levi and I were dragged along for social obligations thinly disguised as family events, such as one memorable picnic at the beach that ended with me bloodying the nose of the snobbish son of the bank's vice-president, who had dared to make a remark about my little brother's Jewish features. Family museum trips were better, but too highly organised to be much fun.

Here, however, Father had been himself. Which was only proper, since he had built the Lodge with his own hands.

The original building had comprised four spacious rooms: an all-purpose sitting room at the front, a grand fireplace and dark-panelled walls, and beside it a smaller room that had served as my father's bedroom in his bachelor days, converted into a billiards and smoking room after my mother came. Behind these rooms were the kitchen, with the table at which we often took breakfast, and the dining room, opening onto a broad stone terrace that nestled between the back of the original Lodge and one side of the two-storey sleeping addition. The newer wing, five bedrooms and two baths, had been added (along with electric lights and hot-water heaters) when he had brought civilisation, in the form of Mother, back from England.

Father had lived in a tent among the trees for the better part of two years during the construction of the Lodge, which coincidentally amounted to the time it took his parents to withdraw their demands that he return to Boston and assume his responsibilities there. He had chosen the trees, helped to cut and haul them, milled the boards, and stacked them to dry. He had learnt a score of trades in the course of the building, become a brick-layer and a glazier, a carpenter and a plumber. He'd rebuilt the fireplace chimney three times before he was satisfied that its draw was clean, and spent a solid month experimenting with the decorative wood-work on the porch railing.

Despite the later additions, this house was his from foundation stones to roof-tree; every time he walked in, he looked around and made in the back of his throat a small sound of profound relaxation. It was, it now oc-curred to me, the precise equivalent of my mother's touching of the mezuzah as she entered the Pacific Heights house.

"Do you want me to open the door?" asked Flo at my shoulder.

"No," I said sharply, then softened it to, "Thanks, but I was just remembering how lovely it was to come here, and get away from the city."

"Really?" she asked dubiously. I laughed, suddenly seeing the rustic building through the eyes of Miss Florence Greenfield, and she hastened to add, "I mean, I'm sure it's a very nice house, and I know a lot of people have summer places or hunting lodges or things, espe-cially with Prohibition and all, but it's just, well, I'm not really a briars-and-brambles kind of a girl."

"Not to worry, Flo—the plumbing works, there are no bears here, and I'm sure we'll find it clean and tidy. It's only for a couple of days, and if it's too dreary you two can always go back early."

But as I stepped forward with the key, it occurred to me that Flo was the one responsible for the transforma-tion of the Greenfield house, and that to a woman with Deco sensibilities, the rusticity of the Lodge might prove a challenge.

The key moved easily in the lock; I stepped across the

threshold: no trace of mustiness in the air. The house was cool, certainly, but as we moved into the rooms I was relieved to find it as tidy and dust-free as it had ever been—clearly the interdiction against trespass in the Pacific Heights house had not extended here. There were even a couple of fairly recent *Saturday Evening Post*s laid on the table between the sofas, just as Mrs Gordimer had used to provide for us. I told myself that Norbert would have informed her that I was coming to California, and therefore a visit of the Lodge's owner to the lake was possible—it was better than thinking that the poor woman had replaced these offerings and removed them, unused, every time she'd cleaned over the past decade.

Flo's cautiously polite noises had turned to honest appreciation as soon as she had seen the interior, and now, as she worked her way towards the back, her voice took on a note of enthusiasm and even—once she saw the view—wonder.

"Oh, Mary, this is perfectly swell! It's like something from a fairy-tale book, the flowers and the lawn and the lake—and look, there's even a boat, just sitting and waiting."

I moved, reluctantly, to join her at the expanse of windows that formed the back wall of the original cabin, and saw that, indeed, the little sail-boat lay ready. One glance at its trim paint told me that it had also been recently placed there—no doubt by the stout Mr Gordimer, grumbling and snapping at one or another of his youthful assistants as they wheeled the vessel out of the boat-house and down to the dock. He'd always knelt, laboriously, to pass a clean cloth over the boat's prow before nodding to himself, then climbed to his knees, turned his back on the gleaming object, and marched up the dock and the lawn with the weight of the world on his shoulders, muttering glum but inaudible invective to himself all the way—most of his conversations were conducted with himself.

I'd once caught my mother smiling at his retreating back; when she'd noticed me watching her, she had winked, as if we shared a secret.

I pulled my eyes from the waiting boat and made myself look at the wide stretch of green that spilled down to the water's edge: my mother's realm. Father had built the house, but Mother had formed the garden, and my dread for this spot was greater than any other. She had spent hours here every day we were in residence, pruning and weeding, planting the flowers and shrubs she had brought from the city, putting into effect the changes she had worked out with the help of Micah—who, as far as I knew, had never set foot here. It was all her, from the tiny pink rose she had placed in the shelter of the apple tree to the dancing fuchsias she had placed in shady corners and the wild-flower seeds she had scattered in the lawn, every inch of it her vision and her labour. I was afraid that seeing the garden without her in it would act like a knife in my heart.

But I had reckoned without the effects of time: What I saw was not her garden. Oh, the bones were there, the trees and shrubs she had planted, the shape of delineation between cultivated and wild, but the flesh had changed beyond anything she had known. The lilac, once a trim and obedient resident of the far corner, now appeared to be making serious inroads on the native growth. Another shrub—a peony, I thought—was halfway to being classified as a tree; the tiny pink rose had all but overcome the apple in a riot of colour; and the English flowers she had nurtured around the perimeter had long ago broken for freedom in the lawn.

The grass, which Mother had always preferred shaggy as compared to the tight trim of English lawn-grass, was nearly a meadow; although it had been mown in the past couple of weeks, pink daisies and yellow dandelions gave it the appearance of a tapestry.

It was startling at first, then reassuringly foreign. And as I began to relax out of my apprehension, two thoughts came to me: that it was indeed magical, as Flo had said; and that it was precisely what my mother had been working towards. I was grateful that Mrs Gordimer had not inflicted her tightly pruned system here.

My ruminations were interrupted by a voice previously unheard here—Donny's, coming from the next room.

"I don't know about you girls, but I could sure use a drink after that drive."

"Oh, yes!" Flo exclaimed. "A nice long drink, sitting on the lawn, watching the sun go down, that would be heaven. There probably isn't any ice," she added sadly.

"There probably isn't any booze," Donny commented, his voice saying that this was clearly a more serious problem. "I knew we should've brought along something stronger than fizz. All I've got's my flask—I don't suppose we could unearth the local boot-legger at six o'clock on a Sunday afternoon?"

"There should be both," I said, and followed his voice into the kitchen.

If the Gordimers had laid out the magazines and the sail-boat in anticipation of an unannounced visit, they might well have put milk in the ice-box, tea in the cupboard, and bread in the bin. I pulled open various doors and found them occupied as I had expected, so I took the ice-pick from its customary drawer, wiped off its rust on the clean dish-towel that hung below the sink, and handed it to Donny.

"Chip off some bits from the block in the ice-box. Flo, you'll find glasses in the second cupboard there. And unless the mice have figured out how to use a corkscrew..." I laid my hand on the tea caddy that sat on the set of narrow shelves along one wall, and tugged. Then I tugged harder, hanging my weight against it. Flo and Donny both stared, no doubt wondering both why the caddy had been glued down, and why I so wanted it off. Slowly, the apparent canister gave way, tipping forward: Its tin sides concealed, not tea, but a lever for unlocking a sliding door. With a grinding protest of gears long un-oiled, the caddy folded itself face-downward on its shelf. I stuck my fingers against the edge of the shelf, pulled hard, and the entire wall of shelves trundled slowly to the left and vanished behind the cupboards.

I turned to grin at my amazed companions, both of them crowding to see beyond my shoulders. "My father had an oddly elaborate sense of humour," I explained. "He used to offer my mother a glass of tea, and this is what he meant."

"And that in the days before the Volstead Act!" Flo said.

"Even more appropriate now," I agreed. I started to move forward into the dim hidden closet to peruse the bottles, then stopped dead at a tinkle of glass skittering across the floor. "Don't come in, there's glass on the floor. Some of the beer bottles probably exploded in a hot spell. However, apart from that, there appears to be pretty much whatever you like," I said to Donny. "Gin?"

"Any vermouth? I could make us a shaker of martinis."

I'd never had a martini, but I obediently handed out the bottles. While he and Flo searched the cupboards for a shaker of some kind, ending up with a decidedly rustic

Mason jar, I found a broom and swept up the shattered bottles—two of them. I also gingerly took the remaining three out to the dust-bin, although they were probably no hazard in the cool of that day. When I returned, I was checking over the other contents of the hidden closet when an arm snaked past me holding a cold, clear glass.

"Cheers," said Flo. I took the glass, lifted it in response, and took a swallow. After that, I stood where I was for a while until my eyes had stopped watering. Flo studied the shelves with her own clear eyes. "What a nifty little room, Mary. Like a safe-room."

"More or less. My father figured that there would be long stretches where the house was empty and didn't want to leave things out in the open to tempt passers-by. Not that there's anything particularly valuable here, but there's the candelabras, and a nice set of old silver in that chest, and two or three of the cameras he used to fiddle with."

"Ooh, and a phonograph! Does it work?"

"I should think so, although the music will be old."

"How sweet, we can lace up our whalebone corsets and tap our toes decorously to the old songs. Donny, be a sport and wrestle that old Victrola out onto the lawn, would you?" She followed him, clutching a stack of recordings in one hand and her drink in the other; I ran a last eye over the shelves, made a mental note to find some oil for the mechanism, and wrestled the door shut, tipping the tea canister back upright to lock it.

We drank rather a lot that evening, between the martinis, the wine Flo had brought for our picnic dinner, and a bottle of very old brandy from the hidden store-room. We drank and we laughed and we listened to the music of another generation, Flo and I taking turns dancing with Donny on the uneven stones of the terrace. When it was dark, we placed candles in the three tarnished candelabras and ate our picnic on the lawn. The night was so still that the candle flames scarcely moved, and the occasional moth drawn by the light was soon extinguished. Afterwards, we returned to the terrace, where Flo and Donny danced in and out of the light. They found a tango, a dance that had been new and racy during my family's last two summers here, and set about it with great seriousness that soon gave way to laughter. I realised that I was rather drunk and very tired, and that before too long I would become maudlin; to top it off, we hadn't made up the beds.

With a sigh, I put down my glass and went to see about sheets and things, only to find that the ever-efficient Mrs Gordimer had made up every bed in the place except that of my parents' room. I took my own childhood room, not even seeing the walls or tables, simply divesting myself of spectacles and shoes and tumbling in between the sheets, there to weave gently to and fro on a sinking ship into the depths of unconsciousness.

And struggled up from the dark comfort of sleep at the sound of a voice.

"Huh?" I asked sensibly.

"I said," came Flo's voice, "do you want a sleeping draught?"

"No, thanks," I told her, and put my head down again.

I came awake again in the quiet hour before dawn, when a faint light brought shape to the undrawn curtains. As my mind returned to me through the fog of the previous night's drink and the deepest night's sleep I'd had in ages, three thoughts came with it.

The first was that the years spanning the ages of fourteen and twenty-four were long indeed. In my case, they had been longer than for most people: Very little remained of the girl whose hair-brush lay on the table, whose books inhabited the shelves.

The second came, wryly, as, "And being the married matron here, I was supposed to act as chaperone." I had no idea where Flo and Donny ended up, and frankly had no intention of looking into the matter.

Last was the thought that had me sitting up in bed and patting along the bed-side table for my spectacles: *hidden room.*

I had searched every inch of the Pacific Heights house on Saturday and found nothing there that joined up with the third of my dreams, the dream of walking through a house and showing its rooms to my friends, all the while aware of the key in my pocket, the key to a hidden apartment. I had searched my family house both literally and figuratively, looking for an actual, physical concealed hideaway or even a place that possessed the same sensation of secret and personal knowledge, and found neither. My father's library had contained the closest facsimile of that sensation, but when I folded myself up beneath his desk (abashedly, checking first that the door was bolted) and curled my legs to my chest, it had not been the same.

But the casual expertise with which I had reached for, then worked, the hidden-door mechanism off the kitchen—even though I could not remember ever being allowed to work it myself as a child—had contained precisely that blend of the hidden and the known, the important buried within the everyday. I wanted to see that room again, now.

Once upright, I discovered that not only was I unsteady, but I was dressed in the same crumpled trousers and shirt I had worn from the city the day before. I cast the garments off and took my childish bath-robe from

the wardrobe, thinking to slip out to the motor and retrieve my possessions, but one step outside my door and
I nearly went sprawling over the valise. With a silent word
of thanks to the hard-headed Donny, I carried it inside,
scrubbed myself with a cold cloth in the bedroom's flowered basin, and dressed in warm trousers and a pull-over
sweater. I picked up a pair of shoes and tip-toed down the
stairs, where I became aware that Donny was behind the
door to the first guest-room, the one with the largest bed.
Demurely, I stepped into the main wing of the house before I could locate my other guest by her snores, shutting
the connecting door behind me.

To my mother, one of the great blessings of the Lodge
had always been the relative lack of servants. We ended
up roughing it, yes, but we were also granted a degree of
privacy we rarely found in the city. Not that Mother did
all the work herself—just that my father before her had
trained the Gordimers to slip in and out like the elves of
a fairy-tale: Meals appeared as if by magic, dinner dishes
she didn't feel like washing up were miraculously restored to their shelves by morning, clothing left in the
hampers materialised a day or two later, freshly ironed.

The polite fiction of our independence here was
maintained by the unspoken agreement as to the times
of day we would be absent from kitchen and bedrooms.
Mrs Gordimer and a changing régime of assistants let
themselves in once in the afternoon, then in the evening,
during which times the dishes were made clean, the cupboards and wood-box filled, and the oven stocked with
an evening meal. The other times of day we fended for
ourselves, leaving a note on the kitchen table if we had
any request.

Thus without a maidservant's help, I laid a handful
of kindling atop the stove's embers and put the kettle

on, finding an unopened tin of MJB coffee in the cupboard beside a fresh packet of Lipton's tea, a jar of Mrs
Gordimer's blackberry jam, and similar basics. While
the water was heating, I stepped into my shoes and went
onto the terrace.

The last stars were fading as the sky grew light; the
lake was a sheet of black glass with a mist gentle over its
surface. Everything was so completely still and utterly
magical, merely drawing breath seemed a disturbance.

After a time, the sound of water boiling drew me back.
With a regretful glance at the calm, I returned to the
house, opening the noisy packet of tea and wincing at the
clatter of the cup and the suck and snap of the ice-box
door. Unearthing a thick travelling-rug in the cedar chest
near the entrance, I carried it and my milky tea outside.

I must have spent an hour there on the tapestry lawn
that flowed into the lake, sipping my tea, wrapped in the
fragrant blanket, watching the morning come. The fish
began to rise for insects, dotting the sheet-glass water
with rings; a tall white bird stood in the reeds near the
dock, perusing for frogs. The beauty of the moment
made my bones ache with pleasure, and when at last the
morning's ethereal perfection had faded and it had become just another lovely day, I felt complete and calm in
a way I had not for many weeks.

I gathered up my cup, draped the now-damp rug over
a bench where the sun would soon hit it, and went inside to look at my father's hidden room.

I worked inside the room for an hour before the
sound of water in the pipes betrayed a guest's waking. I
made haste to shut the secret door and went to wrestle
with the tin-opener, and had the coffee finished by the
time Flo came in, yawning and tousled and looking far
more beautiful with her skin pink from sleep than she

did with rouge and paint and immaculate hair. I poured her a cup of coffee; she mumbled something that wasn't quite words, drifting away into the sitting room. A suspiciously brief time later, Donny came through from the sleeping wing, dressed in a white 'Varsity sweater and plus-fours. He, too, accepted coffee, although he was somewhat more communicative than Flo, dropping into a kitchen chair and, after asking my leave, sticking a cigarette into its holder and lighting it.

"This is a peach of a place," he said. "My parents have a summer house, but since every one of their friends has a house in the same square mile, it's just like being back in the city, only cooler."

"Where is that?" I asked.

"In Chicago. They're still there, in spite of the winters. I've tried to get them out here, but they're sure the place'll shimmy down around their ears."

"Yes," I said with a grin. "Half my friends in England assume that San Francisco collapses on a yearly basis."

"Flo said you're in London?"

"I do have a flat there, but we live on the south coast. I also spend a lot of time in Oxford."

"That's right, she said you were a, whatchamacallit, bluestocking."

"She probably said I spent my life with my nose in a book."

"Something like that. Can't manage it, myself. Books, I mean. Ever since I graduated, anything but a novel brings me all out in hives."

He had a nice laugh, pleasantly crooked white teeth, and—although he'd taken a minute to make the razor-sharp part down the middle of his hair and slick it into place—a nicely rakish blond stubble on his square cheekbones. He might not be much of a one for books, but in addition to being restful on the eyes, he was intelligent, thoughtful, and seemed to care a great deal for Flo. I was, theoretically, a member of the same "jazz generation" as the rest of Friday night's party, but in truth I hadn't known many of this sort of social animal with any intimacy, and hadn't expected to find a solid foundation beneath the self-consciously blasé pleasure-seeker. Maybe it was because Donny was a little older; maybe he was just made of stronger stuff.

Hearing our voices, Flo re-appeared. "Morning," she said, taking the chair between us. "Is there any more coffee?"

Donny reached for her cup and stood up; as he went past, he mussed her already on-end hair affectionately. "Not a morning girl, my Flossie."

"Hell, I'm full of pep," she protested, then yawned.

He poured her coffee, placed it in front of her, then started opening various cupboards and taking things out. "How do you like what my old man calls 'cackle berries'?" He held up a pair of eggs.

I placed a half-hearted objection, saying that I really ought to be doing the cooking for them, but Flo said, "Donny loves to mess around in the kitchen. It's going to drive the cook bananas, when we're married."

"I didn't know," I said. "Congratulations."

"Oh, we haven't set a date or got a ring or any of that hooey," she told me. "When we do, Mummy will take over, and it'll be just another rotten bore. We'll probably elope, but right now we're having too much fun. Plenty of time to be respectable when our livers give out."

I shot a quick glance at Donny; he was breaking the eggs into a bowl, but from the side of his face, I thought perhaps the wild boy of the Blue Tiger might be more ready for the ring than his girl-friend was.

"Well, in any case," I said, "it's a good thing he likes to cook, because otherwise you'd be eating burnt food chipped from the pan. I am no chef."

Donny scrambled the eggs with some herbs that I hadn't noticed growing along the outer wall of the cabin—at least I assumed they were herbs and not some poisonous weed. The eggs tasted good, whatever the herbs' Latin names, eaten with sausages from the ice-box and toast heaped with Mrs Gordimer's jam. We ate on the terrace, which gathered the morning sun nicely. When our plates were polished and the toast basket was empty (Flo having pressed the last pieces on me) I cleared the table and made more coffee, returning to find Flo stretched out on one of the deck-chairs with her face to the sun, eyes closed like a cat.

"I'm gonna bake in the sun all day," she declared.

"You'll get horribly red and sore," Donny warned her.

"Oh, don't be wet, Donny. I don't care. I think I'll just move down here to the sticks and turn into a turnip."

"A red turnip," he commented.

"There should be a couple of beach umbrellas in the boat shed," I offered. "If they haven't fallen to pieces. And canoes, a badminton net, and lawn bowls, if you're interested."

The umbrellas hadn't fallen to pieces, not quite, and when Donny came across the lawn with a pair of them across his shoulder, he said that the shed's other forms of entertainment seemed in decent shape as well. He drove the pole of the most promising umbrella into a place in the lawn chosen by Flo, raising its ribs gingerly. The fabric had a few holes in it, but it held, and Flo spread a rug underneath it and settled down with a sigh of satisfaction. He installed the other one nearby. We all lay down, and lethargy descended.

Thirty-five minutes later, the lack of stimulation drove all three of us into motion. I was the first to tire of watching the humming-birds in the fuchsias.

"I'm going to see if I can find something to read. Can I bring either of you anything from the house?"

Donny leapt up with an eagerness that betrayed his own growing need for action. "I'll take a stroll into the village and see if I can find a paper," he declared.

"Mrs Gordimer will be happy to get you one," I offered.

"Nope, I'll stretch my legs and then I can be a sloth the rest of the day. And I want to know how the baseball went." But before I could comment on how unlikely and wholesome an interest in baseball was in a jazz-baby like him, he added, "I've got some money riding on it."

Flo, too, was on her feet. "I'm going to put on my bathing suit."

Donny left in the direction of the village, Flo disappeared into the house and came out in a skimpy bathing costume, settling onto her rug, and I returned to the hidden storage room. I searched every inch of its walls, examined every object on the shelves, pushed and manipulated every shelf and hook, but nothing gave way, no concealed entrance or trap door came to light, to lead me into the locked rooms of my dream.

There was nothing here.

When Donny came back, the bounce in his step proclaiming how the scores had gone, he too changed into his costume and persuaded Flo to bathe in the rather murky waters. After a while, I scrubbed my hands and went down to the umbrellas, where I found Donny had arranged three of the deck-chairs from the now sundrenched terrace. He and Flo lay sleeping, hair damp from their swim, chairs three decorous feet apart, faces turned towards each other in slumber.

I smiled, and sat down in my own chair, remembering only as my backside hit the wood that I had neglected to bring a book from the house.

But I stayed where I was, effectively alone on the lawn, nothing to distract me but the sound of two men in indistinct conversation from the other side of the lake.

What had the hidden-room dream meant, if not an actual, physical place?

Dreams, I knew, were not some mythic message from Beyond. Dreams are speech from the unconscious mind, messages couched not in the logical terms of daylight consciousness, but in a twilight narrative of glimpsed images and impressions. Repeated dreams, worked over and over, generally had a purpose: In my case, the flying-objects image had taken me by the hand and eventually led me to the realisation that I had been in San Francisco during the earthquake, thus opening up an entire segment of my childhood that I had closed away. The second dream, that of the faceless man, was rooted in a specific incident that clearly had terrified my six-year-old self, an event that had rested unquiet over the intervening years until I could finally bring it to light and put it to rest—I felt certain, thanks to Holmes' discovery of the old woman's reminiscences, that that particular nocturnal visitor would trouble me no more.

Both dreams had their origin in frightening incidents, two events that had been wrapped about and reshaped by my unconscious mind to soften their sharp edges—until, triggered by the realisation that I was heading to the place where both had occurred, like bits of psychic shrapnel they worked their way to the surface.

But the third dream appeared to be without

antecedent. I could find no concealed rooms, either here or in Pacific Heights; moreover, the dream had always been very specific: I knew about the rooms, and needed only to put the key to the door and step inside. Yet in both houses I had actively searched, and although memories awakened as I went along—freely and comprehensively in the Lodge, piecemeal and grudgingly in San Francisco—in neither place had I felt that throb of recognition that told me I was getting close to the door.

Perhaps Tom Long had been right. When I'd heard those precise Chinese accents telling me of Matteo Ricci's memory palace, I'd been frankly indignant, that this stranger might presume to see into my mind. But maybe I'd been too quick to dismiss his suggestion that the hidden rooms were not of stone and wood, but were located in the recesses of my mind.

Like an object so familiar to the eyes it goes unseen, I had habitually walked past my own history, freely displaying the rest of the house to all and sundry, knowing yet not knowing what lay behind its surfaces. My entire childhood had become a self-inflicted blind spot—I had complacently passed by the locked rooms of my past for so long, fingering the key in my pocket, that I no longer knew where to find the door.

I sat where I was for a long time, staring unseeing at the lake. The sun crept its way onto my toes and up my ankles. Eventually, Flo and Donny stirred, bantered, rose. They raced down the lawn and down the dock to dive into the lake, which looked so lovely and cool that I changed into my own very conservative bathing costume and joined them. Afterwards, we took some lunch, and when a breeze came up we experimented with the little boat, ending up using the oars more than the sail. Sunburnt and replete with the pleasures of childhood, we returned to a house that was fragrant with beef and onions, a rustic casserole left in the oven for us by Mrs Gordimer. We hurriedly rinsed the lake water from our skin and changed into our dinner wear, then threw ourselves on the food as if we had not eaten in days.

Later, when the dishes were virtuously dried and put away, we lit the citronella candles on the terrace and took our coffee out there.

Flo eventually broke the long silence, crossing the legs of her heavy silk lounging pyjamas and giving a sigh of contentment. "Golly, what a swell day this has been, Mary, just the tops. Thanks for letting us crash your party."

"It's been a pleasure," I told her in all honesty. An unexpected pleasure, I could have said, but did not. "Thank you both for coming with me."

"You did look pretty down. On Friday, I mean. I don't know what was wrong, but you looked like a real flat tyre before you got some bubbly into you."

She was too polite to ask, but I could see no real reason not to tell her why I'd been troubled—after all, I'd told a relative stranger that same night. "I had some bad news, Friday morning. An old friend of the family died."

"Criminy, Mary, why didn't you say—"

"Oh, she died a long time ago, it's just that I only found out on Friday." Flo's expressions of distress faded to a more appropriate level—after all, how close a friend could this have been, if it took me so long to hear about it? A question, indeed, that I had been asking myself. "She was the doctor who helped me, after the accident. A, well, a psychiatrist. I was in pretty bad shape then, mentally as well as physically, and she helped a lot. I'd hoped to see her, but I discovered she actually died within a few weeks of the time I went back to England in the winter of 1914. She was murdered."

"Murdered! How absolutely dire! What was her name?"

"Ginzberg. Leah Ginzberg."

"But—wait a tick. That sounds familiar."

"She was famous, wasn't she?" Donny asked. "That was just after I came out from Chicago, and I remember a buzz about it. She was killed in her office, wasn't she?"

"That's right," I said. "I wouldn't have said she was famous, but your friend Jerry knew of her. Or was it Terry? Terry, right. He and I were talking while I was resting my feet at the dance, and it came up."

"Gosh, yes!" Flo exclaimed. "I remember now, she *was* famous—the Lady Mesmerist, they called her."

"She did use hypnosis sometimes," I agreed.

"There was some trial, wasn't there?" Donny's voice went thoughtful as he searched his memory. "She'd helped some girl come up with a memory, and the cops were making a stink, saying she was turning the courtroom into a vaudeville stage."

"Really?" I said doubtfully. Flo chimed in.

"Wasn't that the girl claiming she had been assaulted? Mummy wouldn't let me see the papers, but I snuck them out of the trash. Yeah, they were saying the only reason she was making the charge was because she wanted to be an actress and thought it would get her noticed. Like the Fatty Arbuckle case, only that was later. And this girl didn't die."

"She was a dancer—chorus line, not ballet," Donny added, for my sake, "and told everyone she'd been knocked cold during the attack, and forgot the details. And your doctor friend helped her remember them— only the police said it was all hooey, that she'd just helped the girl come up with a story for why she hadn't made the charges when the attack happened instead of waiting nearly a year."

"I suppose that makes sense," I told them. "Dr Ginzberg used hypnosis to help me put together what happened during the accident—I'd sort of…" My voice trailed off as I was hit hard by what I was about to say. With an effort, I finished the thought: "I'd pushed it away, even the parts I could eventually remember. So yes, she was probably accustomed to working with helping people retrieve their repressed memories."

I found myself smiling, a little sadly, at this last. A patient invariably feels that the intense relationship she forms with her psychiatrist is entirely unique and essentially personal; it is always a jolt to realise that it is also one of a score such relationships the psychiatrist holds simultaneously: a part of the job.

Donny lit a match, his handsome face coming brightly into view then fading into a mere outline in the glow of the cigarette. "Didn't they think one of her loonies went nuts in the office and killed her? I don't remember ever hearing who it was—the papers are never as good in following up a story as they are in telling you in the first place, are they?"

"It was never solved," I said. Both of them went quiet at this reminder that we were speaking of a friend, not an anonymous victim. Then Flo stirred.

"What happened with the girl's case?"

"I think it was dropped," Donny answered. "Yes, there was some hokum about the man having the doctor killed, but wouldn't he have knocked off the girl instead?"

"Wonder what happened to her?"

"She went back to work. Used to be one of the dancers at the Tiger, in fact."

"The Blue Tiger, where we were Friday? Is she still there?"

"She wouldn't be, no—she'd be too old even for the chorus now."

"Billy's no spring chicken," Flo commented, in what sounded like an objection.

Billy? I thought, then: Ah. Belinda Birdsong, the saucy chanteuse.

Donny gave a snort, and said, "Billy was old when he was in short pants."

Hmm. Another Billy, then. Unless this was another of the slang turns my American contemporaries used, where a girl was "old man" and a man "young thing."

Flo giggled. "Don't be absurd, Donny. Billy never wore short pants; he was born in a skirt."

"Wait a minute," I broke in. "Are you saying that Belinda Birdsong is a man?"

My two companions flew into gales of laughter, making me realise that I'd sounded like someone too ancient, or too naïve, to have imagined such a thing as a man acting as a woman. "No, honestly," I protested, "I've seen men impersonating women before, but a person can usually tell. Are you sure?"

This set them off again, into the sort of choking noises that can only come from a risqué joke. "Oh, yes," Donny got out at last. "No mistake."

"Do you care to tell me why?"

The cool edge to my question reminded him of his manners. "Sorry," he said. "Didn't mean to ... That is to say, yes, I'm sure Belinda's a man, 'cause I saw his, er, fittings one evening. I was walking by his dressing-room when someone threw open the door at a ... revealing moment."

"I see."

"As did I. Gave me quite a trauma, I tell you, seeing the, er, lengths the boy would go to conceal—" A slapping noise came out of the darkness as Flo chastised him, and I made haste to move the subject on a step.

"I'm impressed. Their throat usually gives them away, the Adam's apple, you know, and a degree of exaggeration in their manners. He's very natural."

"They all are."

"What, you mean the others on the stage were all men, as well?"

"Not the chorus line, but the three other singers, yes."

I'd never even suspected it. Alcohol, of course, was partly to blame for my lack of perception, and the room's thick, smokey air, but on reflection, I decided that the reason I had failed to notice was that, in England, such acts as I had seen were generally in small and seedy cabarets, not in a glittering palace the size of a warehouse with a big, slick jazz band to accompany its internationally known singer.

"Well, fancy that," I said in the end, vowing to myself never to tell Holmes of my failure. We sat beneath the stars and the sliver of new moon, speaking of other things, and after a while Donny brought out a ukulele and sang in a surprisingly sweet tenor a bouncy melody assuring us that "It Ain't Gonna Rain No Mo'," some of the words of which escaped him, and another tune (this one sung in a startling imitation of a Negro woman) about Mamma going where Papa goes. He played songs I did not know and others of my childhood, and although the ukulele has never been one of my favourite instruments, under the stars and beside the lake that night, it seemed the only appropriate music in the world.

Eventually, when the moon had slid beneath the hills and the Milky Way was a bright smear across the firmament, we took ourselves to bed.

Chapter Nineteen

Tuesday was a day of leisure, an unlooked-for holiday from care, during which we at last eased into the attitudes appropriate to a summer house. The weather cooperated in the venture, with a slight high fog to keep the sun from waking us too early, then burning off to present us a day worthy of the Riviera. Flo and Donny appeared, yawning and tousled, to exclaim in appreciation of the sparkle off the lake. Flo turned on her heel and went back to don her bathing costume, and while Donny was studying the potential contained in the cupboards, she trotted down the lawn and to the end of the dock where she stood, pulling on her red bathing cap, before launching herself off the end into the water.

Donny produced griddle-cakes (apologising all the while for the lack of some spice or other that his mother used and which, he claimed, defined the dish) until we were groaning, and we then merrily abandoned the mess in favour of reading in the lawn-chairs.

They had both brought novels, although at the moment both were buried in other things. Flo was reading one of the *Saturday Evening Post*s that Mrs Gordimer had left in the sitting room, chuckling over an F. Scott Fitzgerald story called "How to Live on $36,000 a Year." I glanced automatically at the book beneath her as I settled onto my chair. "Heavens, Flo," I said, "what is that door-stop of a book you've got?"

"It's *Ulysses*," she said with a giggle. "A friend bought it in Paris and smuggled it in disguised as a five-pound box of Swiss chocolates. Have you read it?"

"Not yet."

"They say it's hot stuff."

"It had better be, considering the size of it. And what's that you have, Donny?"

"Cross-word puzzles," he replied, holding up a peculiar book that had come with a pencil attached to it. "Just hit the shops, and a friend said it was going to be all the thing. Can't see them catching on, myself. They're tough."

The more ordinary-looking book on the grass underneath his chair said *The Plastic Age*, by someone named Marks. "I presume that's a novel?" I asked.

"You bet," he said. "Everyone's talking about it—nearly got itself banned for the hot bits. The story of a fellow's undergraduate years. What about you?"

"A book on feng shui. It's a kind of Chinese philosophy." I saw their faces go blank, and thought I should perhaps redeem myself a little. "I did read a book on the boat out that had been banned for years. Have you read *Jurgen*?"

They'd heard of it, wanted to know how "hot" it was, but I had to admit that the moral outrage of the censors probably had less to do with the petting scenes than with the fact that it was gods who were doing the petting. Donny trumped my bid of *Jurgen* by saying casually that he'd met Scott Fitzgerald at a week-end in France the previous summer, but as I'd found Fitzgerald's stories a somewhat tedious glorification of childishness—and American East Coast aristocratic childishness at that—I had little to say. Eventually I returned to my Orientalia, they to their stories, and the sun continued its complacent way across the sky.

We ate lunch, and then Donny wanted to try the canoes. Flo protested that the sun was too hot, but he offered her one of his long shirts, and that (along with a wide straw hat from the house) mollified her. They paddled, they swam, I joined them and sat out, and then it was somehow evening, and the happy melancholy of physical repletion coupled with too much sun settled over us. We had a drink, and dinner, and played billiards in the front room until the worst of the mosquitoes had been driven off by the citronella.

Around ten o'clock Donny proposed another swim. Flo and I begged off, but he was set on it, and strode down the lawn into the darkness. After a minute, we heard a splash, then the rhythmic sounds of arm strokes.

"Do you suppose he went in fully dressed?" I asked Flo. He was by no means drunk, so I wasn't worried about his safety, but I was curious.

"No, there'll be a line of clothing down the lawn come morning," she told me.

The sound of his strokes faded and grew dim, then nonexistent. "He seems a strong swimmer," I said dubiously.

"Gosh, you don't need to worry about Donny—for two bits he'd swim across the Golden Gate. You'd never know he had scarlet fever when he was a kid, would you?"

"It doesn't seem to have affected him."

"It did, though. He tried to join up in '17, but they wouldn't have him. A dicky heart. That's when he came out here—he was too wild about it to stay at home where all his friends had joined up, had to get away. Bit sensitive about it, you know?"

"I won't say anything."

"Crazy, really, he's strong as an ox. Hell, they even took my father, who was old."

"Yes, your mother told me he'd been killed in the war."

"Bet she said he was her husband, too." I heard her chair creak and protest as she sat up suddenly, then heard the sound of her cigarette case opening. In a minute, the flare of a match lit her face.

"Do you mean to say they weren't married?" I asked tentatively.

"Oh, they were married, just not by then. They divorced when I was tiny, maybe five, but she never tells anyone that, like it's something shameful. He used to come around and ask Mummy for money, after she inherited Granddad's packet, but we never saw much of him in between. You know, once upon a time he was great friends with your father."

"He was?"

"I think they went to school together, or maybe university, I don't know. In fact, I was thinking today that my daddy probably helped yours build this place. I remember him telling me stories about living in the woods, building a log cabin and fighting off the bears."

"More likely raccoons," I murmured, considerably distracted by the revelation.

"I always thought it was just talk, but looking back, I have to say that most of his stories had some kind of truth behind them. More illustrations than inventions, you know? And I know the two of them were pals, 'way back when, long before our mothers were."

"But what happened? Or have I just forgotten him?" Yet another gaping hole in my memories?

"You probably never knew him. Your father didn't see much of him after they both got married. Things change, I guess. And I know your mother didn't like Dad—I haven't a clue why, but Mummy let it slip one time, when she was mad at him. 'Judith was right,' she said. 'He's not to be trusted.'"

"My mother didn't trust him?"

"Maybe because he was part of your old man's wild youth. That's what happens, isn't it, when people tie the knot? They put nooses around each other's neck and pull them tight? Tell them they can't see their old friends, can't go out and be wild, have to have babies and a white picket fence?"

"Not always," I said distractedly. "But what—"

But Flo had worked the conversation around to the question that bothered her, and would not be set aside. "Tell me, Mary. What's it like, being married?"

"In what way? The restrictions, you mean? I haven't found—"

"Not just that. The whole thing. I haven't...Donny and I haven't...you know—done it. We've come pretty close, but even when I've been pie-eyed I think about how he'd look at me, after. It wouldn't be the same, would it?"

That rather answered the question of whether or not they were sharing a room. I cleared my throat. "Er."

"Oh, I don't want the birds-and-bees stuff; I know all that. It's just, I can't decide if I should wait."

"What stands in the way of your getting married?"

"Just . . . everything!" she cried, her glowing cigarette-end making a great sweep through the air.

"Picket fences and nappies?"

"Exactly!"

"Have you talked it over with Donny?"

"He says he's glad to wait, that he wants what I want. If I knew what I wanted."

"But you're afraid he'll change his mind and become a tyrant once you're married?"

"Men do, don't they? Once you're pinned down they go off and there you are, raising the babies and getting fat and bored to tears."

"Flo, look—sure, some men do that. But from what I've seen of Donny, he honestly loves you, and if something bothered you, and he knew it, he wouldn't force it down your throat." I hesitated, then said, "Just because your father was irresponsible, doesn't mean Donny will be."

"Dad wasn't irresponsible," she retorted instantly. "Just a little . . . childish. He was great fun—I always loved it when he visited; it was like having another play-mate. But Mummy got so absolutely grim whenever he came around, it made me wild to see, and I would look at her face and think, I never want to feel that way, never want to be forced to, I don't know, grow up I guess, if that's how it makes me look."

I began to see why my own mother wanted nothing to do with Flo's father, although I couldn't see why she would have banned him outright.

"So you think he wouldn't, look at me differently, I mean?" she asked hopefully.

But I was not about to take that degree of responsibility. "He probably would, Flo. How could he not? And you would look at him differently. The question is more, would it lessen how he looks at you, and I can't answer that one."

She gave a little sigh, and the glowing ember sagged to the ground. "No, I suppose not."

"Flo?" I said, hesitant about offering advice. "You know, one thing I have found, that it helps a lot to have some kind of interests outside of the marriage itself."

"Easy for you to say. I had to have help getting through high school."

"You did a magnificent job converting your house."

"I did, didn't I?" she said proudly.

"What about that?"

"What, decorating? You mean as a job?"

"As a profession you love. You have the skills, and you have the social contacts necessary. Think about it."

"Hm," she said. "I will."

The sound of splashing reached us, but before he got close enough to hear our voices, I hurried to ask, "But tell me, Flo, what happened to your father? If he didn't die in France, where is he?"

"Oh, I think he did die in France, just not the way Mummy says. You see, he wrote to tell her that he was going to join the French army, which by that time was taking pretty much anyone, even broken-down men in their late forties. He'd been living in Paris—he had a half-sister there, about fifteen years younger than him. His father had left his first wife and remarried—divorces seem to run in Daddy's family. Anyway, that was the last we heard from him. Rosa, his half-sister, wrote at Christmas, 1918, to say that he had gone missing in action in September, three months before. So I suppose in the end, he became a little more responsible after all."

"It sounds like it."

"Anyway, I'm sorry he's gone. He wasn't around a whole lot, but he was fun."

We sat in silence for a moment of eulogy, then Flo jumped to her feet and picked her way down to the water. In a minute, the swimmer got close enough that she could speak with him, and the two joked and carried on like... well, like an old married couple.

Two hours before dawn on Wednesday morning, I sat bolt upright in my bed while the dream of the hidden apartment faded before my eyes, to be slowly replaced by the dim outlines of my childhood room in the Lodge. I'd only had the dream once or twice since arriving in California, and this time it took place in a house similar to that of the Greenfields', except that the vining Art Deco motifs were actual vines growing up the high stone walls, and the thin greyhound statues were living creatures, mincing about on their impossibly thin legs. It was as if some long-lost jungle temple, overgrown with creepers and saplings, had been chosen to host a party of the fashionable crème of Society.

I had, as usual, been walking through the rooms showing my unlikely house to half a dozen acquaintances, passing through the orangerie (where three quizzical black-and-white monkeys peered through the overhanging branches at us) before inviting them to admire the proportions of the great hall (whose corbels and beams, on closer examination, proved to be the mighty trunks and branches of some enormous clinging trees). We went past a fireplace, across whose twelve-foot-high mantel stretched a panther, and a billiards room where the game was being played with clear crystal balls, before turning towards the noble staircase leading to a long gallery. Then someone in the party said, "What's that?"

"That" was a half-opened door revealing a library of extraordinary richness. Walls twenty feet tall laden with leather-and-gilt spines; high, angled work-tables displaying precious Mediaeval manuscripts; racks of ancient scrolls and papyri; long gleaming tables calling out for scholars and behind them a glimpse of soft leather chairs inviting a more leisurely read before the fire.

In other words, Paradise.

But in the dream I merely shrugged, pulled the door shut, and said, "It's nothing important." I then went on to show my companions the intricacies of the decorated stairwell.

Nothing important? How the hell could Paradise be unimportant? And why was this third dream still with me, lingering at my shoulder like some telegraph boy awaiting a reply? The other two dreams had politely faded away as soon as their messages had been delivered. If I had accepted the message of this one, that the hidden rooms represented the portions of my past that I had closed away from myself, then why hadn't it drifted away as its brothers had? Instead it had returned, with greater urgency and detail than ever—my dreaming mind could not have been more insistent had it grabbed my shoulder and shouted in my ear, but for the life of me, I could not decipher its meaning.

One thing was clear: I would have no more sleep that night. Putting on my glasses and dressing-gown, I padded downstairs to make myself a cup of tea.

I took it out onto the terrace and sat in the darkness, but the night air was uncomfortably cold and damp, and before the cup was halfway empty I retreated inside, at something of a loss.

I missed Holmes. The realisation surprised me somewhat, since it had only been three days, and we were often apart for far longer than that. Perhaps it was Flo's talk of marriage, perhaps my need to converse with someone who spoke my language, but at that moment, I'd have given a great deal to have him sitting across the kitchen table from me.

Leaving the tea on the table, I went upstairs to retrieve one of the books I had brought with me; halfway down the corridor I paused, and turned towards the stairway.

My parents' bedroom was at the rear of the addition's upper floor. I had not gone in the room on Sunday, merely glanced through the door-way, seen that Mrs Gordimer had not made up that bed, and shut the door. Now, before I could reconsider, I opened it and stepped inside.

The light from the hall-way showed me a slice of the room: floor-boards, carpet, bed, lamp-shade, wall. I made my way around the bed to the lamp on the night-table, and switched it on.

A simple room, considerably smaller than its counterpart in Pacific Heights. A single, built-in wardrobe for clothing, a small dressing-table for my mother, a private bath-room, and, on the opposite side of the room, French doors leading out onto a balcony wide enough for two chairs and a low table. And between the doors and furniture, bookshelves.

Those shelves, laden and much used, made this room more a boudoir than a chamber for sleeping. Books in

the bedroom—serious books, and in great number—
were considered an oddity; that I had known even as a
child. However, I did not know, then or now, if my
mother's intentions had been to bring the best of the
outer world into her private chambers, or to keep her
private life insulated from the world.

In either case, this room was where she spent what
free hours we gave her. My father would take us swimming or out in the boat, and when we looked back at the
house, Mother would be here reading, either on the balcony or just inside the glass doors. And it was not that
she was shutting us out, for we were welcome to join her,
with our own books or choosing one from her shelves.
Other activities, board games or cards, were taken elsewhere; books from the shelves generally remained in the
room, with cautious permission granted rarely for their
removal. It was a room where my mother's worlds over-
lapped. A holy place, as it were.

Odd, I reflected: In Pacific Heights, I thought of books
in association with my father and his library; here, it was
my mother's books that dominated, while my father
pursued more active forms of entertainment.

I went forward to the shelves, finding them as neat as
they had always been: spines pulled evenly half an inch
from the edge, a book-end at the right end of each row
to allow for additions, every book, large or small, novel
or theological treatise, English, Hebrew, or other,
arranged by the author's last name. I had asked her
once, when I was first reading—was I six? No, it must
have been the previous year, if we had gone to England
shortly after the 1906 fire—how she could order names
when they were in different alphabets, and she had
showed me how to transcribe Hebrew letters into
their Roman equivalents. Thus, I saw הלל stood easily

between Hightower and Hindermann. I used the same system on my own shelves. When, that is, I could be bothered to shelve them properly.

The tight ranks of the books and my ingrained hesitation to borrow from those ordered shelves stayed my hand from reaching out and plucking one or another from its brothers. Instead, I wandered away to look over the rest of the room. The bath-room was bare and bright, its tiles clean and the usual detritus of such places—soap, bathtowels, and shaving equipment—tidied away, no doubt by Mrs Gordimer. Now that my attention was finally brought to the subject, it occurred to me how difficult it must have been for the woman to know just how to go about her cleaning duties. Regular dusting and the occasional scrub, yes, but what to do with the stubs of soap left by two dead people? Sliding open the top drawer of the chest beneath the wash-basin, I found Father's razor and soap-brush, and below it Mother's hair-brush and pins, but little of a more ephemeral nature.

On a sudden thought, I left the bright tiled room and walked over to the narrow door into the clothes closet. It smelt of cedar, but faintly, and although the clothes were still hanging there, they had all been pushed to the far ends of their rails, as if that was as far as Mrs Gordimer had been prepared to go without further orders.

I sat for a while at my mother's dressing-table before I could take up the tarnished silver powder-box that had waited ten years for the return of its owner. I pulled up the top and waited until the faint upsurge of powder reached my nose: a pang, nothing more, not even when I lowered my face to the powder and drew in a full breath of it. The still, small voice of my mother was not in the powder, nor had it been in the bedroom itself, nor in the house. A whisper of the voice, faint as a ghost, came from the shelves of her most beloved books, and so I went there and waited, unaware of the quiver of tears in my eyes until they spilt down my face.

Damn you, I told my mother's shade, why did you have to agree to come down here that last time? Why hadn't you pushed a little harder, insisted that the thousand and ten jobs in San Francisco made a trip down here impossible, that we could as easily have a final family week-end in the city? Why?

I caught myself before the maudlin tears could overwhelm me. She hadn't meant to die, hadn't meant to take Father and Levi with her; it wasn't her fault that I had been left alone in the world. No one's fault at all, except my own.

Cleaning my glasses on the shirt of my pyjamas, I issued myself orders: Get a book to read, go down and make yourself another cup of tea, since that one on the table is sure to be cold as ice. Pull yourself together.

I took a volume at random from the shelves before me, spoiling their pristine order, walked around the bed to turn off the bed-side light, then went out of the door, shutting it quietly but firmly, and descending the stairs to the kitchen.

I settled at the table with my fresh tea and the book, but I did not open it. Instead, I stared over the top of my cup at the shelves that were also a door and at the tea canister that was a lever, not really seeing either.

The more I thought about it, the more I felt that Mr Long's suggestion had been in the right direction: The concealed apartment was in no earthly mansion, but rather lay within the walls of Matteo Ricci's memory palace, and the reason I could let myself into it with such ease (at least, I could in my dream) was because I had placed it there myself: built it, closed the door on it, turned the key in its lock. The hidden apartment was my past, the childhood I had locked away and forgotten almost completely under physical pain coupled with the shock of abandonment and the wretchedness of guilt. I alone, the least worthy of the four Russells, had survived: better by far to walk unburdened and amnesiac from the desert of my past than to carry around the lush memories of what I had lost.

Yesterday my intellect had begun to accept the meaning; nonetheless, that morning's version of the dream had all but shouted at me, "It's not that simple."

Not that the interpretation was wrong, just that an intellectual recognition did not take it far enough.

A badly burnt creature will forever shy away from fire; until two weeks ago I had shied away from my past, denying the very possibility that I had gone through the events of 1906, allowing it to remain concealed behind the later trauma of the accident.

And yet, the victim of fire often remains perversely fascinated with flame, incapable of leaving it alone. And so my scarred mind had found reason to bring me, first to San Francisco itself, and then to this lakeside retreat by way of a piece of road that I'd had no intention of revisiting: Unwanted journeys all, yet each step of the way, each painful brush of memory, had brought to me a degree of mastery and self-respect. The prod of one object after another in the Pacific Heights house had made me wince, but I had also felt the dormant pieces of my past begin to unfurl and come alive within.

Then, when I had begun the journey down the Peninsula, the process of memory had changed. To use the image my dream had provided, this place had been an entire self-contained apartment, fully furnished with the people and events of the past, waiting for me to step inside and finally claim it.

And so it had proved: Coming here, I had known what the village would look like before we drove into it; I had anticipated Mrs Gordimer and her work, known what the Lodge would look and feel like before I turned the key, and been able to lay my hands on specific items without having to pat around blindly for what logic told me had to be here. I *remembered* this house, in a way I did not my more permanent home in Pacific Heights, where each event, it seemed, had to be laboriously prised open, each person and memory all but chiselled from the walls.

The Lodge, I thought, was how memory was supposed to work: fully and openly, not grudgingly and piecemeal.

So then why was the third dream so damnably insistent? Not a physical hidden room, not the general opening up of my past—what? What was it I hadn't yet explored, what did I still shy away from confronting?

(Their deaths) my mind whispered to me, but before the phrase was complete I was already on my feet and moving to the kettle, reaching for the tin of coffee, wondering even if Flo had left one of her cigarettes downstairs because although I didn't normally smoke I found myself craving one, the nicotine and the calming ritual of lighting and puffing.

While the coffee was brewing I went to my bedroom and put on some warmer clothes, then took a cup outside where I could sit on the terrace and watch the stars fade, but as soon as I had sat on the low stone wall and drawn my feet up the whisper came again.

(Their deaths.)

I jumped down from the wall, took a swallow of the scalding brew, and set the cup down again, where it clattered so badly it nearly leapt from its saucer. The air of the terrace was suddenly cold, and I hugged my coat around me and walked to the end of the stones and back again, pausing again to take another drink from the cup that persisted in shaking between my hands. I paced to the end of the terrace and back again until I began to feel like some lion in its cage, then abandoned the coffee and the terrace and set out blindly across the wet grass.

(They died) and Yes, damn it, they died, and the immediate cause of their deaths was my irritable adolescent self tormenting my brother and forcing my father to take his eyes off the road. Only he shouldn't have done so, because he was an experienced driver and almost never did that, he'd driven across the country and never got into trouble, not once, and it was a terrible road but he knew it was a terrible road and he was well used to it.

But other people who knew the road went off it as well, as evidenced by the thin insurance man clambering around on the rocks in precisely that spot.

Odd, I thought idly, to happen across the investigation of a motor accident when it was a motor accident that had brought me to that place. And then I heard the voice begin to speak in my ear again and I made a violent turn to shake it off, dimly aware that the ground beneath my feet was sloping down.

(They—)

All right—Yes, they died! Mother, Father, Levi, they all died, but then again people did, all the time. Dr Ginzberg had died, and Mah and Micah, all the time people died. Although actually, no, come to think of it, it wasn't all the time, it was all at the same time that they'd died.

An odd coincidence, I conceded; and with that word, I was suddenly aware that I was beginning to have a bad feeling about this.

My feet were at the edge of the dock, and I stepped onto the worn boards, listening to the stretch and creak of the wood giving under my weight. At the end, I sat down with my boots dangling off the end. The water was still and watchful beneath the marginally lighter sky.

Three dreams. One to drag me by the scruff of my neck up to the events of April 1906, when books flew, objects smashed, the sky burned. The second to bring me face-to-face with an ambivalent figure who had come into the tent in the days following the fire: a man with no features, who simultaneously terrified and reassured me, come looking for my father. And a third to repeat, over and over, the message that I needed only to open the door to find the hidden rooms, that I knew they were there, and had only to stretch out my hand for the latch.

And yes, they died, my family, servants, friend. But my family died eight years after the city burned and half a day's journey south of the place where the faceless man had come into the tent. They died in a snatched moment of leisure before the end of an era, days before my father would go into uniform and my mother would travel east. It might well have been our very last time on that road.

More irony than coincidence, that one.

I shivered in the cold; the air was so still, the lake seemed to be holding its breath; the brief hair on my scalp prickled and rose.

I'd never been as phobic about coincidences as Holmes was—for a man who professed to disbelieve in divine intervention, he was ever willing to follow the tracks laid out for him by Fate. But as I sat on the dock, balancing on the point formed by three intersecting images welling out of my unconscious mind, something else came up and stared me full in the face.

I'd been shot at.

In England, I had enemies; Holmes had enemies; I'd have put an assault down to one of them. But here? Two days after we'd arrived?

Finally, with the sensation of a key's wards sliding into place and an almost audible click, the hard barrier fell away, and I took a step into the hidden rooms of my past.

Where all around me, the walls, the furnishings, the very air shouted at me—

Was it an accident? Or was my family in fact murdered?

Chapter Twenty

Accident, or murder?

With that simple question, the world shifted dizzily on its axis. My father's peculiar will, the deaths of the Longs and Dr Ginzberg, the attempt to assassinate me on the street—all those came together with a clap in my mind. Not that I could see anything resembling a cause, but I had worked with Holmes long enough to see the pattern of a knot forming in the disparate strings around me. Too many deaths, too many coincidences.

Something had happened, Long had said, during the fire of 1906; something that took Micah Long away from his own family during the frantic hours when Chinatown burned, something that changed the relationship between our fathers, an event that may have driven my mother back to England for six years.

An event that, two years after our return, sent their motorcar off a cliff.

And that within four months had extinguished the

lives of three individuals in whom various Russells might have confided.

And which, ten years afterwards, caused someone to lower a gun on the only surviving Russell.

The Russell who was currently sitting in a completely exposed position as the sun climbed towards the surrounding hills, with her only weapon buried at the bottom of her valise.

The stupid Russell who hadn't thought to look behind her since giving a token glance to the street outside the St Francis on Sunday morning.

I scrambled to my feet and scurried towards the house as if I'd heard a twig break in the woods. Inside, I locked the terrace door, then went rigid, waiting for a careless motion or uncontrolled breath to betray an intruder. The house was silent, and the only dampness on the stones of the floor was from my own feet. I slipped up the stairs of the bedroom wing and cautiously nudged open my own door, but the room was empty.

I felt slightly more secure with the pistol resting in my trouser-band. I stuffed my possessions into their bags any which way, then went upstairs to bang on the door of Flo's room.

No response: I had my fingers around the knob when I heard a befuddled whimper from within. "Flo, we need to go as soon as we can. I'll get the coffee ready, but you need to wake up now."

Donny's head had already emerged from the door behind me.

"Something up?" he asked.

"I think I should be back in the city right away. I'm making coffee."

I had just taken the percolator from the heat when Donny appeared, dressed, combed, and shaved.

"Can you take a cup to Flo?" I asked. "I don't know if she'll come out of her coma without it."

He looked at me oddly, but did not say anything, just carried the two cups away. Eventually Flo joined us, picking at the toast I laid before her and drowning her sleepiness in caffeine.

When her eyes were somewhat clearer, she fixed them on me. "What's the rush?" she demanded. "I thought we were going to have a nice swim before we go?"

"I just need to be back in the city," I said, the flatness of my tone brooking no argument.

Flo blinked, and Donny cleared his throat. "Well, then, if you girls want to pack up your things, I'll put the umbrella and chairs back into the boat-house."

"Never mind them, the Gordimers will take care of everything."

I stood up. Flo and Donny, after exchanging a glance, did the same. Without waiting to see if they did as I asked, I picked up the key-ring from its hook and walked out of the front door.

The dirt drive to the road had only the Lodge and, up at the road itself, the Gordimers' house. I went to the back door and knocked, knowing at this time of day they would be in the kitchen. Mr Gordimer opened it, dropping his sweat-stained hat over his head as he did so; the odour of home-cured bacon and fried eggs washed over me, making me smile involuntarily as I held out the keys.

"We're off this morning. Thank you for watching over everything so carefully."

He took the keys from me and passed them over his shoulder to the figure behind him. I greeted his wife, whose stern face softened as she said, "I'm sorry we didn't have a chance to chat, Mary. I hope everything was satisfactory?"

"Absolutely perfect."

Gordimer gave a sort of rumbling sound preparatory to speech, then came out with, "You'll be selling up?"

"I haven't decided yet. I'll most likely sell the place in the city, it's ridiculous to keep it standing empty, but if you two are willing to go on with the upkeep here I'll hang on to it for a while longer."

"Of course we're happy to keep it tidy and safe for you," Mrs Gordimer said, "for as long as you like. And if you want to have your lawyer drop us a line again to say you're coming, we'll put the milk in the ice-box, like always."

"I appreciate it, Mrs Gordimer. And any of the bigger maintenance jobs that come along, I trust Mr Norbert's good at approving them."

"Oh, yes, there's never been a problem. Last year when the roof started leaking—no, I'm a liar, it was two years ago now—all I had to do was drop a line and suggest it was a job too big for Willy here on his own and Mr Norbert wrote right back to say we should hire whoever we liked and send him the bills. Willy wanted to do it, of course, but we hired the son-in-law of Mr Jacko—remember him, at the post office? His daughter Melinda married a nice hard-working boy from San Mateo and though of course they live over there, the boy was happy to bring his crew here for a few days and do the job. With Willy to supervise, of course."

Willy—Wilson, his name was, and the diminutive did not suit him—looked slightly abashed that he had not mounted the assault on the roof by himself, but I was glad his wife had put her veto on his active participation. I nodded my appreciation and made to ease myself back from the door, lest I be caught in the snare of Mrs Gordimer's words for the entire morning.

"Well," I said, "it's lovely to see you two looking so well, and I'm sorry I can't stay longer. My friends decided that they have to get back, so we'll be off."

"That is a pity, but I do understand, young people today are so busy. You just leave everything there, I'll pop in later and tidy it all away."

"That's very good of you, Mrs Gordimer. Perhaps I'll manage to get down again before I leave." I threw this last down as a sop to distract her, although it was a blatant lie. I had no intention of coming again, not for years. Maybe not ever.

Mrs Gordimer's continued barrage plucked at me, but slowly I moved back, further and further from her range.

However, it was Gordimer himself who stopped me. With another rumble, he summoned the following words: "Had some people here, asking questions."

My feet, halfway down the steps, stopped feeling their way backward. "People?"

"Man and a woman. Few weeks ago."

Mrs Gordimer's head inserted itself between us, staring at her husband in outrage. "There were people here and I didn't see them?"

"Day you left for your sister's. I was working on the boat-shed door, after dinner one night. Nearly dark. They came around the house, bold as brass. I sent them off."

"Can you tell me about them? Did you get their names?"

"Nah. Just told 'em to leave."

"What did they look like?"

"Didn't see him close, he stood off down the lawn with his back to me, like he was too good to do any talking. Had grey hair. She looked vaguely familiar.

Maybe forty, taller'n him. Old-fashioned hair—up on her head, you know?"

Like mine, until three months ago. "What colour was it?"

"Brown, I think. She had a hat," he added, which I assumed was meant to explain his lack of certainty as to colour.

"And you think you saw her somewhere before?"

"Dunno. Maybe just her picture."

"Anything else you noticed about them? Beard, eye colour, jewellery, that sort of thing?"

Gordimer took off his hat and scratched his balding pate in thought. "He'd a moustache, saw it when he turned just a little to say something over his shoulder. Never liked moustaches, myself," he added, a surprising digression for a man so chary of words and opinion. "Wore a sparkly ring, diamond, like, on his pinkie. 'Bout my height. Wanted to be taller—wore those shoes with the soles. Foolishness." My, my: Mr Gordimer really hadn't cared for his visitors. "The woman. About as tall as you, not quite so skinny. Brown eyes. Pretty voice. Southerner. Not him."

I reared back. "A Southerner? You're certain?"

He shrugged. "That drawl. Magnolias and juleps. Iron underneath."

I continued to gape at him, not only flabbergasted by the news, but by the simple fact of my neighbour speaking so many words. I scarcely noticed the addition of this third perceptive judgement until later.

However, the effort appeared to have drained him. I pressed for more detail, but he had given me all he had, or all he could manage to convey, because his words were replaced by shrugs and hand gestures, and a look of panic crept into his eyes. In the end, I took pity, and thanked him. He looked vastly relieved.

There was one other question, however, and for that I looked to his wife. "What day would this have been?"

The words that had been stemmed by her husband's unnatural loquacity burst forth as Mrs Gordimer provided me with the saga of her sister's debilitating illness in an unspecified part of the anatomy, with more details than I thought entirely necessary, but the essential detail of the day managed to creep in as well: March the thirtieth.

I thanked her, thanked him, and continued my backward retreat until I was safely out of the garden gate and the crunch of drive-way gravel was under my boots.

We drove away from the lake-house on Wednesday a different trio from that which had arrived on Sunday. Then, my apprehension had been so great, my two companions could only tread quietly around me; now, I was so eager, even anxious, to be back in the city I paid almost no attention to my surroundings; Flo sat in the front seat with her shoulders set in an attitude of pure disgruntlement, with Donny beside her at the wheel, silent and puzzled.

As we started up the drive, I swung around for a last look at the Lodge. I did not know if I would see it again, but I was grateful for the days here. Grateful, too, that my companions had proved so easy to get along with, other than Flo's occasional spasms of overly solicitous behaviour, pressing on me toast and sleeping draughts.

When the last corner of mossy shingles was swallowed by the trees, I faced front again.

We passed through the bucolic little village and wound through the hills towards the sea. The original plan had been that our return would cross the hills to the faster road that ran up the eastern side of the Peninsula, but before we could turn in that direction, I leant forward and put my hand on Donny's shoulder. He tipped his head to listen.

"I know it's rather out of the way, but I'd very much like to stop at that garage we passed on Sunday."

"Which one is that?"

"In the little town, Serra Beach."

"Oh, right," he said dubiously. "I'd thought to go back by way of Redwood City—along the Bay. Serra Beach would mean the coastal road again."

"Would you mind awfully?" I asked, piling on the helpless female tones, then put in the knife. "It's the very last place we spoke, my parents and I, before the accident."

He exchanged a quick glance with Flo in the seat beside him, then faced forward again. "No problem," he said over his shoulder. "If that's what you want."

"Very good of you," I said, and settled back in my seat, too occupied with my thoughts to see much of the passing scenery.

The accident site appeared up ahead of us, looming above the sandy beach where we had talked with the insurance investigator. The beach was sunny today, but deserted, with neither bread van nor closed touring car parked on the side of the road. When we got to the top of the hill, I scarcely glanced at the place where it had happened; my mind was taken up with the coming garage.

Donny pulled up to the petrol pump and all three of us got out of the motor. The boy who came out to help us was too young to remember much about the events of 1914, far too young to have built up the garage on his own. I asked him if the owner was there.

The boy glanced at me curiously, but could see no reason to fend me off. "My uncle's around the back, working on a transmission."

The mechanic looked as if he was doing battle with the transmission, or being eaten by it. The dismantled vehicle lay strewn all about, the body lifted to one side, the engine hanging from a gargantuan tripod, and the underpinnings—drive-shaft crossed by two axles—lay atop a pair of outstretched legs. I stopped short, wondering if I should summon help to lift the weighty object off a dead man, but then the legs convulsed and, marginally more reassuringly, a string of dire imprecations emerged from the wreckage. Someone that eloquent, I thought, could not be *in extremis*.

"Er, I beg your pardon?" I said loudly.

The imprecations paused, the convulsing legs began to push against the paving stones, and one arm wrapped around the drive-shaft, pulling its owner into open air.

A grease-blackened face glared at me. "Yeah?"

"I'm very sorry to interrupt you, but I'm looking for the gentleman who owned this establishment back in 1914."

More of the torso emerged, and a rag was waved across the visage, making no discernible difference, although beneath the film he appeared not much older than I. "That would've been my brother, Dick," he said. "I helped out, and took it over after he was killed back in '20."

"Would you have been here in September 1914?"

He cocked his head and fixed me with a long, thoughtful gaze before deciding to get to his feet. The rest of him was no less greasy, and I had to stop myself from retreating fastidiously when he climbed over his project and came over to stand in front of me. He tugged a cap from the back pocket of his overalls and pulled it on. Thus equipped for a formal interview, he squinted at me. "Why do you want to know about September 1914?"

It was my turn to look thoughtfully at him. Was it the date itself, or my asking, that had caught his attention? When in doubt, fall back on the truth, or a close facsimile.

"I was in a motor accident then, just down the road from this place. I wondered if anyone might remember any details about the day."

The black, shiny surface before me shifted as his expression changed. "You were in that car?"

That car. "I was."

"You're the girl."

"I was, yes."

"Well, I'll be da—Sorry, miss."

"So you do remember it?"

"Yeah, and I'm sorry to tell you you're too late. I already gave it to him."

"Gave what to whom?" It was an effort to speak over the sudden pounding of my heart, but I didn't know if it was excitement or apprehension.

"The insurance man."

"Insurance—you mean the tall man with the hair going white?"

"Bad cough."

"That's the one. What did he want?"

"Didn't want much of anything at first, just asked

questions about the accident. But when I told him what I'd done, what I had, he got more interested in it than in his questions."

"What you'd—" I drew a breath, let it out slowly, and began over again. "Mister—what is your name?"

"Hoffman," he replied, automatically sticking out his filthy paw. Without hesitation I took it, and took also the grubby rag he handed me afterwards.

"Mary Russell," I told him. "Might we sit for a moment?"

"Sure, over here."

I did not look too closely at the condition of the bench he offered—they were, after all, merely clothes. "Mr Hoffman, could you tell me about the insurance man and what you gave him?"

"Fellow came by late Saturday afternoon, asking about that accident just like you did. At first I didn't have the faintest what he was talking about—it'd been ten years, after all—but then after I'd shook my head about a dozen times it was like it shook something loose in my skull and a little bell started to ring. Anyway, I was in the middle of saying No, I don't know anything, when it hit me, sort of like, 'Oh, *that* accident!' So I said, Now wait a minute, that was the car whose tyre I changed, and started rummaging around in the back where I keep all the odds and ends I might need one day. Only took me a little while, and there it was. Little dusty, of course, but clear as day."

"What was it?"

"Oh, right, you haven't seen it. It was part of the braking system of a 1914 Maxwell, almost as clean as when it came off the factory floor, except it had a slice halfway across it that sure as shooting wasn't put there by the factory, and it had broke the rest of the way."

My face must have told him that, though I was a female, I understood not only what a brake rod was, but what a cut one meant. He nodded encouragingly, and told me a long and apologetic story about how his brother had seen that perfectly good chassis sitting there getting beaten by waves and decided that it might as well be salvaged for parts before the ocean took it. As they'd been dismantling it some months later, the remaining half of the brake rod came to light. His brother had found it, showed him what it had meant, and stuck it on the shelf.

"Why didn't you give it to the police?" I asked.

"We did," he answered indignantly. "Next time the town cop come by, a day or two later, my brother and me showed it to him, told him where we'd got it. He was more interested in the fact that we'd helped ourselves to the car—as if there was anything left of it, it was less of a car than a heap of scrap. By the time he left, he was saying he'd have to ask his sergeant about charging Dick and me with theft. Had us a little worried, I won't lie. But nothing happened after that. And when nothing happened, I sure wasn't about to stick my neck out a second time and risk getting me and my brother arrested over something that had maybe or maybe not happened four months before. So we just left it on the shelf for safekeeping and shut up about it, and after a while I just plumb forgot."

"Until the insurance man came asking." Asking about that accident, not one of the previous December.

Hoffman nodded. "He sawed off the end and took it away with him. The end I had, anyway."

"It was only half?"

"About eight inches of rod cut about three-quarters of the way through. The rest of the way it'd tore, like I told you. Our local Deadeye Dick said it was a piece of junk, that it broke in the wreck. But I know cars, and I know brake rods, and even when I was a kid I could see that it wasn't just a break that happened in going off the cliff. My brother was right—someone sawed nearly through it. Couldn't be no accident or flaw in the steel, and sure as hell—pardon, miss—wasn't from no scraping rock."

"I believe you," I told him. He settled back on the bench, his ten-year-old indignation soothed by my agreement. I continued. "Did you notice anything about the insurance man? I don't suppose he gave you his card?"

"Come to think of it, he did—should be near the register somewheres, that's where he found me."

"Had you seen the—" I caught myself before I could reveal that I knew that the man had come in a hired bread van "—the car he came in?"

"Wasn't a car, a white bakery delivery van, out of the city. Never seen it before."

We talked a while longer, but he knew nothing else about the purported insurance man. I was about to thank him for his time and rejoin my companions when I realised that I'd been so distracted by his unexpected information about the insurance man and the brake line, I'd nearly forgotten the question that started it all.

"About the accident, ten years ago. Apart from the brake rod you found later, was there anything about the day itself that stuck in your mind?"

"Long time ago," he said.

"Yes, I understand. Well, thank you—" I started to say, but he was not finished.

"...and you know how it's hard to be sure about

details, when things happened, unless you pin them down at the time?"

"Yes?" I said by way of encouragement, settling down again on the hard seat.

"Well, after we found the brake rod—and remember, that was months later—end of December, first part of January—I got to thinking back. Like I said, I'd been the one patched the car's tyre, and when I heard a little later that it'd gone off the cliff just down the road, all I could think of was I hadn't fastened the wheel down strong enough and it fell off and I'd killed them. Can't tell you what a relief it was to see all four wheels still on the car— the rubber melted, of course, but there. So the day itself made what you might call an impression on me, you understand?"

I nodded encouragement.

"It's like there's a light on the day, and yeah, I forgot about it there for a while, but once I thought about it again, I could see a lot of details. Like those wheels, and where Dick stuck that hunk of rod, and that it was the afternoon a girl I was sweet on come by and brought me a cake she'd made, that kind of thing, you know?"

I nodded again, wondering where this tale was leading us.

"So, one of the things I remembered later, I'm pretty sure it was that same day, but if you told me it wasn't, I couldn't call you a liar, you know what I'm saying? But I think it was the same afternoon that the man with the scars was there."

It was a good thing I was already seated; the *thump* of reaction would have put me on the ground. "Scars," I repeated breathlessly.

"Yeah, burn scars, all over his face. Not real heavy, you

know, and his eyes and nose were okay. Just that the skin was funny-looking, all shiny."

"And his eyebrows were gone."

"Not completely, but they were kind of patchy, like his moustache. Even the front of the scalp was uneven, like. And they weren't pink, so they probably weren't new. I was sixteen then and the war had just started up so it was in all the papers, and when I saw him I wondered at first if he'd got them in the war, then realised it was probably just some kind of accident."

"What did he want?"

"Nothing, as far as I could see. I'd just finished putting the wheel on and noticed him standing about, and he was still there when I'd moved the car and helped another customer. So I mentioned it to my brother, thinking maybe the guy was looking to steal something. Dick laughed at me, said I'd been reading too many cheap stories, look at the guy, did he look like someone who needed to steal things? He went over and talked to him, turned out he was just waiting for a ride he'd set up. And his ride must've come, because he wasn't there next time I came out."

"But you remembered the fellow, later."

"When that cut rod got me thinking, yeah. But like I said, I can't be a hundred percent sure it was even the same day, just around then. And the guy didn't look like someone who'd crawl under a car with a hacksaw."

"Dressed well?"

"Yeah, like a dandy."

A dandy. "Did…by any chance, was he wearing a diamond ring?" This was feeding information to a witness, but it couldn't be helped, and imagination or no, I didn't think the mechanic was terribly suggestible. The grimy face looked startled, then the eyebrows came down in thought. "He was, now I come to think about it. How'd you know?"

"A friend mentioned him," I told him, more or less truthfully: The scars explained why Mr Gordimer's grey-haired intruder with a diamond ring had kept his back turned, only revealing his face when he spoke over his shoulder, showing a scrap of moustache. "You haven't seen him since?"

"That I haven't, and I think I'd have noticed."

"I imagine you would," I said. "Can we just check the insurance man's business card?"

He led me inside the tiny building, rooting around in his cash-drawer for a minute before coming up with a slip of white pasteboard identical to the one the man had given me on Sunday. I handed this one back to the garage owner, thanked him, and gave him a card of my own with the telephone number of the St Francis on it, in case anything else should occur to him. Before I left, I asked, "The boy outside, is he your brother's son?"

"He is. Four years old when his daddy joined up. I'm raising him as my own."

I went back into my hand-bag and laid a ten-dollar bill on the counter. "I'm sure there's something the boy needs. This is a thank-you from an English citizen, to one who made the great sacrifice."

He took the money, shook my hand again, and watched me walk away.

Around the side of the garage, I found a water tap and a bar of filthy soap stuck onto a nail, and absently scrubbed at my palms, my mind caught up in the sensation of pressure, of memories unseen, and the inner echo of that morning's voice murmuring: *They died.*

Clearly, the Southern woman and her scarred companion had hired another agent. Still, I'd have expected their "insurance man" to be more than a few days ahead of us. Gordimer had thrown the pair off the lake property five weeks ago—why hadn't they come to the Serra Beach garage at that time? If they were looking to retrieve any evidence of their murderous sabotage of my father's motorcar, why wait until I was breathing down their necks?

I joined Flo and Donny at the car, but before I got in, I turned to study the garage and its adjoining café.

Something was missing here; either that, or I was missing something. Trim building, petrol pumps, big gum tree growing around one side, a general air of prosperity; the air smelt of eucalyptus oil, the sea, petrol, and frying meat from the café; the sounds were the chugging of the pump, the cries of sea-birds, voices in conversation, a dog somewhere barking in play; I couldn't put my finger on what should have been there but was not.

"Do you see something missing?" I asked my companions. When they did not answer, I glanced around and saw their expressions, which were frankly concerned. Belatedly, I realised that my peremptory commands of the morning, given without explanation, had left them wondering as to my stability.

"It's okay," I said with a rather forced laugh. "I know I've been a bit lunatic this morning, but really, I simply remembered that there was something I needed to do in the city, and hadn't made other arrangements. Sorry I've been so pushy. And here, well, I'm trying to remember what it is."

Both of them dutifully turned to study the front of the garage. Donny cleared his throat and suggested, "These kinds of places sometimes have signs standing out in the road," but that did not feel right. With a sigh of resignation I climbed into my assigned seat.

My thoughts were so distracting that all the way back up to the city, I was scarcely aware that I was not the one driving.

Back at the St Francis, I invited them in for a cup of tea. They hesitated, then Flo said that she knew it was early but she'd really like a drink, and so they left their car with the valet and came in. The waiter brought their "tea" in long-stemmed glasses with an olive in each, although I stuck to the more traditional English stimulant. I excused myself for a moment to go up to the room, but there was no sign of Holmes, and the only message was from Mr Braithwaite at the hospital, giving me the information I'd asked for regarding Dr Ginzberg's death. I read it, noticed the house keys on top of the dressing-table and pocketed them, then went back downstairs.

I made an effort to redeem myself and be friendly and relaxed, but when Flo and Donny left, amidst a flurry of affectionate cries and kisses worthy of her mother, I felt a great burden depart with them. I waved them away, thought about the empty room upstairs, thought too about the possibility that Holmes could return at any time, and asked the man for a taxi: If the keys were here, Holmes was not at the house, and I could have some quiet in which to meditate.

During the short trip into Pacific Heights, I considered what I would do with the remainder of the day. After I had absorbed some silence, I would go to police headquarters and locate the officer who had investigated Dr Ginzberg's death, whom the note identified as James Roley. Then I would locate the bread company whose van that false insurance agent had hired, find out at what garage their van had spent the previous day, and hunt down the man through the garage's mechanic.

The taxi stopped in front of the house, and I paid the driver and got out, walking briskly up the walk and working the key without hesitation, then locked the door behind me.

I took one step, and froze: There were lights in the house, and movement.

My hands dove for my hand-bag of their own accord, slapping at the clasp and fumbling for the cool touch of the revolver before Holmes appeared at the far end of the hall-way. I straightened, allowing the weight to slip back inside, and gave a startled laugh as I started down the hall.

"Why didn't you bring the keys with you, Holmes? Did your pick-locks need practice, or did you have a copy—"

My voice strangled at the sight of the well-dressed figure sitting before the library's fireplace: legs as awkwardly long as Holmes' own, skeletal fingers on the chair's arm, an incongruously healthy head of red hair going grey at the temples: a man I'd last seen driving away from the beach at the base of the cliffs.

In an instant, with no fumbling, the gun was out and level. "Holmes, move away from that man. He's working for the people who killed my parents."

Holmes did not move, and I glanced briefly at him, keeping the gun steady.

Why the devil was my husband positively grinning—and with what looked remarkably like relief?

BOOK FOUR

Holmes

Chapter Twenty-one

The previous morning, Tuesday, Holmes had been up long before dawn. With Russell safely retired to the lake-house for another thirty-six hours, Holmes was free to sit amongst his cushions behind closed curtains and drink his morning coffee in solitude, raising as much of a stink as he wished with the black and reeking tobacco he preferred for times of ratiocination.

The question was not so much a matter of whether or not he *could* convince Hammett to work a play of deception on his erstwhile employer, as whether he *should*.

The note sent to Hammett by the woman with the Southern accent had said that she would telephone to him on Tuesday morning at eight o'clock. By that time Hammett would need to decide: Should he openly decline her offer of employment and arrange the return of her money, or use the opportunity to lay a trap—feeding her false information, stressing the importance of a meeting?

Clearly, the trap was desirable, but pressing this

ex-Pinkerton to be the active cause of the woman's downfall was fraught with delicate ethical considerations. As Hammett had put it, "If I get the better of a guy who's been cheating me, I've got no problems with helping myself to his wallet. But if I take his job and then sell him to someone else, that's worse than stealing, it's plain dirty. A verbal contract's still a contract, and it's got to be broken before it can be ignored."

Holmes did not know if he ought to force the deception on him. Doing so ran the risk of alienating Hammett completely, having him simply declare a curse on both their houses and go home to the Underwood on his kitchen table.

Actually, Holmes reflected, knocking the first pipe out and reaching for the tobacco, on closer consideration the question might actually be whether he *could* convince the man to turn coat.

In the end, the previous evening he had simply presented his case for bringing the lady—or even her agent—into the open, that she might be located, identified, and assessed. Then he had left Hammett to make up his own mind.

Holmes tried to console himself with the idea that, even were Hammett to decline the job, she would have to venture into the open to retrieve her cash. Of course, if she had any sense, she'd write the money off rather than risk exposure; whether or not she did so would in itself tell him a great deal.

When he had exhausted the possibilities of Hammett's telephone conversation, Holmes removed his mind from that and turned his thoughts to his father-in-law's will, his mother-in-law's garden journals, and the tantalising words on the burnt scraps of paper.

The hands of the clock moved with agonising slowness. Holmes sat, motionless for long periods on the cushions, his hooded eyes glittering in the dim light of the room, and waited for his telephone to ring.

At sixteen minutes after the hour, the device emitted the strangled burble that was its mechanical equivalent of a throat-clearing, and he snatched it up before it could go on to its ring.

"Yes," he demanded.

"She 'phoned, right on the dot of eight," Hammett's voice told him. "I told her I couldn't take the case."

"I see." Holmes was not surprised.

"She wasn't happy about it. Cursed me in a couple of languages, and I had to raise my voice to ask her where I should send her money. She finally heard me, said I should keep it for a while, that maybe I'd change my mind. Said it like a threat. So I had to tell her that, if I didn't hear from her by Friday morning, I was going to tack the envelope up to the entranceway of the apartment building and leave it there for anyone to help themselves to."

"What was her response?"

"She just said she'd be in touch and hung up. With a bang. When I got the exchange, the girl said that the call had been put through from a public office on the other side of town, but when I called there, the woman had left already. She's pretty good at this."

"I expected nothing less. Hammett, it might be a good idea—"

"Yeah, I know, I'll need to be back here before my wife comes home with the kid for lunch, just in case we have a visitor with a gun. But I think I'll use some of your money to send them both down to Santa Cruz for a couple of days. She's been talking about going. Once they're out of the way I'll be yours for what you need."

"You might also make sure you don't leave any notes concerning the case lying about in the open."

"I'll do that. So, what do you want me to do this morning?"

"How far did you get on the Ginzberg death?"

"Found the man in charge; he was tied up with a fresh case."

"I'd like to have something to give Russell on that when she gets back tomorrow. See what you can do with it."

"Right you are. You need me, I'm at police headquarters 'til noon, then back here."

"And I shall check in with the hotel during the day, to ask if any messages have been left me," Holmes told him, then, "Hammett?"

"Still here."

"I was thinking of placing an advert in one of the papers, asking for information regarding the delivery of an envelope to your address. That lad might be able to tell us something."

"Are you asking my opinion?"

"I suppose I am," Holmes said, rather surprised at the fact.

"Then I'd say not. Later, maybe, but doing it now, you'd risk scaring them off. You'd also be risking their getting to the kid first."

"You feel they could remove him?"

"Yeah, I do."

"I'm afraid I agree with you, Hammett. Thank you." Holmes set the earpiece back on its hook, and pulled back the curtains to let the day in. He leant his shoulder against the window-frame, staring unseeing down at the street, weighing his options—or, rather, weighing his opponent's options. His picture of her was more blank space than anything else, but he did not have the impression that the woman had unlimited resources. Her efforts had been too focussed for that, and her fury at Hammett's refusal indicated that she had rather a lot tied up in him—although her anger could as easily have been due to the waste of time rather than money. However, there was also the fact of her overgenerous payment to Hammett: In Holmes' experience, someone with a great deal of money was less likely to misjudge the cost of a thing, or of a person.

All in all, he thought that the woman's resources could well be somewhat stretched, and she would want that money back. He considered his available stock of Irregulars: Hammett was not only noticeable but known to the woman; Long would stand out anywhere outside Chinatown; the lad Tyson could not be trusted to keep to the shadows—he would want to sail in, guns blazing.

No, there was nothing for it: time to recruit.

Holmes went to the trunks that had been stashed, as he'd insisted, not in the hotel store-room but against the back wall of the bedroom. He unearthed the one he wanted and, sorting through the layers of clothing Oriental and Western, eventually put together a costume that would be unremarkable in the part of town he intended to visit. The lift-man looked at him askance, but said nothing.

His first task was to determine if a surveillance of the Hammett apartment was even a viable proposition—watching the front door of an apartment building was of little use without a detailed description of the quarry. He sought out the delivery alley that ran in back of Hammett's building, and was gratified to find that the fire-escape doors possessed small windows at each level. By the judicious rearrangement of dust-bins and the hook of his walking-stick, he scrambled onto the metal escape and moments later was looking straight down the hall-way at Hammett's door.

Humming a tune under his breath, he dropped out of the heights and went out to recruit a platoon of Irregulars.

The modern fashion for universal compulsory education had put a distinct cramp into the style of a consulting detective. In his Baker Street days, he'd been regularly able to summon a group of street arabs to serve at his beck and call, but now—and particularly in this democratic republic of America—all his most valuable resources were parked behind desks, chafing at the restrictions and wasting their most productive years while their heads were filled with mathematical formulae they would never use and the names of cities they would never visit.

Fortunately, the truant officer who worked Hammett's neighbourhood did not appear to be among the most stringent. Three streets away from Hammett's apartment, Holmes heard the sound of children's voices from down an alley. He sauntered down the dim recesses between two buildings until he could see their figures, gathered in a lump against a brick wall. Then he halted, leaning against the wall and taking out his cigarettes. He lit one, to ensure that he had their attention, and they went silent for a moment while they considered the necessity of flight.

Children, Holmes had found, were like wild dogs: Liable to slink away at the merest threat when encountered in their solitary state, in a pack they were curious, intelligent, potentially vicious, affectionate to their friends, and immensely loyal to the pack leader. Sure enough, before the cigarette was halfway down a small child was standing in front of him, just far enough away to dance out of reach of the walking-stick. Holmes studied the end of his cigarette, and stifled a yawn.

"Say, mister, what do you want?"

Holmes turned his head as if noticing the child for the first time. "Are you the boss-kid here?" he asked.

"Nah," the young scout admitted.

"Then my business isn't with you," he told the infant, and went back to leaning against the wall.

The child returned to his pack; whispers gave way to a sharp command; the sounds of their game resumed—penny pitching, Holmes heard, rather than dice or cards. He came to the end of his cigarette, ground it out under his heel, and leisurely lit another; it wasn't until the third time his match flared that the pack leader's curiosity overcame him.

He was a lad of about ten years, by no means the tallest of the half-dozen children, and not quite the oldest. His heritage owed something to both Ireland and Mexico, but he'd have fit right in among the Whitechapel urchins Holmes had known for so many years: scuffed shoes, too-short trousers, too-long coat, and a tweed cap worn at a rakish angle. Holmes had to conceal his smile with the cigarette, while waiting for the boy to speak.

"What do you want?" the ruler of the alleyway demanded.

"I need a job done," Holmes told him. "I thought maybe you'd have an older brother who'd be interested."

As he'd anticipated, the boy ignored the open acknowledgement that he was the pack's leader and fell for the implication that he was not man enough for the "job." He drew himself up to his full four feet and bristled.

"I got two older brothers. One's a drunk and one's in prison. Which one do you want?"

"By the sound of it, neither of them. I need someone who's wise enough not to fall into a bottle and bright enough not to get caught when he does something slick. How smart are you?"

"Smarter'n you, mister, if you think I'll fall for that guff."

"Up to you. I need a job done, and I'm willing to pay, but if you're not interested, I'll find someone else."

"What kind of job?"

"The kind of job that takes brains and the ability to keep his friends under control."

The boy looked at the friends in question, standing in a knot just a little further down the alley. Then he looked back at Holmes, and took a couple of steps closer. "Like I said—what kind of a job?"

The negotiations that followed would have done a wigged barrister proud, but in the end, Holmes had bought the day's services of the boy's pack: keeping constant watch over the Hammett door, running a messenger to the St Francis if anyone came to the apartment, and following discreetly when the intruder left.

"You'll need to be wary of the boot-leggers on the ground floor," he warned his new lieutenant. "They may stand watch in the evenings. And if an intruder comes, you are not to approach him, or her as the case may be. You will follow, *at a distance,* for as long as you can. If she—or he—gets into a taxi, don't try to run behind or draw attention to yourself by trying to hail a taxi of your own. Just get the cab's number and we can later find where the driver went. Er, I am correct in assuming you can all read numbers?" The scornful snort the lad gave out reminded Holmes of Russell; it also satisfied him, and he went on. "If she goes into a shop, one of you go around the back to make sure—"

"Mister," the leader interrupted with infinite disdain, "we know all this. My uncle runs a betting shop, and when one of his customers don't pay up, sometimes he asks us to help lay hands on the guy. You're doin' what he calls 'Teaching granny to suck eggs,' whatever that means. Sounds disgusting, but that's what you're doin'."

Holmes beamed at the boy and reached out a hand to pat the disreputable tweed cap, then changed the gesture to the offer of a hand-shake, which the lad eyed curiously, then accepted. "You give me hope for the coming generation," he said. "You needn't continue all night, as the man who lives there will be at home, but if nothing has happened today, I'd like you back here tomorrow. Same rates. I'll come back here first thing in the morning, to pay you what I owe you and receive your report." He handed over the agreed-to retainer of two dollars and left the pack to their work.

At the end of the alleyway, he stopped to change his neck-tie for one less gaudy, reverse his coat so that its staid side was facing out, snap the brim of his hat down into dignity, and brush the dust from his trouser-legs and shoes.

He entered Chinatown with the appearance of just another stray from the financial district, looking for a late lunch.

It took a while before Long could extricate himself from customers, a while longer while they settled into the corner of a tea-house, and even longer before he grasped what Holmes was asking.

"You think there is treasure buried in the Russell garden, and you want me to help you find it?" He was too polite to sound openly incredulous, but it was in the back of his voice.

"I believe there is something of importance hidden in

the grounds, yes. Consider, if you will, three points. First, Charles Russell wrote a codicil to his will shortly after the fire, making it nearly impossible for any outsider to gain access to the property, a thing most easily explained by the presence of something either valuable or incriminating on the premises. Second, a thorough search of the house interior gave us nothing. And third, your family, long and faithful though their service seems to have been, appears nowhere in the house records after the summer of 1906. There was no mention of them in the will, no cheques made out to them in the account registers after that time, no official link whatsoever that I have been able to uncover.

"Taken separately, none of the three pieces of information leads to much in the way of a conclusion. Taken together, the indications would be that the thing Charles Russell wished to conceal was not in his house, but in the garden. And how could he hope to keep a buried object hidden from a gardener as skilled and conscientious as your father? He was forced to take your father into his confidentiality, but to protect him, he cut all evidentiary ties between himself and the Long family. He paid their salaries in cash, he made no provisions in his will for them, and he and his wife refused a signed document when she lent your parents money to buy the bookstore. So yes, I believe there is something buried in the garden, something your father knew about. Something too sensitive to be locked into a bank's safe-deposit vault, where it would come to light on Charles Russell's death."

"You may be correct, Mr Holmes, but I assure you, he did not tell me about it."

"I should be very surprised if he did. However, I should also be surprised if you could not find it."

"How? What would I be looking for?"

"I have no idea."

"Then how do you know that it is there?"

"This threatens to become a circular argument," Holmes said. "I know it's there because it's all that explains the facts. My wife tells me that astronomers posit the existence of an invisible planet by the effects it has on the orbit of other celestial bodies. Thus do I posit the existence of this object."

"I see. Mr Holmes, I have been in the garden a few times, yes, when I was very young, but I doubt that now I could even find where my father had his vegetables growing—the place is a jungle, I saw that much the other evening."

Holmes hunched forward over the table, and spoke in a low voice. "Mrs Russell kept a detailed record of the work done in her garden, including a yearly sketch or map of the arrangement of flower-beds and paths, the addition of major plantings, and so on. There is a volume for every year, beginning with the spring of 1903. The years she spent in England, 1907 to 1911, are missing, but there is one made dated March 1906, and one made in the autumn of 1912 after her return."

"None of them, I would assume, have a spot marked 'X' with the Stevensonian suggestion to 'dig here'?" Long asked it with a smile.

"Alas, no. However, I believe your father may have acknowledged the presence of some object of supreme importance in the arrangement of the garden itself, whether he was instrumental in its concealment or simply told of its presence after the deed was done."

"How do—ah." Long sighed. "You are thinking of my father's commitment to the principles of feng shui."

"Precisely," said Holmes. "I am suggesting that, were one to analyse the adjustments that were made, the replacement of the fish pond, for example, and the shift of the rock-garden, one might work backward to find the source of the perceived problem. That, to a knowledgeable eye, the re-channelling of the earth's energies that was done some years ago might point to a specific source." He watched closely until he was satisfied that Long understood, then sat back to let Long think.

After a while, the bookseller shook his head. "I could look at the garden drawings and see if anything catches my eye, but I am a neophyte, and if my father did the thing correctly, the changes would be quite subtle. After all, there is little purpose in hiding a thing if you then place a large arrow over its location. He would have consulted a practitioner of the arts."

"Did he know such a man?"

"He did. He used him to arrange the fittings in the bookstore, in fact. But the man was very old, and died years ago."

"That is unfortunate," Holmes said. "However, perhaps if we were to give those maps to another with that knowledge, might he be able to perceive the place that your father would have been . . . protecting?"

"It is possible. The classical principles of feng shui are laid down in history, and although each practitioner has his or her own style, the formulae should be the same. Would you like me to find out?"

"Very much." As the alternative would be to reduce the entire garden to something resembling the trenches of northern France, any guidance, however idiosyncratic, could be of value.

"I know a man who can do what you need, if anyone can. Would you care to wait here while I go and see if he would consider taking the consultation?"

The phrasing and the way in which Long nervously

adjusted his tie and cuffs indicated that the person he intended to ask was of an exalted rank, not at all the sort of person a casual Westerner could drop in on. Holmes told Long that he was happy to wait, and he settled in with his tea, tossing down countless tiny cups of the scalding beverage while the citizens of this town-within-a-town scurried back and forth across the window. He was impatient: The clock was ticking, and it was beginning to look less and less likely that he would get this thing settled before Russell returned.

When Long came back, he wore the face of unsuccess.

"He is out of town," he reported. "A new restaurant in San Jose has a complicated set of problems. He is not expected to return until tomorrow. I asked to be notified as soon as he comes back, but if you prefer, I can find another practitioner."

"Would the other be as good?"

"No," Long said simply.

Holmes rapped his tiny cup rapidly on the table a number of times, then pushed it away from him, sitting back in his chair. "Very well, then; tomorrow."

"Will you call?"

"I shall either call by your shop or telephone to you, after noon."

"I shall be there."

Holmes left the tea shop and walked down the street, but there he stopped, a large barrier of indecision on the bustling pavements. In the end, he turned abruptly back and walked in the direction of his telegraphist. Not that he expected a response from Mycroft, who would have received the second telegram less than twenty-four hours before, but only the careless leave a possibility unattended due to assumptions.

To his surprise, the busy man responded to his arrival

in the door by slapping an envelope onto the counter-top. To his greater surprise, once he had redeemed the thing and gone out to the street to open it, it was not second thoughts from Watson, but from Mycroft:

DEAR BOY FAR EASIER TO GIVE ALL DETAILS AT
BEGINNING AND DON'T MAKE ME GUESS BUT
BASED ON GUESSWORK AND WORKING BACKWARD
FROM RUMOURS SENT ME FROM OUR FRIEND IN
ADEN I BEGAN ENQUIRIES REGARDING FURTHER
ACTIVITIES OF ANY PERSON OR PERSONS
UNKNOWN WHO MADE HASTE TO INTERCEPT
YOUR BOAT IN MARSEILLES OR PORT SAID OR
CAIRO. ONLY ONE SUCH LOOKED PROMISING
NAMELY WOMAN IN PARIS BEGAN SEARCHING
FIFTH JANUARY FOR FLIGHTS TO EGYPT FOUND
PILOT AND ACCEPTABLE WEATHER MONDAY
SEVENTH ARRIVING PORT SAID EARLY HOURS
OF TUESDAY EIGHTH. COST UNKNOWN BUT
CONSIDERABLE. DESCRIPTION QUOTE TALL BUT
WOMANLY UNQUOTE LATE THIRTIES BROWN HAIR
AND EYES SPOKE FLUENT FRENCH AND ENGLISH
WITH QUOTE SOUTHERN AMERICAN UNQUOTE
ACCENT NOT CERTAIN IF MEANS SOUTHERN USA
OR SOUTH AMERICA SORRY O THE PROBLEMS OF
FINDING GOOD HELP. LET ME KNOW IF I SHOULD
EXTEND ENQUIRIES TO THE BOAT WHICH DOCKS
HERE THURSDAY. NEXT TIME BE FORTHCOMING
EARLY TO YOUR BIG BROTHER. ALL WELL HERE
LOST TWO STONE.   MYCROFT.

Holmes laughed aloud with pleasure at the undimin-ished authority of Mycroft's voice. He did not care to think of the world without his older brother, who in January had looked very ill from his heart attack.

He went back inside to send a return message of thanks and to assure Mycroft that it would not be necessary to interview the staff of the *Marguerite* at this time. No doubt Mycroft could extract more detail from the pursers than Watson had, but he did not think it necessary.

Telegram sent, he made his way back to the house, let himself in with the key he'd had cut the previous day, and settled in for a minute study of the household accounts. These covered the period from 1890, when Charles Russell had arrived here after university, until the close of 1913—later records, he figured, would be with Mr Norbert.

He had looked these over before, gleaning from them such information as when the Russells had come here after their marriage, when Judith Russell had left for England, and when the Longs had first begun, then ceased, to appear on the books. Now, however, he read more carefully. Making notes, he turned back from time to time as he tried to piece together the portrait of a family.

He laboured all the afternoon and far into the night, breaking away only to make two telephone calls to the St Francis from his new Italian friends down the street, but there were no messages. On his second trip down, the owner of the café urged a dinner on him, and he returned to the accounts refreshed by a nice scallopini and a litre of powerful Italian coffee.

He discovered many fascinating truths about the Russell family, but only two that stood out in his mind for the purposes of the investigation. Both of those were associated with the father of the young lady currently sharing a house near a lake with Russell. In 1892, before he had gone to Europe and met his wife, young Charles Russell had made out a cheque for $750 to Robert Greenfield, with the notation "for help with building cabin." Then on April 22, 1906, he had written another to the same person, for $7500. Against this had been noted "repayment of loan."

He closed the last book near midnight and went to stand, only to stop halfway upright, biting off an oath. He eased his back through a series of cracks, feeling like an arthritic grandfather. "I'm getting too old for this," he muttered, although he'd been saying it for years now, and did not really believe it. He stretched and popped his joints, then let himself out of the house, moving with the determined ease of a man who had never known discomfort.

Early Wednesday morning he went around the back of Hammett's apartment building and found that his Irregulars had been organised into an efficient body of surveillance operatives. The urchin at the entrance of the alleyway spotted him coming down the street, and gave out a shrill whistle that had the leader waiting for Holmes at the base of the fire-escape.

The boy reported that they had seen no one all day, not until the tall man who lived there came home about four o'clock and his wife and the little girl about an hour after that. They'd stayed in all night, except when the woman had stepped out to the little market up the street for milk and bread at six and the man had brought the garbage down to the alleyway around eight. In the first case, two of the boys had followed her, in the second they had all faded away into invisibility behind the cans.

"And I know you said we weren't to keep watch all night," the lad told him, "but I figured that if they all got murdered in their beds during the night, you'd like to know who done it. That maybe there'd be a bonus, like," he added cheekily.

Holmes hid his grin and counted out the previous day's pay, then added half as much again for the night duty. "You'll stay on during the day, when they leave?"

"You pay, we stay," the boy told him. "We'll hunt you down if anything happens."

"You're doing a good job. I only hope you go back to school when this is over."

"School's a waste of time."

"That may be so, but university isn't, and you have to get through school to get to university."

The look of scepticism shooting out of those dark eyes would have given a priest doubt, but Holmes had seen it before. He tipped his hat to the boy, then paused. "What's your name, lad?"

"Why do you want to know?"

"Because gentlemen do not address each other as 'Hey, you.' "

"Gen'lmen, huh? Okay, it's Ricky. Rick Garcia."

"Mr Garcia, it is a pleasure doing business with you. My name is Holmes. I shall try to return this evening, but you know where to find me."

"Okay. 'Bye then, Mr Holmes. See you later."

Holmes' eggs had just been placed before him when a bellman came to tell him there was a telephone call for him. It was Hammett, suggesting that they meet.

"I'm just taking breakfast. Would you like to join me?"

"Sure, that would be fine. I'll be there in ten minutes or so."

Hammett arrived, looking as well-dressed and cadaverous as ever, just in time to see the dignified Englishman half-rise from his chair, eyes popping at some article in the paper before him, and then ball it up and hurl it to the floor. The entire restaurant fell dead silent; the only people moving were the maître d' and Dashiell Hammett.

"Sir, what is it?" begged the hotel gentleman. "Is there anything—"

Holmes raised his eyes and found Hammett standing in front of him, then looked further and noticed that every pair of eyes was avidly waiting to see what this dignified Englishman would do next. He gave a sharp little laugh, waved away the maître d', and dropped back into his chair. Hammett scooped up the armful of newsprint and sat across from him.

"Don't like the news?" Hammett asked laconically, straightening the pages.

The older man scowled furiously at the day's *Chronicle*. "Hammett, if ever you find yourself bound to a literary agent, for God's sake make sure the man isn't utterly barking mad."

"Literary agent?" Hammett asked.

"I cannot get away from the man. I sit peacefully over my poached eggs and toast, wishing only the gentle news of the latest poisoned-chocolates case or Babe Ruth clouting his homer, and who should stare out at me from the pages of a newspaper from a city halfway across the world from my home but Conan Doyle."

During this monologue, Hammett had been paging through the crumpled sheets with some difficulty, interrupted by the waitress taking his order and the bus-boy cleaning up Holmes' spilt coffee, but at last he found it:

Conan Doyle Lauds, Hits S.F.
Likes City's Beauty; Abhors Spiritual Void

Hammett read the article with close attention, learning that the writer's recently published account of his *Second American Adventure* included the lament that he had found San Francisco to be a far less psychic city than Los Angeles. At the article's inside continuation, he read aloud the author's regret over "San Francisco, with its very material atmosphere," and ending with his judgement that the city left "much room for spiritual betterment."

By the time Hammett reached the final resounding phrase, he was finding it difficult to control his laughter. Holmes looked storm-clouds at him, until the younger man protested, "Hey, you might have had to come to Los Angeles instead of here."

Holmes' glare held, then softened, and he relaxed into his ruffled feathers. "That is very true," he admitted, adding, "I like your town more and more, Hammett. Any town whose people have the sense to laugh at Doyle's infantile philosophy can't be too bad."

Hammett raised his coffee cup. "Here's to San Francisco."

Holmes, casting a last disgusted look at the paper Hammett had folded up onto the unoccupied chair, tore his eyes and his attention away from the outrage and asked Hammett if he'd heard anything during the night.

"Not a thing. Looks like she's cutting her losses and I'll end up nailing the envelope onto the front of the building like I told her. But like I said, my wife's taken the kid off to Santa Cruz for a couple of days with friends. I'm at your service."

"What did your police detective have to say about the Ginzberg death?"

"A fat lot of nothing. Not even any prints on the statue that bashed her. Some kind of bird carving it was, an owl maybe, from Rhodes or Crete or something in the Mediterranean. Seems she collected bird sculptures from all over."

"If you haven't exhausted your friends' patience there, how would you feel about having the police lab look at a set of prints?"

"From where?"

"I found them on an otherwise pristine toilet-pull in the house. They appear to belong to a woman—ours probably has no record, but just in case."

"Okay."

"Then later, why don't you come by the house? I've arranged something that might interest you."

"Yeah? What's that?" Hammett's plate arrived and he picked up his utensils.

"Oh, I suppose you might call him a Chinese fortune-teller." Hammett shot him a dubious glance before bending to his food. "There's also this," Holmes added, and slid Mycroft's telegram across the table.

The thin man read it carefully, then asked, "What are these two stones he's lost?"

"Stones? Ah, that's a British weight measurement; fourteen pounds is a stone. My brother's doctors have him on a slimming diet."

"Got you. You think that's your gal he's found, that she's followed you all the way here?"

"It would fit. She lives in Paris, sees mention of my

name in the Saturday *Times*, scrambles desperately for a means of getting to Egypt ahead of our boat—the weather was vile, which added to her difficulties. She finds one on Monday for a considerable price and boards the ship in Port Said. While we're sailing down the Suez Canal and Dead Sea, she keeps mostly to her cabin while finding as much about us as she can. Then we get to Aden, when she gets off—possibly having arranged with an associate to meet her there and set up a booby-trap. The bazaar isn't that large, so that if we were going to disembark for the afternoon, there was a good chance we'd walk past her trap eventually. I have a friend there I can ask to find out, for a fee."

"But she missed."

"*If* it was an attempt in the first place, and not just a shaky balcony," Holmes added, to be fair.

"As you say," Hammett noted. "But by that time, she knew you were headed to San Francisco. So while you and your wife were in India, she came on here."

"Where she broke into the house, found some papers and burnt them, and lay in wait for our arrival. Which, again, seems to have made it into the papers."

"But what's she after? Other than your dead bodies, that is?"

"That I hope to learn this afternoon at the house."

"Well, there's an offer I can't pass up. Give me your finger-prints and I'll see what I can do with them, and meet you at the house later. What time?"

"I am not sure, but perhaps four?"

"I'll be there."

And he was. At ten minutes before the hour, Hammett stood on the door-step listening to the bell fade and the foot-steps approach. Holmes opened the door with a magazine in one hand, an object that caused

Hammett to do a double-take: It was a copy of *Smart Set* from the previous year, an issue containing Hammett's set of brief reminiscences, "Memoirs of a Private Detective."

Hammett looked from the magazine to Holmes. "How on earth did you find that?"

"A news-agent agreed to search for your stories. I was curious," he said, sounding apologetic.

Hammett began to chuckle ruefully. "Have you met Waldron Honeywell yet?"

"The gentleman with the poor opinion of the specialised skills of one Sherlock Holmes? Yes."

"Sorry about that. It's what sells."

"Well, Mr Honeywell is not altogether mistaken. May I offer you something to drink while we wait?" Holmes asked.

The two men settled into Charles Russell's library, waiting for Long and his feng shui divinator, smoking, drinking coffee with just a little whiskey in it to keep out the cold, and slowly easing into the shared talk of professionals concerning tricky investigations and foolish criminals. At four-thirty in the afternoon, they heard the front door come open and Holmes stepped into the hall-way, and in an instant, into the library swept Russell, looking magnificent and furious as she pulled a gun on the greying ex-Pinkerton, shouting at Holmes to stand away from the man who worked for those who had murdered her family.

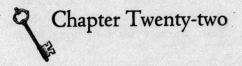

Chapter Twenty-two

An invalid Hammett might be, but the man had nerves of steel.

His bony hands tightened over the arms of the chair when the weapon first appeared, then they relaxed, curled loosely over the leather. He did keep a close eye on the pistol while Holmes stepped forward to explain: It was a decorative object, but big enough to mean business.

"Russell, this is Mr Hammett. He was clambering around on those cliffs at my instigation. I've hired him as an Irregular in your absence; hope you don't mind?"

The silvery barrel wavered, as if it might decide to point at Holmes for a while, then sank towards the floor. "*You* hired him," she said flatly.

"He knows the ground here better than I, and I needed an assistant."

"When did you make this arrangement?"

"Saturday," he admitted: an exaggeration, as it had been little more than Friday night.

"Saturday. And you didn't think to mention it to me that night, or even Sunday morning?"

"We had a great deal to get through on Saturday as it was. And in the morning, you were busy, I was busy. I'd have told you—it hardly mattered if you did not know."

"It would have mattered just now if I'd shot the man," she retorted.

Hammett gave a little snort of laughter, and her eyes went to him. In a moment, the gun went back into its hand-bag and she came up to him, hand out. "Mr Hammett, pleased to meet you. I apologise for my ill manners."

"Miss Russell. Don't worry about it. You have remarkably steady hands on a gun."

"For a girl, you mean?"

"For a hand. More people get shot by twitchy fingers than ever get aimed at."

"I try to avoid manslaughter when I can. Mr Hammett, if you are working for Holmes and not our two opponents, then I take it you retrieved the brake rod of my father's Maxwell?"

"Safe and sou—" he started to reply.

"*Two* opponents," Holmes broke in. "You say that as if you've identified them."

"Yes," she said, sounding rather pleased with herself. "I believe you'll find that either your assistant here is keeping something from you, or else he got so excited about the evidence that he forgot to carry through with the interrogation of the Serra Beach mechanic."

"Yeah, I was afraid of that," Hammett said with chagrin. "I didn't remember until later that night that there were questions I'd forgotten to put to him, but it was too late to go back, and the garage wasn't open Sunday. I should've run him to ground at his home."

"Well, I nearly did the same," Russell admitted generously. "And I didn't even have a lovely piece of solid evidence to distract me."

Hammett's haggard face pulled into a grin that matched hers, but Holmes was impatient.

"Tell me about the two."

"Can we sit down? I've had a tiring day, steering from the backseat."

"Certainly. I had the sweep in yesterday; we can even light the fire. Would you care for whiskey, or coffee?"

"Is it the same coffee we found in the house?"

"No, I found a charming Italian gentleman up on Columbus Street who permitted me to buy some of his freshly roasted beans."

"Such domesticity, Holmes. Coffee would be lovely."

As she passed the small table, Russell scooped up the drooping petals of her flower arrangement and tossed them onto the bones of the fire she had laid but not lit the other day. Borrowing a match from Hammett, she set it against the dried kindling and stood back cautiously, but indeed, the chimney drew cleanly. Holmes pulled over the desk chair, and the two men settled their glasses on the table alongside her cup, then took out their tobacco pouches.

With the crackle of flames and the odours of coffee, spirits, and tobacco—Hammett's cigarette joined by Holmes' pipe—the library was transformed from a habitation of ghosts into a place where civilised conversation might take place.

Holmes cleared his throat. "What made you decide that your parents were murdered?"

Her eyes went sideways to the third person in the room, as if to ask how much they were to say in front of him—but then, Holmes would not have asked if he had not meant her to answer. "You mean, seeing as how I've been fighting the idea for days now?"

He would have said somewhat longer than that, but he merely nodded.

"Too many oddities, piling up on each other. The codicil to the will, my parents' behaviour in the years after the fire, three related deaths immediately after theirs that were clearly murder, the shooting here. But mostly it was the dreams: The dreams were pushing me to something, all the time. I finally got there."

"So tell me about your two villains," Holmes suggested.

"Yes," she said. "The two villains. A woman with a Southern accent, and the faceless man—only he is now merely a man with facial scars." Then she paused as a thought occurred to her. "Er, Holmes, before I get into that, why are you here?"

"We are awaiting Mr Long and a friend of his, who may be able to point us towards the solution of one of our mysteries."

"Oh yes? What time will they be here?"

"With any luck, before it is too dark outside to see the trees."

"Will we need to see the trees?" she asked, then held up her hand. "Never mind, I'll find out soon enough." And without further questions, she told the two men about her days at the Lodge. She kept it to the essentials—the lack of anything resembling evidence in the hidden storage room, Mr Gordimer's two visitors, her revealing conversation with the Serra Beach garage mechanic, the conversation with Donny and Flo that revealed the extent to which Dr Ginzberg had been known as a doctor with a speciality in helping patients retrieve memories. She did not bother telling them about her other conversations with Flo and Donny, as those were not pertinent to the matter at hand.

Holmes listened with his hands steepled and his eyes on the flames, his face showing nothing of the relief and pleasure surging through his veins. Russell was awake at last, returned to her normal clear wits and keen vision. Although he had to admit that even half asleep, she'd managed to turn up as many items of vital importance as he had working flat out. When she had reached the point in her narrative where she'd decided to come here, she sat back and said firmly to Holmes, "Now it's your turn."

He began by giving her the telegrams, explaining how his own had started the exchange. He told her about meeting Hammett, although he left a great deal out of the manner and precise time of their meeting, not wishing to get side-tracked into the reasons he had been following her on the Friday night. He described the cut brake rod, safely in the bank vault, and his growing conviction that her father had concealed something in the garden. He then turned the floor over to Hammett, who described how he had become involved, how he had been caught and recruited by Holmes (he, following Holmes' lead, also avoided specific mention of time and place), and spent the next few days searching crash sites and interviewing police officers.

"And," he finished up, "just in case you're wondering, I had a second conversation with the lady who'd tried to hire me, telling her I wasn't working for her and asking her where I could send her money. She hasn't gotten in touch yet, but I told her that if she didn't fetch it by Friday, I'd be putting it out for the birds to find.

"Which reminds me," he said, turning to Holmes, "are those children yours?"

It never even passed through Russell's mind that the man might be referring to any biological responsibility. "More Irregulars, Holmes?"

"It seemed a good idea to keep an eye on the Hammett apartment," he replied, then added in disappointed tones, "I expected the lads to be more invisible than that."

"Oh, they're good, all right—anyone who doesn't know the area would never think twice. But it's my own block, and I happen to know there aren't any kids of that age right there. Especially not kids who just stand around in groups of two or three, and don't seem to wander off much. Although I'll admit that if I hadn't already been thinking of getting someone to watch my door, I probably wouldn't have noticed them."

"I'm glad to hear that."

Hammett reached for his pouch and papers again, glancing at Russell as he did so. "I had a couple of questions for you. Your father was going to join the Intelligence branch when he joined up?"

Russell shot a surprised glance at Holmes, who returned it evenly, as if to say, *Yes, I told him nearly everything.* She shrugged, and said to Hammett, "That's right. He had a slightly bum leg which would have made it difficult to do a day's march with a full pack, but he spoke both German and French, he had travelled extensively in Europe, and in addition his father had gone to school with one of the generals in charge of Intelligence, or at any rate, what eventually became the Intelligence branch."

"But you don't think your father could have picked up an enemy through those connexions?"

"What, German spies and assassins in San Francisco, just two months after the war started? I shouldn't have thought so. As far as I know, he hadn't done any work at all for them yet, and he didn't even have any links with the Presidio. But would I have known if he did? Probably not."

Holmes turned to Hammett. "Do you know anyone inside the Army here?"

"I might. Don't know if he'd know, or talk if he did, but I can find out."

"It might be worth asking. Just to eliminate the possibility."

"I gave your toilet-pull to my police friend," Hammett told him. "Nothing yet, but it's not exactly a fast process, and like you said, the prints are probably not in their files."

"There's a project for the future," Holmes mused, "developing a central and quickly accessible registry for finger-prints."

"A hobby for your retirement, Holmes," Russell commented.

But before the men could get any further in the planning stage of such a thing, the bell sounded. As Holmes went to let in Mr Long and his mystery-solving friend, Russell glanced at the window, and saw that the trees were still clearly visible.

Five hours later, when Mr Long's feng shui expert pushed himself back from the paper-laden library desk, the trees in the garden behind him had not been visible for some time.

His name was Ming, and he was a doctor of some kind or other, although apparently not including medical. Long's every gesture made it abundantly clear that the old scholar was one of the most important individuals in the Chinese community, and that it was an unheard-of honour for the practitioner to come to a Western house for a consultation. The three barbarians expressed their proper gratitude, which the scholar waved aside with a gracious hand. He seemed, if anything, amused at Long's solicitous behaviour, and interested in everything around him.

Particularly in Holmes. The old man stood before the English detective with an enigmatic look on his ageless features, the lips beneath their wisps of beard twisted in what might have been distaste, or amusement. His first words did not make the attitude any clearer.

"This low-born servant is unspeakably honoured at this opportunity to meet the English High Prince of Hawkshaws," he said. His audience looked startled, at the flowery speech as much as at this unlikely reference to low detective fiction; even Long seemed taken aback.

Hammett got the joke first, and let loose a snort of smothered laughter. Holmes, looking more closely at the visiting sage, deliberately continued extending his hand, a motion that had been interrupted by the man's flowery words.

"The Savant of the Breath of Dragons is of course welcome to take amusement at the expense of this humble thief-taker," he replied, and Ming nodded, the twist of his mouth finally becoming a smile.

Dr Ming was a thin, elderly gentleman with white hair that flowed from his high forehead down over the collar of his beautifully cut Western suit, a back straight and flexible as bamboo, and delicate hands that seemed to fold themselves together into the sleeves of an invisible robe. His English was fluent and precise, although accented, and he emanated a Mandarin sensibility in everything he did, from opening the cover of one of Judith Russell's garden journals to picking up a cup of the pale green tea Long had thought to bring with him. Watching him make notes with his silver mechanical pencil was like witnessing the art of a master water-colourist, the meditation of precise and delicate strokes.

He was not, however, speedy.

Holmes explained what he was hoping for. He described the document they had found in the fireplace, and its possible meanings (leaving aside the potential interpretation that implicated Charles Russell as the author of blackmail—undue complications were not for the moment) and then pulled up the stack of Mrs Russell's journals, one for each year, to show Dr Ming the drawings they contained. He presented his theory that Charles Russell, most likely with the knowledge of his wife but certainly with the assistance of the gardener Long, had concealed something of considerable importance in his garden before he had died: the garden that, as Dr Ming could see, was now so hugely overgrown as to be unreadable, and very nearly impenetrable.

When he had explained all this, he asked his question: Knowing that the man in charge of the garden, Tom Long's father, was devoted to the precepts of feng shui, and knowing that Mr Long would have wished to help conceal and protect this important article, could a comparative study of the garden before and after 1906 suggest to Dr Ming where precisely the item might have been buried?

Dr Ming asked, "Is this an item of importance, or one of value?"

"It could be either, although I suspect to Charles

Russell, its importance would not have lain strictly in its monetary value. He was a wealthy man."

Dr Ming tucked his hands into their invisible sleeves and meditated on the open journal before him, that with the date of March 1906. He meditated for so long, and sitting so still, that Hammett began to think the old fellow had drifted into a nap, and Russell found herself wondering if, despite his earlier fluency, he actually understood English as well as he had seemed to.

Finally he took his hands apart and looked into Holmes' eyes. "It may be possible," he pronounced. He turned to Long to suggest that another pot of tea be assembled, began to unpack a collection of papers and writing implements, and asked the room in general, "I shall need the precise time of birth of the owner of the garden."

Fortunately, Holmes had come across just such a document in his search through the family papers, or all might well have been lost before it began. The aged scholar merely accepted the information as if such knowledge was a given, and pulled the first of the garden journals towards him.

After an hour of studying the sketches and journals, he began to transfer certain pieces of information to the sheets of paper he had brought, using as reference a drawing that looked like a highly complex cross between a compass and maze. He murmured from time to time in his own language. Long sat on the edge of his chair, unwilling to relax in the great man's presence. Little else happened.

After two hours, Holmes directed Hammett to an upstairs bed for a rest while he and Russell strolled down to the Italian café, bringing back an assortment of food. Dr Ming plucked curiously at a plate of noodles with a pair of chop-sticks he pulled from his case, but seemed unimpressed with what the Italians had done with the product. Another hour after that, and Dr Ming was on his third pot of tea ("Quite a three-pot problem," Russell had murmured to Holmes), frowning slightly with the intensity of his excitement, and giving tiny nods of the head from time to time.

Finally, four and a half hours after he had begun, he raised his head to Holmes and said, "Yes."

"You know where it is?"

But he would answer the question in his own way. "When my friend here explained your problem, it was of interest to me, this matter of anticipating how another man might read the energies. Of course, it simplified matters considerably when I found that the woman whose garden this was left the country shortly after the item was buried. Therefore I could assume that the considerable changes made between her drawing of 1906 and her subsequent one of 1912 would reflect entirely the work of Mr Long Kwo. You see where he has extended the pond a few feet here, and planted a red-flowering bush there?

"You no doubt wonder at this superstition," he said, carefully not looking at Hammett, who had been sprawling back in his chair for several minutes, as if to put as much distance as possible between himself and this nonsense. "It seems to the Western mind absurd to believe that the manipulation of material objects can change the nature of human emotions, expectations, and perceptions. Yet a room with walls the colour of a peach will make a person feel entirely differently from an identical room whose walls are pale blue. That is a minor example of the precepts of feng shui. In a painting, a small brush-stroke, a specific shape and colour placed in a key position, can change the balance of the whole; in life, a small adjustment in precisely the right place and time may have more effect than an enormous effort elsewhere and later. We use a, hm, mythological language to speak of these adjustments and effects, but that does not mean we believe that there are actual dragons living under the earth."

Under the force of those sparkling eyes and sensible words, even Hammett had to withdraw his scepticism. He pulled back his out-stretched legs and sat nearer upright in his chair, and Dr Ming went back to his notes.

"The difficulties—your difficulties—arise with the question of whether the item you seek was considered important, or if it was valuable. If he was seeking to protect a thing of monetary value, the adjustments made would reflect that, whereas if, for example, the thing he concealed could be detrimental to the public reputation of the family if it were found, then the adjustments would stem from an entirely different set of considerations."

Holmes controlled his impatience, for scholars must be allowed their full explanations. However, it seemed that Dr Ming's caveats were brief.

"I believe, looking at what Long Kwo has done, you will find he shared with his employer the attitude that the matter's importance lay not in its monetary value, but in how it affected the family's welfare and social standing—what is called 'face.' If it *is* a thing merely worth money, you may find it in this area." His silver pencil darted out to add a neat little square to the drawing he had made of the garden's bones. "However, if its power lies in its preservation of face, it should be in this place." The second square was on the other side of the drawing. Just where the worst of the bramble thicket lay.

Holmes saw Long and the scholar of feng shui out to

the car that had waited at the kerb for them all this time. He bowed to the old man, thanked him, asked Long to have the bill for the services sent to the St Francis, and went back inside.

"Too bad Conan Doyle didn't meet that man," he muttered. "It might have made him think differently about San Francisco's psychic energies."

Russell looked up from the desk where she was collecting the journals and scraps of paper. "Sorry?"

Holmes shook his head to indicate it was nothing of importance, and began to transfer the used cups and glasses onto a tray. With an armful of journals, Russell paused in the door-way and said, "It is too dark to go bashing around in the garden."

"I agree," he said to her obvious relief. "We shall return at first light. However, let us bring the good doctor's treasure maps with us."

If their opponents were so set on whatever might or might not lie out in that wasteland that they would tackle it in the dead of night at the cost of much bloodshed and injury, Russell would almost have been inclined to let them have it. Almost.

When she had returned her mother's journals to the front parlour, she folded Dr Ming's map into her pocket. They walked back to the hotel by a circuitous route of Holmes' devising, reached it without interruption, and took their leave of Hammett.

Early in the morning, Holmes dressed and went to see to his Irregulars. He found their interest flagging, but they bounced back with an infusion of cash and the reassurance that it would be either that day, or not at all. Young Mr Garcia assured him they wouldn't take their eyes off the place, an assurance rather spoilt by his subsequent discovery that the very young lad who was supposed to be watching at that moment was instead standing at his elbow, unwilling to miss anything. However, as Hammett had not yet left the apartment, no harm was done.

By seven o'clock, the two detectives-turned-archaeologists were at the house. Both were dressed in their toughest, most impenetrable clothing, but the bramble thicket laughed at them, inflicting a thousand scratches and punctures. Hammett appeared shortly after eight, and although he expressed his willingness to pitch in, he seemed not unhappy to be assigned a seat and the position of look-out. Later in the morning, Long came walking down the drive, although he, too, ended up sitting in the sun while Russell and Holmes took turns with the saws, branch clippers, and spades they had found in the garden shed. Hammett rolled and smoked one cigarette after another and began to tell them about a story he was writing, its protagonist an operative in a detective agency rather like that of the Pinkertons, only more efficient and ethical. Long contributed suggestions from his own broad reading of the literature of the masses, while the other two sweated and cursed and drew themselves mental goals, after which they swore to move the hunt over to the other marked square, the one where Dr Ming had suggested mere money might lie.

Well past several of those mental goals, but before the final one could be reached, Russell's spade hit something metal.

All four of them went still. Without taking up the tool, Russell squatted and brushed at the crumbly soil. She slipped off the leather gloves (also from the shed, and half eaten by mice, but better than nothing) to feel around the base of the spade. In a minute, she tugged at an object a foot long and half that wide: a biscuit tin, surprisingly heavy, freshly dented and rusty around the corners. She handed it to Holmes, who most manfully waited as she dug around to see if there was anything else. Almost immediately, her fingers encountered a second such object, equally weighty, this one advertising the contents as chocolates, which she wrestled out of the ground and gave to him. Two seemed to be all, and she followed Holmes along the path-way they had hacked and to the kitchen door, where they kicked off their dirt-encrusted shoes and went into the scullery to scrub the worst of the grime from their hands while Hammett and Long spread one of the house's dust-cloths over the table.

Russell sat down before the two tins, sucking absently at a bleeding place on the side of her hand. Holmes clattered around in the kitchen drawers until he had found utensils to prise and rip, and did so.

Although they had been digging in the place indicated for something of importance, the first box contained money. Some of it was paper, tied together in three bundles, but the weight came from the coins, mostly silver but a few of very old gold. Hammett whistled; Long sat back in surprise; Holmes and Russell looked inscrutable and turned to the other tin.

This one held money as well, but in addition to coins it had a white cloth with bright red markings on it. This was wrapped around what proved, upon unfolding the cloth, to be a fist-sized tangle of jewellery—a dozen or more gold chains, four completely plain gold rings, three loose diamonds, two rubies, and half a dozen sapphires, of various sizes and conditions. Holmes tugged the cloth free and spread it out, revealing it as an armband with a red cross painted onto it. He dropped it back into the box, and poked at the knot of chains, saying, "I should think that finding the original owners of these would be extremely difficult. Particularly as some of it appears to have been taken from people who were bleeding."

They studied the brown stains clotting a couple of the chains, all four faces registering various degrees of distaste. Then Russell nudged the valuables and Red Cross arm-band to one side to prise with her finger-nail at the flat oil-cloth shape that lay beneath, tugging its corner to work it loose from the jewellery, laying it on the dust-cloth to unfold the wrapping.

Inside lay the carbon copy of a letter, typed on an Underwood machine with a crooked lower-case "*a*": her father's type-writer; her father's words.

Chapter Twenty-three

August 22, 1914
San Francisco, Calif.

To whomever this may concern,

At the end of October, I, Charles David Russell, intend to enter into the employ of the United States Army. However, to do so without having cleared my conscience of the events of April 1906 would make me and the work I intend to do vulnerable to the sorts of pressures often considered blackmail.

I have kept silent for the past eight years. The events involved two other men as well, and the contagion of a felony would have blighted their lives and honors. Since neither man has chosen to come forward under his own initiative, I feel I may not reveal the names here. I shall merely refer to them as Good Friend—GF—and PA—Petit Ami.

GF and I had been friends in our youth, almost as close as the brothers we were sometimes taken for. And although like brothers we went our separate ways under the complications of maturity, I retained an affection for him, and felt that I owed him a considerable debt, for his friendship and his stalwart assistance when I needed both friend and help. I say this to explain the call the man had upon me, although we had not been close in the years since my marriage, or even seen each other for some considerable time.

I need not describe the general happenings of that day in April. My family was shaken from its beds shortly after five o'clock in the morning as the rest of San Francisco was, although—being blessed with a heavily built house with its foundation on rock—we did not suffer as much as those in the lower areas. Nonetheless, the house was a disaster and a highly dangerous place for children, being now carpeted with broken glass and with gaping cracks in the walls and ominous sags in the heavy plaster ceilings over our heads. Along with most of our neighbors, we moved out of doors on that first day, and when the tents began to reach us the following day, Thursday, we moved into Lafayette Park until such a time as our house could be declared either safe or unliveable.

I spent the three days of the fire in the same way that most of the able-bodied men did, namely, providing transport to the wounded while my supply of gasoline lasted, and afterward digging through rubble for survivors and helping the professionals to battle the flames. We rescued those who were trapped, collected the bodies of those who were beyond mortal help, and attempted to make a path down the streets for vehicles and carts to pass, to carry the injured or possessions.

As far as I can determine, the mayor's order to shoot looters on sight was announced within a few hours of the earthquake—an irony, considering how much the man had himself stolen from the city coffers. Official numbers of those looters actually executed were ludicrously low—I myself witnessed three such shootings, none of which were in the least justified. The police and soldiers were as maddened as the rest of us, the difference being that they were armed and had received orders to be free with their bullets.

The first afternoon, Wednesday, having spent the bulk of the day laboring downtown, I drove back as far as Van Ness, left the car there, and walked the rest of the way into Pacific Heights to assure myself that my family was well and to see if I could find something to eat. I found my wife and children in good spirits, and she told me that PA had been by shortly before that, to see if we were well and to reassure us that his own family was uninjured. She had told him where I had gone, and he said he would be back later to talk with me.

I retrieved food and drink from our damaged home and helped my wife build a fire-pit in the front garden out of the overly plentiful fallen bricks from our chimney, then returned to the house for bedding, which we spread among the trees in the garden. The house creaked and groaned as one walked across the floor, and I was not at all certain that it would endure another major shaking.

We ate our meal, settled the children beneath the stars, and then, very late, PA returned. Completely exhausted, he was, badly shaken by an experience he had endured. A soldier, seeing him walk down the middle of the street, had turned his rifle on PA and declared that he must be a looter. When PA protested that he had gone nowhere near any shop, the soldier prodded him with the gun, then put him to work in a gang clearing a fallen hotel. PA was willing to do the work, but he was not a young man, and the labor was harsh.

Eventually, long after dark, the soldier was replaced and PA could slip away. He was becoming extremely concerned about his family, but as the fire was traveling in that direction, he made his way back into Pacific Heights to rest before trying to circle the flames for home. He fully expected to be accosted at any moment by one of the roving bands of soldiers, many of whom, it should be said, were drunk, having themselves looted nearby liquor stores and taverns. But he made it to us, looking half dead with exhaustion.

We fed PA and urged him to stay with us that night, for the soldiers and self-appointed vigilantes among the population would surely be even more aggressive under cover of darkness than they had been in daylight. I pointed out that although it looked as though the fire was nearing his part of town, in the darkness and without identifiable landmarks, it could easily have been a mile to one side. I assured him that surely the flames would be extinguished during the night, and that his wife and son, intelligent and capable individuals, would without a doubt be safe until the morning—safer than he would be were he to set off then and there. He did not wish to remain, but as I was making my argument, we heard a volley of shots from down the hill, and he had to concede my point. We gave him blankets and went to sleep ourselves, certain that in the morning a degree of normality would have been restored.

Instead, of course, matters deteriorated. The fire spread, the air was rent by the sound of explosions as building after building in its path was brought down, gunshots were heard throughout the day. My own family was safe, being in an area far from the fire and with sufficient numbers there to drive off intruders (official or otherwise). I talked it over with my wife, and we decided it best that I accompany PA across town, thinking that two responsible individuals might stand forth against the mob. We set off, intending to reassure ourselves as to the state of PA's family (whom he had not seen since the previous afternoon). The view from the Heights was other-worldly: to the east, the fires of Sheol, to the north, all appeared completely normal. We made our way north along Franklin, so as to put off as long as possible the hell that waited for us on the other side of Van Ness. Eventually, however, we had to turn east, but we only made it as far as Larkin before we were shanghaied again and put to work on a rescue attempt.

It was a toppled apartment building, and we could hear the weak cries of women and children from its depths, trapped there for more than twenty-four hours. I regret to say that, although we succeeded in rescuing several from their living tombs, some of the wretches were still trapped inside when the flames came.

We were forced to retreat from the intense heat, and I for one was grateful that the roar and crack of the burning building obscured the feeble cries of its victims. Still, it is that moment of failure that lives with me, in memories of that terrible time. That, and one or two others, which I will come to soon.

PA and I collapsed for a time and poured water down our parched throats, turning our backs on the fire as if we could deny its existence. Only then did we notice the angle of the sun through the smoky pall, and found to our astonishment that we had been fighting that doomed apartment building for going on six hours. It was nearly two o'clock—I had to put my pocket-watch to my ear to be certain it was going—and we had not come anywhere near PA's home. Again we set off to the north, giving wide berth to the hotly burning mansions on Nob Hill, but climbing to the top of Russian Hill in order to determine where the flames were, that we might avoid them—neither of us wished to be pressed yet again into fire-fighting duties.

The vision of the city stretched before us

was like something from Dante, an ocean of ruin set with broken towers that clawed their way upwards like skeletons attempting to rise from their graves. Great pillars of smoke gathered over several places, the highest with hot red fires at their base, others low and wide above smouldering wreckage.

I commented to my friend that the pillars of smoke must be visible for a hundred miles, but when he did not answer, I saw that he had attention only for his home.

It was no longer there. From our feet to the sea, only Telegraph Hill remained, and it appeared embattled. PA would have run straight down to the smoking ruin that was his home had I not brought him down in a flying tackle, and shook him hard, repeating over and over again that he should think: His family would not have been taken unawares by the flames. They would have moved before it, as tens of thousands of others were doing. We needed only find whether they had gone north, or east.

Flames were working their way towards the north. The only thing to do was to go that way as well, as far as we could, and hope we met neither flames nor press-gangs. We nearly ran down the side of the hill, until I seized PA's arm and pointed out to him that two men walking might appear less criminous than two men sprinting away from the wealthy neighborhood.

We walked, quickly, working our way towards our destination. My friend knew all the paths and short-cuts here, as it was a route he traversed daily, and he led me surely through delivery alleys and the foot-paths that cut through hillside gardens. Twice we heard shouts behind us, but with a twist and a turn we would be out of sight again.

We came to an area of pleasant homes between the Italian district and the docks, homes in the process of being emptied by their owners under the watchful eyes of a pair of soldiers. We nodded to them, keeping our hands in our pockets and walking straight down the center of the street to show our innocence, and although we ran the gauntlet without coming to harm, the two soldiers adjusted their long rifles over their shoulders and sauntered after us. We turned a corner and had just stepped into a rubble-strewn alley when there was a rapid and surreptitious movement ahead.

We both stopped dead, caught between some unknown threat and the two soldiers at our backs. PA was turning to ask my opinion when I heard my name being called from ahead.

It is at this point that my "Good Friend" enters the story. I had not seen him in two or three years, was not even certain that he was still living in the city, but we were brought face-to-face here in this deserted alley. He walked up to me and offered his hand.

I took it, said his name, and asked him if he lived here now, but something about the way he answered, or rather took care to avoid answering, led me to interrupt his glib reply with the warning that soldiers were probably on their way to ascertain that we were up to no harm.

Immediately, he grabbed my arm and pushed me down the alley towards where he had come, doing the same with PA, hurrying us ahead of him. His urgency coupled with the awareness of the rifles at our backs proved contagious, and PA and I stumbled over the bricks and tiles until he jumped ahead of us and slipped into an invisible hole between a wall and a shed that had been thrown against it. It was pitch black inside, and GF hissed at us to be silent.

In a minute or so, we heard voices outside, and the two soldiers came down until they were standing just at the entrance to our lair. In the end, they decided that there was nothing here worth stealing anyway, and went back the way they had come.

GF collapsed into nerve-taut giggles, only pulling himself out of the state when I told him that we would be on our way.

"But you mustn't," he told me. "I need your help."

"With what?"

"Hiding some stuff."

I somehow knew in an instant what his attitude of mischief meant. Although we had not been close for years, I knew him of old, known him as a brother when we were both careless youths. In that setting, and being fully aware of what was going on in the city, it took no great leap of imagination to see that the "stuff" was not something rightfully his, that in the confusion and turmoil he had helped himself to the contents of some abandoned shop or jewelery box, and stashed them here. That my old friend was a common thief and a looter.

I pulled myself away and led PA away without saying another word to GF. PA and I did not speak about what we had seen, merely went on through the disorder until we came near to his home.

His neighborhood was aflame. We stood staring, as if we had never seen such a thing before, and gaped at the firemen struggling to coax a trickle out of the hoses. Then PA saw a friend of his, and pounced on him, demanding where the residents had gone.

"To the docks," the man replied, and we set

off again, circling around until we found the refugees of my friend's neighborhood, thousands of them milling about with their meager possessions.

PA turned to me and told me that he could find them from here, that I had to leave and see to my own family. I refused to go until we had some news of his wife and son, but it was not until nightfall that we found a man who had seen them settled into a tent in the nearby Army base. This time PA was adamant: He would not have me accompany him, but told me that he would find them, and send word to me that they were well. He turned his back and walked off, and reluctantly I went my own way.

His family, I will add here, was unharmed, and although his house burned to the ground, his wife and son had managed to rescue the things they valued most, and guarded them throughout the flight and to their new canvas abode.

I reached home very late that night, to find my family missing. But a neighbor, taking his turn walking guard up and down the sidewalks, directed me to the park, where the Army had provided tents. My family was happy to see me, and I slept that night under canvas for the first time in many years, too tired for the nightmares to reach me.

I didn't tell my wife about seeing GF, not then anyway. She was friends with GF's wife, primarily because we had children the same age, but GF himself was a sore point with her, and I didn't want to go into it then and there. In truth, I did not think there was anything to go into.

Friday I spent with the rescue crews, although by the end of the day, the tacit agreement was that we would retrieve whatever bodies we might without risking our own life and limb. The fires would take care of the others.

We fought hard, and all that day and into the night the explosions continued in the determination to create a fire-break the flames could not breach. Van Ness was most peculiar—a flat and smoking wasteland on one side while appearing grotesquely near normal on the other. We staggered off to our rough beds that night knowing we had done all we could.

And won. Saturday morning the news came that no new fires had broken out, in spite of instances of the clumsy use of black powder that set off the very fires it had been meant to prevent. We held our breath lest the wind come up and fan the embers, but it did not. By Saturday afternoon we began to think that the worst was over. Now it was a matter of

reconciling ourselves to the Aegean stables—
we who in three short days had already come to
loathe the feel of a shovel.

We would be a long, long time bent over picking up bricks.

Abruptly I realized that I was no longer a
boy of twenty, able to spend all day in physical
labor—my back ached, my hands were ripped
raw, I had cuts and burns at a dozen places on
my arms and legs, and I couldn't breathe without coughing up black. I took to my bed, cud-
dling my two small children to me with the
pleasure of life itself, while my wife read to us
from some nonsense child's book.

The children fell asleep, and I was not far
from it when my wife, seeing my eyes beginning
to close, told me that she was going to our
house before the sun set to retrieve some waterproof garments, as the sky looked threatening. I could not of course allow her to go
alone, so I forced my blistered feet back into
their boots while my wife asked the neighbor-
ing tent to keep an eye on the children should
they wake.

We walked hand in hand through the cool
evening. The wind had shifted, coming in from
the sea to drive the worst of the smoke in the
direction of Oakland; indeed, I thought, rain
appeared possible.

We found our waterproof coats, and I went

upstairs and brought some toys and books for our daughter to keep her from fretting if the rain should last. Between one thing and another, it was nearly an hour before we left the house with our armloads of provisions. We took a detour to the edge of the high ground, to look at the darkness falling across the city, and found the familiar view profoundly eerie—few lamps, no street-lights, just the outline of the Fairmont Hotel on the opposite rise, and below us a great stinking expanse of blackness, the fires out at last. We must have stood there looking at the foreign landscape for twenty minutes, and when we got back to the tent, we found the entire area in a state of writhing turmoil.

In our absence, someone had come looking for me, and frightened my daughter. Her screams had awakened all the infants in the vicinity, and they had raised their voices in chorus, along with half the women, all the men, and most of the dogs. We soon got her soothed and I went to ask if anyone knew who the intruder had been, but he hadn't left his name, merely said (or rather, shouted, over Mary's roar, which had been of fear but had quickly turned to one of indignation) that he would come back later.

The most glaring characteristic of the man, all agreed, was that his face had been

burnt, and that his thick ointment and bandages rendered his face invisible.

A burned face could have been any of the
men I labored with over the past few days, so I
thought nothing of it. He did not come back
that night, or the following morning, and it
was not until noon on Sunday that I found who
it was.

During the night, the rain had come down
hard, Nature's cruel joke on our heartbreak-
ing efforts against the fire. Had it begun
earlier, the city might have been saved, but it
came on Sunday, to turn the ruins into a sodden black slop-pit. Even our tidy green park
was a sea of mud, and we needed shovels to direct the runnels and creeks out from under
our feet.

As I walked through Sunday's drizzle down
the drive beside the house, intending to fetch
tools from the gardener's shed, I heard something move inside the house.

It could have been the foundations settling, or a precariously balanced whatnot
taking its final plunge, but it was a sound,
and I stopped to listen for more. Nothing
came, but I walked around the back just to
check that the door was locked, and found it
was not.

I hesitated, since I knew there was a gun
inside and that if an intruder had found it, I

would be in trouble. But then I turned the handle and took a step inside, and shouted for them to come out.

I wasn't expecting an answer, and certainly not the one I got. Which was a voice calling from upstairs, "Charlie? Is that you?"

It was my Good Friend. I asked him what he was doing there and how the hell he got in, the oath startled out of me by his unexpected presence in my home, and he reminded me that I'd given him a key long ago, and that he'd never taken it off his ring. I'd forgotten that he had a key, but indeed, before I married I'd given him and two or three other of my friends keys to the door, in case I was away when they needed a place to sleep. That had been years ago, but they were the same locks, and clearly the key still worked.

As we called to each other, he had been coming down the stairs. When we met in the gloom of the hall-way, a great deal became clear: His face was shiny with smears of white ointment, his eyebrows and lashes had been burned away, and he had a bandage around his head.

"Hey, you're the one who scared my little girl!" I accused him, and he immediately began to apologize for it, saying he'd never thought about how his appearance would strike a child, certainly never thought the kid would be alone in the tent, and he'd left as soon as he saw there were people that she knew who could look after her, so as not to frighten her any more. So he'd come here, and found the place empty, but he'd desperately needed a place to sleep so he'd let himself in and dragged the guest bed over to a spot where the plaster had already fallen down.

He ended by saying he hoped I didn't mind, and that he'd been careful not to light a fire anywhere.

"I guess not," I told him, and asked what he'd done to his face. He touched it gingerly and said he'd done it on Friday night when the fire he was working on hit a stash of kerosene and blew up in his face. "Knocked me top over teakettle," he said with a laugh. "I woke up in the hospital tent twenty-four hours later, and since I could walk and remember my name and that Teddy Roosevelt was President, they kicked me out, since they had a dozen others who needed the bed worse than me. My boarding-house is gone, so I thought you wouldn't mind."

"Of course not," I told him.

"There's one other thing," he said, and the way he said it made my sympathy for his plight fade.

You see, when we were young, we'd gotten

into a number of scrapes. Just through high
spirits, but it would begin with a dare and a
look, and even beneath the white grease and
the bandages he wore, the look he gave me now
was the same he'd give me when he had something really outrageous in mind. And I remembered the "stuff" he'd needed help with, and I
immediately stepped away from him.

"GF," I said, "I have a family. I can't do that
kind of thing anymore. You're on your own."

"It's nothing at all," he told me. "Hey, my
face really hurts. You got anything to drink
in this mess?"

That was the moment I should have ended
it. I should have told him no and showed him
the door, taking his key as he left. I should
have, but I did not. He was burned and I'd seen
far too much in the last few days to put my old
friend out on the street. Before I knew it we
were sitting in the library with a candle and
a bottle of good whiskey, talking about old
times.

It turned out his "stuff" was a tin cookie
box that he'd tripped across right in the middle of Geary Street the first morning.
Because it was heavy enough to trip him, he'd
taken a closer look and found it packed to the
gills with cash—bills, coins, even gold. No
names on it, no identifying marks, no body
lying nearby. "So I kept it."

"It's not yours," I told him in disgust. "You'll have to put up a notice and ask somebody to identify it. If they tell you what kind of money was in it and how much, it'll be theirs."

"Well, there's a little problem."

"What's that?"

"I kind of added to it. It'd be hard to know what was there originally and what went in as time went along."

"Jesus wept!" I shouted at him. "You're a damn thief."

"I guess," he said, "but I've got to tell you, it all came from people who won't miss a hundred dollars here or there. All of it. And I can't give it back, there's money there from maybe ten places."

I dropped my head in my hands, feeling sick.

"Charlie, I really need a new start." He was pleading. "You know about my wife and that mess, and I can't get any money, and without money you can't make money. You've got to help me."

"You disgust me," I told him.

"I know."

"Where is the box now?"

"Well, that's the thing. It's buried in your garden."

I nearly hit him, bandages and all. If I'd

had the gun, I'd have shot him dead, I was so angry. He saw it, and put up his hands as if to say "Whoa."

"Now look, Charlie, I couldn't very well just leave it sitting on your kitchen table while I went up to sleep, could I? I just buried it under a bush to keep it safe for a while."

"You buried your looted cash in my garden." I couldn't believe I'd once been close to this idiot.

"Just until I can get it and go. I'm off to France. My half-sister lives there now, she said I could go stay with her and help manage the business—she's got a nice little bar and cabaret in Paris. Anyway, I was thinking about it even before all this happened. This town has been a curse for me, Charlie, you know that."

I did know that, as it happened. He'd had a lot of bad breaks, and only some of them he'd brought on himself. His final blow had been when his wife had divorced him, then six months later inherited a packet.

I stared into my glass for a while, and then I asked him, "How much do you suppose is in your box?"

"I'm not sure. Maybe about three thousand."

I thought he was absolutely sure, but I didn't call him on it. I was tired, and I was tired of him, but on the other hand I felt so incredibly lucky, having seen all those poor souls dead, mangled, and homeless while my family had come through unscathed, that I could not bring myself to judge him. "If I give you a check for five thousand dollars, will you go to France and leave me alone?"

"Charlie, I can't ask you to—"

But of course he allowed himself to be talked into it. I'd find a way to return the money to its owners somehow, or donate it to the orphans, but buying GF out seemed somehow appropriate, as if it placated the Fates that had passed me over. I hunted down my checkbook, wrote him his check, and told him I didn't want to see him again, ever. And to leave his key with me. He took the thing out of his pocket with a hurt expression and put it on the table, then grabbed my hand and made me shake his, told me he'd buried it under that statue with the book, and ran away like I'd given him a set of wings.

It was madness, I know, to do that, but he'd been like a brother once, and in the last few days we'd all walked through hell.

It was only later that I heard the whole story—or rather, heard some, read about parts of it in the papers, and guessed the rest, but by then he was gone and I was stuck.

It seems that on the Friday night after the

quake, a cop had seen him going into a house whose residents had been ordered out just ahead of the fire. There were actually two cops together, but they split up when they heard the distinctive crash of a breaking window on the next street. One went to investigate that, the other followed GF, and when the cop came through the back door after him, GF panicked and bashed him with the fireplace poker. It killed the man, or anyway GF assumed it did, but instead of just running away, he thought he'd conceal the evidence by burning the house. What was one more burning building when the whole city was up in flames?

But being GF, a couple of problems came up. The first was that the bottle of gasoline GF found in the pantry and poured around the floor didn't just burn when he set a match to it, it went up like high explosive, shooting GF out of the house and scorching off all his hair. The other problem was, the fire shifted and didn't eat up that street, so after the fire died down, there was one house burned among a bunch still standing. And in that house was a dead cop with a broken skull and a fireplace poker lying next to him.

GF had buttoned the box of money inside his shirt to leave his hands free when the gas went off in his face, and when he picked himself off the ground and found he could walk, he did so. Eventually he more or less passed out, and was taken to a hospital tent, but as soon as he came to on Saturday he figured it wouldn't be healthy to be a scorched man with a box full of money.

So he came to me.

And I bought his way to freedom, leaving me with a tin box so badly dented that I understood why the hospital workers hadn't looked inside—when I dug it up, I had to use a hammer and screwdriver to get it open. It had money in it, but only about $1700, and some of that had what looked to me like blood on it. Talk about your blood money.

The other thing it had was a band of cloth with a red cross painted on it. Dressed as a rescue worker, GF had gone in and out of houses under the pretense of looking for injured people, when all the while he'd been robbing them blind.

I felt wild when I held that cloth in my hands and realized what it meant. Then later, I got to thinking about the problems I had, and I began to feel even worse. I was stuck with the damned box. If I gave it to the authorities and told them the honest truth, I thought that I'd probably be charged—if not with the actual stealing, then at least with aiding a felon. If I took the box away and threw it off a ferry, I risked getting caught with it red-handed, and wouldn't that be fun to explain? Plus, if I got rid of it and GF came back to shake more money out of the Russell tree, I couldn't use it as a threat to get rid of him—surely there'd be his finger-prints or something in that box that would—I started to write "hang him," which is a little too close to the bone. But I couldn't leave it where he'd put it—what would stop him from sneaking in one night and digging it up? I could take it down to the Lodge and drown it in the lake, but something about introducing that box into that setting made it feel somehow polluting.

So in the end I talked it over with my friend—I should say, my true friend—PA, and he agreed that it would be best if we just buried it again quietly and said nothing. But not in the same place—we talked about where to do it, and he had a fellow in to do some mumbo-jumbo over it, and we hid it deep, where only he and I know.

A year or so later, the gardener uncovered another box, this one with pictures of chocolates on the front. It had money in it, too, and jewelry. It also had a gun. PA and I buried it in the same place as the first, but without the gun—that I did get rid of.

The whole thing was just a disaster, and it didn't even end with seeing the back of GF. I told my wife about it a few weeks later, which I probably shouldn't have done—she always had some odd notions about GF, from the very first time I'd brought her home, she'd never taken to him, never liked having him around. When she heard about what he'd done, and that I'd buried his stash, she became convinced that he would return one night and do something to us, maybe even threaten the children, to get it back. I got quite hot at that, the idea that I'd be friends with such a man—it still seems to me that robbery and panicked manslaughter in the midst of anarchy is a far cry from cold-bloodedly threatening friends, but my wife is as strong-minded a person as I am, and we had words. It took me years before I could talk her into coming home again.

So there's my story. I haven't seen GF since, although I think he's been around, because once in 1910 we found someone had been digging where he'd buried the two boxes. For all I know he's dead, but I wrote a letter to his half-sister last week, saying that if he was still alive and she was in touch with him, I wanted him to know that around the end of October, the U.S. government would "know the details of an incident that took place in 1906." The events of those days have been allowed to fade somewhat, but it was murder, after all, and it wouldn't be too hard to figure out who GF was, if they wanted to come after him. I thought it only fair to warn him that the U. S. of A. might not be a comfortable place for him.

Like I said, he was my friend, once, and frankly I don't know that we weren't all pretty insane those days of the fire.

I've also told PA all this, and he agrees it's best. I'll try to keep him out of it as best I can, and I've long since removed all mention of him from my official documents, my will and such, even though he had nothing to do with it until it was all over.

So there it is, my life of crime. I may be over-scrupulous in revealing this, but I would not care to be put into a position involving the security of the nation with this vulnerable point in my past. If it alters the judgment of my superiors as to my fitness for the proposed position, so be it.

Yours sincerely,
Charles David Russell

October 1, 1914
San Francisco

ADDENDUM:

I leave next week for Washington, D.C., and will take the above with me to present to my superiors. I shall bury a copy with the two tin boxes as well, less for insurance than by way of explanation, should someone ever come across the incriminating contents and wonder.

The day after tomorrow, I'm going down to the Lodge, to close it up for some time. Most people here believe the war will be over in a few weeks, but I have been to Germany, I know the strength of her people, and I do not think so. I do not know if I shall ever see my beloved lake again, and I have a sentimental wish to visit it one last time before I go. My wife says she has too many things to do here in San Francisco, but I hope that she will reconsider and that she and the children will join me at the place where we have spent so many blissful days of family unity and pleasure.

I have had no word from the man I called GF, nor from his half-sister, although considering the disruption France is currently undergoing, I do not suppose that is surprising.

Well, I have done my best by him, and can only hope that his life since we last met has been lived in a manner to recompense his sins.

As for my own, we shall soon see.

Signed,
Charles Russell

BOOK FIVE

Russell

Chapter Twenty-four

"The letter was written and sent to France the third week of August, just after the war began," Holmes remarked. "And the accident that killed your family occurred the third of October. Even in the first month of war, mail was getting through, particularly to Paris. 'Good Friend' would have got the letter within a week. He could have made it back here from Paris with time to spare."

"His friend," I said bitterly. "A man he helped out of a tough place, a man with whom he shared a wild..." My voice shifted tone as my mind tore itself from the immediacy of my father's presence and began to process the information it had been given, now and in recent days. I finished "...wild youth."

"Petit Ami, or 'PA,' could only be Micah Long," Holmes observed, too taken up with his own thoughts to notice my distraction, "considering the references to hiding things in the garden and the fellow's protective 'mumbo jumbo' of feng shui. And as Charles Russell himself says, it shouldn't be too difficult to come up with a name for the other. Particularly after one has had a close look at the household records, in which is noted a cheque for seven thousand five hundred dollars, written just days after the earthquake. Your father seems to have held the charmingly innocent notion that changing the amount of the cheque in the letter would mislead anyone investigating the evidence of the accounts book."

I stood up abruptly. "I have to go. I'll meet you back at the hotel."

I was out of there before he could stop me, striding down the streets with neither hat nor coat. I pulled the ornate bell, then banged on the door when it did not open instantly. When Jeeves appeared in the opening I pushed my way inside.

"Where's Flo?" I demanded. "Miss Greenfield? Is she still in bed?"

The abruptness of my entrance and the lack of delicacy in my question reduced him to jerky little protests, which I overrode ruthlessly. "I need to talk to Flo this instant. Where is her room? Oh, never mind, I'll find it myself."

The house-maid he summoned sprinted up to me after the sixth door I had opened, and said breathlessly, "This way, miss, er, ma'am."

I'd have found the room eventually, but I did not bother to thank the little maid, just marched past her towards the formless shape on the bed. "I'll bring coffee!" the poor girl squeaked, and slammed the door.

"Flo!" I said loudly, shaking where I thought her shoulder would be. "Flo, wake up, right now. I don't have time for your morning dithers. Flo!"

My shout brought her bolt upright, staring around

in a panic. She dashed her hands across her eyes as if doubting their evidence. "Mary? What on earth—"

"Flo, do you know a man with a scarred face?"

"What?" It came out more like, Wha? With an effort, I resisted the impulse to slap her awake.

"A man with scars on his face, burn scars."

"What of it?"

"God damn it, Flo, who is he?"

"My father," she said, her pretty face screwing up in confusion. "What about him? Mary, what a state you're in! You look like you've been rolling in the garden!"

I sat down abruptly on the bed, ignoring her fastidious protestations. "Your father had a scarred face?"

"Yes, it was sort of puckered, like. He got burned rescuing people in the great fire. Mary, what are you doing here? What time is it? Oh, golly," she said, squinting at the clock on her table, "it's not even noon. Do you know what time I hit the hay?"

"Flo, I really don't care if you haven't slept in a week. What did your father look like?"

"He used to be handsome once," she replied, and settled her back against the head-board in resignation, although I watched her closely to make sure she didn't fade into sleep again. "At least, that's what Mummy says, and the picture she has of him is kind of dreamy, in an old-fashioned kind of a way."

"How tall was he?"

"Oh, yes, his height. Poor Daddy, he was so sensitive about it. Used to wear shoes to make him taller. Oh, thank God!" she exclaimed as the house-maid backed in with a tray of coffee. "This feels like one of those horrible dreams you keep trying to wake up from and it drags you back."

"Just a little more and I'll let you go back to sleep," I said ruthlessly. "What about a ring?"

"A ring?" she said uncertainly, her cup paused in front of her mouth.

"A pinkie ring with a stone."

She took a gulp, gasped a little with the heat of it, then wheezed out, "How did you know that? He never used to, but when I saw him later, he had it. I always figured it meant he'd made it big after the divorce. Although it was a little flashy."

"You mean, he didn't wear the ring when you were small and they were still married, but he did later on? When did you see him, later?"

Her face took on a look of childish shiftiness and she glanced at the door, where the maid had just gone out. "I didn't."

"Flo, I know you saw him. When was it?"

"Mummy didn't like it."

"I won't tell her. When?"

She let out a gusty breath. "Just every so often. After the fire, I didn't see him for a long time, and when he came back he sort of scared me, his face I mean. But then I could see that it was him, and he told me that he'd gotten it rescuing people, so it was all right, sort of. Sad, I mean, and not nice to look at, but he was so brave and that mattered. But not to Mummy."

"Your mother wouldn't let you see him?"

"She didn't like it. They had a bad divorce, you know, and later on he kept asking her for money. But I didn't see why that should mean I couldn't see him. He was fun, you know?"

"Do you remember what years you saw him?"

"No."

"Flo, please. Try."

She screwed up her face again, thinking hard. "He was here for a couple of my birthdays—that's in September," she added, "the twenty-fifth. He was here for my tenth, and I think my twelfth—yes, it was pretty much every other year."

She was the same age as I, born in 1900. "And your fourteenth?" I asked.

"Oh, yes, he brought me a very pretty pearl necklace from Paris that year," she said happily. "I told Mummy they were good fakes that a friend had gotten tired of and gave me, but they're real, and they were from him."

I rubbed my face, suddenly tired. Flo's father, who had been my own father's close friend in his youth, whose crimes during the fire had driven the final wedge between them, had been here immediately before the accident.

"Tell me," I said, "do you know a woman, she might have been an acquaintance of your father's, who is taller than he is by several inches, and younger, with brown hair she wears up on her head?"

As descriptions went, it did not go very far, Flo's quizzical expression seemed to say. I began to tell her it was all right, but she surprised me.

"Not a friend, but his sister used to have long brown hair she wore up."

"Sister? The one who owns a night-club in Paris?"

"I don't know about that, but last I heard, she lived in Paris. She was actually his half-sister, that's what he told me, a lot younger than him. Didn't look a bit like him, and Daddy kind of flirted with her, which was a bit strange. Still, she was nice enough to me, sent me pretty things to wear. When Mummy didn't catch them and take them from me," she said, and yawned. She added,

"Although she must be some kind of old maid, to be so devoted to her half-brother. Hung on his every word."

The "sister" sounded less and less like a blood relation, but I suppose it hardly mattered. "Do you have a photograph of either of them?"

"Sure, why? Mary, what is going on?"

I thought that I preferred her stupefied by sleep.

"I think your father may have been involved in something criminal."

"Oh, bunk! Have you been talking with Mummy? She's got crime on the brain when it comes to Daddy."

"No, I haven't spoken to your mother. May I see the pictures?"

I thought that the only hope was if I did not pause for explanations, but simply overwhelmed her with peremptory demands. It worked, in that it got her out of bed to pad in her pyjamas over to her childhood bookshelves and draw out a picture album.

She'd hidden the photos of her father behind harmless snapshots of friends and holiday scenery. One of him, young and handsome, with hair as light as my father's (blond hair on a guest-room pillow, the machinery in the back of my mind noted: blond enough that his face would not show much of a stubble some days after it had been burnt) holding a black-haired baby girl in his arms: Flo had her mother's hair. The second photograph showed Robert Greenfield some years later, turning his scarred face slightly away from the camera as he lay on a deck-chair with some stretch of the Mediterranean behind him; a third showed him later yet, his body beginning to thicken and his hairline receding, standing beside a handsome, somewhat taller woman dressed in pre-war fashion—but when I took my eyes from their figures to study the background, my knees gave way and I had to fumble for a chair.

The photograph had been taken at the Lodge.

"Who's she?" I asked Flo, although I thought I knew already.

Flo squinted at the photo. "That's Aunt Rosa. Daddy's half-sister. She came to California a couple of times. Look at that hat—this must've been taken before the earthquake."

"When was her other visit?"

"Hell, I don't know. I was maybe eight or nine. Yes, that was when Daddy went away."

("Looked familiar," Mr Gordimer had told me—he had in fact seen her before, nearly twenty years earlier.)

Flo pressed other snapshots into my hands and I was dimly aware of glancing at them, but when I looked up again she had gone back to her coffee and was sitting cross-legged on the bed, brushing her hair vigorously.

"I'm going to borrow this one, Flo," I said.

"Ninety-three, ninety-four," she chanted.

I put the others on top of the album that lay on the shelf and walked towards the door. Her hair-brush clattered to the floor as she jumped off the bed and came after me.

"No, you can't borrow anything if you don't tell me why you want it. Here, give it back."

She made to grab it from me, but I held it out of her reach, looked straight into her eyes, and said, "Don't."

She took a sharp step back, her eyes going wide and hurt at the force of my tone. "I'll return it," I said, and walked out.

I heard her call my name as I went down the stairs, but I did not stop. Jeeves managed to get the door open before I could touch the handle, and I trotted down the steps, not in the least surprised to find Holmes seated on the wall beside the entrance gate, a slim book in one hand and a cigarette in the other.

He watched me come down the drive, and when I handed him the photograph, all he said was, "Her father?"

"And a woman, who may or may not be the half-sister he claims. She runs a cabaret in Paris; he's lived there since around 1908."

"Very good," he said. "Now we have a chance to lay hands on them."

"If we're going to talk to the police, I think I ought to bathe first. I don't look like the most reputable individual."

"Let us go by the house on the way to the hotel and see if Long and Hammett are still there."

We set off walking, but on reaching the next street a taxi went past, slow and vacant. Holmes put up his hand and we climbed in, and he had the driver go past the house to fetch the other two men. Hammett came out with a bundle in his arms, wrapped in a torn piece of dust-cloth. When he settled in, he said, "I didn't know that you'd want to leave this in the house. If you don't want to trust the hotel safe, I can recommend a nice discreet bank for you."

On the way, Holmes asked the driver to stop at a photographic shop around the corner from the St Francis.

"You don't think we should give the photograph to the police?" I asked him.

"I'd prefer to have a copy of our own first."

"Or perhaps a number of copies," I said.

"Quite."

The driver paused at the edge of traffic for Holmes to run inside; he was back in moments. Once at the St

Francis, as I turned on the taps in the bath-tub and went in and out of the rooms with my clean clothing, I listened to the three men discussing the case over the lunch that had been sent up. I shut off the taps and lowered myself into the hot water, lying on my back and allowing my head to submerge until only my face stood above the surface.

Alone at last with nothing but my breathing, I pulled out of my mind the small treasure Holmes and Hammett had given me the night before, and looked at it.

The brake rod had been cut.

Fourteen-year-old Mary Russell had not sent the motor off the cliff. Mary Russell's argument with her brother had absolutely nothing to do with it. The brake rod had been sawed nearly through and when my father had pressed his foot against the pedal to slow the car at the top of the hill, the rod had snapped and the motorcar had swerved to the right, directly at the abyss.

My only sin was being a survivor.

And survival, I thought, might be something I could live with.

After a while I raised my head above the water, and as I scrubbed the grime off my ankles and hands, I listened to the conversation in the next room, following the points of the discussion as they came up, one at a time.

"If Robert Greenfield had one key, he could've had two," Hammett said, his contribution to the question of the house break-in of the previous March. The sequence, I thought, was fairly clear, once one put Flo's information together with the telegrams from Watson and Mycroft.

In January, an American living in Paris—either Robert Greenfield or his "half-sister" Rosa—had picked up a copy of the London *Times* and seen a letter that indicated Mr Sherlock Holmes was taking a quick and urgent trip to the Continent. And as Mrs Hudson had specifically mentioned in her telegram to Holmes that she had received several telephone enquiries concerning our return, we could assume that for the price of a trunk call and a little bit of play-acting—no task for a woman accustomed to the cabaret stage—one of the two had prised the information from the chronically trusting housekeeper not only that Holmes and I were on our way to India, but that afterwards we were headed to California as well.

Exactly what drove the pair into action could only be guessed at—and I noticed that Holmes in the next room made no attempt to do so, although Long and Hammett happily argued about the possibilities: Hammett proposed that the hair-trigger of Greenfield's guilty conscience needed only the tiniest pressure to perceive us as being on their trail; Long thought it likely that the changes in international relations since the War ended meant that France would be more willing to extradite a resident foreign criminal. Personally, I suspected that Flo's father, now a man in his middle fifties, was simply tiring of Europe, wanted to come home, and knew that if he were to be linked to that dead policeman, he would be a fugitive for the rest of his life. He'd tried, back in 1914, to enter the house, and been thwarted by the watch-dogs. This was his last chance to clean matters up.

In any case, the two had reacted instantaneously, scrambling to locate an aeroplane for Rosa—not Robert, whose memorable scars would surely attract the attention of his fellow passengers and, as far as he knew, be recognisable by me. A brief conversation with a ticket-agent would have told them that the only P. & O. boat whose sailing coincided with our hasty departure from

Southern England was the *Marguerite*, which would be in Port Said on the Tuesday. The aeroplane got Rosa there before us. She boarded as Lilly Montera, kept a low profile, and asked questions of various porters and passengers concerning our status and confirming our San Francisco destination. In Aden, the last port before India, she left the boat.

It was just possible that the aeroplane had continued south after leaving her at Port Said, taking Robert to Aden, where he had set up a desperate and unsuccessful attempt at murder. I was still unconvinced that the falling balcony had not been an accident, but it shouldn't be hugely difficult to find out if he was there.

After Aden, either she alone or the two of them would have caught the next boat out, sailing directly to California, no stops along the way—or if she had sailed alone, he would have met her here. They had come to my house by night, aware of the watch-dogs across the street—and as Mr Hammett had pointed out, there was nothing to have kept Greenfield from making a copy—ten copies—of the key before ostentatiously handing the original over to my father back in 1906. (As I worked at my nails with the brush, I made a mental note to have all the locks changed, as soon as possible.) The two of them had spent the daylight hours inside the house searching for anything that might incriminate him; they'd found Father's letter eventually, in the library or my parents' bedroom or in Mother's desk—wherever Father had stashed it before setting off for the Lodge that fateful week-end in 1914. However, the document had led them no closer to the two boxes, and in the end they had given up the search. They had burnt the letter in the fireplace, along with some related newspaper articles, and rested in the beds upstairs until the full moon was bright enough to guide their departing steps. It must have been frustrating, I mused in the cooling water, to know the boxes were out there in the garden, but be unable to locate them.

"Do you think he would have done what he did, had he realised that the entire family was in the car?" This was Long's voice, and the thought gave me pause. Yes, Father's letter had said that he intended to go to the Lodge by himself. He would have told his friends that, and...and perhaps I had mentioned to Flo that my father was going but we were not. It was something I would have done—my adolescent self would have complained in either case: If I'd gone, I was being forced to go; if I hadn't gone, I was being left behind. And Flo's father had been in town just then, with a pearl necklace for her fourteenth-birthday present. She could have passed on the information I had provided....

But sooner or later, after Father had died, Greenfield would have returned to silence Mother. He knew his old friend, knew that Charles Russell would have told his wife what he'd found in the back garden. What Greenfield had done later to the others who might have known, the Longs and Dr Ginzberg, proved that sooner or later he'd have come for Mother.

Probably not Levi, an infant during the fire, only nine at the crash. And possibly not me—I had, after all, lived unmolested in England all those years. But when I grew up and married the world's most ruthlessly efficient detective, it must have caused my father's old friend many sleepless nights. And with the codicil of the will drawing near its conclusion, with it would go twenty years of enforced isolation from snooping strangers—a new owner would surely take the jungle to the ground, and below. And then in January, when I turned with that efficient detective towards California, would have been the final straw—my presence here couldn't be risked.

So, had Greenfield seen the entire family when we stopped at Serra Beach, and cut the brake line nonetheless? Or had he seen only the motor, after Father had dropped the three of us at the café, with none but its driver walking away?

I sat very still, scowling unseeing at the soap-dish. There was something in that thought, a presence in the back of my mind very like that which had pushed at me beside the lake the other morning at dawn, something *(They died…)* that I was not seeing.

(Something…)

But Long's voice broke into my mental search and I lost the train of thought.

"My father was not happy with the idea of concealing the box, but he did so, because he trusted Charles Russell."

Yes: After the fire, the relationship between my father and him had changed, as if something *(something was there waiting to be noticed something was*—but no, I had lost it again)…as if some event had forced a degree of distance in their former intimacy and mutual respect.

I pulled the plug and dressed, in trousers and a clean shirt—no need to appear as an heiress today. When I joined them, Long was just leaving, as his assistant needed to be away during the afternoon and he did not like to close the bookstore unless it was necessary.

"I am very willing to stay and help with anything," he offered, but Holmes shook his head.

"I shall bring some copies of the Greenfield photograph by your shop. If you would care to distribute them throughout Chinatown, that would be a great assistance."

While Holmes walked Mr Long to the door, I picked up a rather dried-looking sandwich and ate it hungrily, washing it down with tepid coffee. Why was it, I reflected, that when one's appetite did return, there never seemed to be anything the least bit interesting to eat?

But I filled my stomach while Holmes and Hammett debated how best to go about the next step, namely, suggesting to the police with their superior resources that they might help us find Greenfield and his half-sister. I piled my things onto the serving tray and went to fetch some boots from the wardrobe, and was sitting at the table lacing them up when the telephone beside me rang.

It took me a moment to understand the voice, as there seemed to be a minor riot going on in the background. "Mr Auberon? Is that you?" I said loudly. "Can you repeat what you said?"

"I'm very sorry to disturb you, madam, but there are some children here who are insisting that they—"

"We'll be down in an instant, Mr Auberon. Tell them that we'll be right down."

I grabbed my coat and headed towards the door, which Holmes already had open, driven there by the urgency of my tone. "It's your Irregulars," I told him.

His face lighted with joy, and as he galloped down the corridor towards the lift he cried, "Come, Russell—the game's afoot!"

Hammett, catching up his coat and walking beside me with more decorum, looked at me askance. "He actually says that?"

"Only to annoy me," I told him, and all but shoved him towards the opening lift door.

The dignified St Francis doorman was attempting with ill success to keep at bay an affront of urchins, denizens of the streets wearing an interesting assortment of extreme and ill-fitting raiment. Upon seeing Holmes, they dodged around the poor man's outstretched arms like so many football forwards and came up short before Holmes, bouncing up and down on their toes and squeaking in excitement.

One long, commanding adult hand went up, and they settled instantly back onto their feet, quivering like retrievers ordered to sit.

"Mr Garcia, you have something to report?"

The lad whipped off his cloth cap and all but saluted. "Hey, mister, sir, they came to the house, and we followed them!" His response set off the others, who chimed in with great enthusiasm but little intelligible detail. He shushed at his fellows with no result, then started slapping at them with his cap. This had the desired effect; rebellion quelled, he turned back to Holmes. "They headed down Market Street. I've got some of my gang on them, but you need to hurry."

Holmes laid a hand on the boy's shoulder and turned him towards the entrance, calling over his head to the doorman, "Taxi, please! Now, Mr Garcia, tell me who came and what they did."

In bits and snatches, interrupted by contributions from the others and by the process of piling three adults and what proved to be only three children into the taxi, we learned that the boy on fire-escape duty had heard a noise from the apartment hall-way just a little before eleven o'clock. Looking in, he had seen a man bent over the lock of the Hammett door, and behind him a woman, looking up and down the hall-way nervously. It had taken the man several minutes to breach the lock (this was imparted with scorn, and the aside that the lad telling this part of the story had an uncle who could have done it in half the time). They had been inside the apartment just a few minutes, and come out with the woman slipping something into her hand-bag. They had pulled the door to behind them, and left in a hurry.

Master Garcia and seven of his boys had been arrayed in wait. They followed as far as Market Street and saw the two turn west; Garcia had then divided his troops: two with him to summon help, the others to follow their quarry.

The lad paused in his story to look at Holmes with wrinkled brow. "I shoulda asked—do you got any two-bits with you?"

"Yes, I have some quarter-dollars. Why?"

"It's just that I told my guys that, if them two make too many turns, we're gonna run out of boys, and they should ask someone who looks like they can use two bits to stand on the corner and let us know which way they've gone. So you might have to hand quarters out to a few bums."

We all three looked at him with respect, and he blushed for a moment before throwing back his head with a cocky expression. "Only makes sense," he asserted.

"How very true," Holmes said. "And when we're through with this, you might talk to Mr Hammett here about local employment opportunities for promising lads."

The taxi drove through the Market Street traffic for nearly a mile before the lad came upright on his seat. "There's Mick! Stop, up there," he told the driver. The man cast a look at Holmes, who nodded. The motor pulled over and arms dragged another boy inside. This one was quite small and so excited he could not get his words to come out in any kind of order until Ricky grabbed his arm and shook him hard. The child gulped in gratitude and loosed a great torrent of words: "They went down Market and they got on a street-car and Rudy said we couldn't get on too they'd see us but then Kurt he said he could hang on the back he did it all the time but I don't think he did I think it was his brother who's bigger than him but anyway he ran over to the street-car and grabbed on and Rudy went with him and then Vince tried but you know Vince he's too fat so he fell off and I couldn't reach the thing it was too tall so Vince and Markie and me got left behind and Rudy shouted that we should wait until you came along and tell you where we'd gone but Vince and Markie said they could run as fast as the street-car and that I should wait until you came along and so even though I can run faster than Vince I did what they said I waited."

The full stop at the end of that sentence came so abruptly, we all took a moment to recover, then everyone in the motor drew a simultaneous breath.

"Good lad," Holmes said, and handed him a bright quarter-dollar. That shut the child up for good—I never heard another syllable from him.

We picked up the boy named Vince a short distance down Market, his plump face red as he stumped along with more determination than speed. He piled into the motor as well (which suddenly began to seem rather warm and crowded) and pantingly informed Ricky that Markie had run ahead but he'd thought he should go more slowly to lead us all when we came. Ricky gave a snort but the rest of us made soothing noises of understanding and appreciation, and Holmes handed Vince a silver quarter with great ceremony.

Just then some oddity in the city landscape caught the corner of my eye, and when I glanced out of the back window, I noticed a thin and ragged boy clinging to the back of a street-car that was headed in the opposite direction. "Is this a generally accepted means of travel for young males?" I asked with curiosity. Several of the others in the motor followed my gaze, and young Rick Garcia gave a great shout.

"Rudy! That's Rudy," he repeated, but Holmes was already in action, exhorting the taxi driver to turn about and follow the trolley. The man grumbled, declared that if he got caught by a cop that it wasn't him that was going to pay the fine, and pulled over to the middle of the wide street to wait for a gap between the on-coming cars. Then just as he began to pull forward, all five of our younger companions began to shout furiously. "There's Kurt!" and "Wait, don't leave Kurt" contradicted by "No, go on, he'll be okay" and "Wait, here comes Markie too, c'mon, Markie, run faster!"

At that, Holmes told the driver to pull over to the side and stop for a moment. He dug two more silver coins from his apparently endless supply and whipped a five-dollar note out of his bill-fold, handing both coins and bill to the leader. "Mr Garcia, I shall have to ask you to leave us here for the time being. I should appreciate it if you would present yourself to the St Francis desk at nine o'clock tomorrow morning for a final accounting."

The boy, naturally enough, protested, but Holmes was already propelling small and angry bodies out of the motor, assisted willingly by Hammett, and he overrode the protests. "Mr Garcia, if you wish to hear the details of what has taken place—*all* the details, even those in which you were not involved—you will appear at the hotel in the morning. If you continue protesting now, I shall give you nothing but your money and send you on your way."

It has always amazed me, how Holmes the bachelor understood so thoroughly the workings of the childhood mind. Here yet again he hit on exactly the thing that got the boys out of the motor without another word of protest. The leader's eyes merely narrowed with consideration for a moment, then he climbed out of the motor. As we drove away from the five standing lads and two more approaching at a run, we heard Ricky's voice call, "If you don't give over, you'll be really sorry."

Holmes brushed himself off and gave me a grin. "I shall, too."

We quickly caught the trolley up, and Holmes had the driver pull just close enough for him to give a sharp whistle, then drop away again. The dangling boy looked around, spotted Holmes, and instantly let go his precarious hold to stand in the midst of the traffic waiting for us to catch him up. Hammett kicked the door open and the boy scrambled in, without the taxi actually coming to a halt. We continued after the trolley while Holmes interrogated his final Irregular.

"You're Rudy, yes? We just dropped your friends down the street. May I take it that the two people you've been following are in this street-car?"

We'd have been well and truly wrecked if the lad said he'd just decided to ride the street-car on a whim, I reflected, but he was nodding. "They got off down near Sixteenth, went into a hotel and walked right out again about two minutes later with a coupla bags, and got onto another trolley going the other way. I left Kurt there to tell Ricky."

"He found us," Holmes reassured him, handing over the shiniest coin yet, this one an entire silver dollar.

"We'll let you out here, lad. And you tell your friends that they should bring their appetites with them in the morning. I'll buy you all the biggest breakfast the St Francis serves."

The boy's expression indicated that he did not often dine in establishments such as the St Francis, and we left him on the pavement, staring in wonder at our re-treating vehicle.

We had the driver dawdle far enough back from the trolley so that our coinciding stops and starts might not attract the attention of the passengers, yet near enough that, if the two spotted us and attempted to fade into the downtown crowds without their bags, we might see them. But no one resembling the man and woman in the photograph Flo had given me descended from the trolley, and it continued up the die-straight path of Market in the direction of the Ferry Building.

The street-car reached the wide boulevard of the Embarcadero, onto which all the piers opened, and en-tered the turn-around in front of the Ferry Building. The afternoon traffic made for a positive anthill of taxis, private cars, bicycles, hand-trucks, and pedestrians. We waited, holding our collective breath, until we saw a man and a woman step down to the street, each carrying a valise; the man's hat was pulled down to hide his face. Holmes slapped some money into the driver's hand and the three of us got out as quickly and as smoothly as we could, trying not to look as if we were interested in anything much, closing casually but rapidly on the terminus.

But the woman spotted us. We were not exactly unob-trusive in a crowd, as even slumped into their coats, Holmes and Hammett towered above everyone else, and I am not far behind. She looked back and she spotted us and grabbed her companion's shoulder; he whirled around, looked straight in our direction, then seized her by the arm and ran, abandoning the two valises on the street. We ran, too, dodging through the traffic to the music of furious horns and the whistles of two outraged policemen, and gained the pavement in time to see the man pull a revolver from his pocket and aim it in our direction.

Knowing intellectually the theoretical inaccuracy of a pistol over a distance of several hundred yards is not the same as knowing one is safe: We all three dove behind the nearest large object until the shot had ceased echoing down the street and the screams and rushing about had started. Three heads slowly emerged, in time to see our quarry climb into a maroon-coloured Chrysler whose terrified driver, hands high in the air, stood in the street and watched his vehicle race off up the Embarcadero without him.

Holmes and I looked at each other, grimaced, and pulled out our own revolvers to commandeer a jazzy green open motor that, although nowhere near as powerful as the Chrysler, was low enough to corner well. Rather to my surprise Hammett, although he appeared eager to stay with us, made no move to shoulder me aside, but threw himself in the backseat so that I might leap behind the wheel. With Holmes shouting thanks and apologies at the man we left behind, I slammed my foot onto the accelerator.

North of Market, the Embarcadero is wide, flat, and straight; they saw us coming before we had gone half a mile. Greenfield accelerated and I did the same, and it looked as if we would keep on at this speed until we flew off the first curve into the Bay or crashed into the walls surrounding Fort Mason. Then abruptly he swerved left and shot into the maze around Telegraph Hill.

"Hah!" came a voice from the back; Hammett leant forward over my shoulder and said, "If they don't know the area, we may have them."

Telegraph Hill loomed ahead of us, too steep for roads on this side, but the motor ahead of us dodged and scurried around its base, avoiding the dead-ends by skill or luck. I kept us on the road and in sight of them, using my horn freely, grateful that this was not an area with heavy traffic. Although we hadn't their engine power, we were better on the corners, and as I grew accustomed to the steering I managed to gain on them a little. We screamed around corners within a hair's-breadth of parked cars and lamp-posts, using the brakes almost not at all; slowly, the maroon motor's number-plate grew ever closer.

I had no idea where I was, and no time to ask. Instead I shouted over my shoulder, "If you have any knowledge of the streets you wish to impart, please feel free."

Hammett said only, his voice tight, "You're doing fine."

After several minutes of circling and dodging through the residential streets, suddenly we were back on the Embarcadero, heading south this time, back towards the Ferry Building. Just before he entered the snarl of traffic there, Greenfield flew to the right, taking some paint off a cable-car, dodged north for a couple of streets, then west. He swerved around a horse-drawn wagon, then with a sharp squeal of tyres shot directly across the nose of a taxi and entered a street I knew all too well.

It was afternoon on Grant Avenue: the crowded, bustling, commercial and residential centre of Chinatown.

Chapter Twenty-five

Chinatown was the worst possible place for a motor-car chase—which, I realised dimly, was why Greenfield had chosen it. He knew that I would have to slow for the vendors, children, afternoon shoppers, and infirm who clotted its streets, although he seemed to have no such compunction. He gained fifty feet in the first two streets by the simple technique of laying hard on both horn and accelerator, hesitating for nothing. I, in the mean-time, received the back-draught of his passage—the grandfather who stepped out into the street the better to see the blur that had just sped past him, the laden bicyclist who teetered, nearly fell, and then caught his balance by veering into my path—so that I was forced to slow and dodge.

"Holmes," I shouted, swerving with one hand and gearing down with the other, "shove your hand on the horn!" But instead, he rose in his seat and shouted for me to stop.

"I can catch them, Holmes—" I protested in grim

determination, but his hand came down to slap mine from the steering wheel and he repeated his command.

I jammed my foot off one pedal and onto the other; our stolen motor stood on its nose with a violent protest of rubber, and had Holmes not been tucked tight against the windscreen he would have been launched over the bonnet into a fruit cart. Instead, the instant the motor sat back on its haunches he peeled himself from the glass and leapt out over the door, coming to rest in front of a diminutive white-headed figure. I couldn't see him at first, since Holmes' shoulders hid him from view, but in a split second a small, dignified Oriental gentleman was in mid-air, feet waving, and then standing on the bonnet of the motor, his scholar's hands out to catch his balance. Holmes scrambled up beside him in a flash, and as his right arm came up with his revolver in it, he put his head down and shouted at the snowy white head, "Tell them to stop that motorcar!"

I do not know if any person in the city could have done the thing except Dr Ming. But Dr Ming it was, there at the place and time we needed him, and with neither question nor even protest. Events proceeded as if they had been meticulously choreographed: Holmes' mouth going shut just as the old man was raising his head to shout; the revolver in Holmes' hand going off, pointing at the sky; the crowded street shuddering into attention, every head turned our way. The old man's voice seemed tiny in the wake of the shot, but his words acted like a spark set to a line of gunpowder. His command sputtered through the nearby pedestrians, then caught as each person turned and passed the phrase on, and on it ran up the street, fizzing and furious as it burned through the residents, coming even with the honking maroon bonnet, passing it, converting itself into motion: A heavy-laden greengrocer's cart began moving, slowly at first but inexorably into the path of Greenfield's stolen motor. The horn cut off as the Chrysler squealed one way then overcompensated to the other before smashing into the cart and a parked poultry lorry at the same moment. Cabbages and caged chickens rained down in all directions as the stunned pair tried to keep moving. Greenfield got so far as to raise his pistol, but the crowd had already closed over them, and the gun went off pointing at the upper window of the telephone exchange, causing a number of trunk calls to come to grief as their connexions were yanked free by startled operators.

We remained where we were while the community brought Dr Ming his two prisoners. The old man had settled down onto the emerald bonnet of our own stolen motor, his hands tucked together into invisible sleeves, and was in placid conversation with Holmes; Hammett gazed at the two of them in frank disbelief; I let myself out of the motor slowly, watching the procession come near.

Greenfield struggled against his bonds of grocer's twine, shouting furiously. His sister had her hands tied as well, and I looked at her carefully, wondering if I had seen her on board the *Marguerite*. She was a tall woman, nearly as tall as I, and although her suspiciously uniform brown hair was slightly mussed by the chase, otherwise she appeared so self-contained, she might have been pausing to answer the queries of a passer-by rather than waiting for the police. Studying her closely, I thought I might have seen her on the ship, perhaps on the night of the fancy-dress ball, but I would not have sworn to it. She came quietly in the hands of her captors, her expression more watchful than daunted; I thought the police needed to be warned that she should be carefully searched.

I wanted to talk to her, wanted in fact to grab her hard and demand what had set her on our heels so resolutely, but then I saw her glance at him, and in that one glance, it all became clear.

Even after all these years, and despite the self-control that was keeping her spine straight and her face untroubled, her weakness was the man beside her. For a brief instant, she looked afraid—not for herself, but for him.

She was not his sister. She might have been his willing slave.

My eyes went to him, as if mere appearance could explain such a lifetime of devotion: Robert Greenfield, my father's comrade-in-youth, who had inspired mistrust in my mother and open animosity in his ex-wife. An ordinary enough figure, other than the scarring on his face, and even that was hardly fearsome.

Standing at the front of the motor, Greenfield's curses only increased in volume, until one of the men nearby drew a length of filthy rag from about his person and held it up enquiringly in front of Dr Ming. Dr Ming deferred to Holmes, who turned to look at me, asking with his eyebrows if I cared to speak with the man before the police arrived.

Greenfield followed the sequence of glances until it ended up with me, at which point his curses strangled in his throat. "Jesus—Charlie?" he choked out, then looked at me more comprehensively. If anything, his face went whiter, and the internal murmur of *something, there was something behind the*—grew loud and louder in my ears.

"You ... You must be the daughter. Mary. Christ, that hair, those glasses ... I thought—" He caught himself up short, and tried hard to summon a crooked grin. "Did anyone ever tell you how much you look like your old man?"

"Before you killed him, you mean?"

The grin slipped for an instant before he retrieved it to buoy his protests, but I was not listening to his words. Instead, I was taken up with his face and the voice itself.

The burn that affected about half his facial skin had erased one eyebrow and part of the other, but had not gone deep enough to reach the muscles and tendons. Below the shiny scar tissue the movement was normal enough, albeit somewhat stiff on the left side.

And the voice—I knew that voice, slightly hoarse and with the flat Boston accent that my father had possessed in a much softer degree. The voice reached in and pulled out the hidden *something*, the room in my memory house that I had known was there, the key I had obediently set aside so thoroughly that I did not even see it.

"You said, 'Don't be afraid, little girl,'" I told him. I had not meant to speak aloud, but the man blinked, so clearly I had.

"What?" he said.

"In the tent. When you came looking for my father and woke me up, you had no face, it was whiter than your face is now and even shinier, and I was frightened. You told me not to be afraid. But I should have been, shouldn't I?"

Greenfield looked at the men holding his arms and again tried to grin. "I was out doing rescue work and got burned, so I went to find your father and see how he was. He'd been a good friend of mine, before he married, and—"

"You were not doing rescue work; you were out robbing abandoned houses and stripping dead bodies."

That silenced him.

"But that wasn't the only time," I continued, speaking as much to myself, or to Holmes, as to Greenfield. "You were there when Father stopped for the tyre-change, weren't you? In Serra Beach. That's the thing I've been trying to remember the last few days, that I caught a glimpse of you behind the garage, slipping behind that big gum tree at the side. You'd been talking with my father, and when I finished lunch and went to find him and tell him we were ready to go, I saw the two of you, arguing. When my father turned and saw me, his face was red and his fists were clenched—I'd never seen him look like that. You ran off. And I asked him then who you were and he told me you were nobody, that it would upset Mother if I told her I'd seen you, that I should try to forget all about you.

"And so I did. God, did I ever. But you *were* there that day, and you cut the brake rod and you killed them all. Just like you killed Leah Ginzberg and Mah and Micah Long, four months later."

At this last pair of names a murmur sprang up, as several of the older residents recognised the Anglicised versions of the murdered couple's names. I walked around the motor until I was standing directly in front of Greenfield, and I wanted to murder him. Then and there, I wanted to gut him and leave him bleeding his life out on the street, for what he had done to six good and loving people. I might even have done so—I was on the very brink of snatching the gun from my pocket or bending for the knife in my boot-top—when something touched my arm. It was the gentlest touch imaginable, the mere brush of a bird's wings in weight, but the faint weight of it settled onto the taut muscles of my forearm and stopped them from moving. I looked down at the delicate old fingers, then into the face of Dr Ming.

"You do not wish to do this," he said.

I did want to do it, I could almost taste the glory of revenge. And then suddenly I did not. The murderous impulse left me, the hand fell away, and as if by a stage cue, the police arrived, bluff and uncomprehending and requiring a great deal of attention, from all of us, for a very long time.

Epilogue

Late, late that night Holmes and I crept back to our rooms at the St Francis. We had persuaded Officialdom to let Long go home, and even Hammett, but at the cost of remaining and explaining, again and again, what it all meant: why Rosa Greenfield's finger-prints had been found on the toilet-pull of my house; why a bullet from Greenfield's gun would match one to be found in a fence in Pacific Heights; why Greenfield's finger-prints were going to be found on coins in the tin boxes in our hotel's safe.

Had it not been for Holmes' name, the bewildered police would have thrown us all out and let us sort it out on the street.

But in the end, Robert and Rosa Greenfield were charged, and we were free to go.

As we walked towards the lift, shortly before midnight, the night man came out from behind his desk and gave Holmes a packet. His hand reached out automatically for it, and as we rode the lift upwards, my eyes idled across the address on the label as if its letters contained some arcane message. It was, I realised only when we were in the room and he ripped open the paper, the urgent reproductions of Flo's photograph that he had left to be copied—only that morning yet many, many hours before.

I went through the motions of hanging up my coat and divesting myself of shoes and the like, then plodded into the bath-room to wash my face.

When I came out, Holmes was sitting with a photograph in his hand—not that of the Greenfields; he held it out in my direction.

"What is that?" I asked wearily.

"Another photograph I left the other day for copying. I'd all but forgotten it."

I sat down to save myself from falling and took the picture from his hand.

A tent city. A woman, a blonde child with a book, a man trudging up the hill, looking as exhausted as I felt.

My family.

I took off my glasses to study my father's face. *Too tired for the nightmares to reach me,* he had written in the document; I wondered if all his dreams had been of the fire.

"Do I look like him?" I asked.

"You do somewhat, without a hat and your hair as it is. To a guilty mind, the resemblance would be startling."

I picked up a copy of the other picture as well, showing the Greenfields at the Lodge, unscarred and not yet embarked on murder. They were standing by the lake, looking over the shoulder of the photographer at the log house that the young and carefree Greenfield had helped his friend Charles build.

"The sun was red," I murmured.

"Sorry?"

"During the fire. Everything was a peculiar colour from the smoke and ashes, and it was terrifying, with the sun a red glow in the sky and the earth shaking and the sound of explosions. But my father came back then and he explained it to me, told me that the booms were just the firemen removing houses so there wouldn't be anything for the fire to burn and it would go out. I understood what he was saying, and when he told me it would be all right, I believed him."

"Your parents were good people," he said. And then he added the most perfect thing anyone has ever said to me. "They would be proud of you."

Not that I believed him, of course. Instead I gave voice to the remnants of my guilt. "If I'd told my mother about seeing Greenfield that day, if I'd said something, I might have saved them."

"I think not. Greenfield was already set on his course. Had you told your mother that you had seen him, it might have caused an argument between your parents, and at most a resolution to confront Greenfield when they returned to the city, but it would not have interrupted the family's progress to the lake. Only Greenfield himself could have done that."

And I could picture it, clearly: Mother's indignation that Father was meeting the man; a family's final minutes tainted by recrimination and regret; the motorcar setting off down the road...

"You would not have changed a thing," Holmes said firmly. This time, I believed him.

I changed out of my day-clothes and settled into a soft bed that seemed to tremble and sway with my tiredness, but my eyes would not close. I looked at the mezuzah, lying still on the bed-stand, and found myself saying, "Holmes, would you mind awfully if we didn't leave right away? I'd like to see my family's graves, and explore the area a little."

"No, I do not mind spending more days here. We've been in California for a week and a half, and I don't believe I've set eyes on a redwood tree."

"And it would also allow you to finish your Paganini research."

"My—ah, yes, my Paganini research."

"There is no research project, is there, Holmes?"

"Not as such, no," he admitted. The bed's sway was magnified briefly as he settled in beside me. I turned to him, closing my eyes with the pleasure of simple human touch.

"Don't let me forget," he said. "I must be downstairs at nine o'clock for breakfast with Mr Garcia and the Irregulars."

"I'm sure that if you haven't appeared, we shall wake to find them staring down at us." He laughed, and stretched to shut off the light. As darkness took over, I had a final thought. "Holmes, what was Dr Ming saying to you?"

"While he was sitting on the motorcar bonnet, do you mean? I apologised for manhandling him so unceremoniously, and said something to the effect of what good fortune it had been to happen across the one person in Chinatown who could summon a crowd's instantaneous response. He replied that the lines of good fortune and the lines of feng shui are often mistaken for each other."

My sleepy brain chewed on that for a bit. "So, what, he was saying that his presence there was predetermined?"

"His words were 'Those who perceive the dragon's path may alter it.'"

I wavered: If the old doctor's presence was deliberate, that would suggest that the Fates—or the old gentleman himself—had not only seen the need for his presence at that precise time and place, but had also envisioned our ability to make use of it.

In the end, I shook the troubling conundrum out of my head and settled into the comfort of the pillow. As I slid towards sleep, I felt, or dreamt, the lightest of touches on my hair, followed by the words, "Ah, Russell, what is to become of me? I find I've even grown attached to this infernal hair-cut."

I felt my lips curl slightly. "That is really most unfortunate, Holmes. I had just decided to allow it to grow back."

And at last I slept, dreamlessly.

·

Afterword

Thanks are due, as always, to the wise and capable people of the McHenry Library of the University of California, Santa Cruz, without whom this book would be a smaller and less lively thing.

Thanks are also due to Dick Griffiths, Jon Hart, and Fred Zimmerman of the Blackhawk Museum in Danville, California. If you want to see Donny's blue Rolls-Royce, that's where it lives.

To Abby Bridge, researcher extraordinaire, and the collections of the California Historical Society, the San Francisco Public Library, and the Mechanics' Institute Library; Don Herron, who knows all things Hammett; and Stu Bennett, who uncovered some insider's guides to the City.

Although none of the biographies of Dashiell Hammett I found, including that written by his daughter, Jo Hammett (*Dashiell Hammett: A Daughter Remembers*), mention this extraordinary meeting of minds in the spring of 1924, from all I can see, Miss Russell captures the man's essence, from the dapper clothes and weak lungs to the man's robust sense of ethics. It should be noted, regarding Hammett's disinclination to sell out his employer in this story, that this desperately ill, lifelong claustrophobe, an old man at the age of fifty-seven, spent twenty-two weeks in federal prison during the Red-baiting fifties because he refused to give up the names of men who had trusted him. As Lillian Hellman said in the eulogy of her longtime lover (which can be found in Diane Johnson's excellent *Dashiell Hammett, A Life*) Hammett submitted to prison because "he had come to the conclusion that a man should keep his word."

No small goal for any of us.

About the Author

LAURIE R. KING became the first novelist since Patricia Cornwell to win prizes for Best First Crime Novel on both sides of the Atlantic with the publication of her debut thriller, *A Grave Talent*. She is the bestselling author of four contemporary novels featuring Kate Martinelli, eight Mary Russell mysteries, and bestselling novels *A Darker Place*, *Folly*, and *Keeping Watch*. She lives in northern California.

If you enjoyed Laurie R. King's LOCKED ROOMS, you won't want to miss any of the novels in her bestselling Mary Russell series, as well as the mysteries in the award-winning Kate Martinelli series. Look for them at your favorite bookseller.

And read on for an exciting early look at Laurie's next ingenious novel, in which San Francisco detective Kate Martinelli encounters a modern-day case—one which very well could have links to Mary Russell and Sherlock Holmes....

THE
ART
OF
DETECTION

By

Laurie R. King

Coming in hardcover
from Bantam Books

LAURIE R. KING

THE ART OF DETECTION

A Novel of Suspense

THE ART OF DETECTION
Laurie R. King

On sale June 2006

Prologue

Kate Martinelli had been in any number of weird places during her years as a cop. She'd seen the dens of paranoid schizophrenics and the bare, polished surfaces attended by obsessive compulsives; she'd seen homeless shelters under a bridge and one-room apartments inhabited by families of twelve, crack houses that stank of bodily excretions and designer kitchens with blood spatter up the walls, suburban bedrooms full of sex toys, libraries filled with books on death, and once an actual, velvet-lined bordello.

She'd never seen anything quite like this.

The outside had looked normal enough, a San Francisco Victorian not far from Kate's old Russian Hill neighborhood, tall and ornately traced with gingerbread decorations. Actually, in its subdued colors it was considerably more sedate than several of its neighbors—the days of fuchsia and viridian Painted Ladies had passed, mercifully, but brightness and contrast were still too great a temptation for many owners.

The first indication of the house's true nature stood just outside the door, a small brass knob below a neat enamel plaque that said, *Pull*.

Kate, feeling a bit like Alice faced with the vial reading *Drink me*, obediently reached out and pulled. When she let go, the little knob jerked back into place and a bell began to clang inside the house—not ring: clang.

The sound died away, with no indication of life within. She rang a second time, with the same lack of result, then she turned around and shrugged at the occupants of the departmental van and the green Porsche, who had hung back until the notification was finished. Since it appeared that the notification was finished before it began, it was just a matter of getting a film record of the house before they went through it, and to have Crime Scene do a quick once-over to be sure the crime had not taken place here. The chances against it were minuscule—why would any murderer remove a body from its own home to dump it?—but the walls had to be checked, the car gone over.

Kate and the Park detective, Chris Williams, split up to hunt down a neighbor with a key. They did not find such a thing, but a neighbor across the street, a man in his thirties with thinning hair and a boyish face, pruning his roses in a button-down shirt and white pullover, told them that as far as he knew, a single man lived in the house. However, he did know the name of the occupant's security company. A phone call and twenty minutes' wait brought a company truck, from which hopped a brisk young woman with fifteen earrings and bleached-blonde hair a quarter of an inch long. She looked at their IDs carefully, made a phone call to confirm that they were who they said they were, then cheerfully unlocked the door for them—or rather she first locked the door, then unlocked it: The deadbolt had not been set, only the automatic lock in the knob itself. Shaking her head at the carelessness of clients, she removed the key from the dead bolt and handed it to Williams, along with the code for the alarm box that her paper said was behind a picture just inside the door. He gave Kate the key and wrestled the door open against the heap of accumulated mail inside, moving rapidly along the walls and pulling aside half a dozen pictures before he located the alarm panel, behind a framed pen-and-ink drawing of two men in old-fashioned dress, walking on a street. He hurriedly tapped out the sequence of numbers, using the end of a pen so as not to obscure any possible fingerprints. The official housebreakers held their breath, and when the alarm did not begin screaming, the woman from the department's photo lab stepped inside and started the video camera running. Kate said to the security woman, "Thanks, we'll hang on to the key."

"My notes say there's a pad upstairs, too, on the door to the third floor study. Do you want me to open that as well?"

"Sure."

The young woman ducked inside and headed for the stairs, with Kate's companion on her heels to make sure she touched nothing. Kate stepped into the victim's house, and with the first breath of pipe tobacco, lavender, and furniture wax, the Wonderland imagery returned, more strongly: She was in another world.

She was also in a remarkably ill-lit world, as the late-January evening was coming on fast and the light switches were even more thoroughly hidden than the alarm panel had been. Tamsin the photographer wandered off through the gloom, playing the camera through the rooms and up and down the walls, but Kate thought her colleague was working faster than usual, as if afraid that soon she would be recording the inside of a cow's stomach. Kate trotted after Williams to get his car keys, went out to get her flashlight from the briefcase she'd left in his car, then knelt inside the door to pile the mail to one side: The earliest postmark was from the twenty-second of January, nine days before. When the mail was in order, she stood and wandered from the entrance foyer with its dangling bell and framed etchings into the shadowy rooms beyond, open-mouthed with disbelief.

The fireplace, for example. It was a cramped, iron-line box that would have spilled any self-respecting log onto the carpet, which she thought explained the shiny brass bucket of black lumps. Except that, this being San Francisco in 2004 and not London in nineteen-whenever, the regulations against burning even the cleanest of anthracite coal were stringent. And so the fireplace was in fact a fake, with black and red pseudo-coals that glowed and pulsed and gave out no more heat than a lightbulb. Still, the coal in the brass bucket—wasn't it called a scuttle?—was real.

Her companion came back downstairs, thanking the security company representative as he ushered her out the door, standing back to allow Crime Scene in, then stepping outside himself to make a phone call. Lo-Tec glanced around and, without a word, got out the equipment to search for organic trade evidence, blood spatter and the like: The darkness just meant he didn't have to switch off lights.

There was not much to see in the lower floor, no sign of blood or disturbance, only the one ashtray to collect, no unwashed cups or glasses. The sound of Williams' voice outside stopped, and he came into the sitting room saying, "The upstairs study wasn't locked, but there's a safe—Jesus…" he said, and stood staring at the walls.

Kate lifted the powerful beam of her flashlight off the laden bookshelves and asked, "You think we can get some lights on in here?"

"There don't seem to be any."

"Don't be ridiculous, there have to be lights. There's one on over the stairs."

"Well, there's things on the wall that look like light fixtures, but I don't see any switches."

Kate played her flashlight beam at the walls, and there, indeed, were fluted glass shapes that could only be light-covers. She walked over to the nearest and peered up at it, frowning, then stretched up an arm to jiggle what looked like a key. A faint hissing noise emerged from the fixture, and she hastily turned the key back until it stopped.

"Hey, Chris, do you see a box of matches anywhere?" she asked. Williams shone his own light around, coming to rest on the mantelpiece. He picked up an ornate little box, shook it, and at the familiar noise, handed it to Kate. "Thanks. Hold your light on this thing for a minute," she told him, sliding the butt of her flashlight into a trouser pocket. Gingerly, she opened the stopcock a partial turn and lit a match, holding it to the place where the hissing noise seemed to originate. With a small pop, the flame ignited, and the gloom in the room retreated a bit. Both cops watched the glowing white bowl of the light warily, but when it neither exploded nor sent flames crawling up the wall, Kate went to two other lights and set them aglow.

"Are those things legal?" her temporary partner asked.

"I've never seen anything like them before," she replied, adding, "outside of *Masterpiece Theater*."

"It reminds me of something," Williams said, looking around the space.

"Yeah. A movie set."

Dark red flocked wallpaper, thick velvet drapes that seemed to suck out the weak dusk light from the windows before it could reach the room—and apparently the air as well, for the atmosphere, though cold, was stuffy. The furniture was of a kind that would have been out of date in her grandmother's time, everything heavy and upholstered except one badly sprung wicker-work chair angled in front of the fake fire. Beside this chair stood a fragile-looking table with an inlaid top all but invisible under a jumble of objects, including two pipes and a laden ashtray that went far to explain the stuffiness of the room. Through the gloom she could see a desk, on one corner of which stood a tall stick-like telephone with the ear-piece on a cord, straight out of the dawn of the telephone era. Even the drinks tray looked as if it had been brought here in a time machine, cut-glass decanters clustered around one of those tall bottles wrapped in silver mesh that swooshed fizzy water into glasses in period movies.

"I know what this is meant to be," Williams exclaimed.

"A museum?"

"Just about. Look at this," he said, and Kate turned to see him studying a heavily gouged patch of the flocked wallpaper—and not random vandalism, she realized, but in lines. "You ever read the Sherlock Holmes stories?"

"No. Well, not since I was a kid." She'd seen plenty of dramatizations on the television, her partner Lee being a serious addict of public television—come to think of it, that was probably where the gas-light wisdom had come from.

"But you know who Sherlock Holmes is." Not waiting for a response, he went on. "There's one story where Doctor Watson mentions that the detective had shot up the wallpaper with the initials of the queen—V.R. Wouldn't you say that's a V and an R?"

Kate stepped back, and indeed, the pock-marks could be interpreted as those letters, although lopsidedly so. "You mean the vic shot a bunch of holes in the wall? And the neighbors on the other side didn't end up in the emergency room?"

With his face nearly brushing the flocking, Williams touched one of the holes, then shook he head. "I don't think he really used a gun. These look too clean, and they're not very deep. More like he punched them into the Sheetrock."

"Plaster," Kate corrected absently. After removing two houses, there was not much she didn't know about old walls. "So the vic was a Sherlock Holmes nut?"

"Looks like."

"Down to the gas lights. And there's the violin on the table over there."

"Wonder how far he took it?"

"Why don't we go see?"

The answer was, he took it very far indeed. A subject of Victoria Regina would have felt instantly at home with furniture, the dusty house-plants (aspidistra? Kate's mind provided), and the fountains of pampas-grass and peacock feathers. The kitchen refrigerator was an actual ice-box, complete with near-melted stub of ice, and the single tap over the stone sink looked a hundred years old. By some chain of thought connected to the plumbing, Kate was struck by an awful idea.

"God, don't tell me this maniac used an outdoor privy." But upstairs was a vintage water-closet, with a flowered porcelain pull-chain to flush its multiple gallons of water. Next to it was the bathroom with a cast-iron claw-foot tub, a peculiar copper device at one end that Kate thought might be an archaic in-line water heater, and a flowered sink with matching porcelain mug, tooth-brush holder, and shaving-brush with foam-encrusted mug. Looped beneath the nearby cabinet was a wide strap with hooks at the ends, an object that stirred faint childhood memories of her grandfather's morning ritual. Sure enough, when Kate opened the cabinet, there lay the deadly artistry of a straight razor with an ivory handle.

She opened her mouth to call to Lo-Tec, then subsided: Gilbert hadn't died of a cut throat.

The other second-floor rooms included a spacious sitting room with a bow window, considerably brighter than the downstairs sitting room, a guest bedroom that looked as if it had never been used, and across the hallway from it, the owner's bedroom. The ornate iron bedstead was painted white, its mattress so puffy it could only have been filled with feathers. The bedside table held an actual candlestick, the lamp over the bed was again gas, and the man's down-at-heel leather slippers rested on a tufted rug with pink roses in the design. The floorboards were otherwise bare, but scrupulously clean, and two free-standing armoires held clothes that went with the house below: a couple of ornate robes, one silk, though slightly more subdued than the one the house's owner had been wearing when he was found, the other quilted velvet, such as Kate thought was called a smoking jacket. Half a dozen somber suits; a number of shirts with buttons instead of collars at the neck and holes on the cuffs for links; dignified silk objects that were more like cravats than neckties; wool trousers with cuffs and buttoned flies; and finally, six pieces of head-gear including two tweed caps, two fedoras, a hard bowler, and an actual, gleaming, honest-to-God black silk top hat.

The shoes to go with this sartorial splendor were arranged on shelves inside one of the cupboards, four examples of the cobbler's art: one pair of brown heeled boots, worn but well-maintained; a pair of polished black leather shoes, not particularly old-fashioned looking (then again, Kate reflected, men's classic shoes didn't change a whole lot over the years); a pair of ornate Moroccan-style house slippers, far less run-down than those under the man's bed; and last, glossy patent leather shoes suitable for evening wear.

It wasn't until they approached the third floor that the twentieth, and even the twenty-first, centuries made their appearance: the light burning over the landing was an electric fixture, so bright it spilled onto the stairs coming up from the first floor as well.

Underfoot, too, there came a marked change of era. In the lower portion of the house, the carpets had been either strips laid down the middle of the hallways and stairs or dark-colored Persian or Turkish rugs atop the polished boards. Here, as soon as one's feet left the half-way landing and started up the last bend, they knew there were in a different place, one that was soft with foam underlay and covered wall to wall with an expensive and modern Berber-style carpet. It extended into some of the rooms, as well, such as the bedroom that lay immediately to the left of the stairs.

This third-floor bedroom was as modern as its carpeting, with box springs and a sophisticated brown-and-tan bedcovering that went nicely with the floor covering. It was a large room, at the back of which was a separate, walk-in closet, holding clothes that could have come from Macy's yesterday: The trousers had zippers, the shirts possessed the normal collars and cuffs, half a dozen pair of shoes covered the gamut of needs (except for athletic shoes—the Sherlock wannabe apparently hadn't gone in for jogging), the neckties were unremarkable, and there was only one hat, a brown fedora. There were no gaps in the row of shows, and all the bare wooden hangers were neatly clustered nearest the door.

Next on from the bedroom was a bathroom, tiled on the floor and half way up the walls. No claw-foot tub here, but instead a glassed-in shower cubicle with chrome fittings. An electric razor stood on the counter next to the sink; the cupboard below held a hair-dryer.

At the end of the hallway, the hall carpeting extended into a sitting room that overlooked the street. Unlike its two brothers below, this one was fitted with electric lights, a matching mocha-colored leather sofa and armchair, two walls of modern books with bright covers, and, behind a discreet cabinet, a combination tape and CD player with an extensive collection of music, most of it classical, with heavy emphasis on pieces for the violin.

Next back from the front, across the hallway from the tiled bathroom, Gilbert had inserted a closet-sized kitchen, considerably more user-friendly than the one on the ground floor. Here was his electric kettle, humming refrigerator, microwave oven, a small gas range. A built-in table would seat two, or four at a pinch.

The final room on the third floor was where the new millennium reigned supreme: Across from the bedroom, Gilbert's study filled the rest of the space on the floor, its lock-pad glowing green to show it was open. Kate turned the handle, and despite the contemporary fittings of this level of the house, it still came as something of a shock to see the blatant display of modernity. True, books covered the wall from floor to ceiling, most of them reference books or antique novels, but apart from the cloth-bound spines, the room was as modern as an electronics showroom: high-tech telephone with answering machine, desktop computer with scanner and printer tucked underneath, a postage meter machine and a combination fax/photocopier to one side. Modern halogen lights hung overhead, and a solid-looking safe was built into the wall over the computer. There was even a second television set with cable and DVD player, in front of which was arranged a miniature island that might have been transported from the house below: A richly glowing Oriental rug sat on the light-colored hardwood floors; on top of it stood a deep maroon tufted leather chair, its matching hassock, and a low table with lion's claw legs, old but beautifully polished. The glossy wood held a small stack of magazines and catalogues, a coaster of inlaid marble from India, a glass with a glaze of dried brown in the bottom, a heavy marble ashtray with ashes in it and a pipe, lighter, and tobacco pouch to one side, and a bare pad of paper with a silver retracting pencil resting on top; the red leather of the chair was worn along the arms and at the tufts of the headrest.

Only later, and then only because Kate told them to look for it, did Crime Scene find the blood among the leather folds.